FORGET ME NAT

MARIA SCRIVAN

graphix
An Imprint of
SCHOLASTIC

For my parents
(the most loving people I know)

All rights reserved. Published by Graphix, an imprint of Scholastic Inc.,
Publishers since 1920. SCHOLASTIC, GRAPHIX, and associated logos are
trademarks and/or registered trademarks of Scholastic Inc.

The publisher does not have any control over and does not assume any
responsibility for author or third-party websites or their content.

This book is a work of fiction. Names, characters, places, and incidents are
either the product of the author's imagination or are used fictitiously, and any
resemblance to actual persons, living or dead, business establishments,
events, or locales is entirely coincidental.

Library of Congress Control Number: 2019947168

ISBN 978-1-338-53825-0 (hardcover)
ISBN 978-1-338-53824-3 (paperback)

10 9 8 7 6 5 4 3 2 1   20 21 22 23 24

Printed in China 62
First edition, September 2020
Edited by Megan Peace
Book design by Phil Falco
Publisher: David Saylor

CONTENTS

Crush 1

You + Me = We 11

Love Songs 23

Falling for You 35

Campaign 51

Brace Yourself 77

The Day before Valentine's Day 93

Stuck on You 99

The Dance 107

Sour Grapes (And Everything Else) 121

Practice 137

Promises 147

Friends 161

Vote 169

Rubber Band 179

Election Results 185

Promises Too 195

Yearbook 209

The Outtakes 223

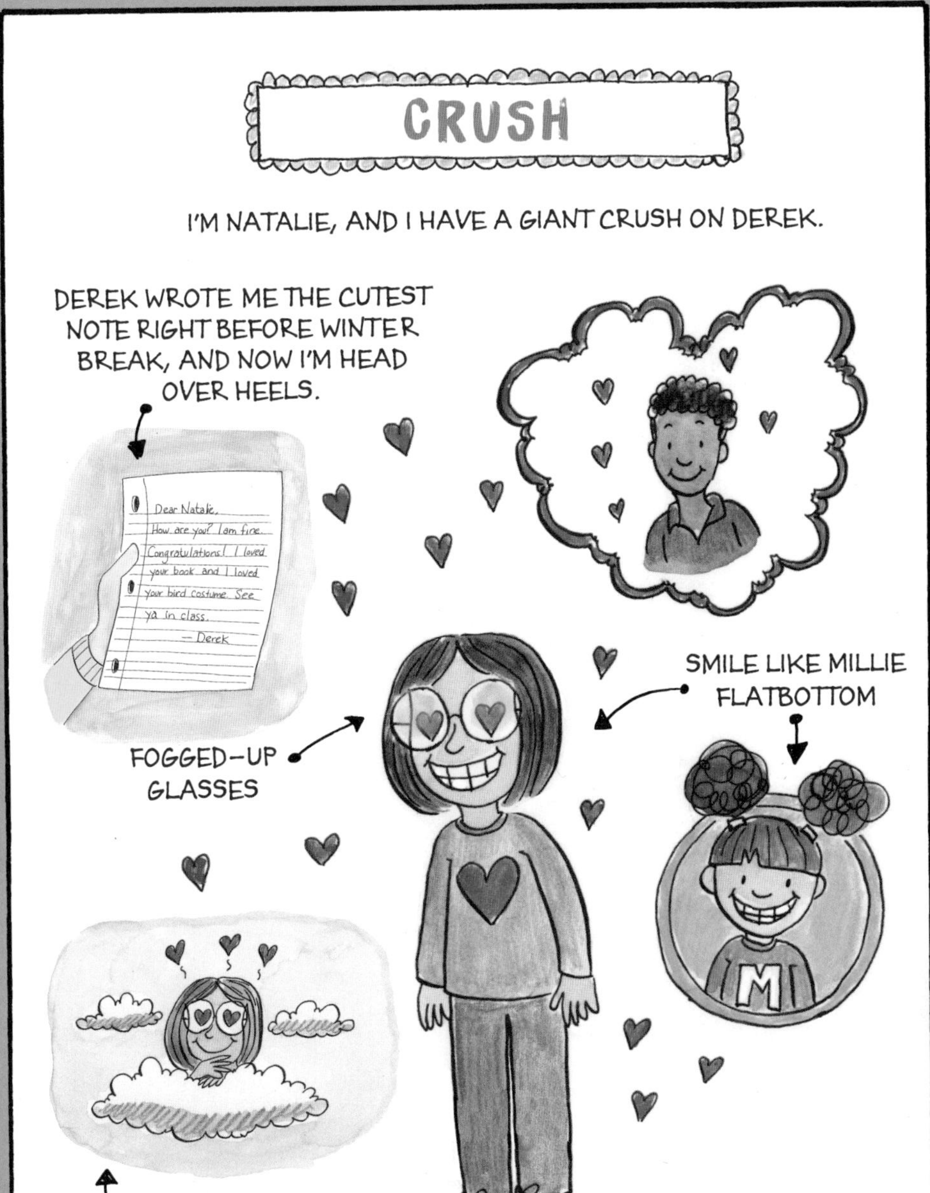
CRUSH
I'M NATALIE, AND I HAVE A GIANT CRUSH ON DEREK.
DEREK WROTE ME THE CUTEST NOTE RIGHT BEFORE WINTER BREAK, AND NOW I'M HEAD OVER HEELS.
Dear Natalie,
How are you? I am fine.
Congratulations! I loved your book and I loved your bird costume. See ya in class.
— Derek
SMILE LIKE MILLIE FLATBOTTOM
FOGGED-UP GLASSES
M
HEAD IN THE CLOUDS

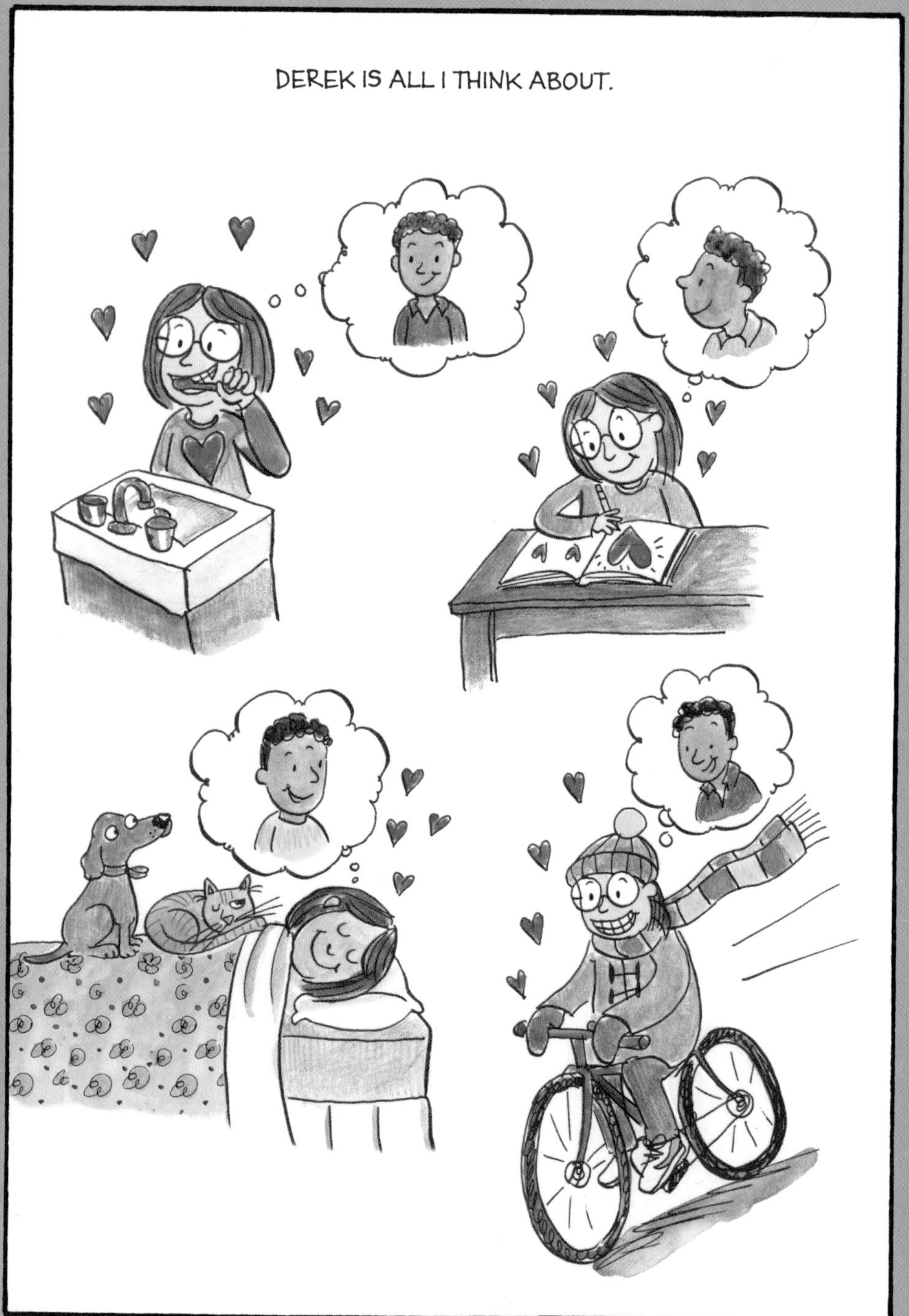
DEREK IS ALL I THINK ABOUT.

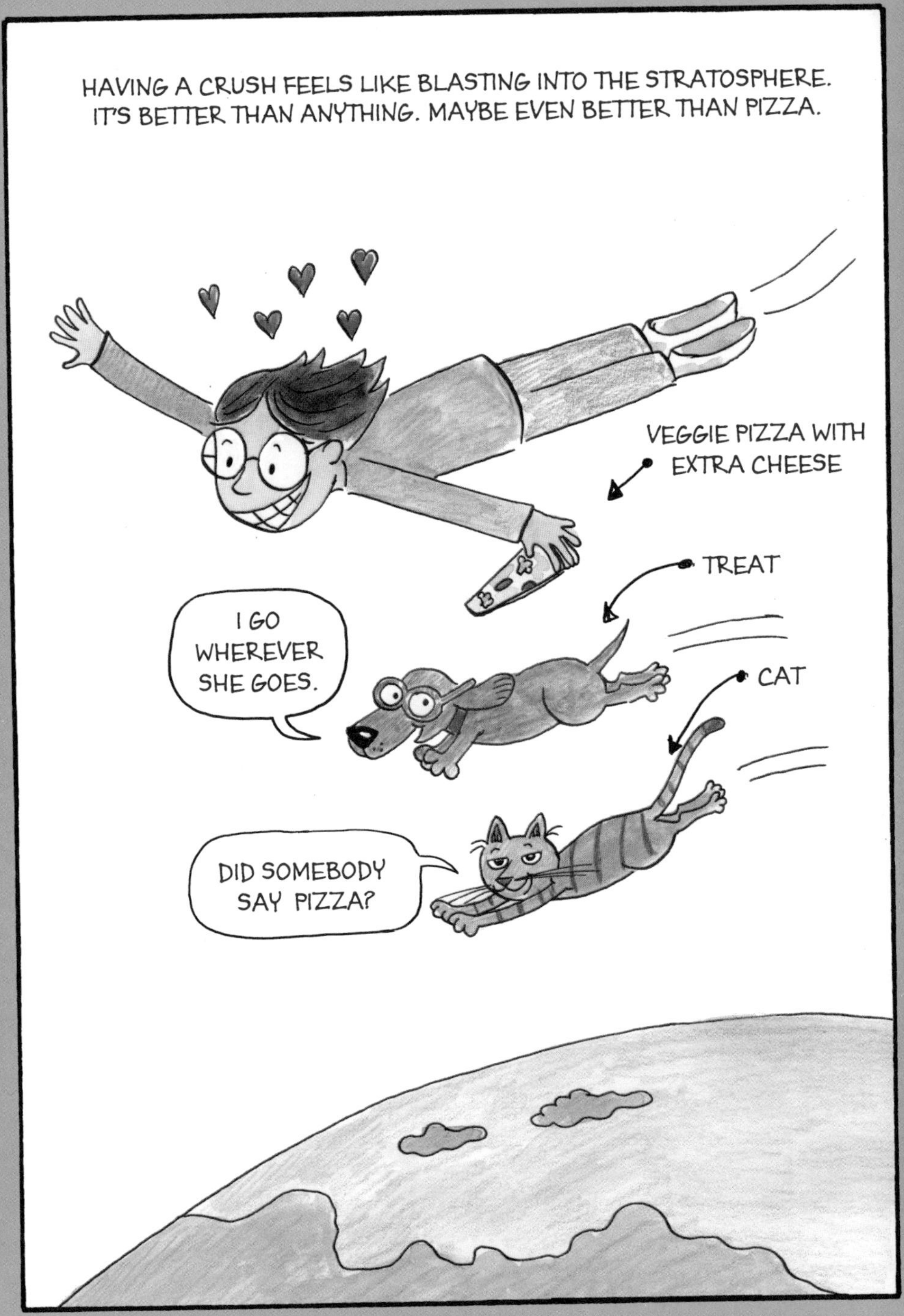
HAVING A CRUSH FEELS LIKE BLASTING INTO THE STRATOSPHERE. IT'S BETTER THAN ANYTHING. MAYBE EVEN BETTER THAN PIZZA.
VEGGIE PIZZA WITH EXTRA CHEESE
TREAT
I GO WHEREVER SHE GOES.
CAT
DID SOMEBODY SAY PIZZA?

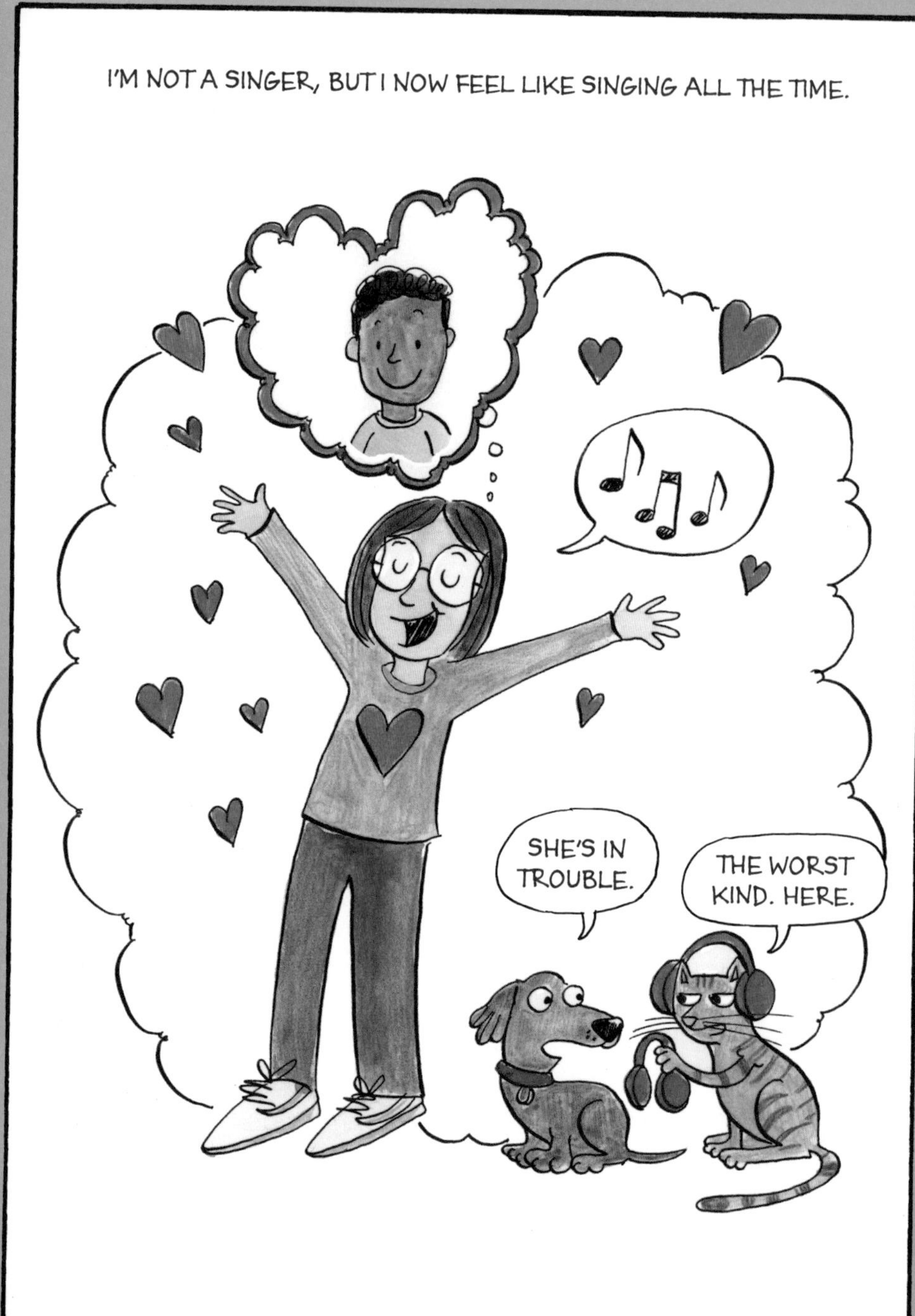
I'M NOT A SINGER, BUT I NOW FEEL LIKE SINGING ALL THE TIME.
SHE'S IN TROUBLE.
THE WORST KIND. HERE.

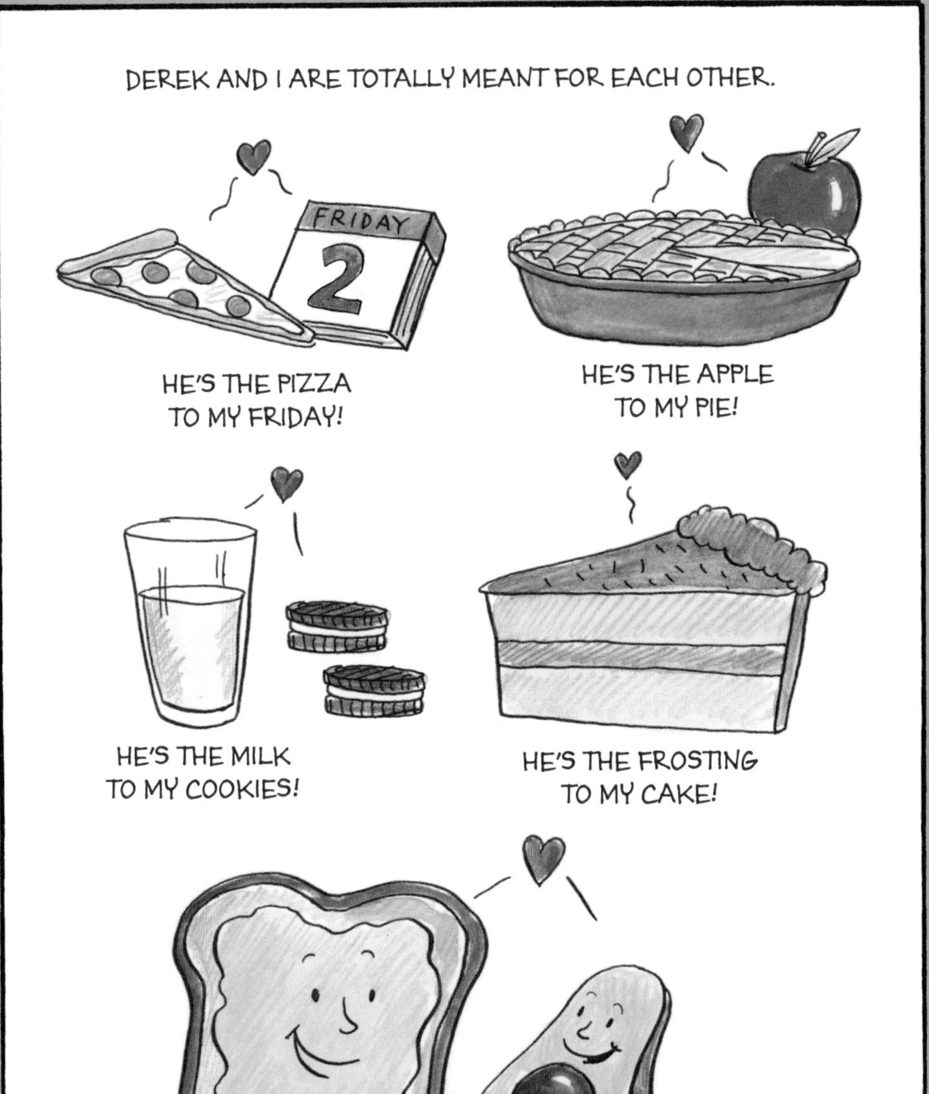
DEREK AND I ARE TOTALLY MEANT FOR EACH OTHER.
FRIDAY
2
HE'S THE PIZZA TO MY FRIDAY!
HE'S THE APPLE TO MY PIE!
HE'S THE MILK TO MY COOKIES!
HE'S THE FROSTING TO MY CAKE!
HE'S THE AVOCADO TO MY TOAST!

HOW TO TELL IF YOU AND YOUR CRUSH ARE MEANT TO BE:

IF YOU THROW A PIECE OF CRUMPLED PAPER INTO THE TRASH AND GET IT IN ON THE FIRST TRY, IT'S MEANT TO BE.

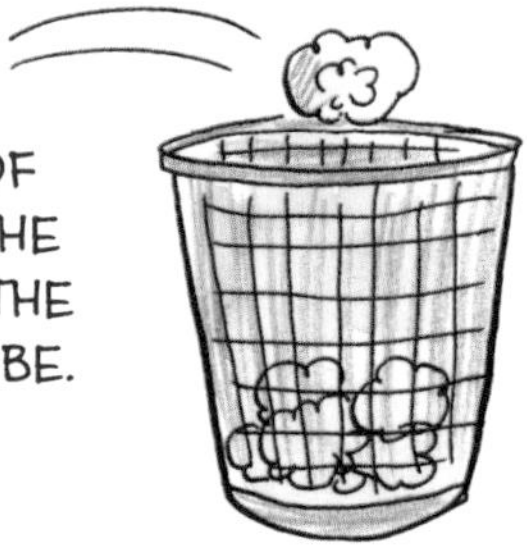

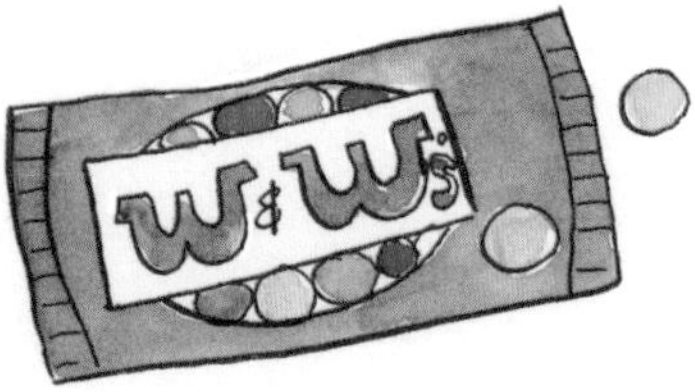
W&W's

IF YOU PICK OUT THE COLOR CANDY YOU CALLED IN ADVANCE, IT'S MEANT TO BE.

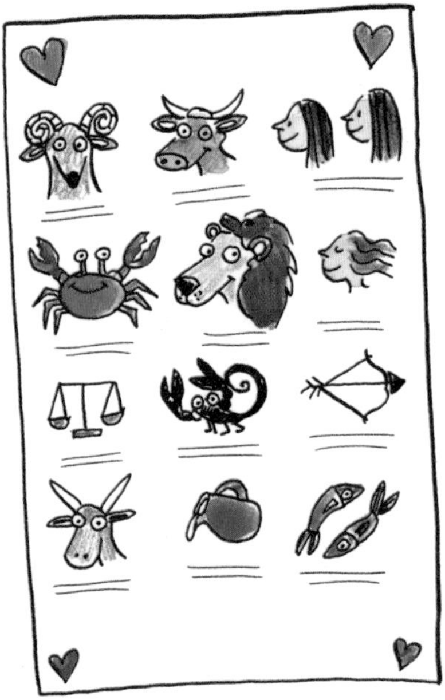

IF YOU READ THEIR HOROSCOPE AND IT SAYS SO, IT'S MEANT TO BE.

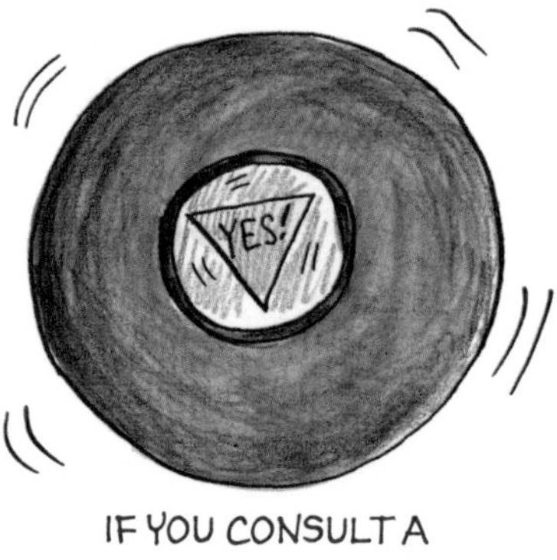
YES!

IF YOU CONSULT A MAGIC 8-BALL AND ALL SIGNS POINT TO YES, IT'S MEANT TO BE.

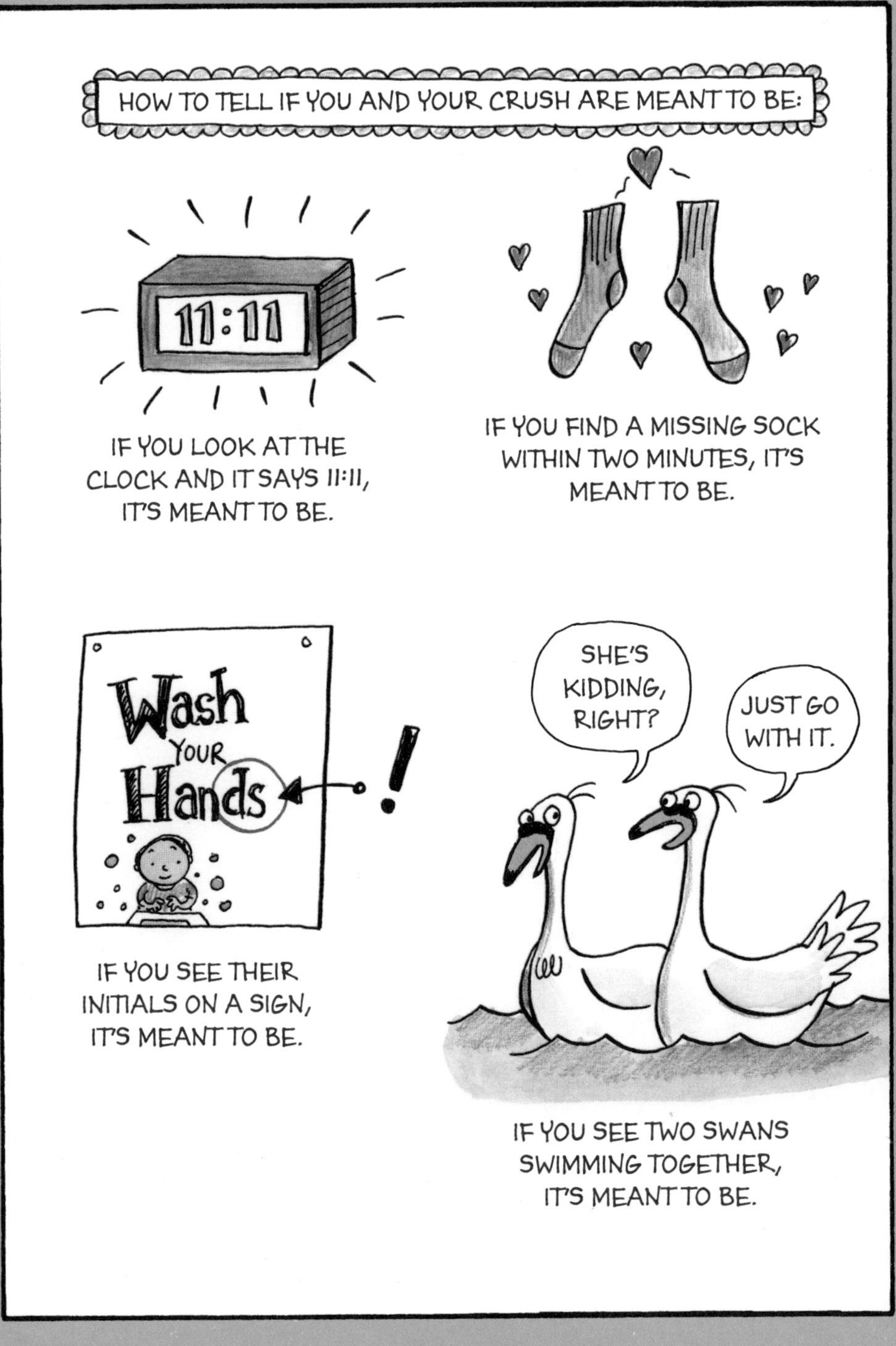
HOW TO TELL IF YOU AND YOUR CRUSH ARE MEANT TO BE:
11:11
IF YOU LOOK AT THE CLOCK AND IT SAYS 11:11, IT'S MEANT TO BE.
IF YOU FIND A MISSING SOCK WITHIN TWO MINUTES, IT'S MEANT TO BE.
Wash YOUR Hands
IF YOU SEE THEIR INITIALS ON A SIGN, IT'S MEANT TO BE.
SHE'S KIDDING, RIGHT?
JUST GO WITH IT.
IF YOU SEE TWO SWANS SWIMMING TOGETHER, IT'S MEANT TO BE.

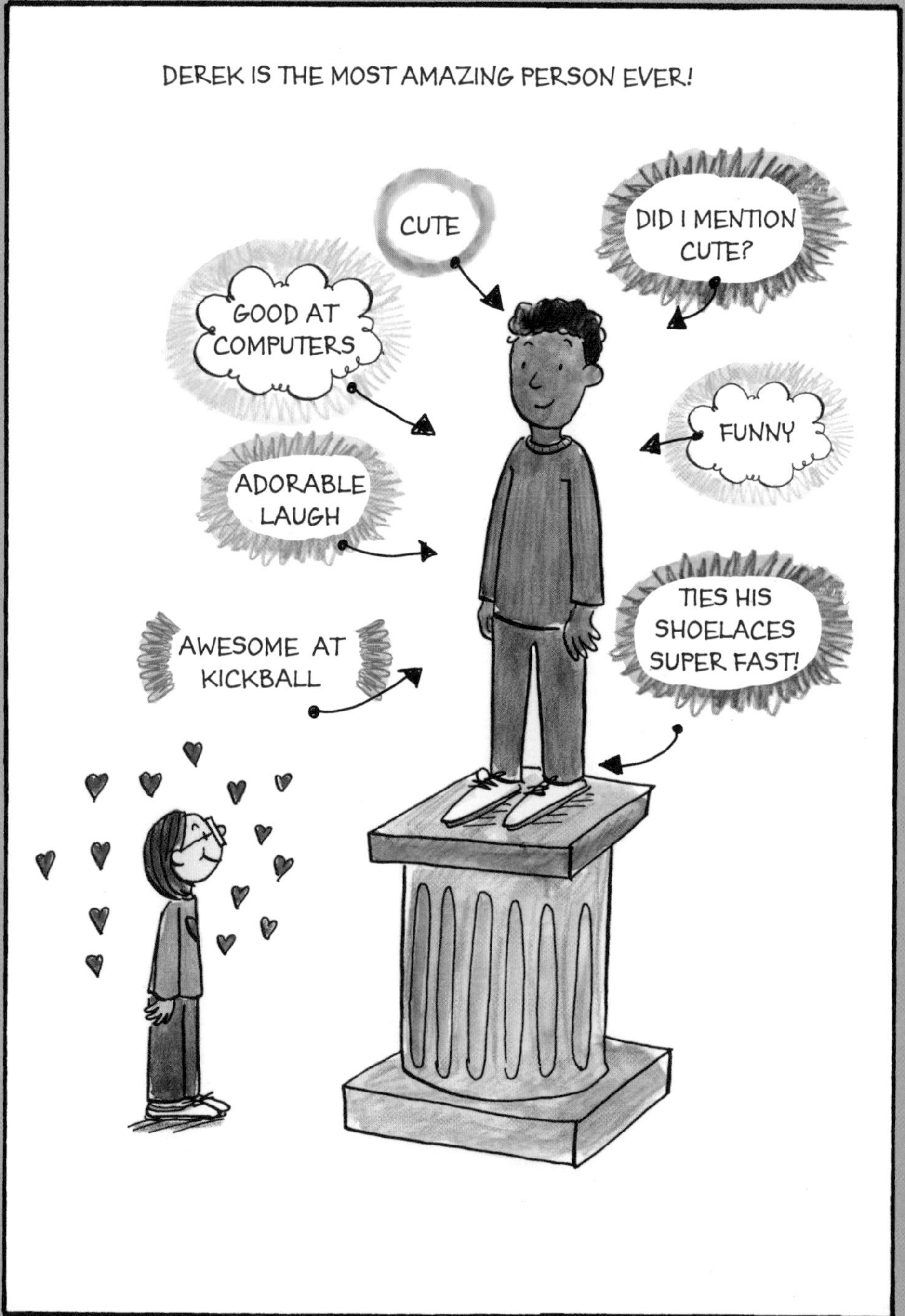
DEREK IS THE MOST AMAZING PERSON EVER!
CUTE
DID I MENTION CUTE?
GOOD AT COMPUTERS
FUNNY
ADORABLE LAUGH
AWESOME AT KICKBALL
TIES HIS SHOELACES SUPER FAST!

WINTER BREAK WAS GREAT, BUT I COULDN'T WAIT TO GET BACK TO SCHOOL TO SEE DEREK.

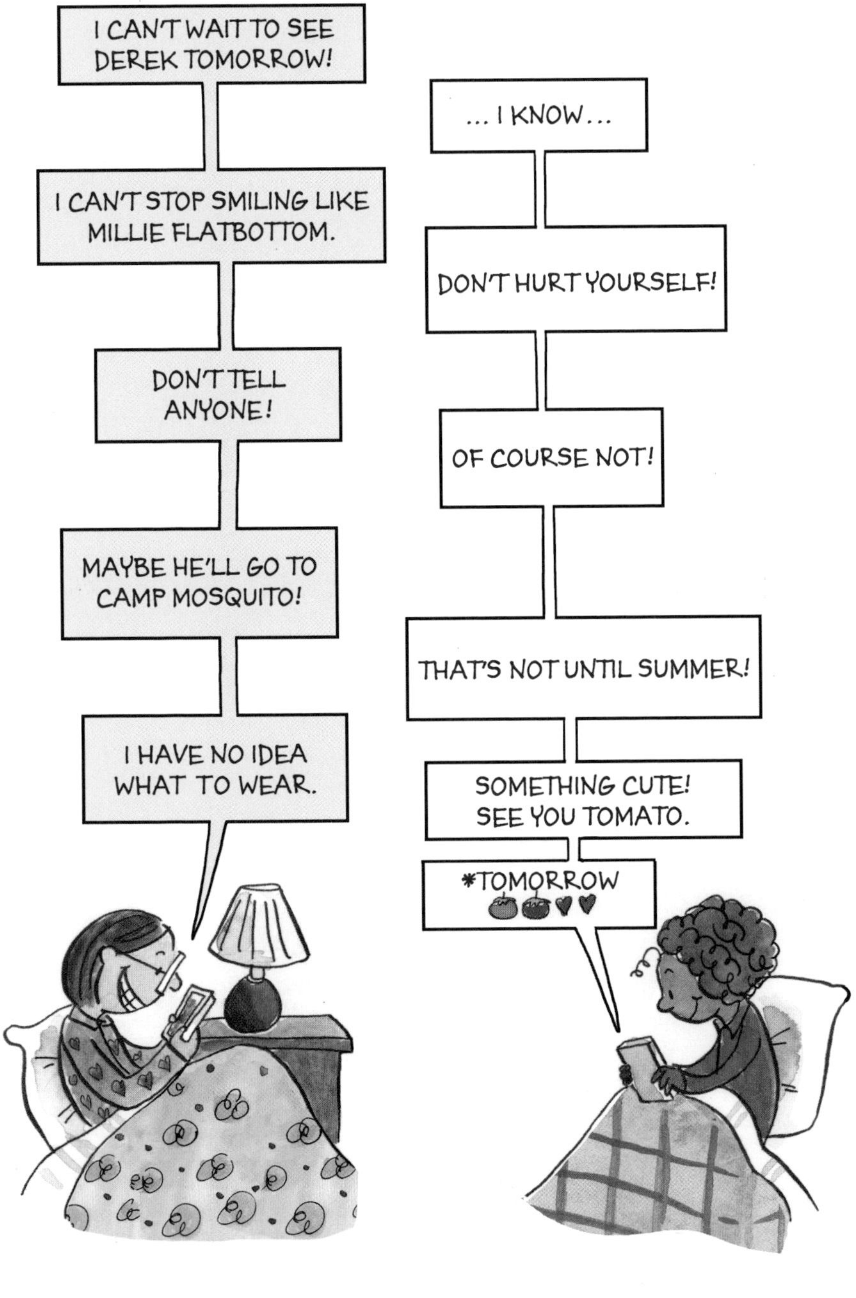
I CAN'T WAIT TO SEE DEREK TOMORROW!
... I KNOW ...
I CAN'T STOP SMILING LIKE MILLIE FLATBOTTOM.
DON'T HURT YOURSELF!
DON'T TELL ANYONE!
OF COURSE NOT!
MAYBE HE'LL GO TO CAMP MOSQUITO!
THAT'S NOT UNTIL SUMMER!
I HAVE NO IDEA WHAT TO WEAR.
SOMETHING CUTE! SEE YOU TOMATO.
*TOMORROW

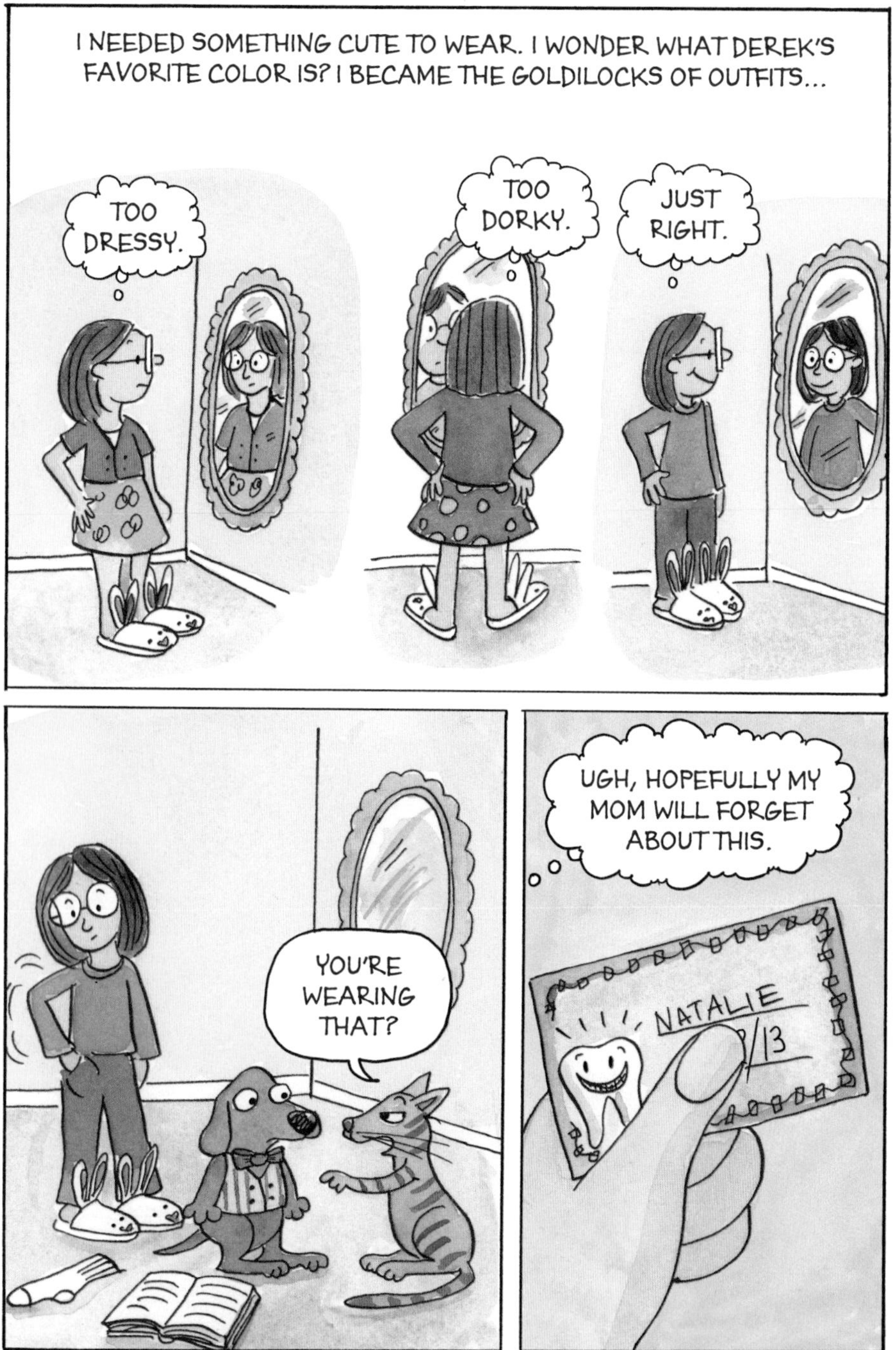
I NEEDED SOMETHING CUTE TO WEAR. I WONDER WHAT DEREK'S FAVORITE COLOR IS? I BECAME THE GOLDILOCKS OF OUTFITS...
TOO DRESSY.
TOO DORKY.
JUST RIGHT.
YOU'RE WEARING THAT?
UGH, HOPEFULLY MY MOM WILL FORGET ABOUT THIS.
NATALIE

CHAPTER 1
YOU + ME = WE

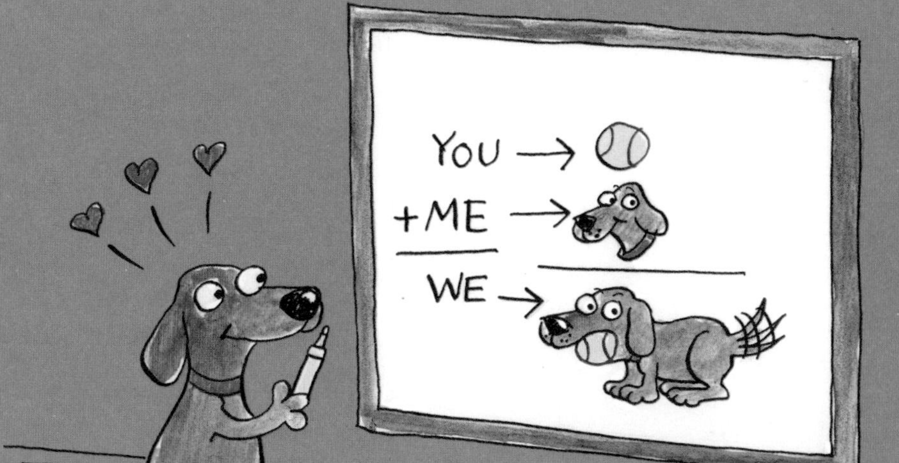
YOU →
+ME →
WE →

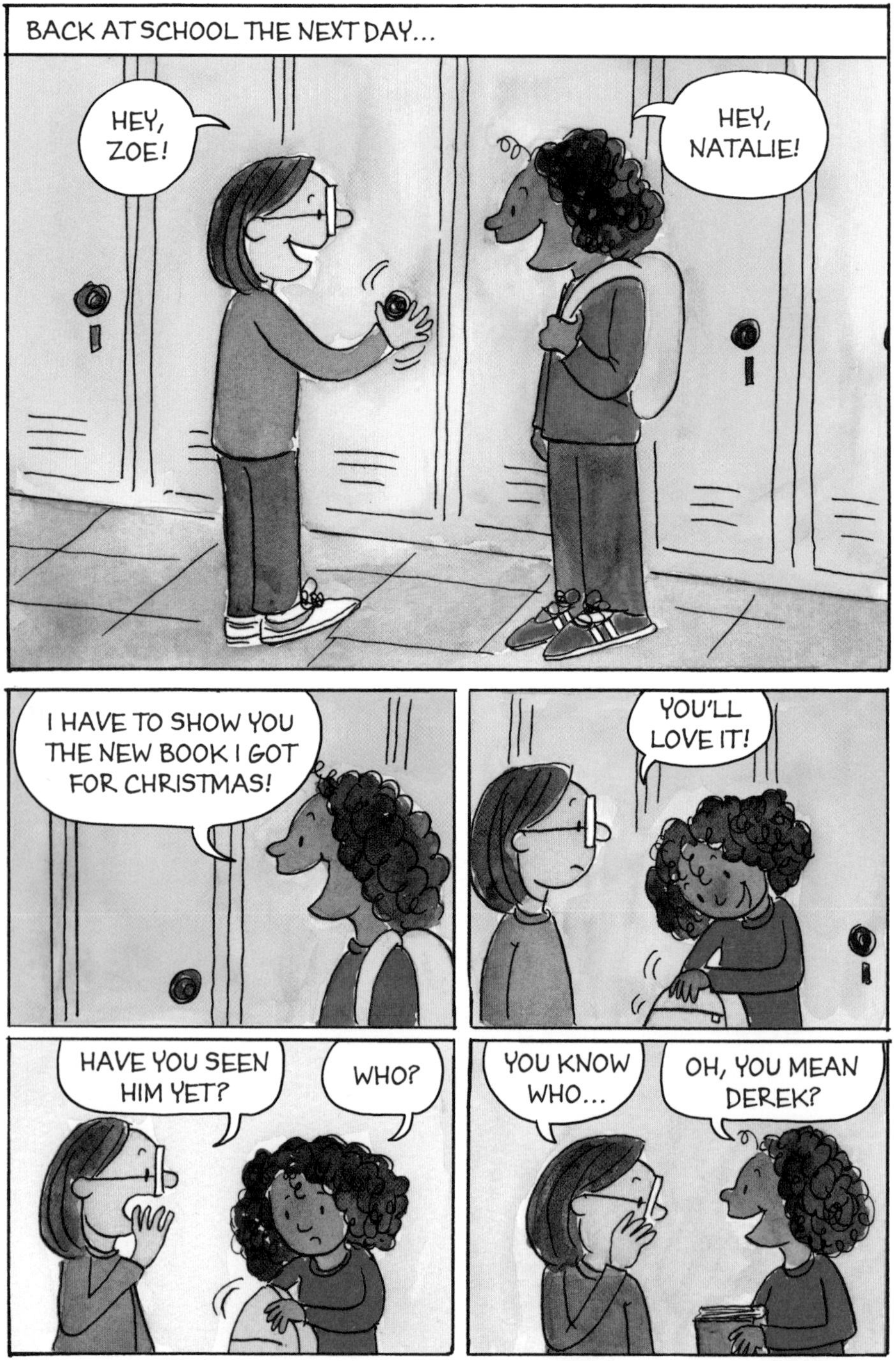
BACK AT SCHOOL THE NEXT DAY...
HEY, ZOE!
HEY, NATALIE!
I HAVE TO SHOW YOU THE NEW BOOK I GOT FOR CHRISTMAS!
YOU'LL LOVE IT!
HAVE YOU SEEN HIM YET?
WHO?
YOU KNOW WHO...
OH, YOU MEAN DEREK?

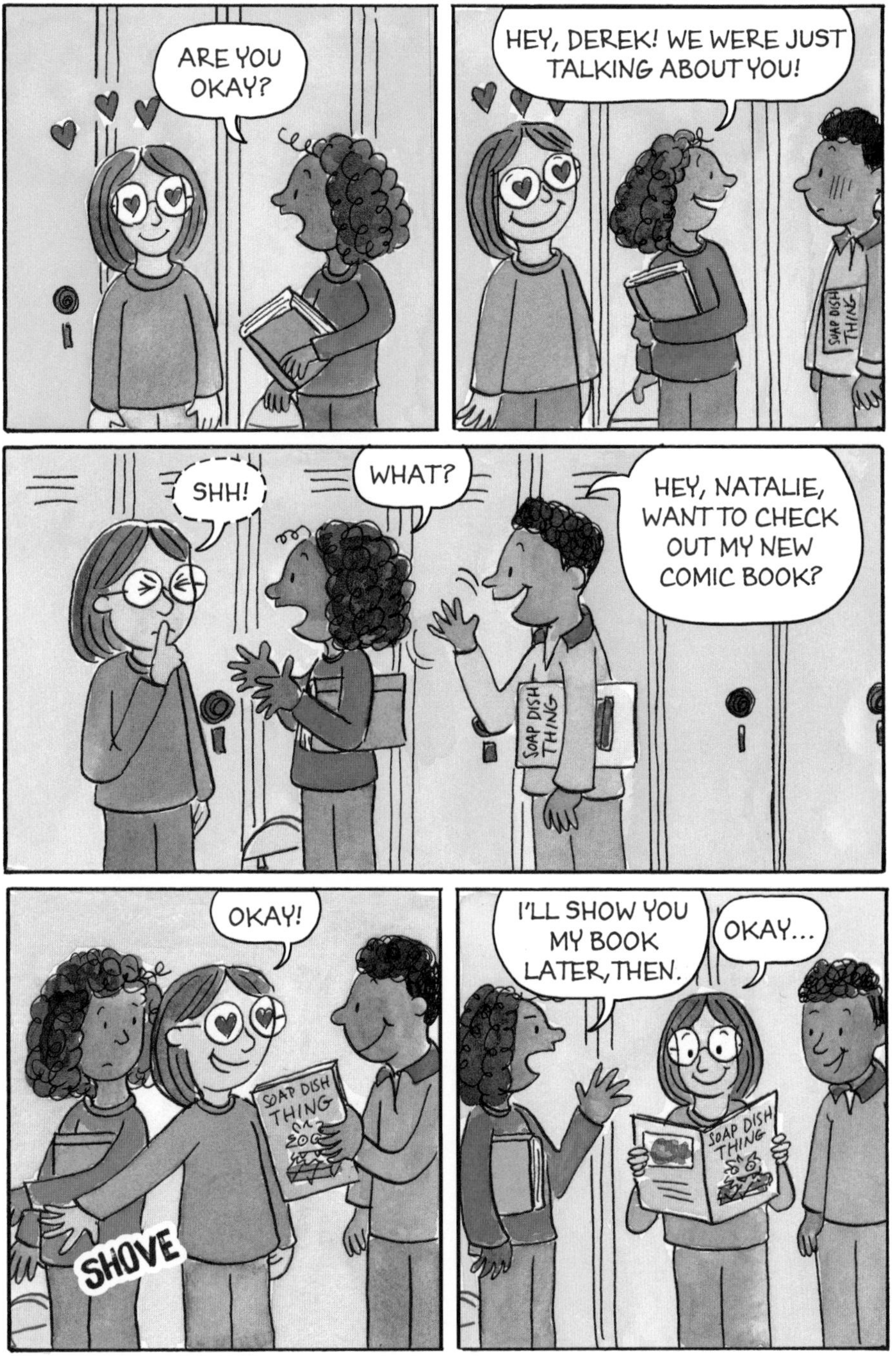
ARE YOU OKAY?
HEY, DEREK! WE WERE JUST TALKING ABOUT YOU!
SOAP DISH THING
SHH!
WHAT?
HEY, NATALIE, WANT TO CHECK OUT MY NEW COMIC BOOK?
SOAP DISH THING
OKAY!
SOAP DISH THING
SHOVE
I'LL SHOW YOU MY BOOK LATER, THEN.
OKAY...
SOAP DISH THING

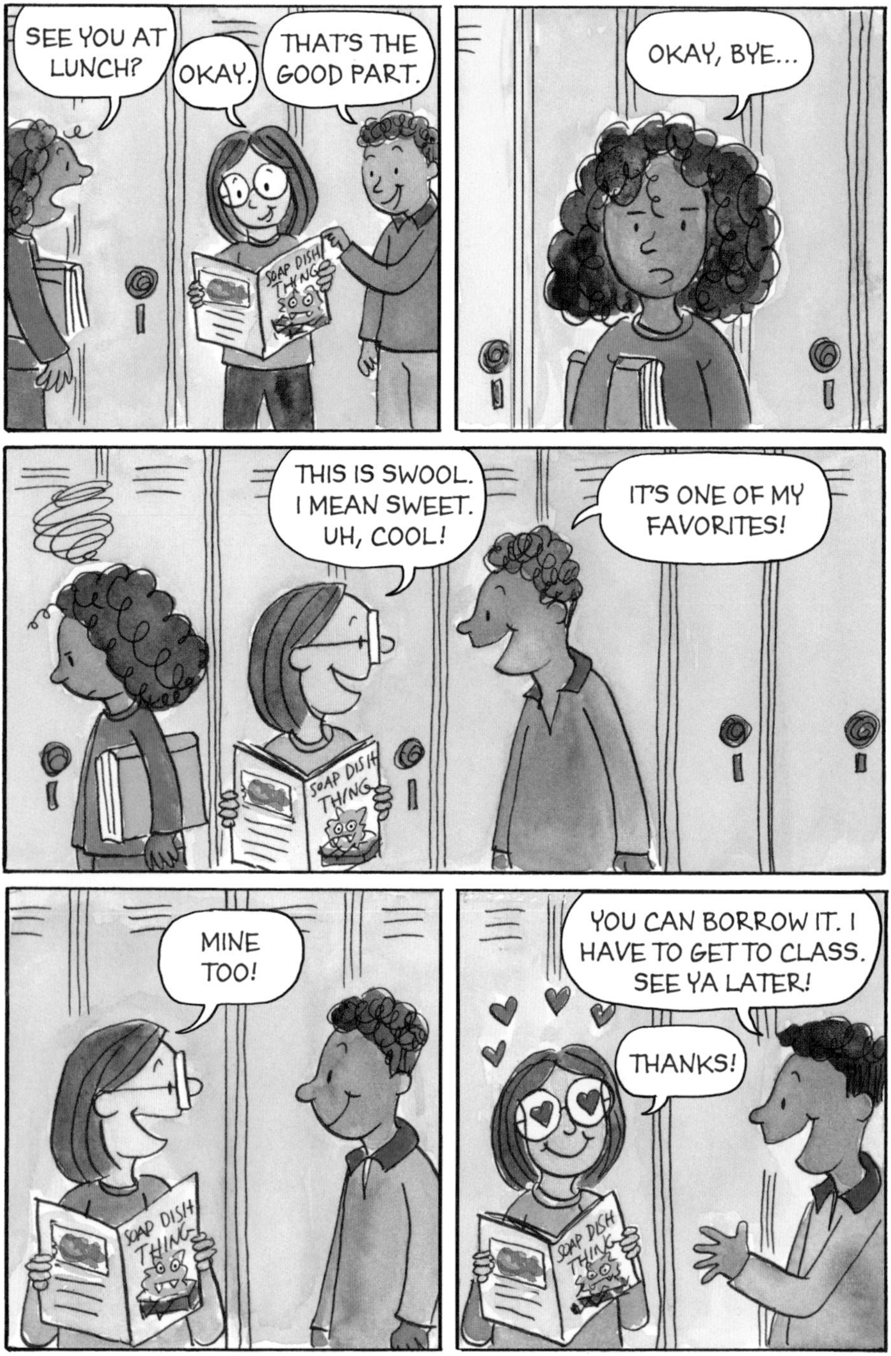
SEE YOU AT LUNCH?
OKAY.
THAT'S THE GOOD PART.
SOAP DISH THING
OKAY, BYE...
THIS IS SWOOL. I MEAN SWEET. UH, COOL!
IT'S ONE OF MY FAVORITES!
SOAP DISH THING
MINE TOO!
SOAP DISH THING
YOU CAN BORROW IT. I HAVE TO GET TO CLASS. SEE YA LATER!
THANKS!
SOAP DISH THING

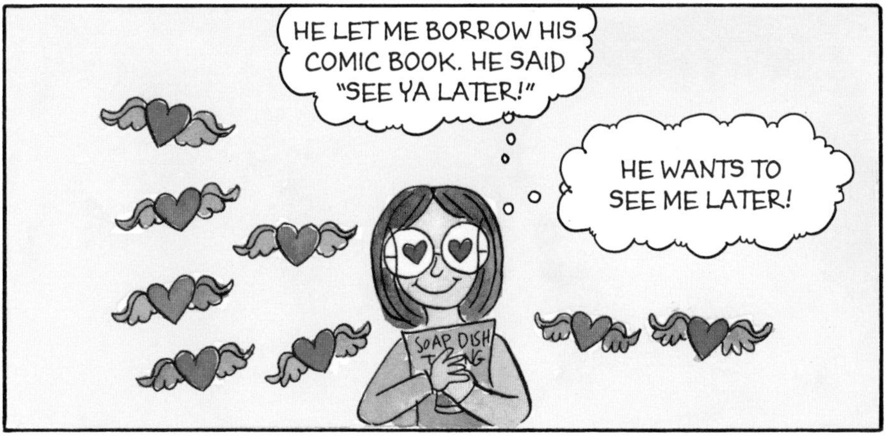
HE LET ME BORROW HIS COMIC BOOK. HE SAID "SEE YA LATER!"
HE WANTS TO SEE ME LATER!
SOAP DISH THING

I FLOATED ALL THE WAY TO ENGLISH CLASS...

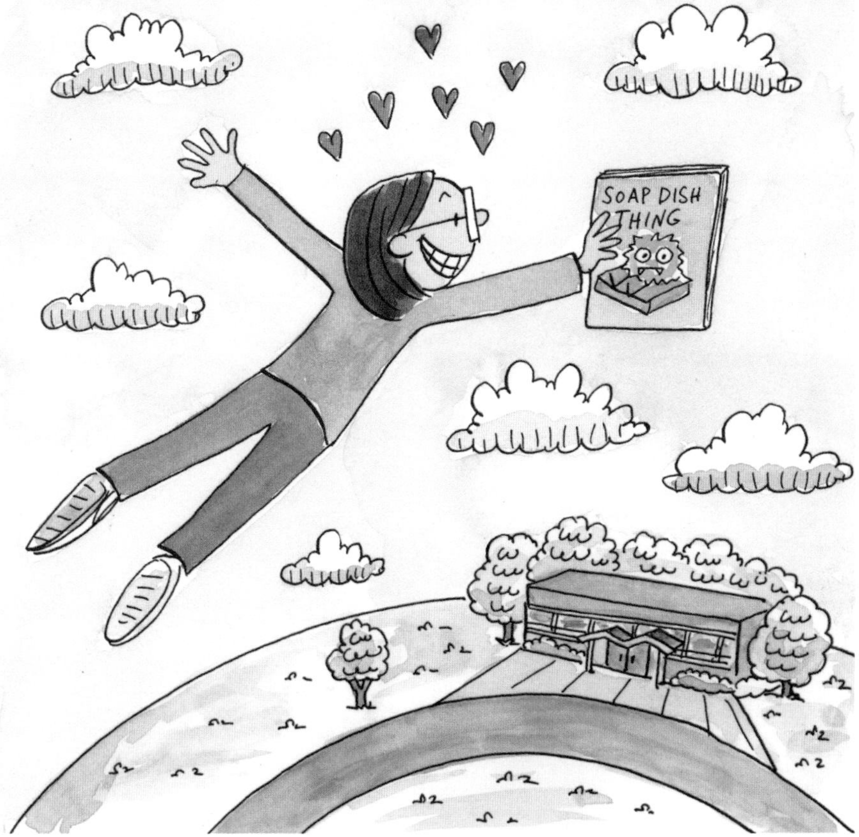
SOAP DISH THING

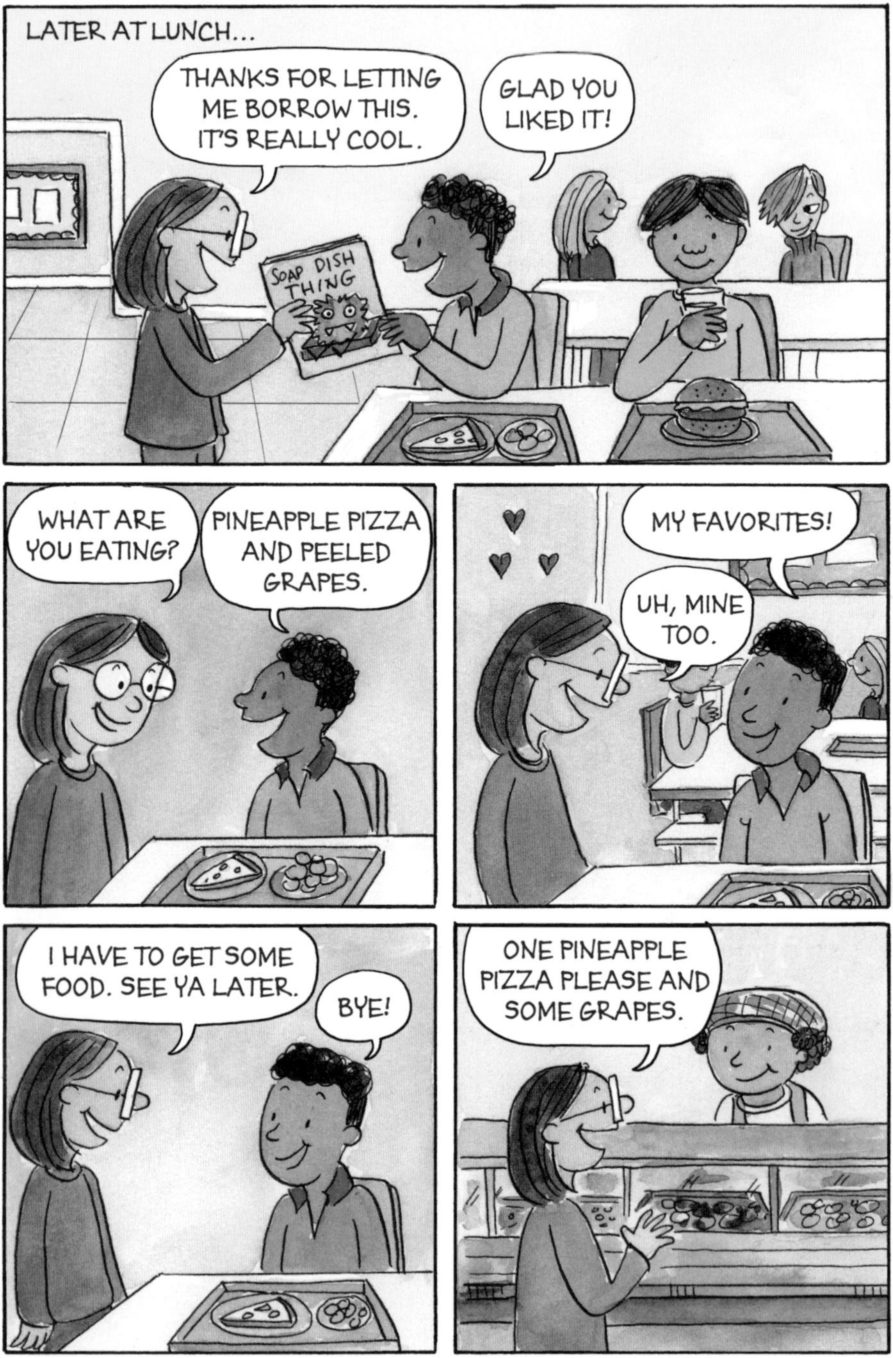
LATER AT LUNCH...
THANKS FOR LETTING ME BORROW THIS. IT'S REALLY COOL.
GLAD YOU LIKED IT!
SOAP DISH THING
WHAT ARE YOU EATING?
PINEAPPLE PIZZA AND PEELED GRAPES.
MY FAVORITES!
UH, MINE TOO.
I HAVE TO GET SOME FOOD. SEE YA LATER.
BYE!
ONE PINEAPPLE PIZZA PLEASE AND SOME GRAPES.

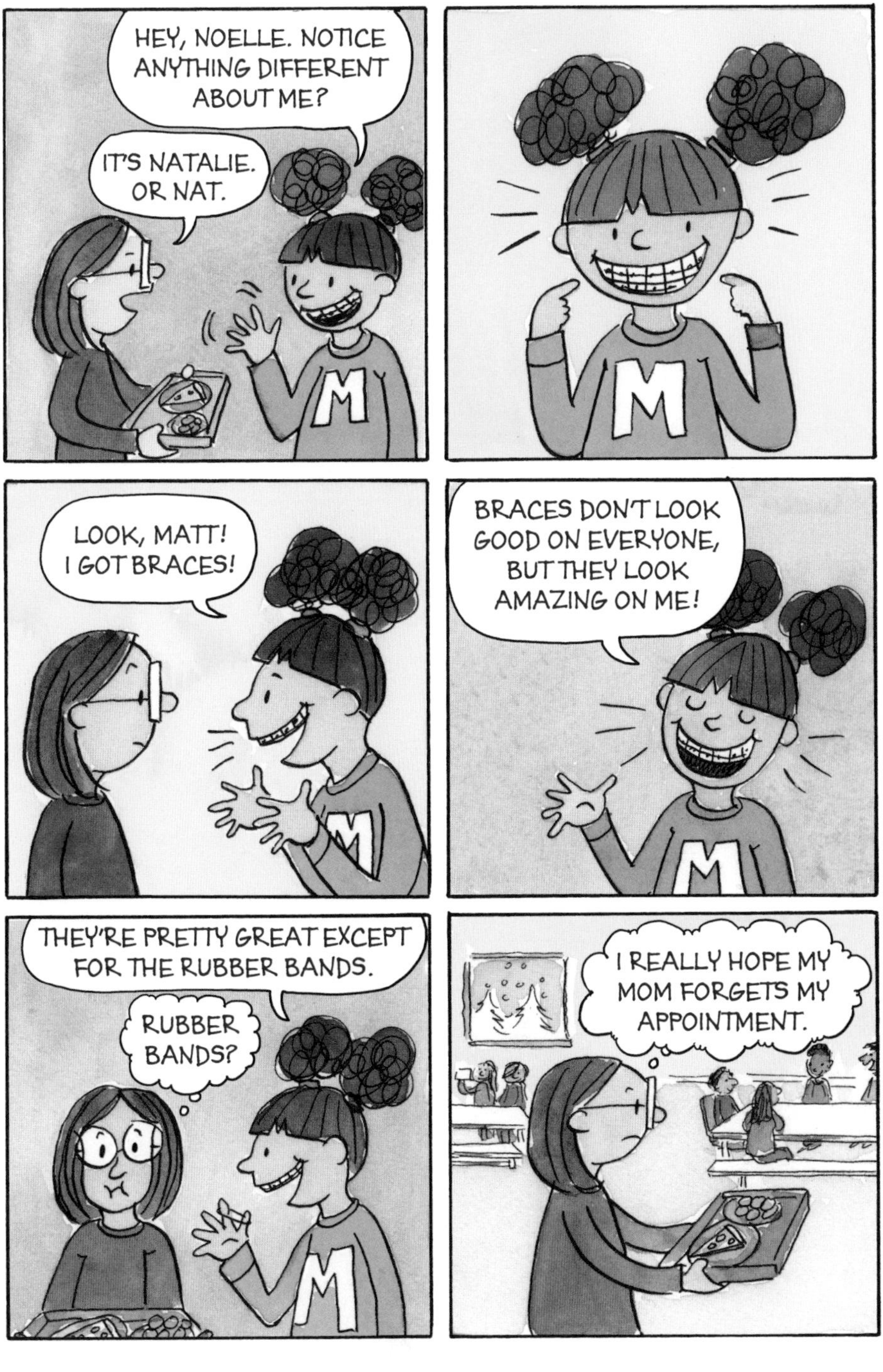
HEY, NOELLE. NOTICE ANYTHING DIFFERENT ABOUT ME?
IT'S NATALIE. OR NAT.
LOOK, MATT! I GOT BRACES!
BRACES DON'T LOOK GOOD ON EVERYONE, BUT THEY LOOK AMAZING ON ME!
THEY'RE PRETTY GREAT EXCEPT FOR THE RUBBER BANDS.
RUBBER BANDS?
I REALLY HOPE MY MOM FORGETS MY APPOINTMENT.

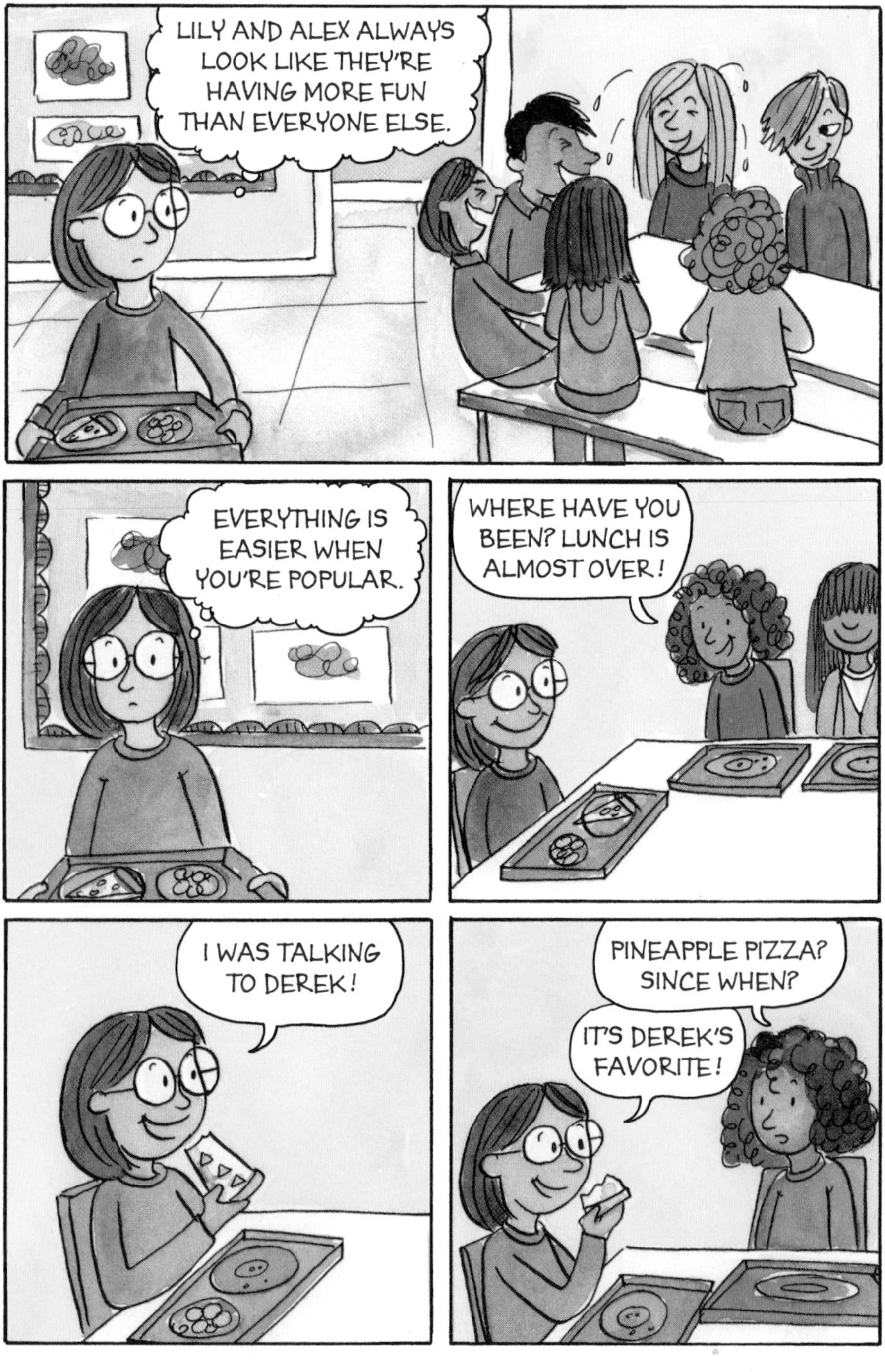

LILY AND ALEX ALWAYS LOOK LIKE THEY'RE HAVING MORE FUN THAN EVERYONE ELSE.
EVERYTHING IS EASIER WHEN YOU'RE POPULAR.
WHERE HAVE YOU BEEN? LUNCH IS ALMOST OVER!
I WAS TALKING TO DEREK!
PINEAPPLE PIZZA? SINCE WHEN?
IT'S DEREK'S FAVORITE!

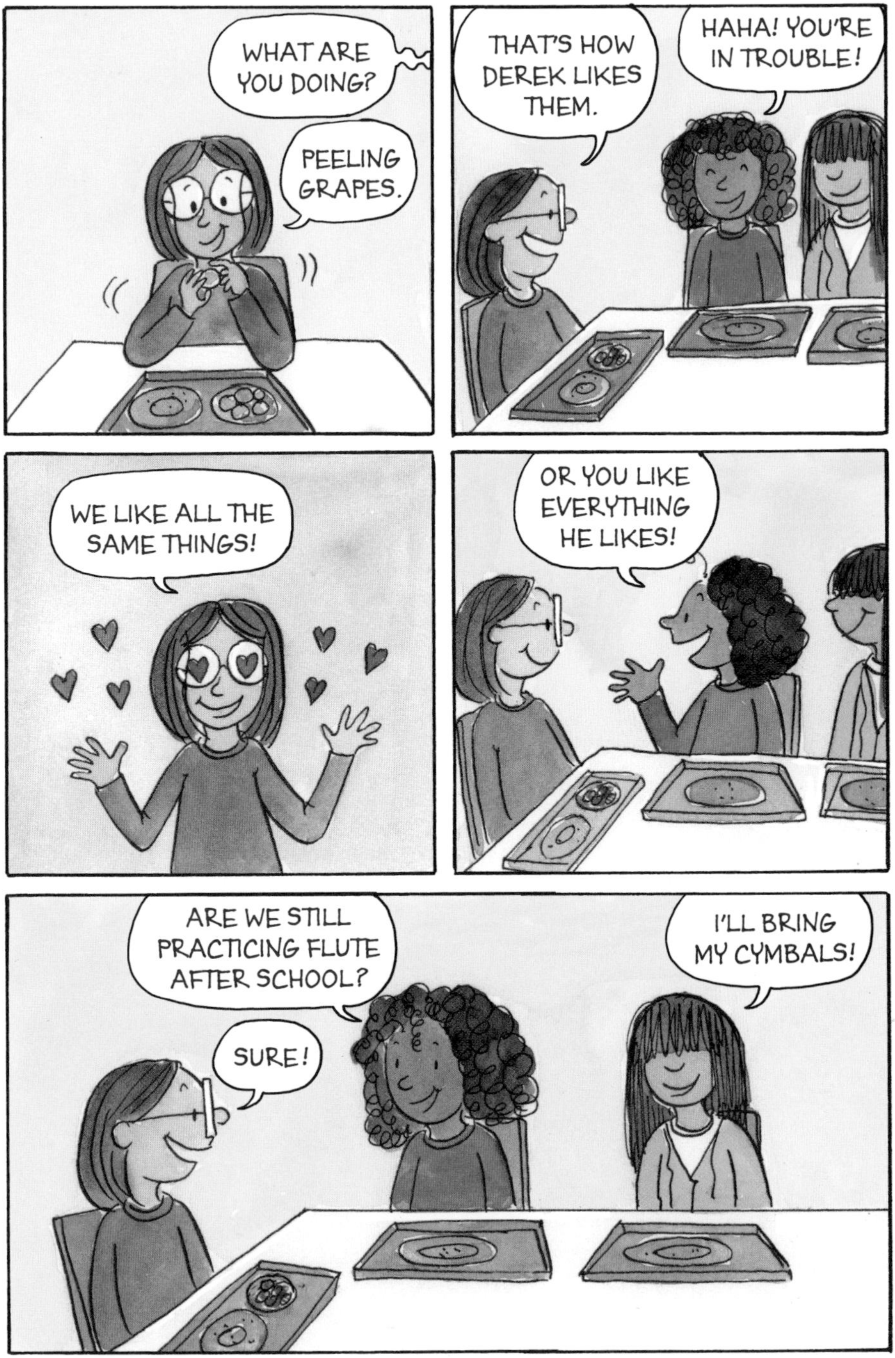
WHAT ARE YOU DOING?
PEELING GRAPES.
THAT'S HOW DEREK LIKES THEM.
HAHA! YOU'RE IN TROUBLE!
WE LIKE ALL THE SAME THINGS!
OR YOU LIKE EVERYTHING HE LIKES!
ARE WE STILL PRACTICING FLUTE AFTER SCHOOL?
SURE!
I'LL BRING MY CYMBALS!

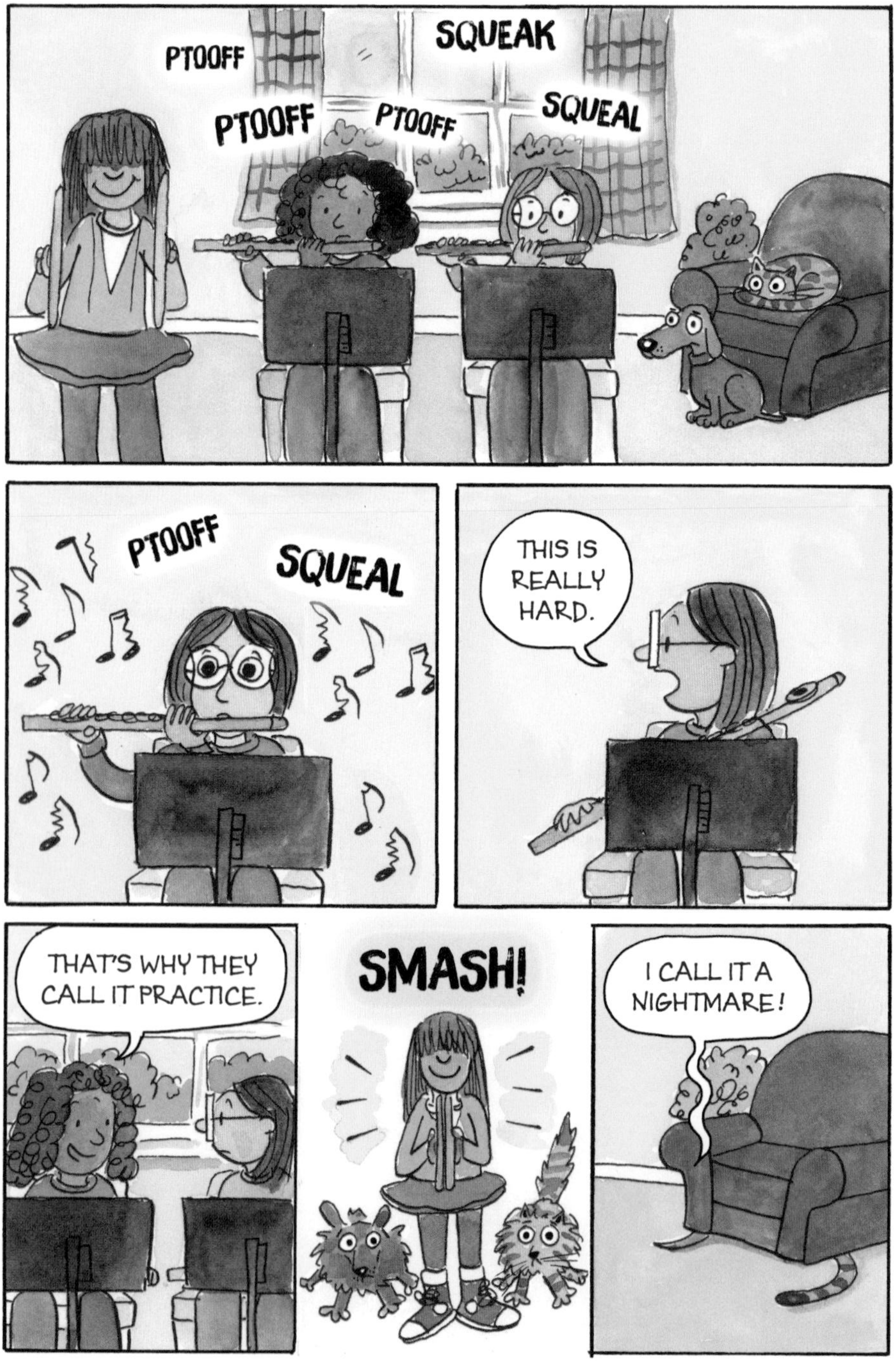
PTOOFF
SQUEAK
PTOOFF
PTOOFF
SQUEAL
PTOOFF
SQUEAL
THIS IS REALLY HARD.
THAT'S WHY THEY CALL IT PRACTICE.
SMASH!
I CALL IT A NIGHTMARE!

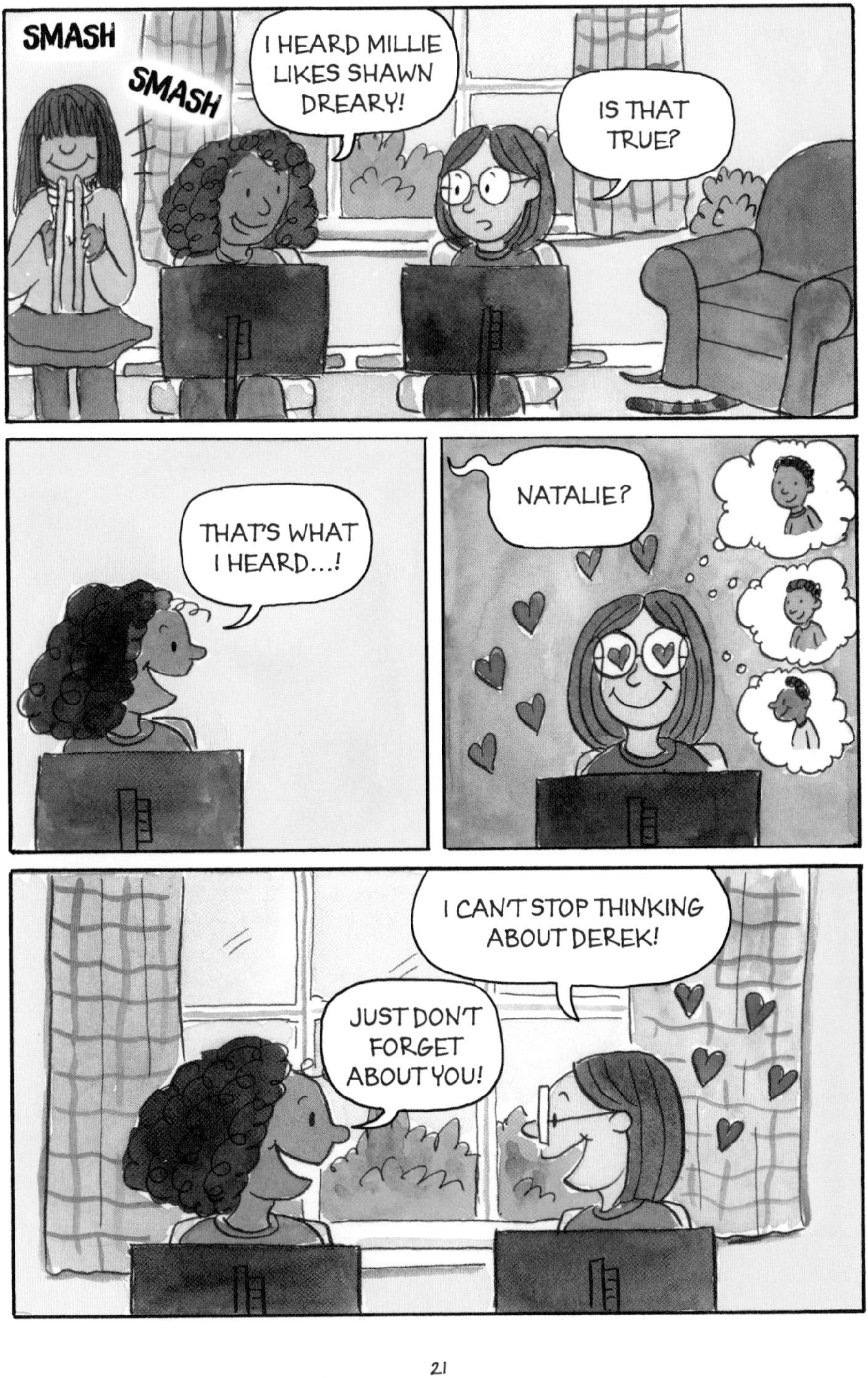
SMASH
SMASH
I HEARD MILLIE LIKES SHAWN DREARY!
IS THAT TRUE?
THAT'S WHAT I HEARD...!
NATALIE?
I CAN'T STOP THINKING ABOUT DEREK!
JUST DON'T FORGET ABOUT YOU!

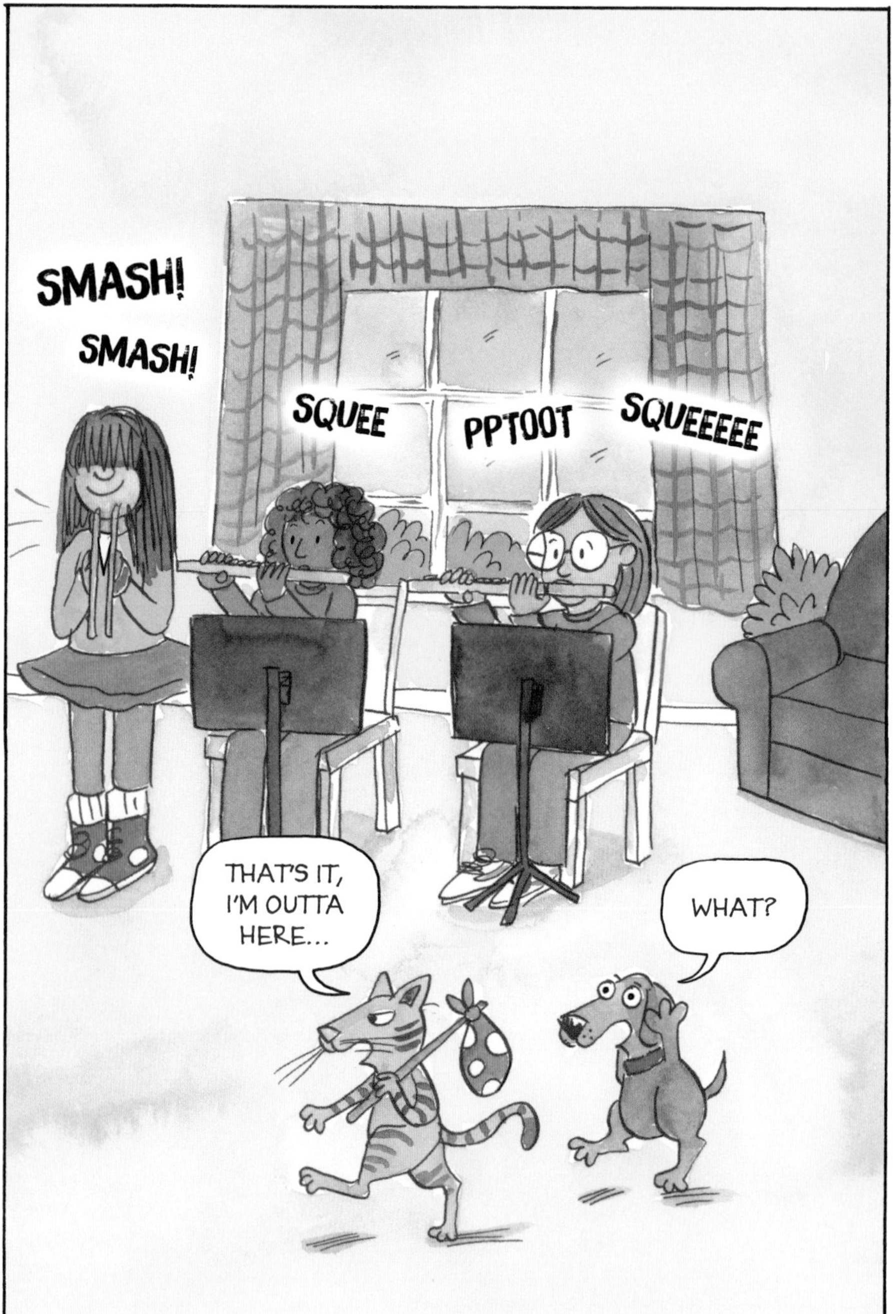
SMASH!
SMASH!
SQUEE
PPTOOT
SQUEEEEEE
THAT'S IT, I'M OUTTA HERE...
WHAT?

CHAPTER 2
LOVE SONGS

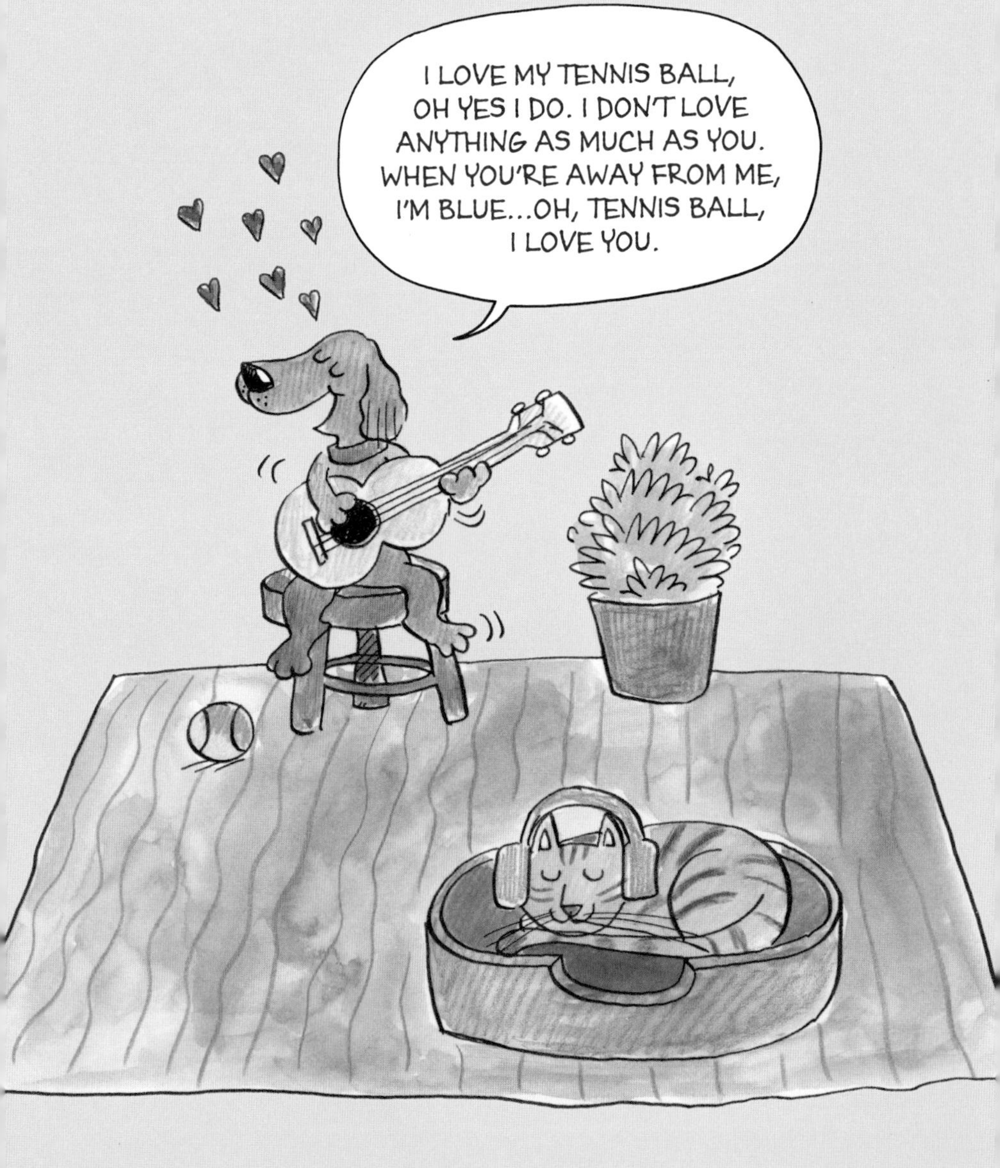
I LOVE MY TENNIS BALL, OH YES I DO. I DON'T LOVE ANYTHING AS MUCH AS YOU. WHEN YOU'RE AWAY FROM ME, I'M BLUE...OH, TENNIS BALL, I LOVE YOU.

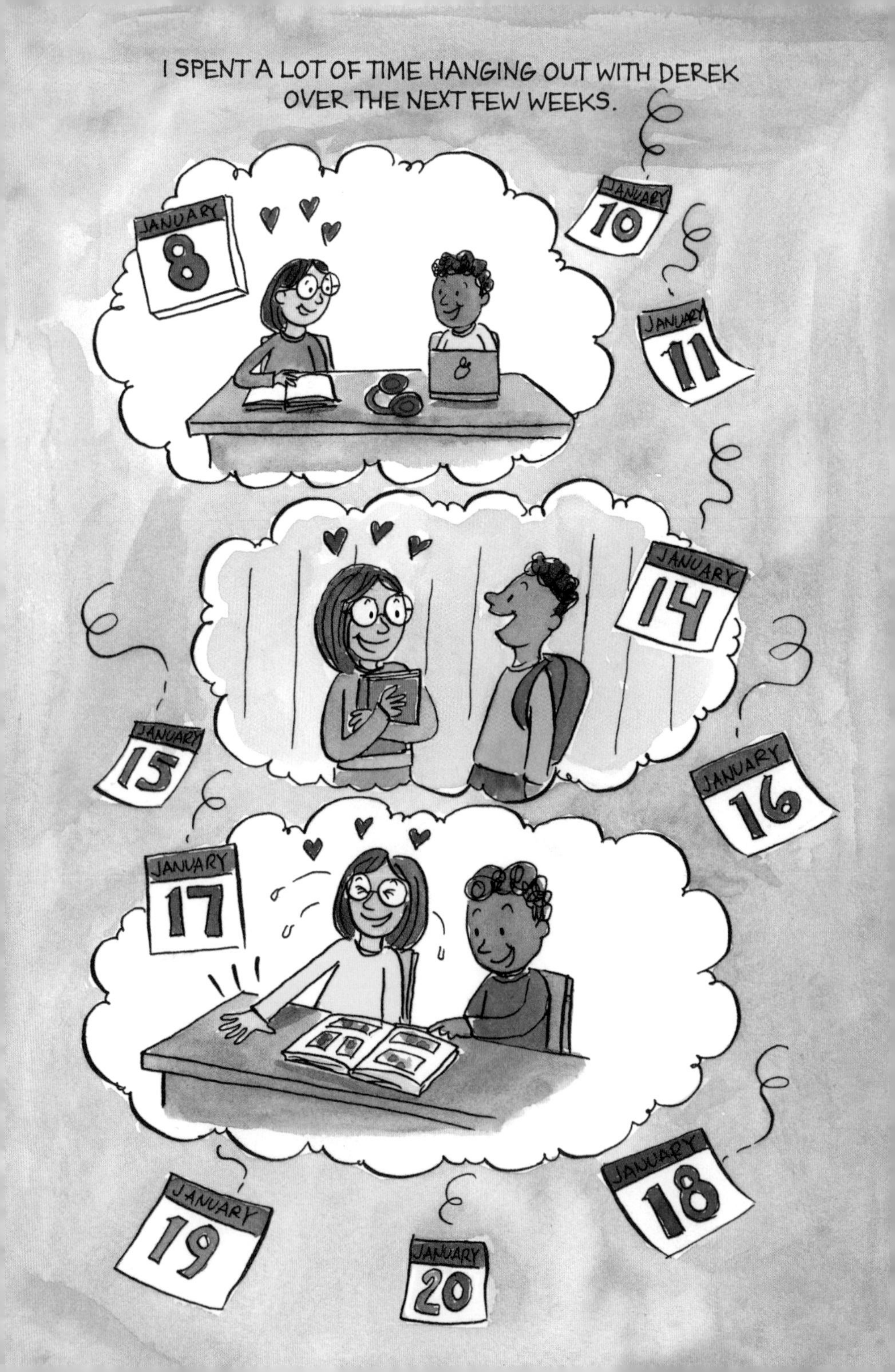
I SPENT A LOT OF TIME HANGING OUT WITH DEREK OVER THE NEXT FEW WEEKS.
JANUARY 8
JANUARY 10
JANUARY 11
JANUARY 14
JANUARY 15
JANUARY 16
JANUARY 17
JANUARY 18
JANUARY 19
JANUARY 20

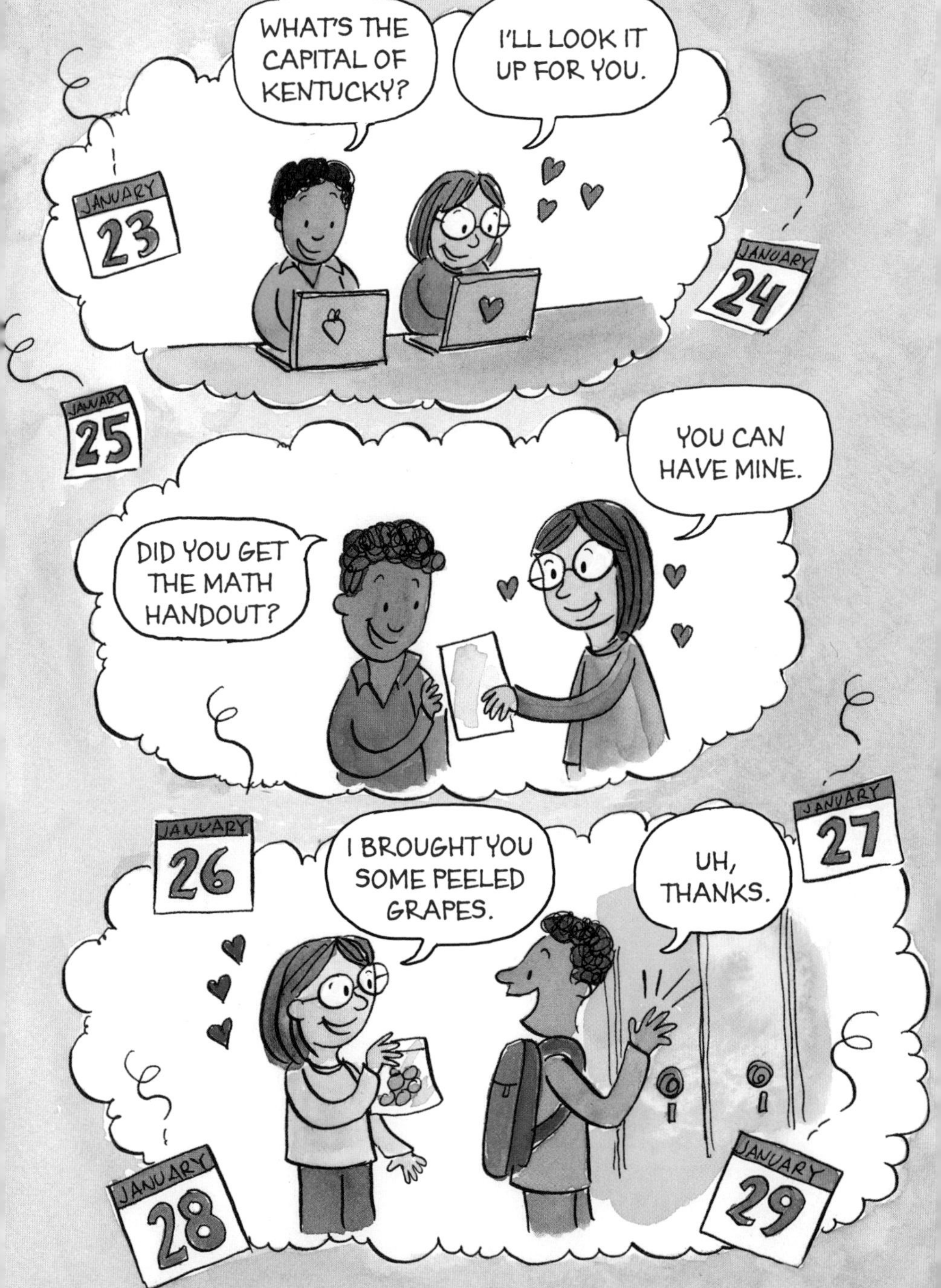
WHAT'S THE CAPITAL OF KENTUCKY?
I'LL LOOK IT UP FOR YOU.
JANUARY 23
JANUARY 24
JANUARY 25
YOU CAN HAVE MINE.
DID YOU GET THE MATH HANDOUT?
JANUARY 26
I BROUGHT YOU SOME PEELED GRAPES.
UH, THANKS.
JANUARY 27
JANUARY 28
JANUARY 29

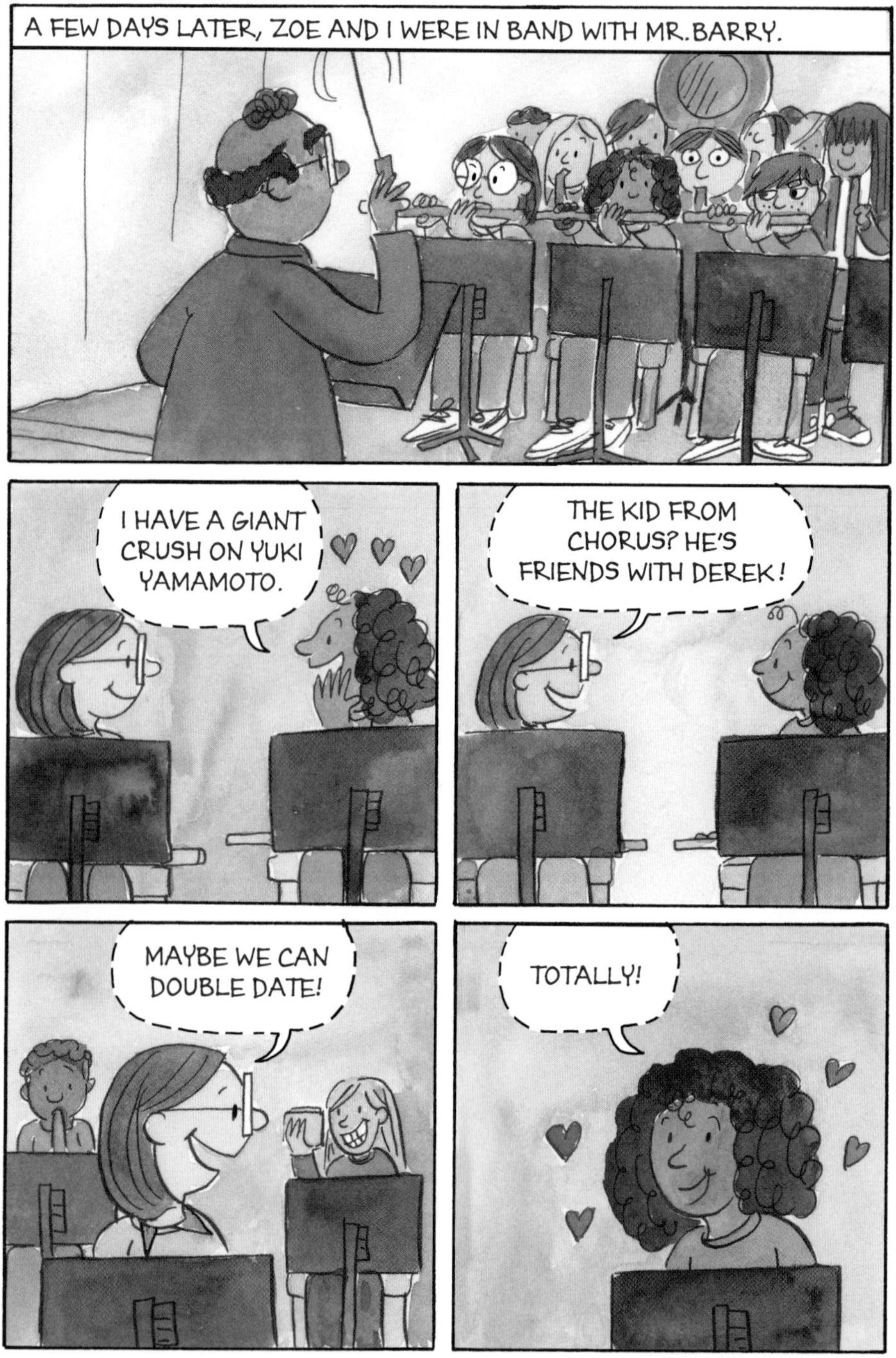

A FEW DAYS LATER, ZOE AND I WERE IN BAND WITH MR. BARRY.
I HAVE A GIANT CRUSH ON YUKI YAMAMOTO.
THE KID FROM CHORUS? HE'S FRIENDS WITH DEREK!
MAYBE WE CAN DOUBLE DATE!
TOTALLY!

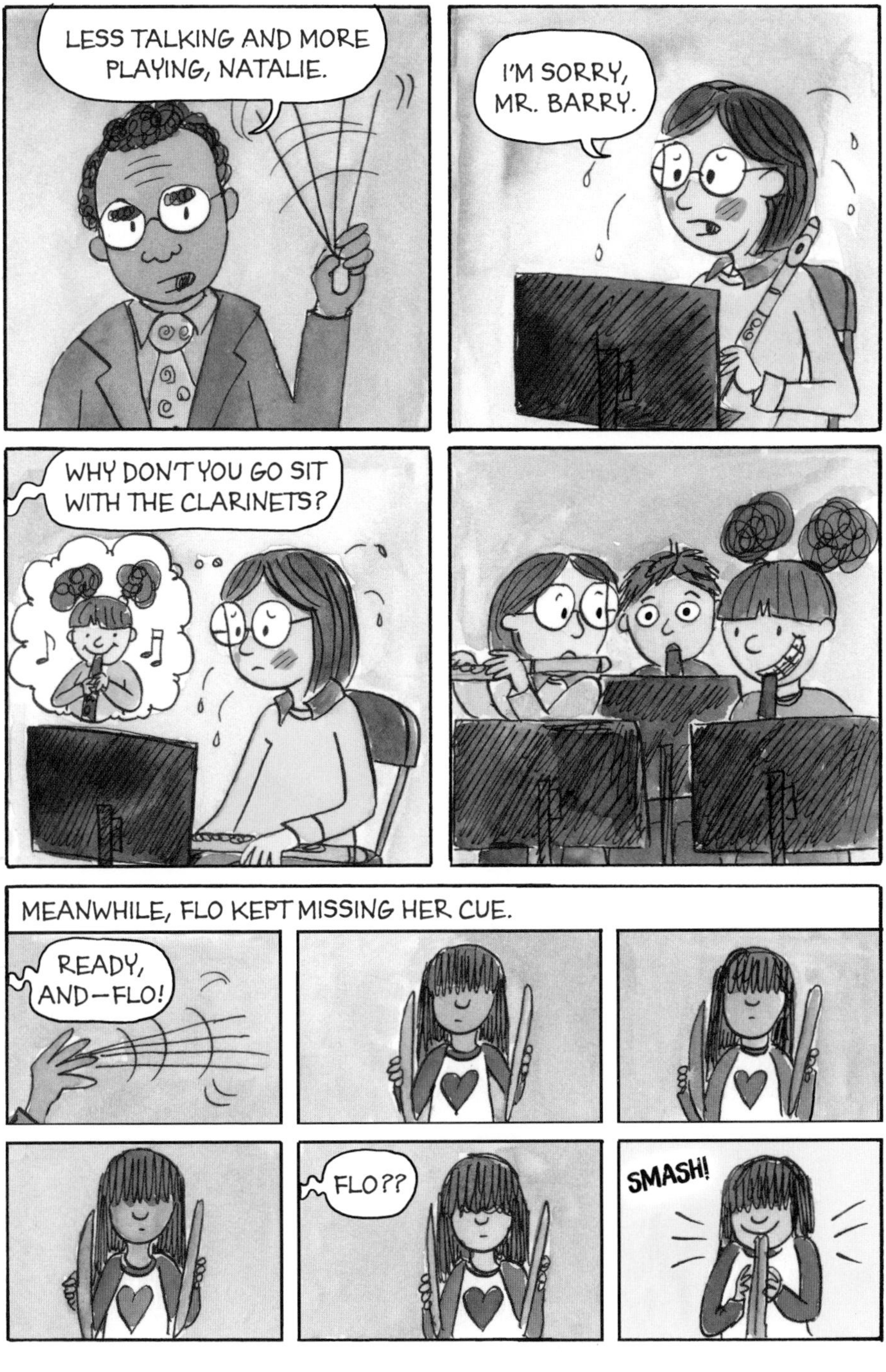
LESS TALKING AND MORE PLAYING, NATALIE.
I'M SORRY, MR. BARRY.
WHY DON'T YOU GO SIT WITH THE CLARINETS?
MEANWHILE, FLO KEPT MISSING HER CUE.
READY, AND—FLO!
FLO??
SMASH!

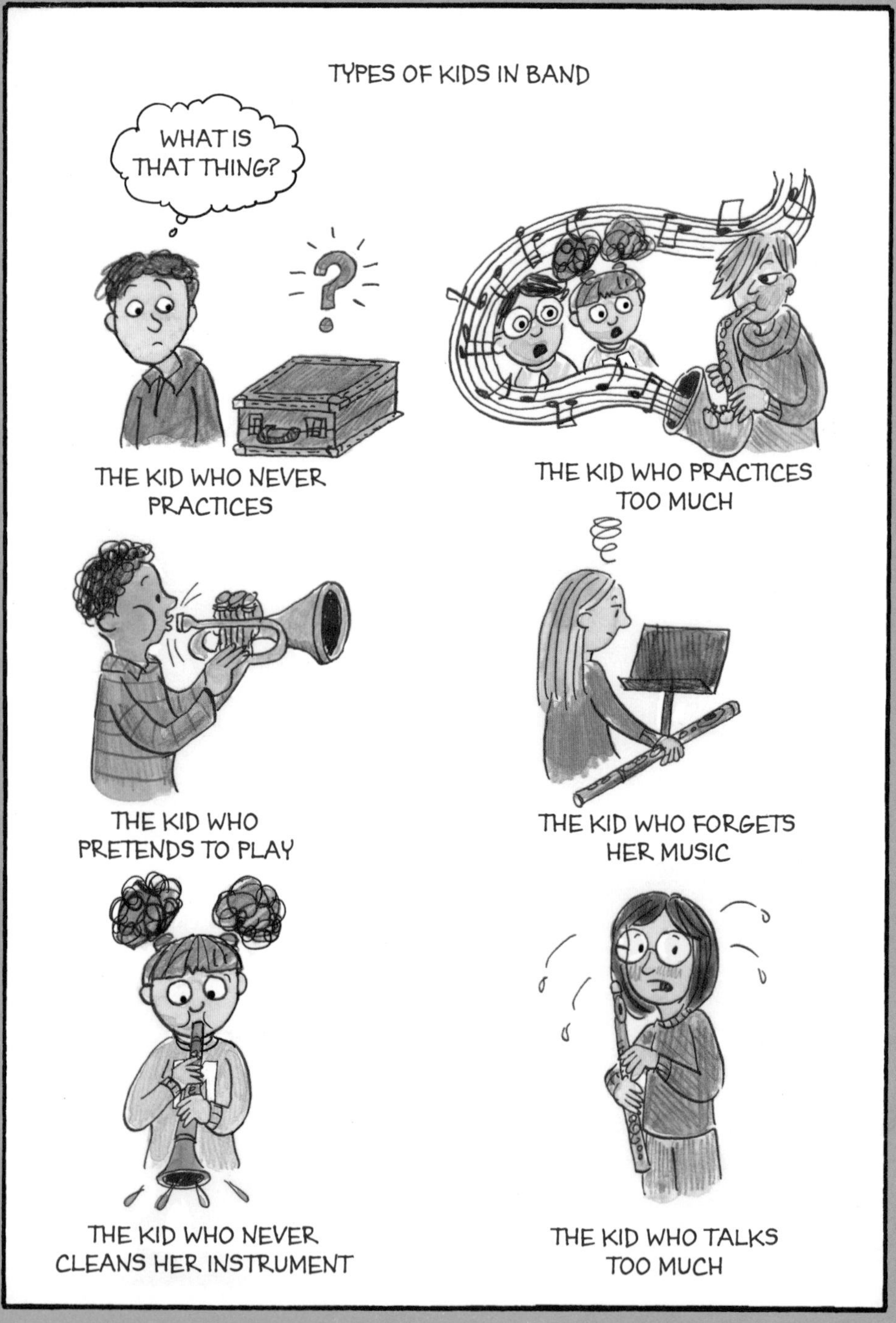
TYPES OF KIDS IN BAND
WHAT IS THAT THING?
THE KID WHO NEVER PRACTICES
THE KID WHO PRACTICES TOO MUCH
THE KID WHO PRETENDS TO PLAY
THE KID WHO FORGETS HER MUSIC
THE KID WHO NEVER CLEANS HER INSTRUMENT
THE KID WHO TALKS TOO MUCH

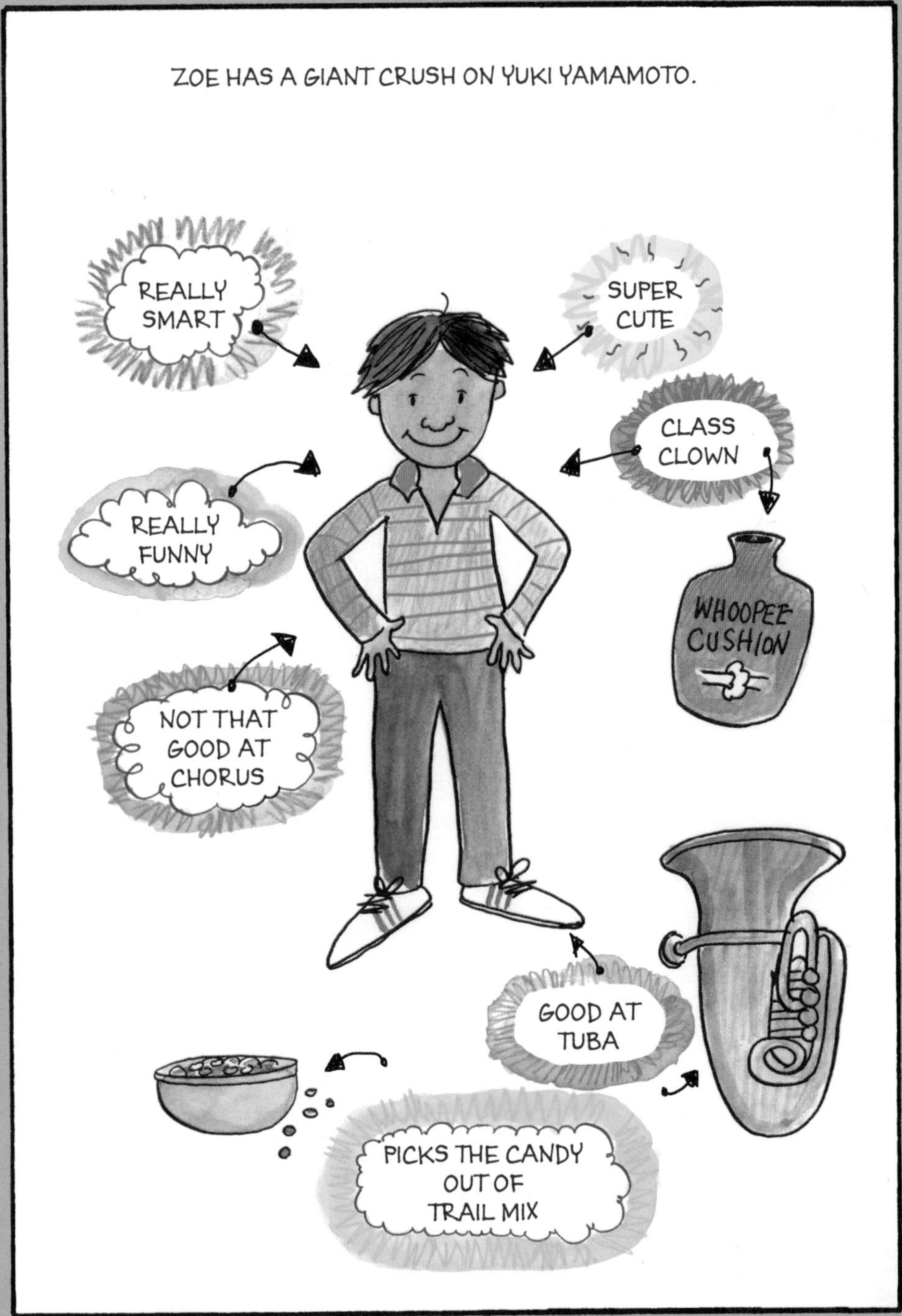

ZOE HAS A GIANT CRUSH ON YUKI YAMAMOTO.
REALLY SMART
SUPER CUTE
CLASS CLOWN
REALLY FUNNY
WHOOPEE CUSHION
NOT THAT GOOD AT CHORUS
GOOD AT TUBA
PICKS THE CANDY OUT OF TRAIL MIX

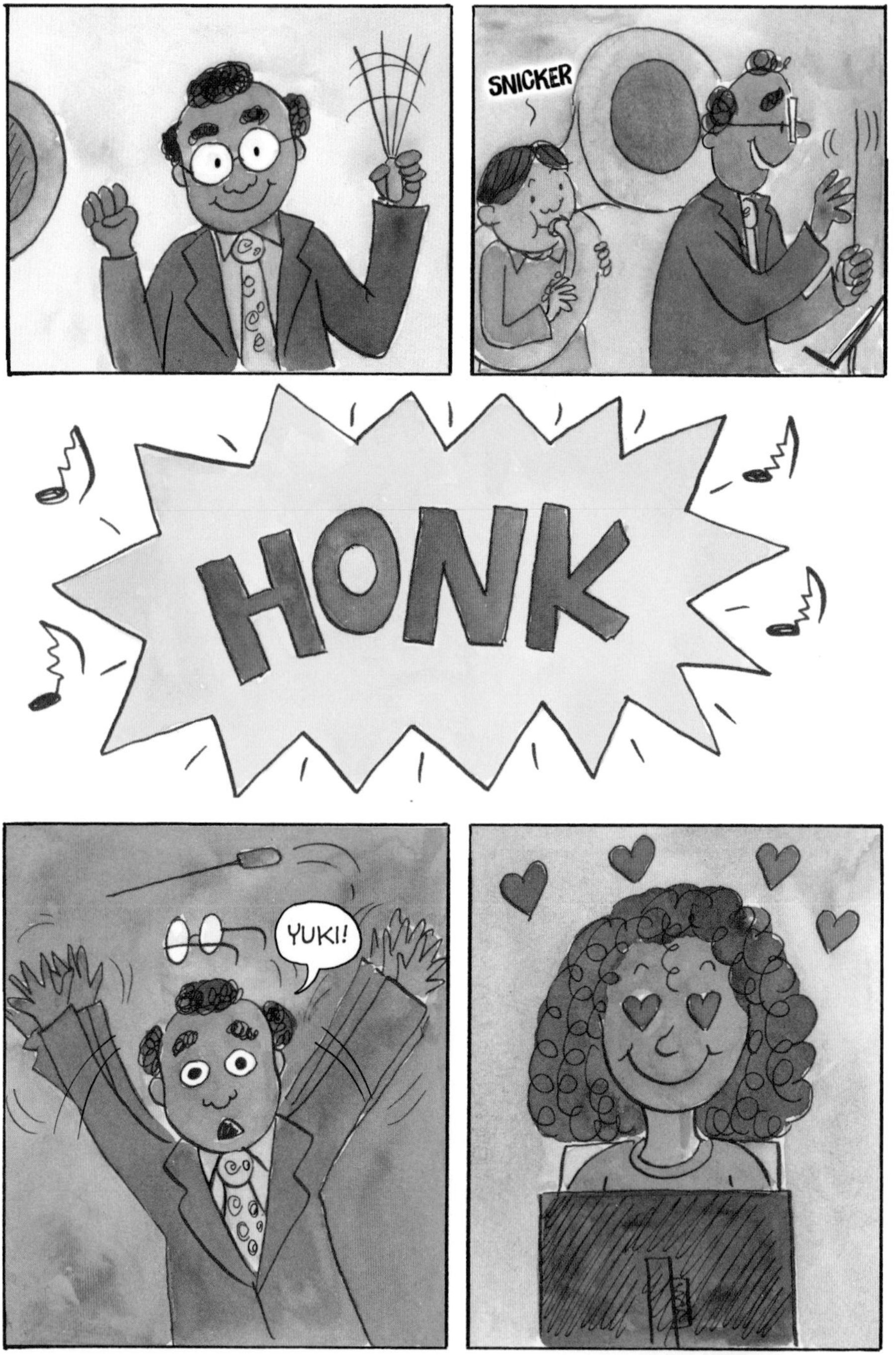
SNICKER
HONK
YUKI!

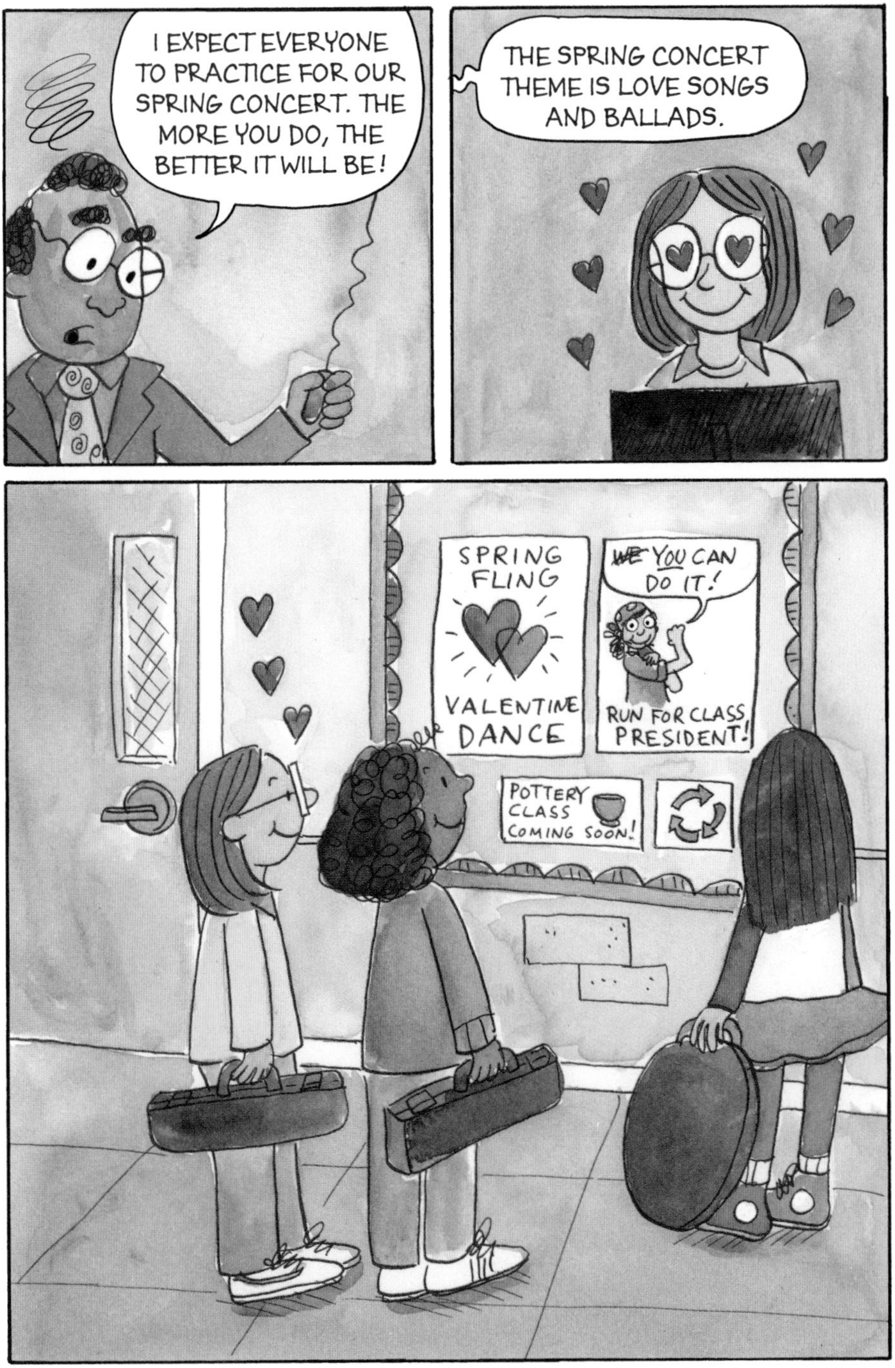
I EXPECT EVERYONE TO PRACTICE FOR OUR SPRING CONCERT. THE MORE YOU DO, THE BETTER IT WILL BE!
THE SPRING CONCERT THEME IS LOVE SONGS AND BALLADS.
SPRING FLING
VALENTINE DANCE
~~WE~~ YOU CAN DO IT!
RUN FOR CLASS PRESIDENT!
POTTERY CLASS COMING SOON!

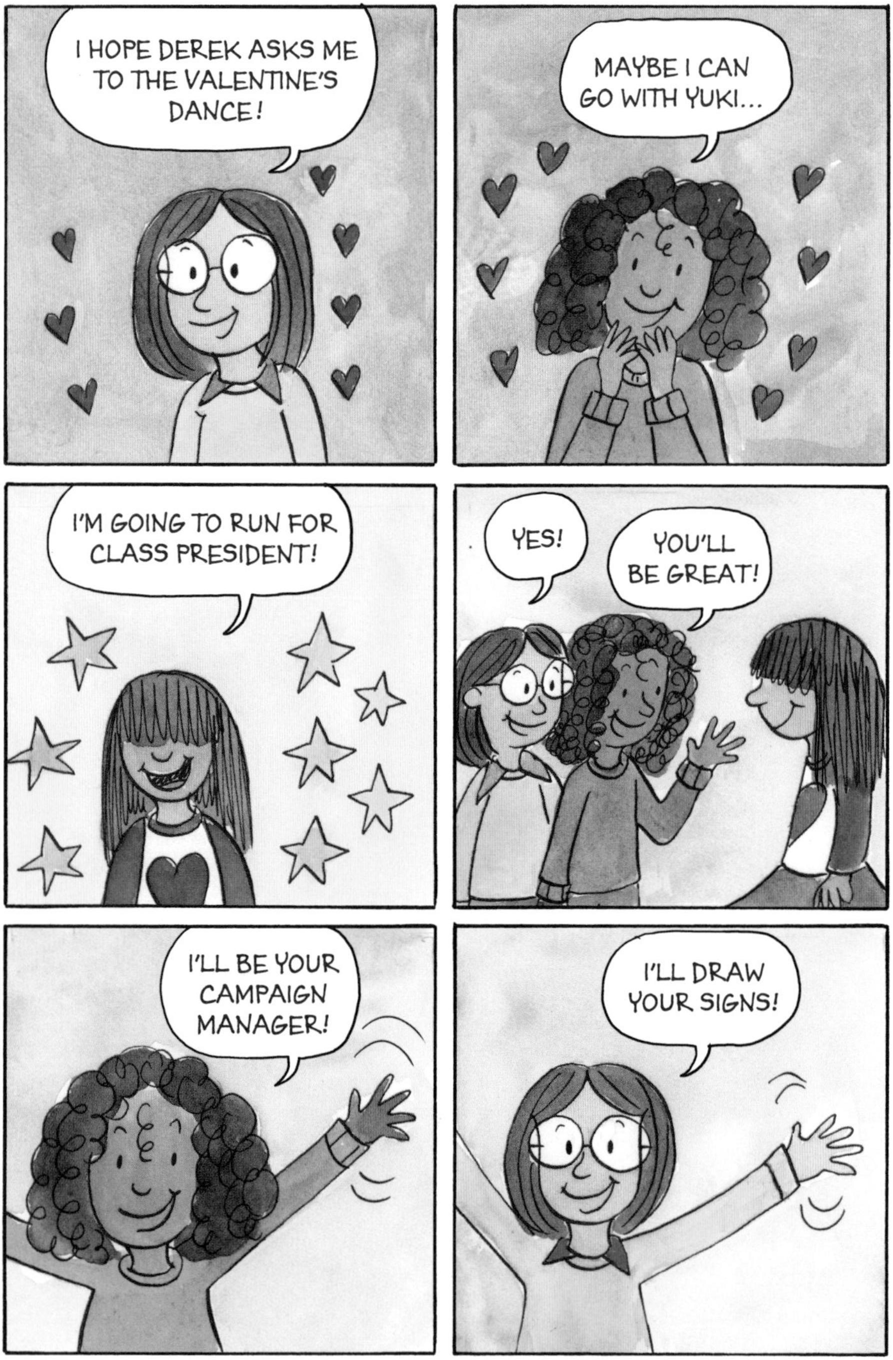
I HOPE DEREK ASKS ME TO THE VALENTINE'S DANCE!
MAYBE I CAN GO WITH YUKI...
I'M GOING TO RUN FOR CLASS PRESIDENT!
YES!
YOU'LL BE GREAT!
I'LL BE YOUR CAMPAIGN MANAGER!
I'LL DRAW YOUR SIGNS!

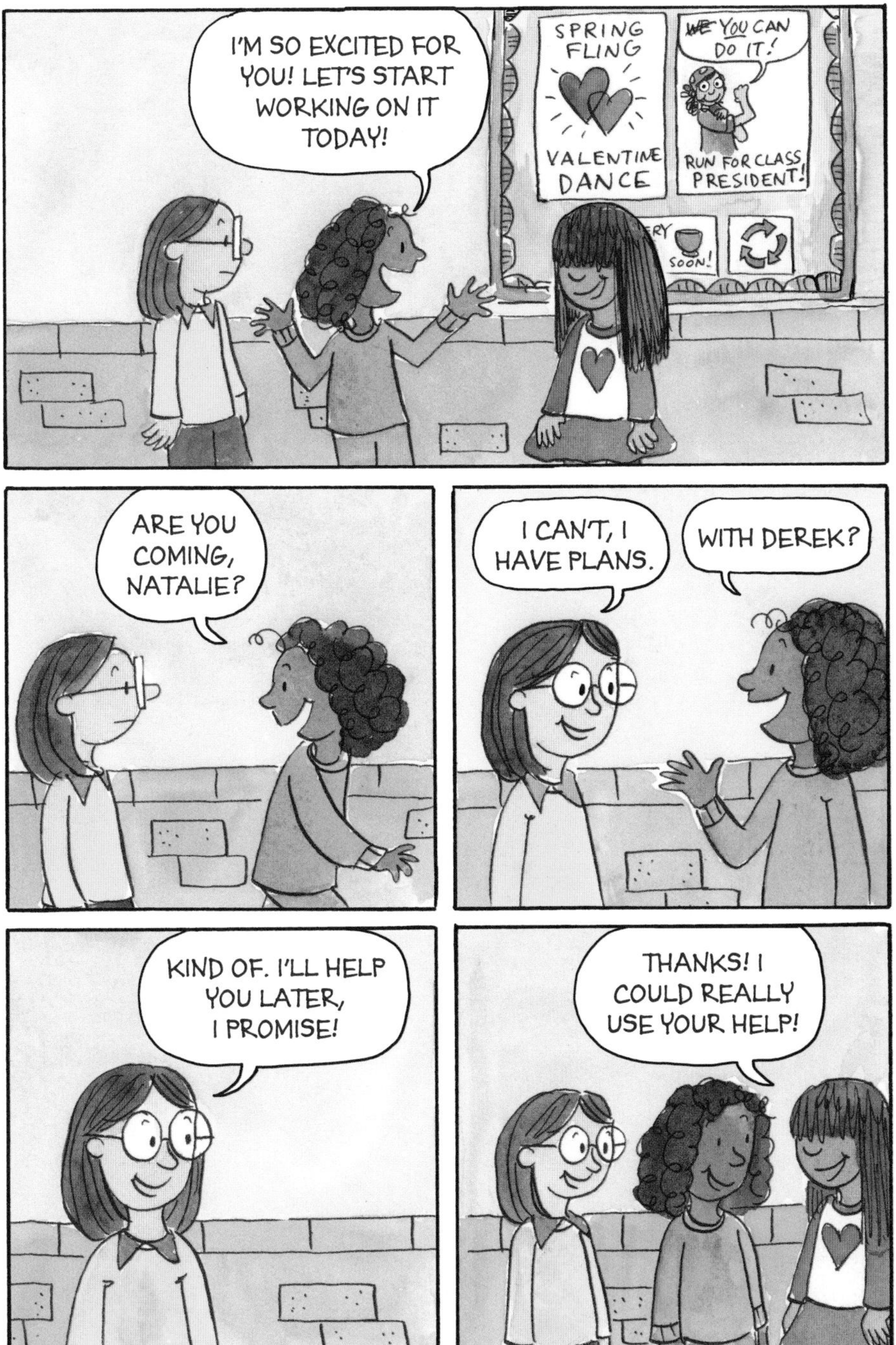

SPRING FLING
VALENTINE DANCE
~~WE~~ YOU CAN DO IT!
RUN FOR CLASS PRESIDENT!
SOON!
I'M SO EXCITED FOR YOU! LET'S START WORKING ON IT TODAY!
ARE YOU COMING, NATALIE?
I CAN'T, I HAVE PLANS.
WITH DEREK?
KIND OF. I'LL HELP YOU LATER, I PROMISE!
THANKS! I COULD REALLY USE YOUR HELP!

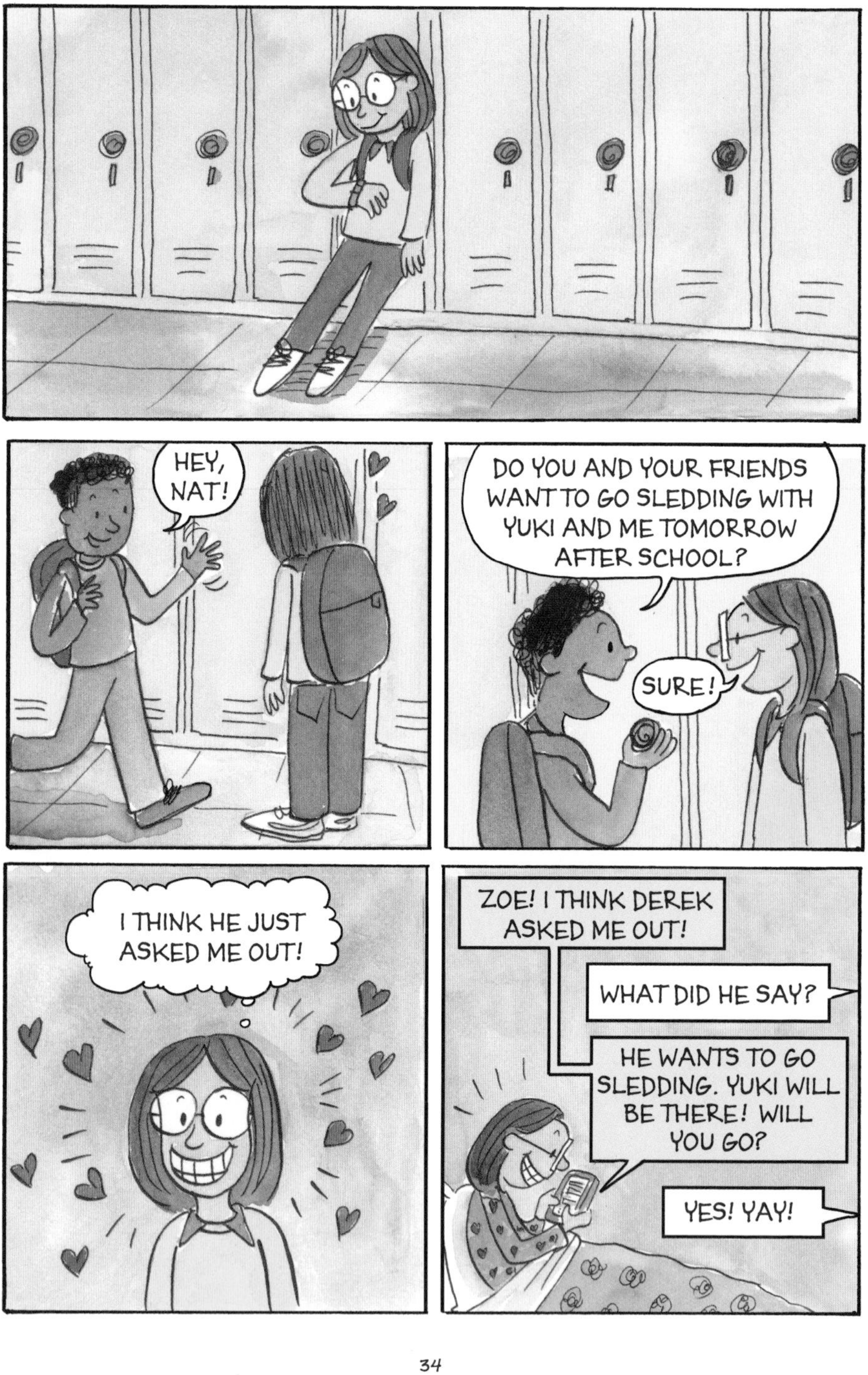
HEY, NAT!
DO YOU AND YOUR FRIENDS WANT TO GO SLEDDING WITH YUKI AND ME TOMORROW AFTER SCHOOL?
SURE!
I THINK HE JUST ASKED ME OUT!
ZOE! I THINK DEREK ASKED ME OUT!
WHAT DID HE SAY?
HE WANTS TO GO SLEDDING. YUKI WILL BE THERE! WILL YOU GO?
YES! YAY!

CHAPTER 3
FALLING FOR YOU

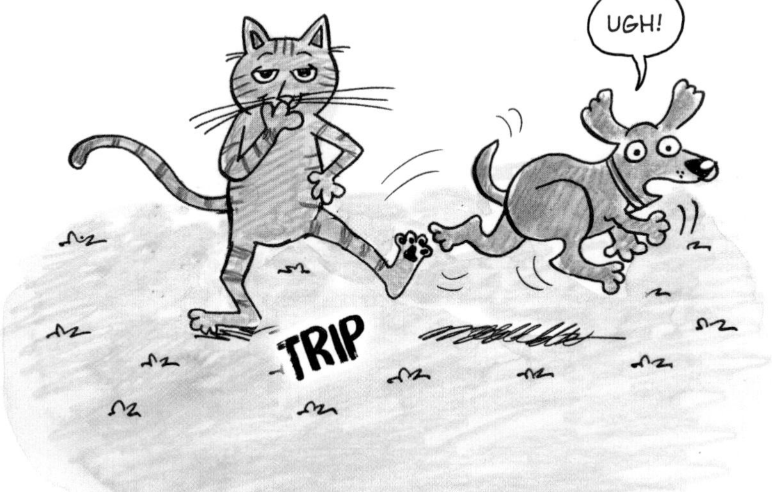
UGH!
TRIP

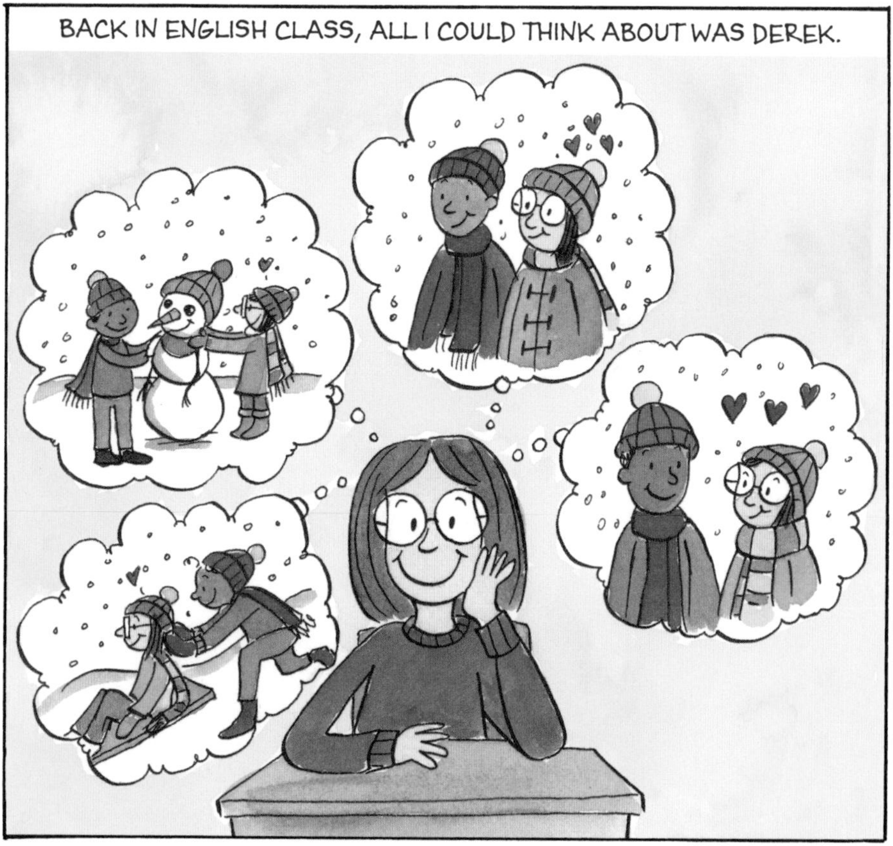
BACK IN ENGLISH CLASS, ALL I COULD THINK ABOUT WAS DEREK.

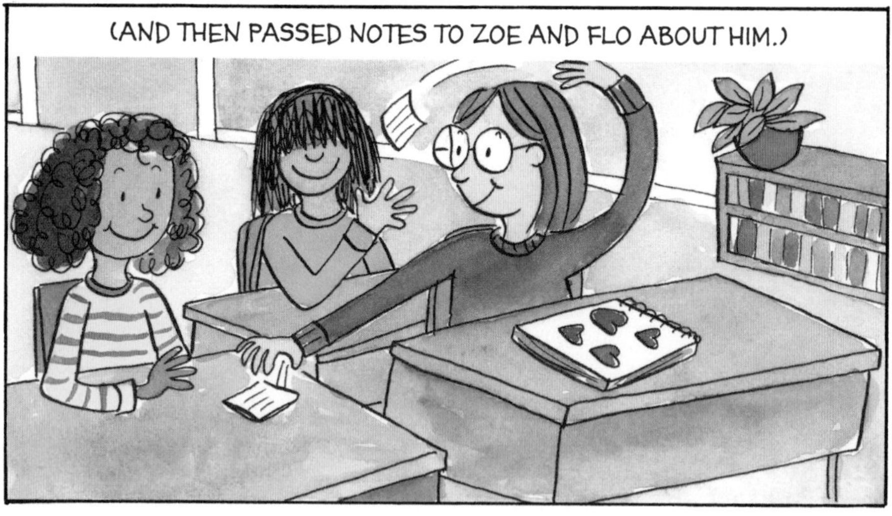
(AND THEN PASSED NOTES TO ZOE AND FLO ABOUT HIM.)

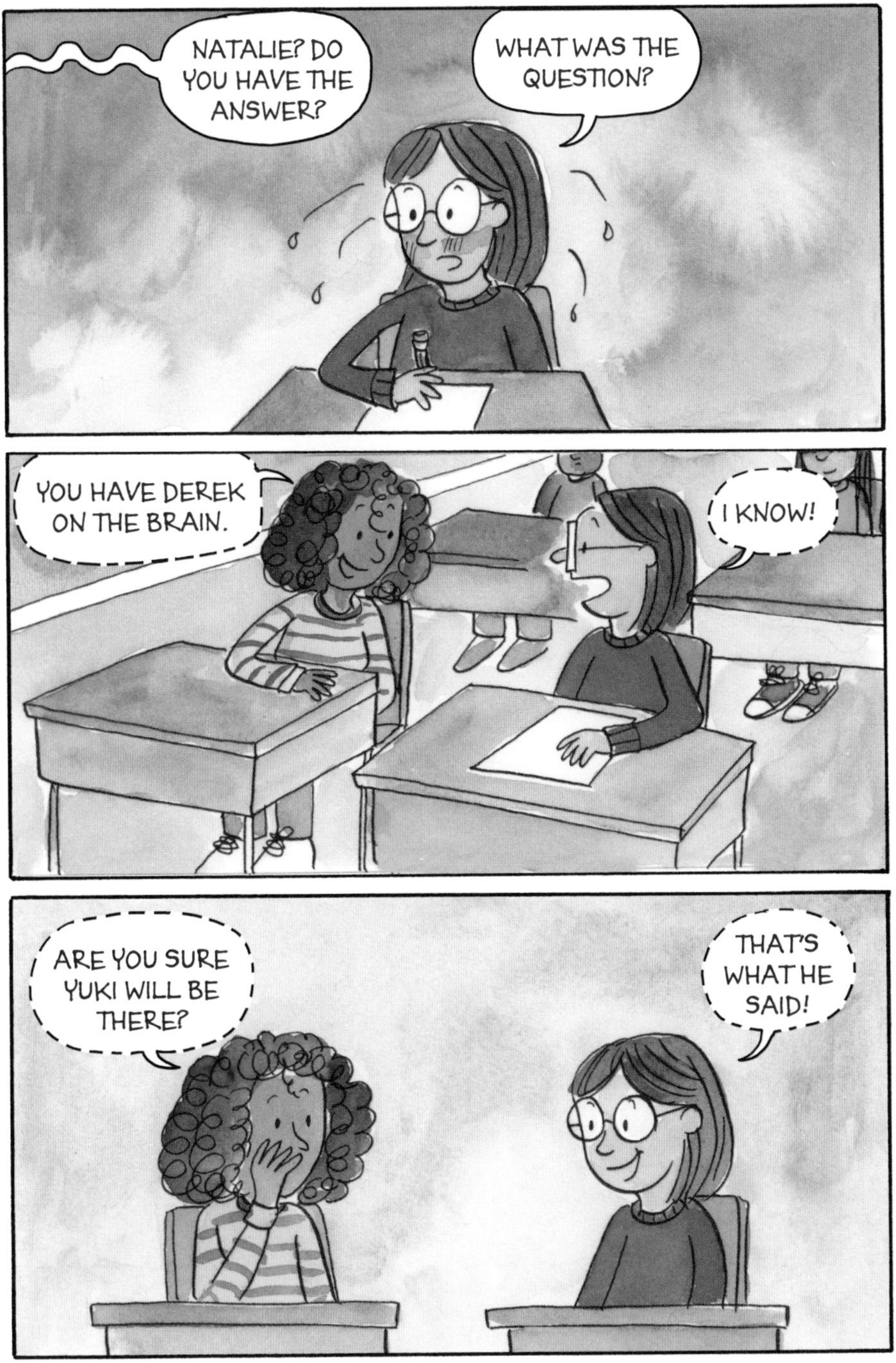
NATALIE? DO YOU HAVE THE ANSWER?
WHAT WAS THE QUESTION?
YOU HAVE DEREK ON THE BRAIN.
I KNOW!
ARE YOU SURE YUKI WILL BE THERE?
THAT'S WHAT HE SAID!

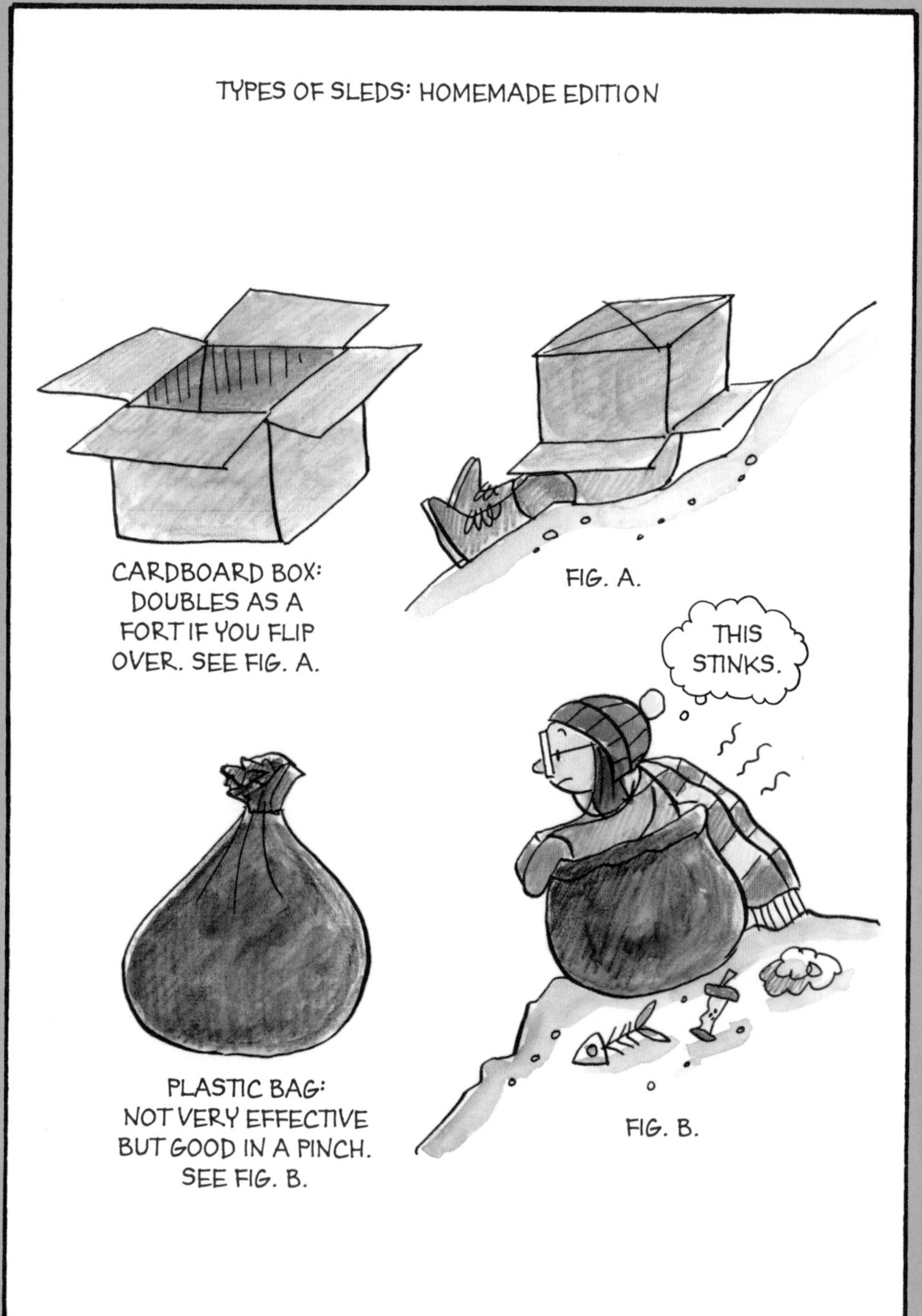
TYPES OF SLEDS: HOMEMADE EDITION
CARDBOARD BOX: DOUBLES AS A FORT IF YOU FLIP OVER. SEE FIG. A.
FIG. A.
THIS STINKS.
PLASTIC BAG: NOT VERY EFFECTIVE BUT GOOD IN A PINCH. SEE FIG. B.
FIG. B.

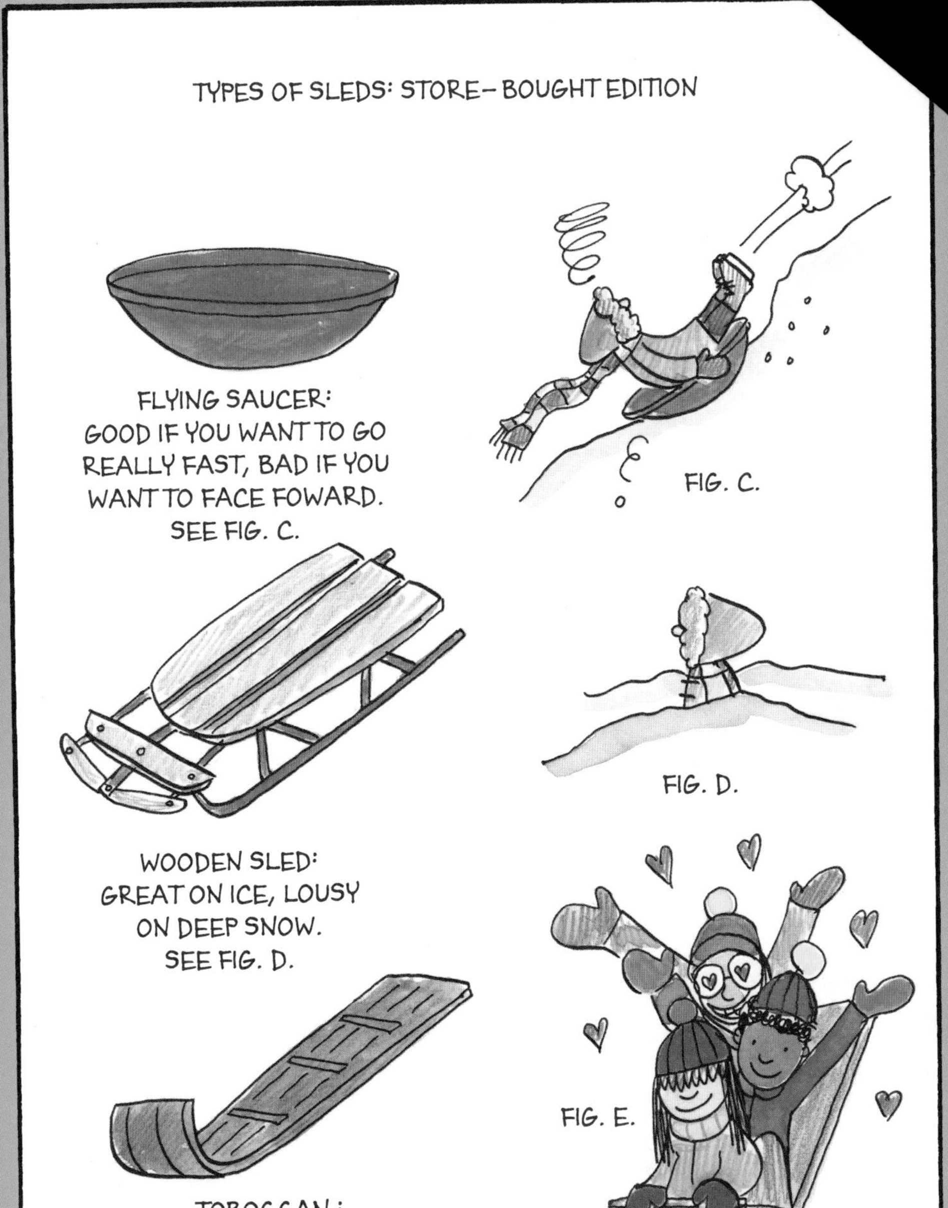
TYPES OF SLEDS: STORE-BOUGHT EDITION
FLYING SAUCER:
GOOD IF YOU WANT TO GO REALLY FAST, BAD IF YOU WANT TO FACE FOWARD.
SEE FIG. C.
FIG. C.
WOODEN SLED:
GREAT ON ICE, LOUSY ON DEEP SNOW.
SEE FIG. D.
FIG. D.
TOBOGGAN:
BEST USED IF YOU WANT TO SIT NEXT TO YOUR CRUSH.
SEE FIG. E.
FIG. E.

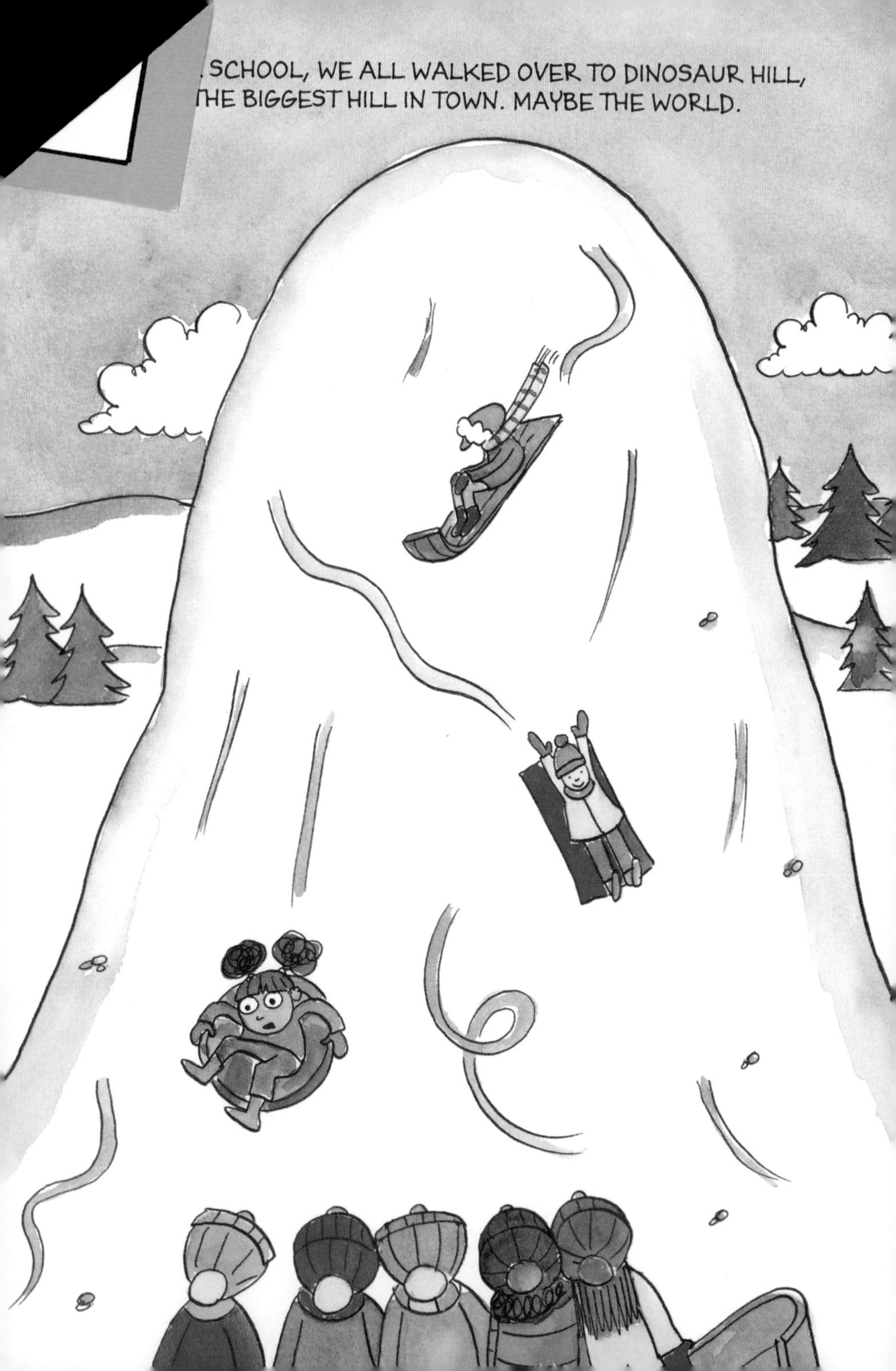
SCHOOL, WE ALL WALKED OVER TO DINOSAUR HILL,
THE BIGGEST HILL IN TOWN. MAYBE THE WORLD.

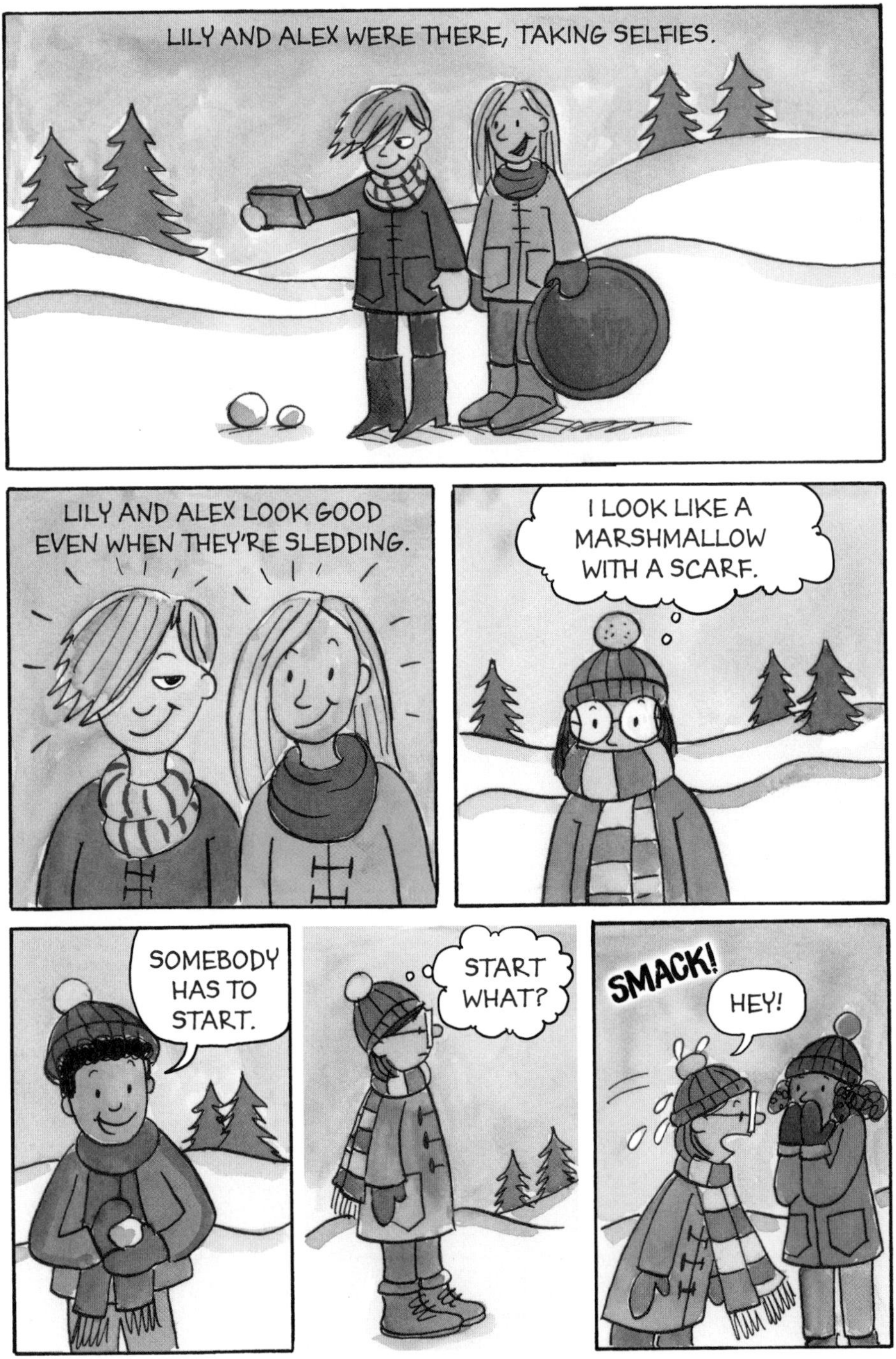
LILY AND ALEX WERE THERE, TAKING SELFIES.
LILY AND ALEX LOOK GOOD EVEN WHEN THEY'RE SLEDDING.
I LOOK LIKE A MARSHMALLOW WITH A SCARF.
SOMEBODY HAS TO START.
START WHAT?
SMACK!
HEY!

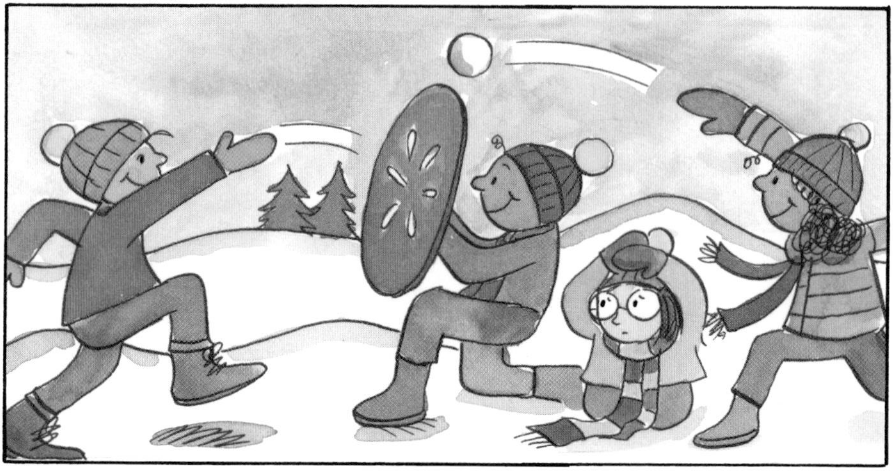

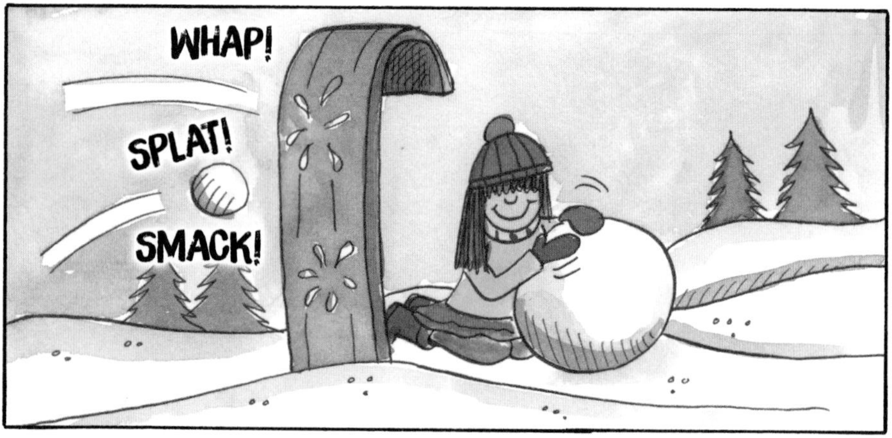
WHAP!
SPLAT!
SMACK!

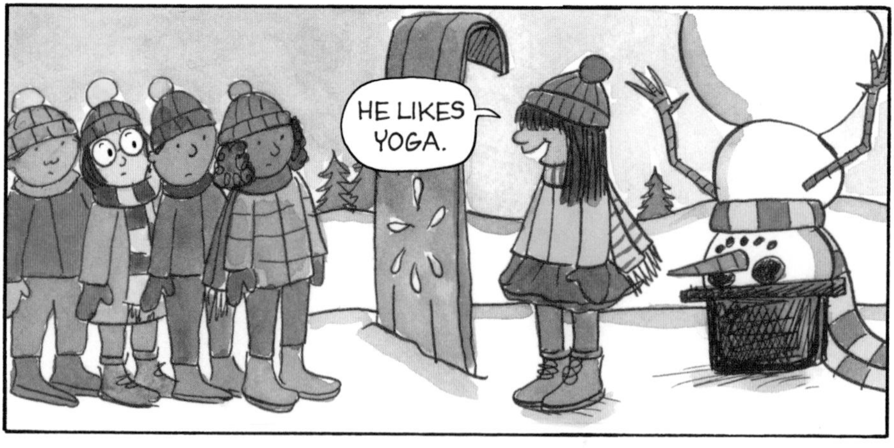
HE LIKES YOGA.

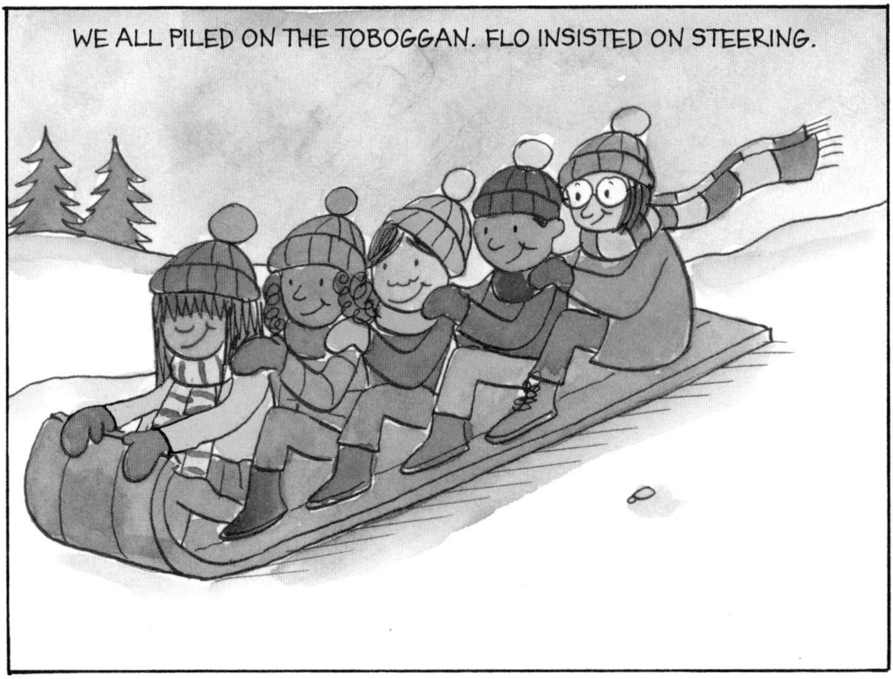
WE ALL PILED ON THE TOBOGGAN. FLO INSISTED ON STEERING.

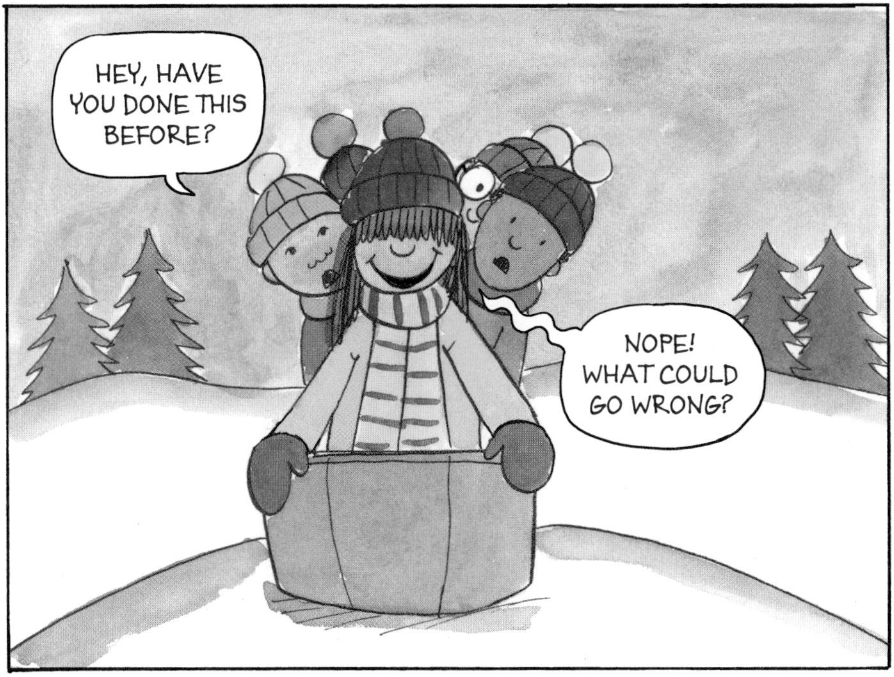
HEY, HAVE YOU DONE THIS BEFORE?
NOPE! WHAT COULD GO WRONG?

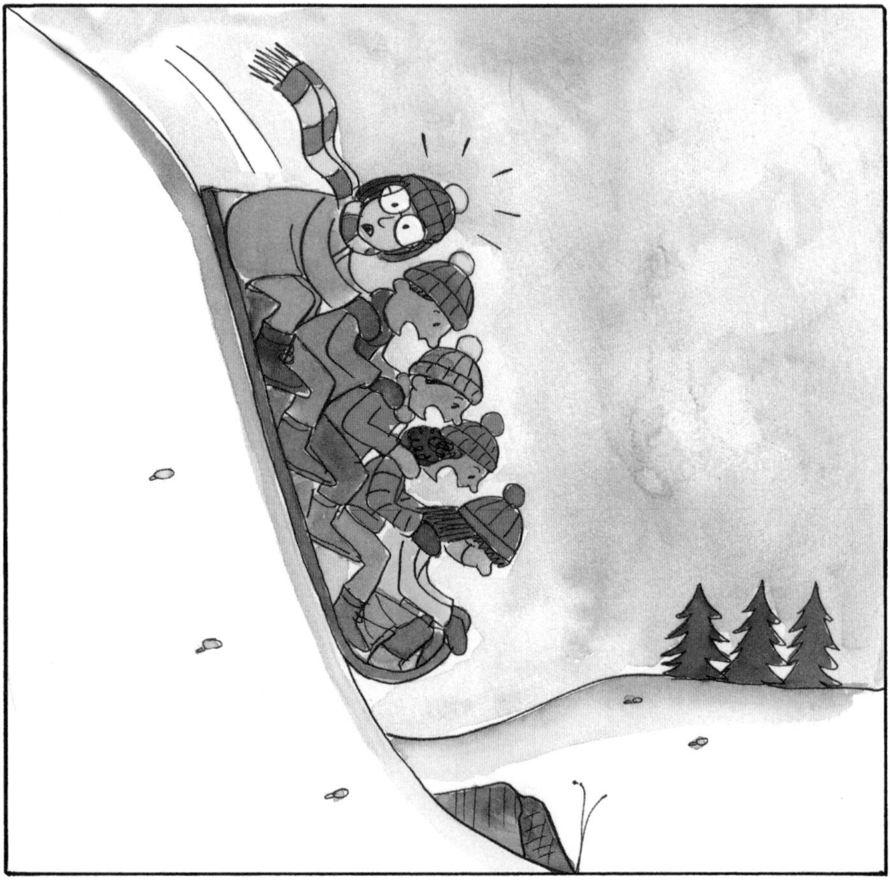

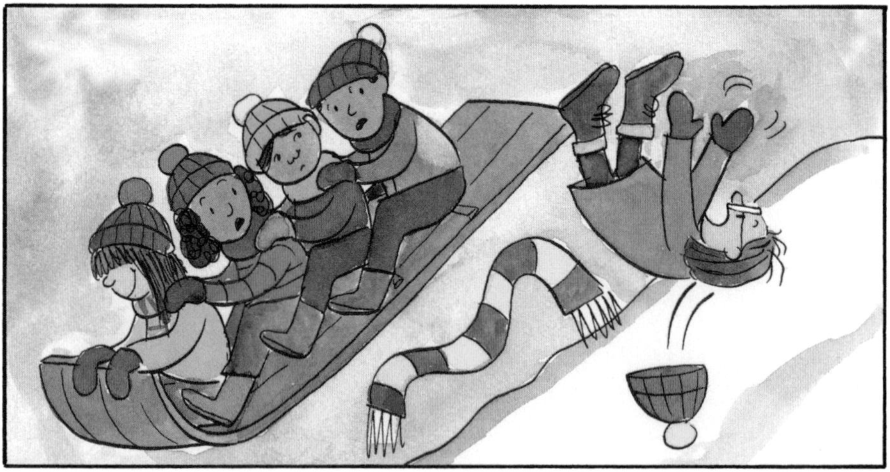

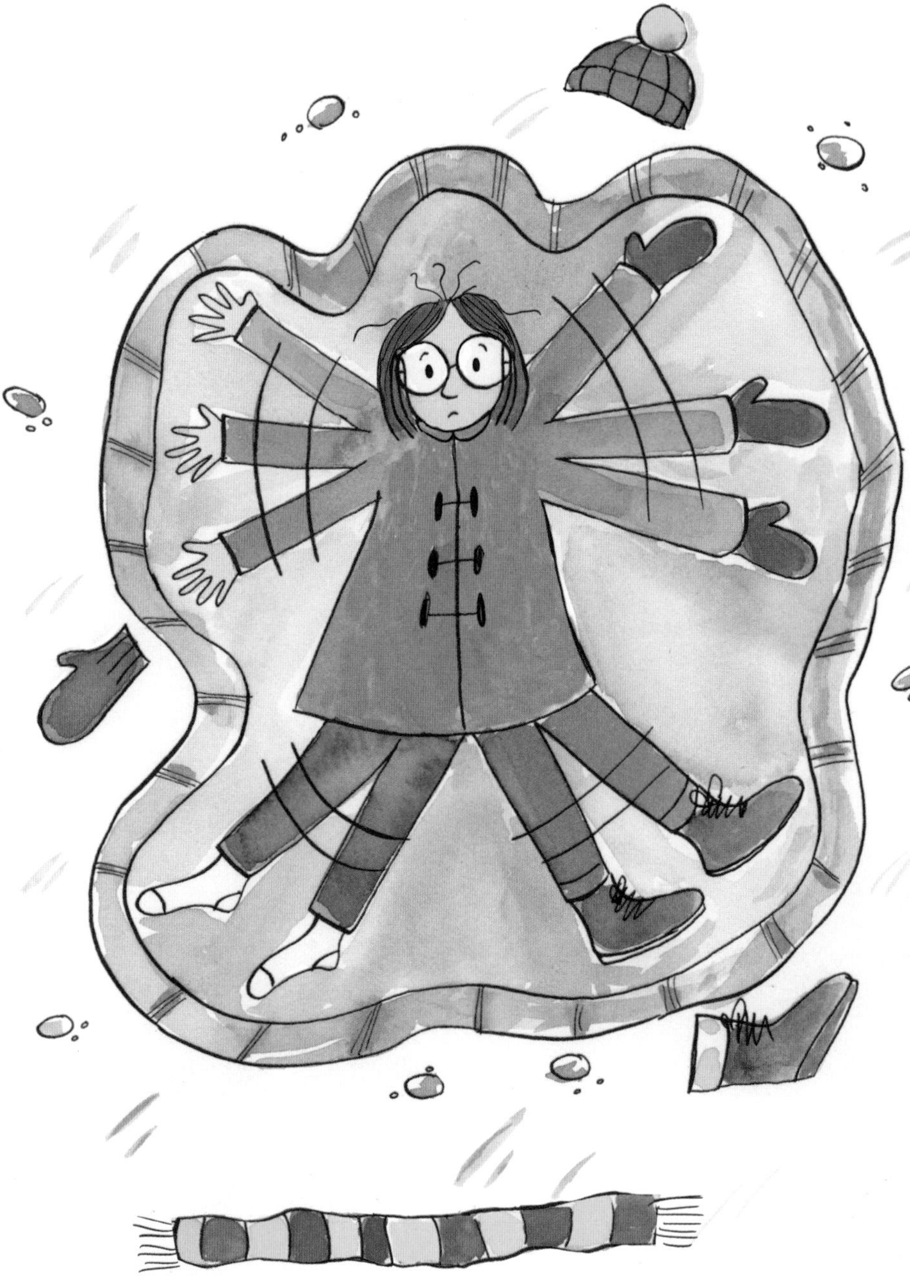

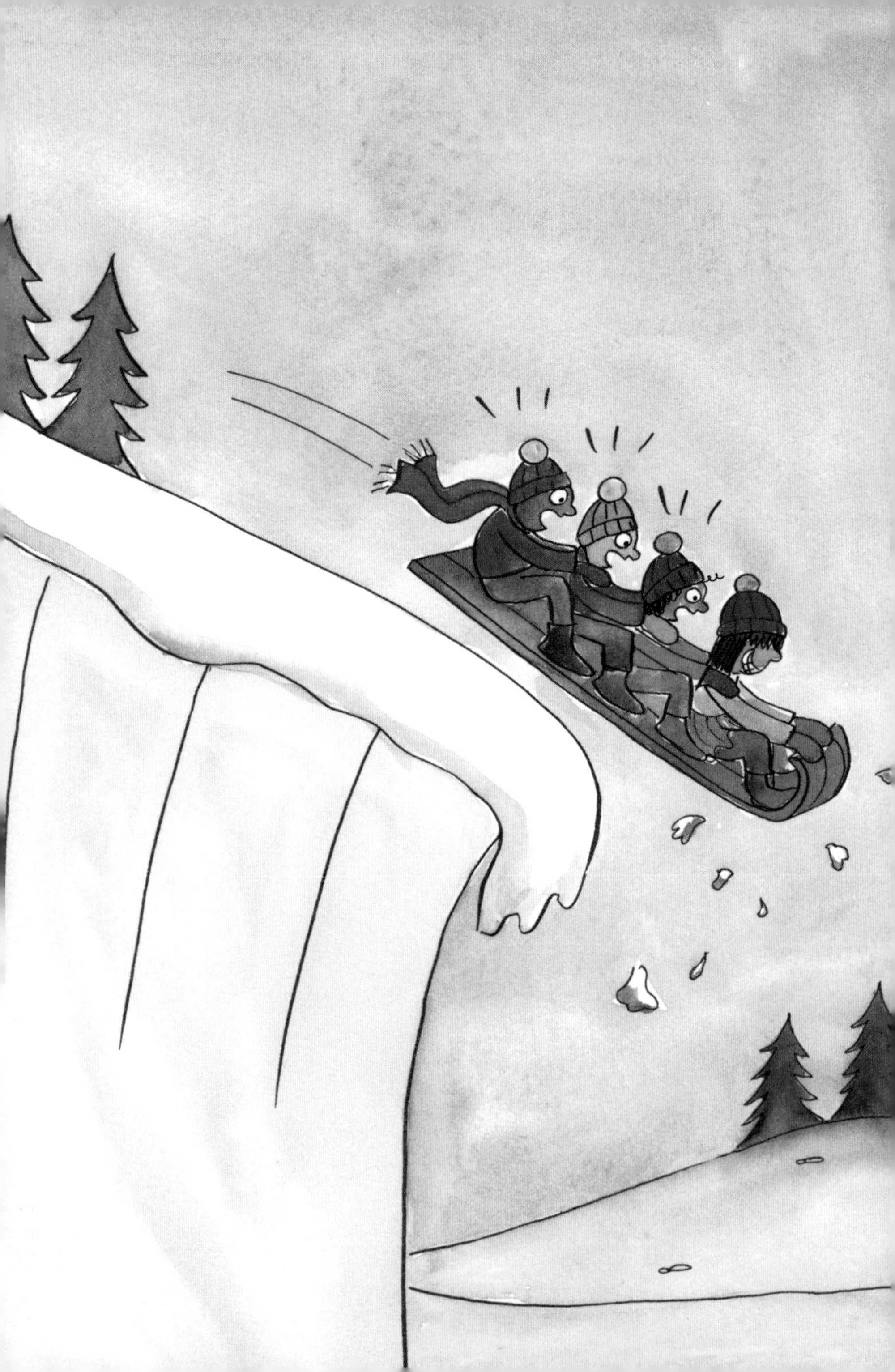

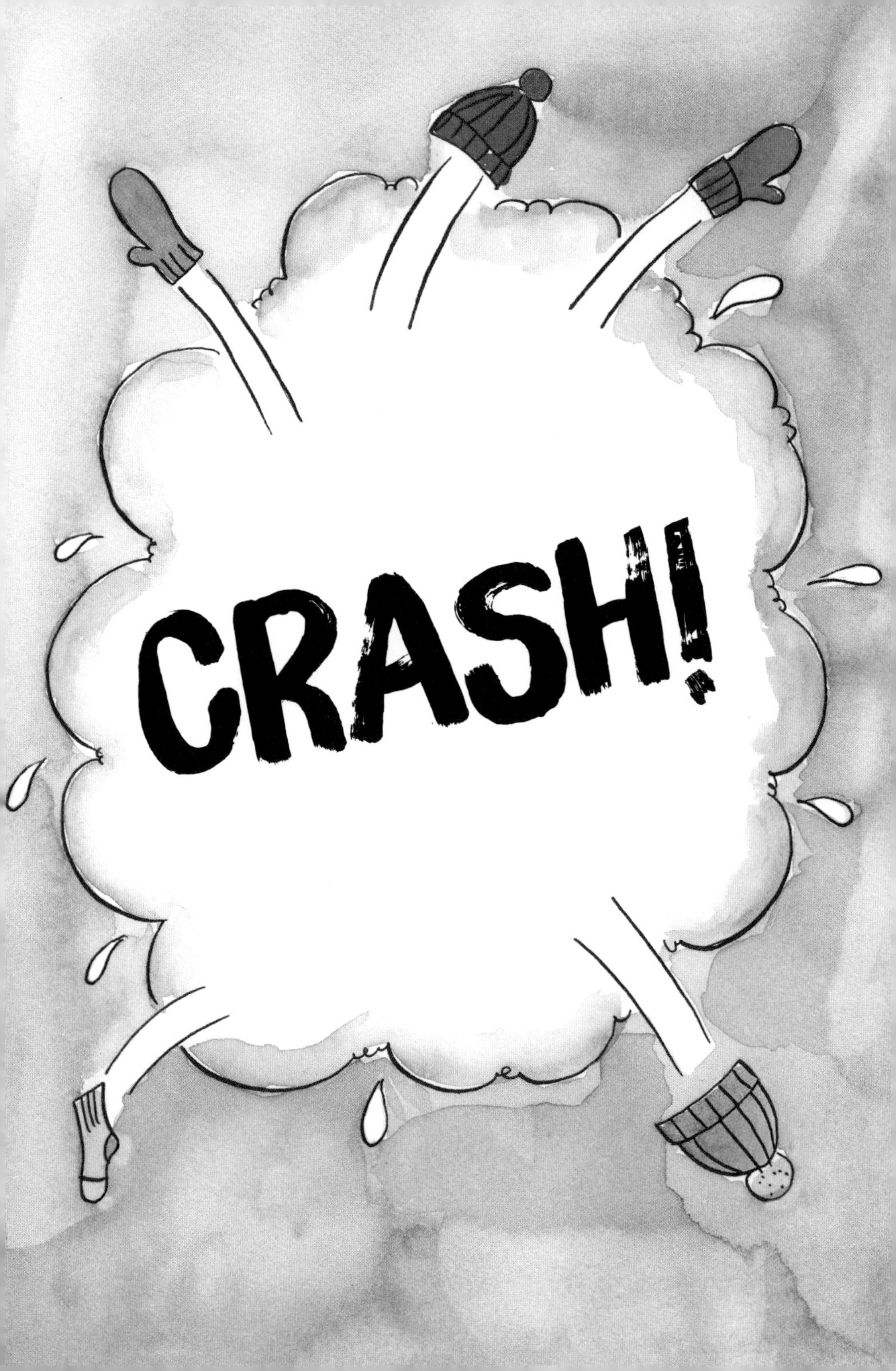
CRASH!

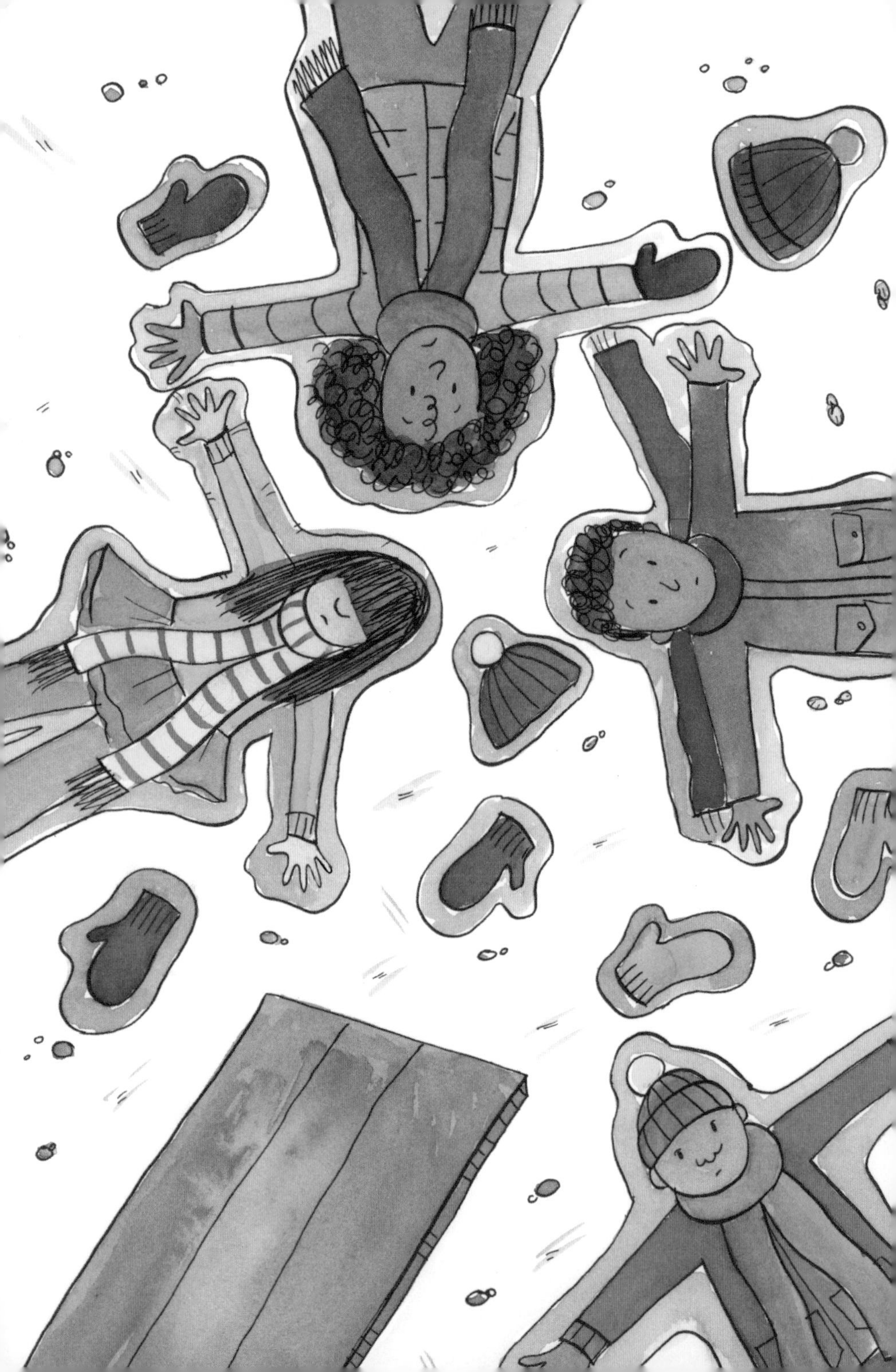

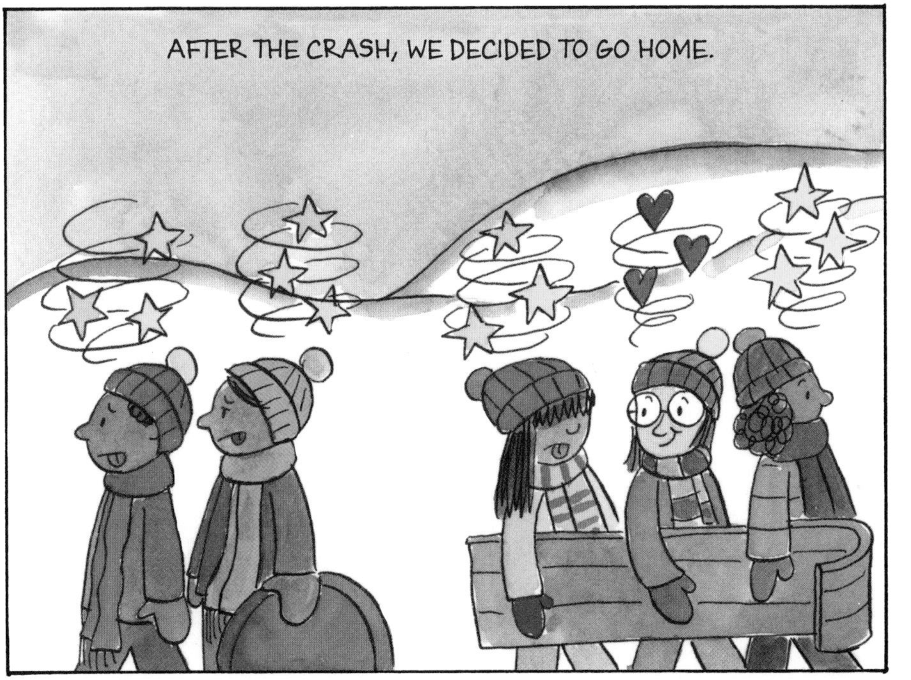
AFTER THE CRASH, WE DECIDED TO GO HOME.

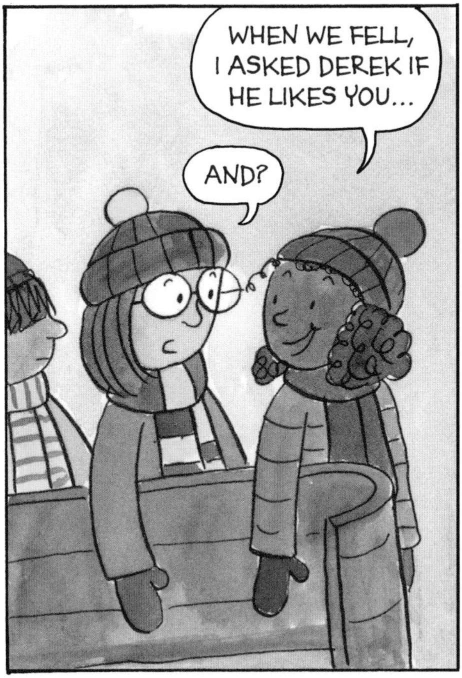
WHEN WE FELL, I ASKED DEREK IF HE LIKES YOU...
AND?

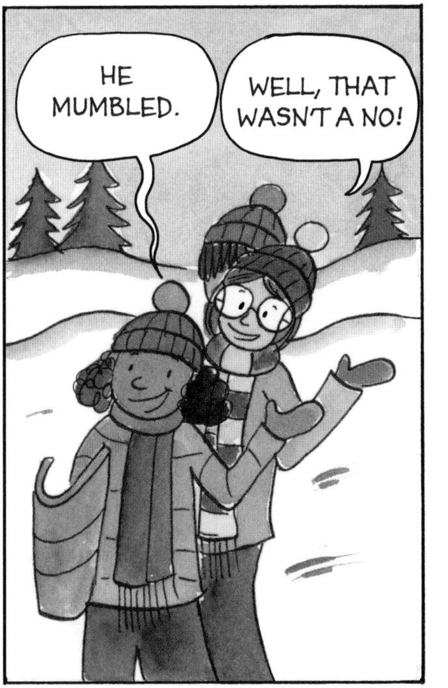
HE MUMBLED.
WELL, THAT WASN'T A NO!

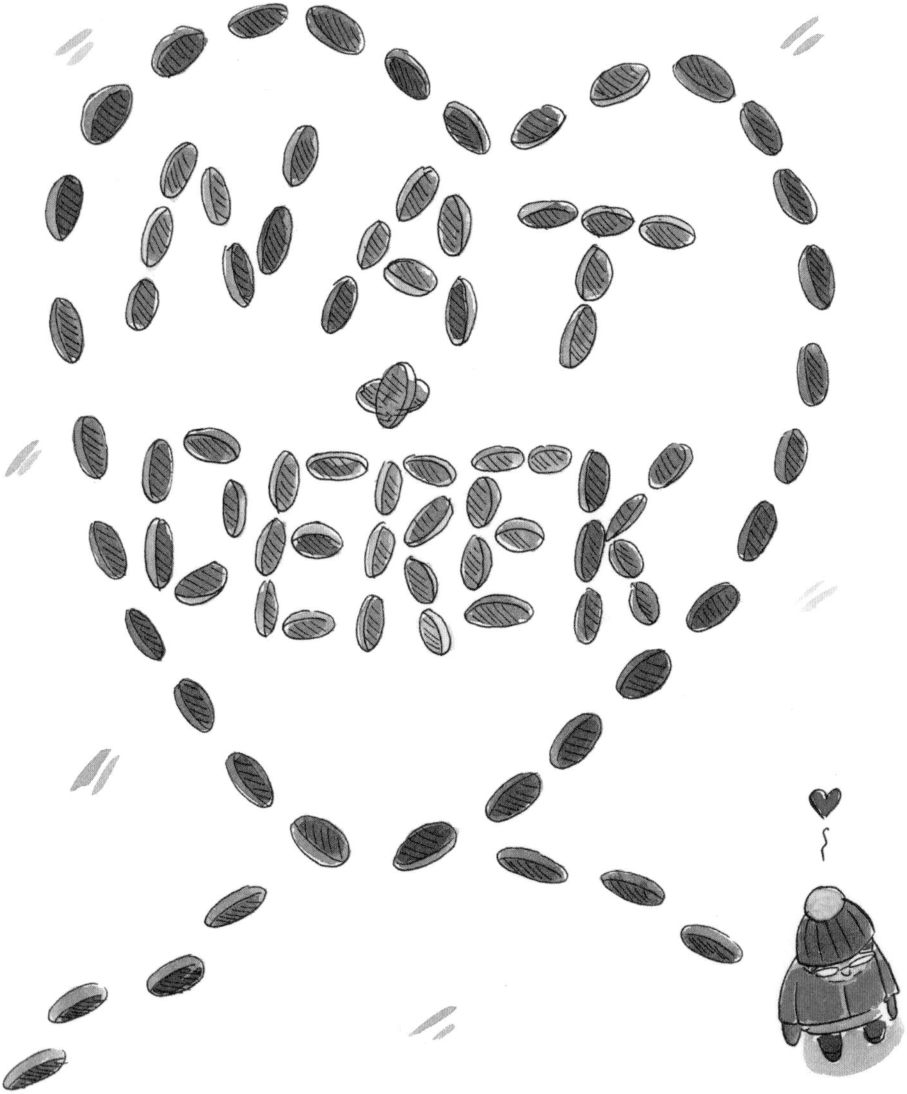
NAT + DEREK

CHAPTER 4
CAMPAIGN

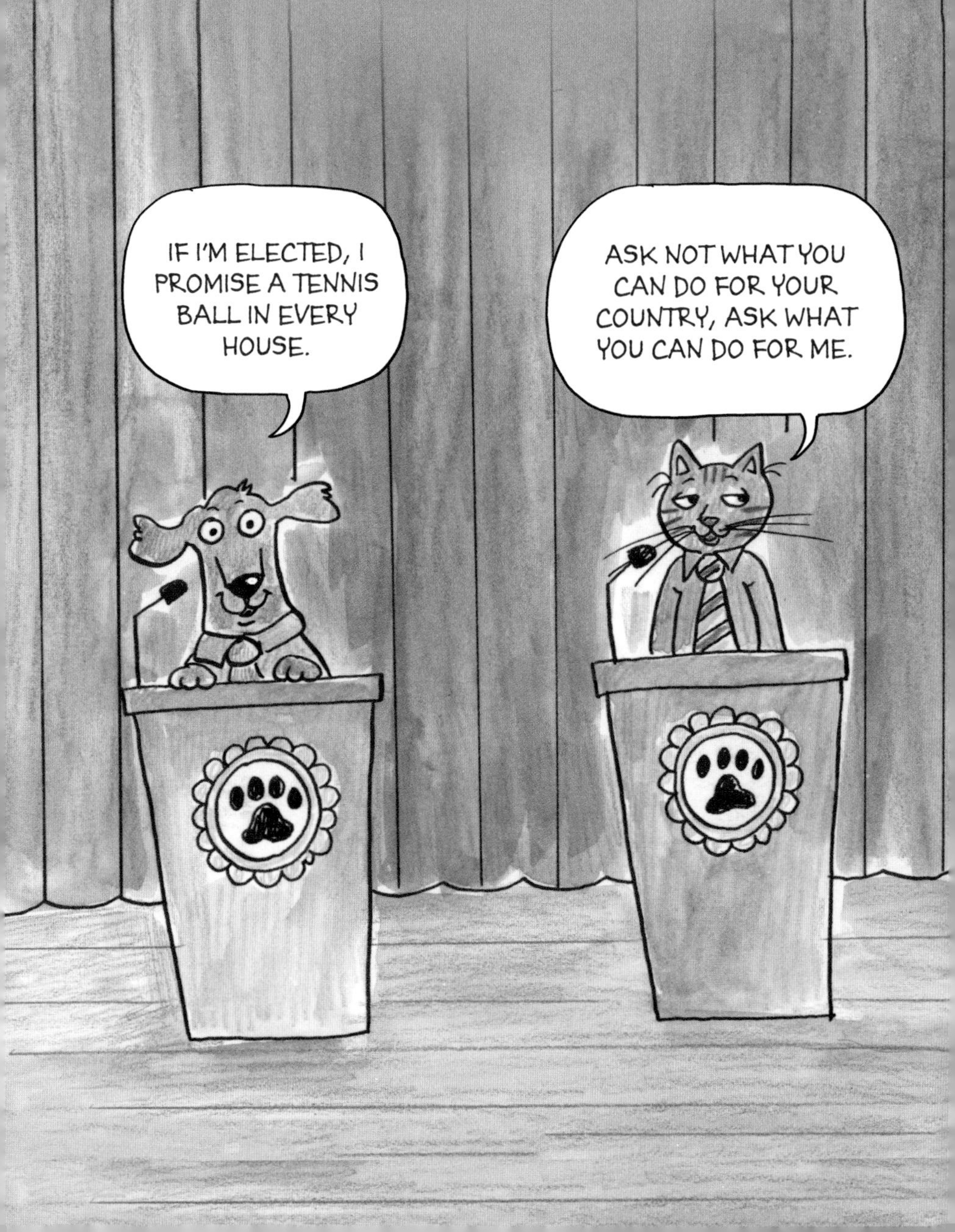

IF I'M ELECTED, I PROMISE A TENNIS BALL IN EVERY HOUSE.
ASK NOT WHAT YOU CAN DO FOR YOUR COUNTRY, ASK WHAT YOU CAN DO FOR ME.

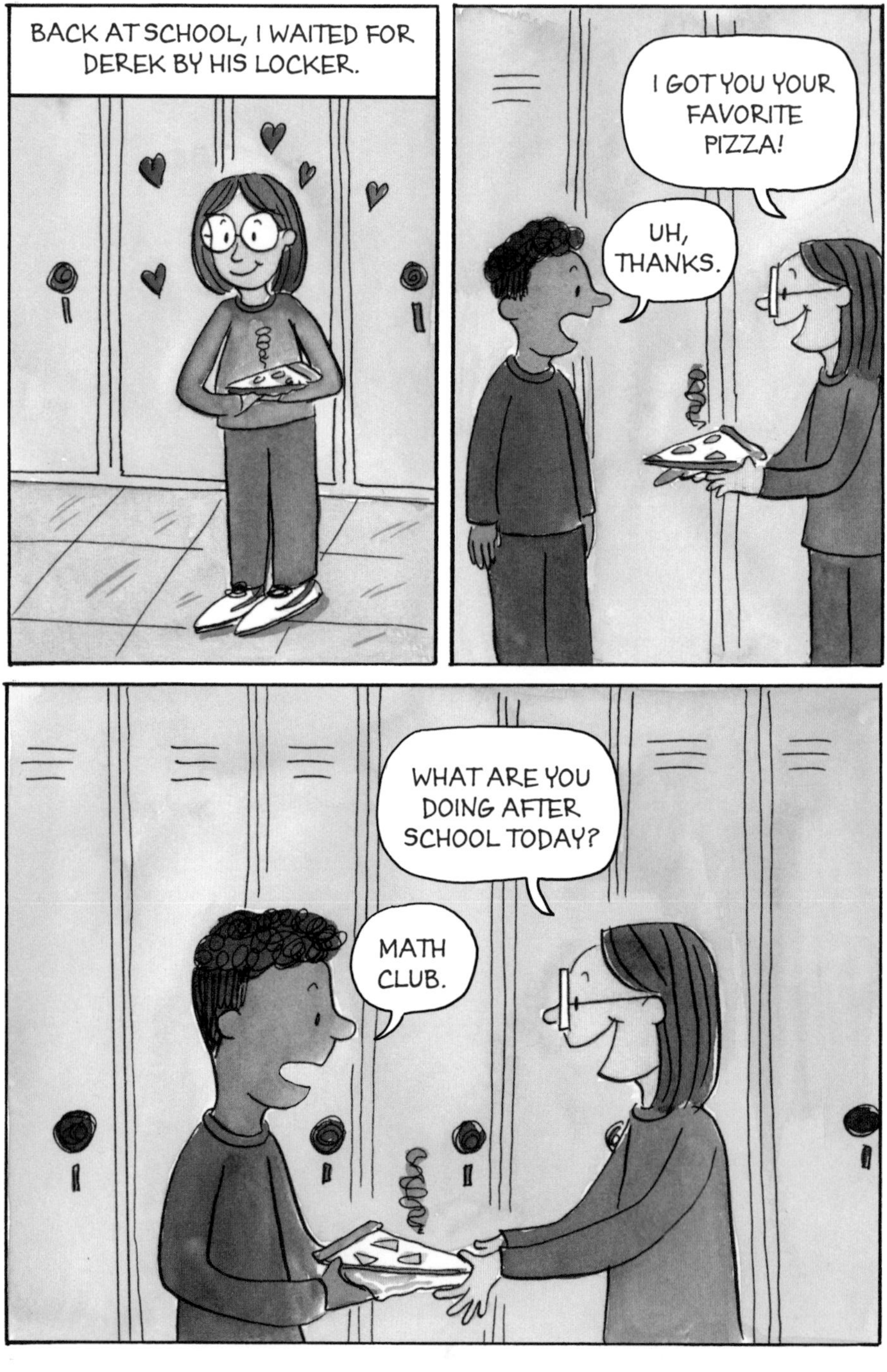
BACK AT SCHOOL, I WAITED FOR DEREK BY HIS LOCKER.
I GOT YOU YOUR FAVORITE PIZZA!
UH, THANKS.
WHAT ARE YOU DOING AFTER SCHOOL TODAY?
MATH CLUB.

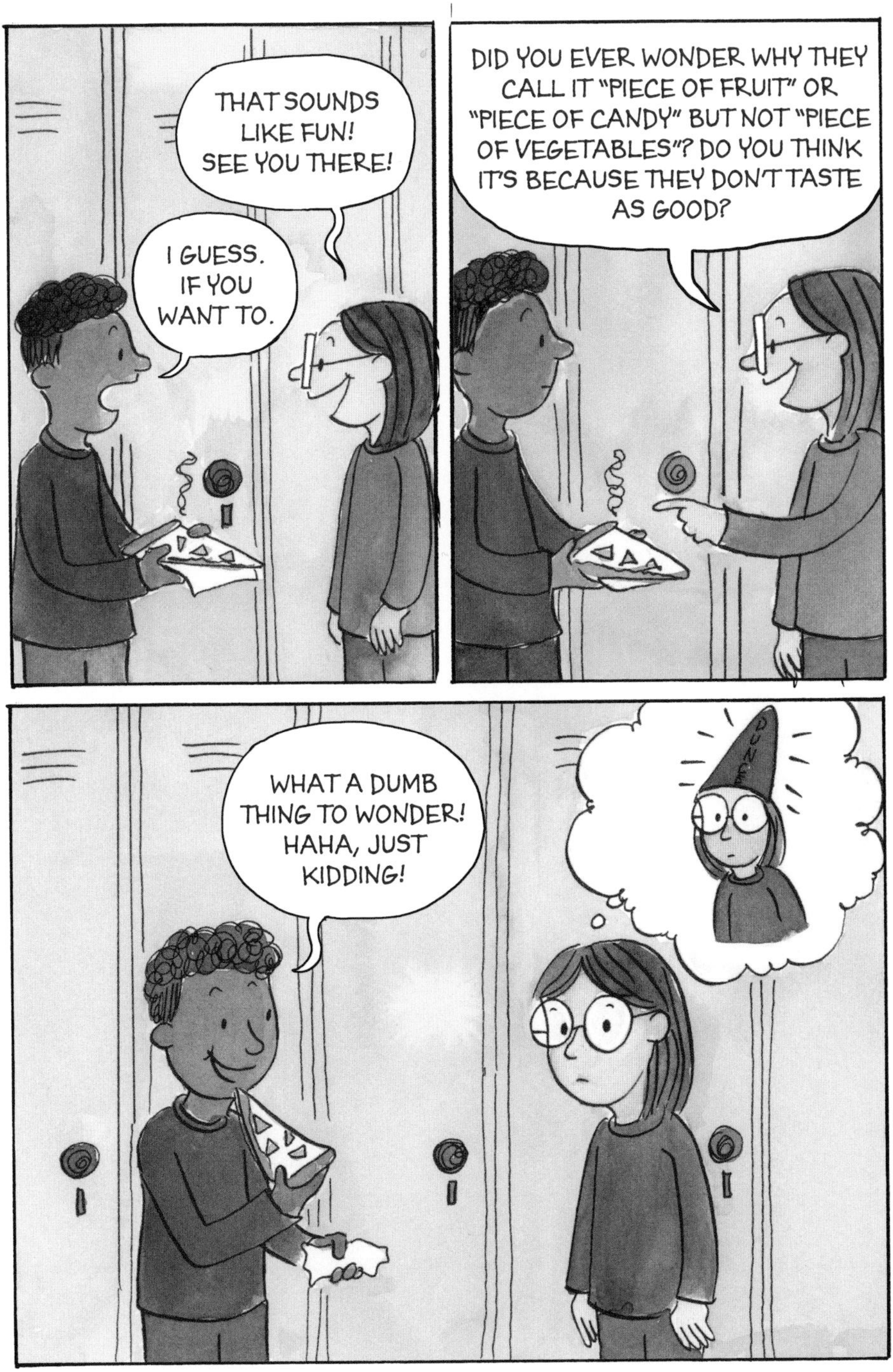
I GUESS. IF YOU WANT TO.
THAT SOUNDS LIKE FUN! SEE YOU THERE!
DID YOU EVER WONDER WHY THEY CALL IT "PIECE OF FRUIT" OR "PIECE OF CANDY" BUT NOT "PIECE OF VEGETABLES"? DO YOU THINK IT'S BECAUSE THEY DON'T TASTE AS GOOD?
WHAT A DUMB THING TO WONDER! HAHA, JUST KIDDING!
DUNCE

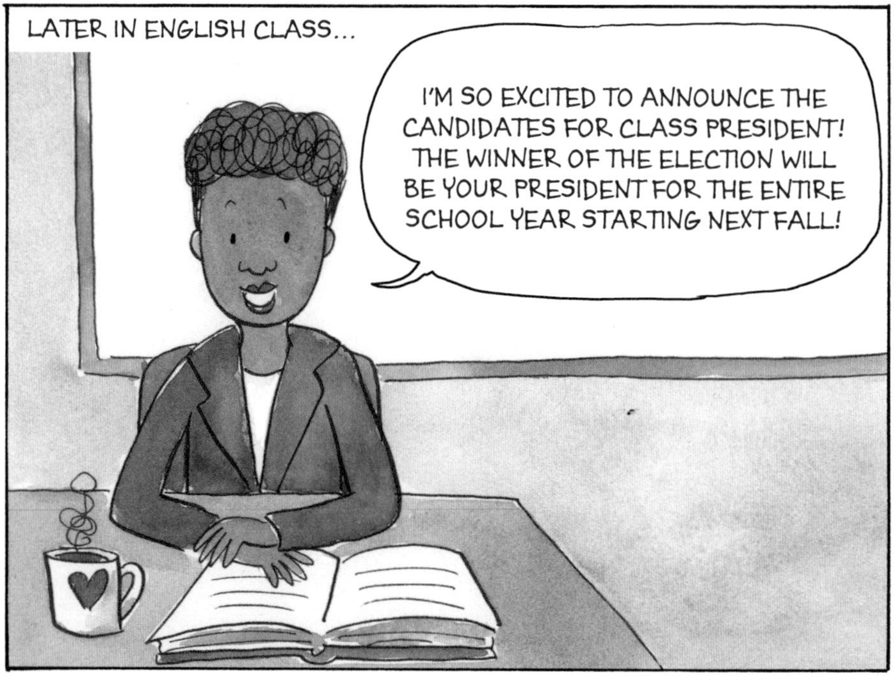
LATER IN ENGLISH CLASS...
I'M SO EXCITED TO ANNOUNCE THE CANDIDATES FOR CLASS PRESIDENT! THE WINNER OF THE ELECTION WILL BE YOUR PRESIDENT FOR THE ENTIRE SCHOOL YEAR STARTING NEXT FALL!

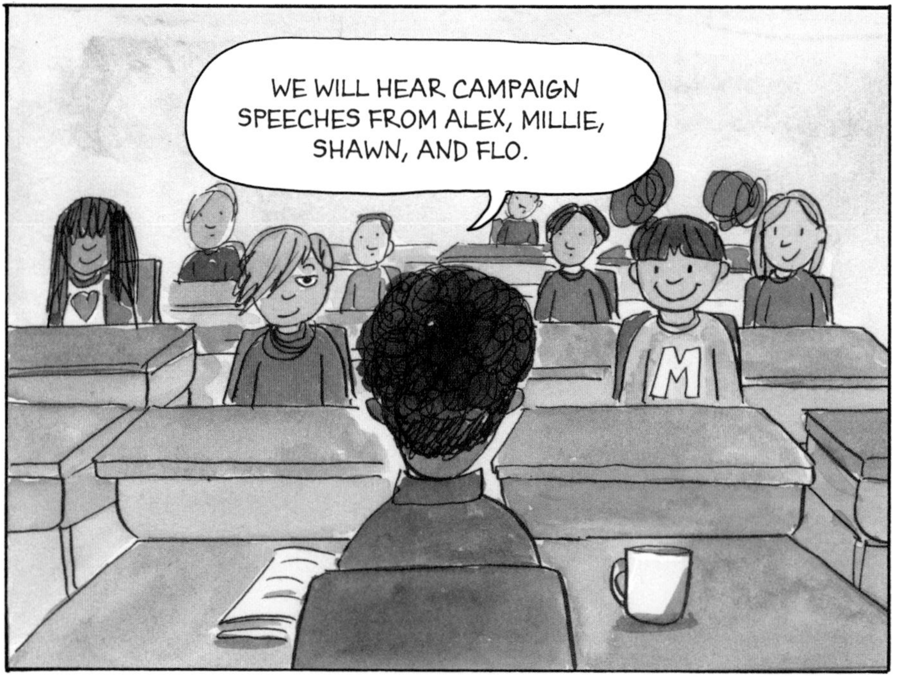
WE WILL HEAR CAMPAIGN SPEECHES FROM ALEX, MILLIE, SHAWN, AND FLO.
M

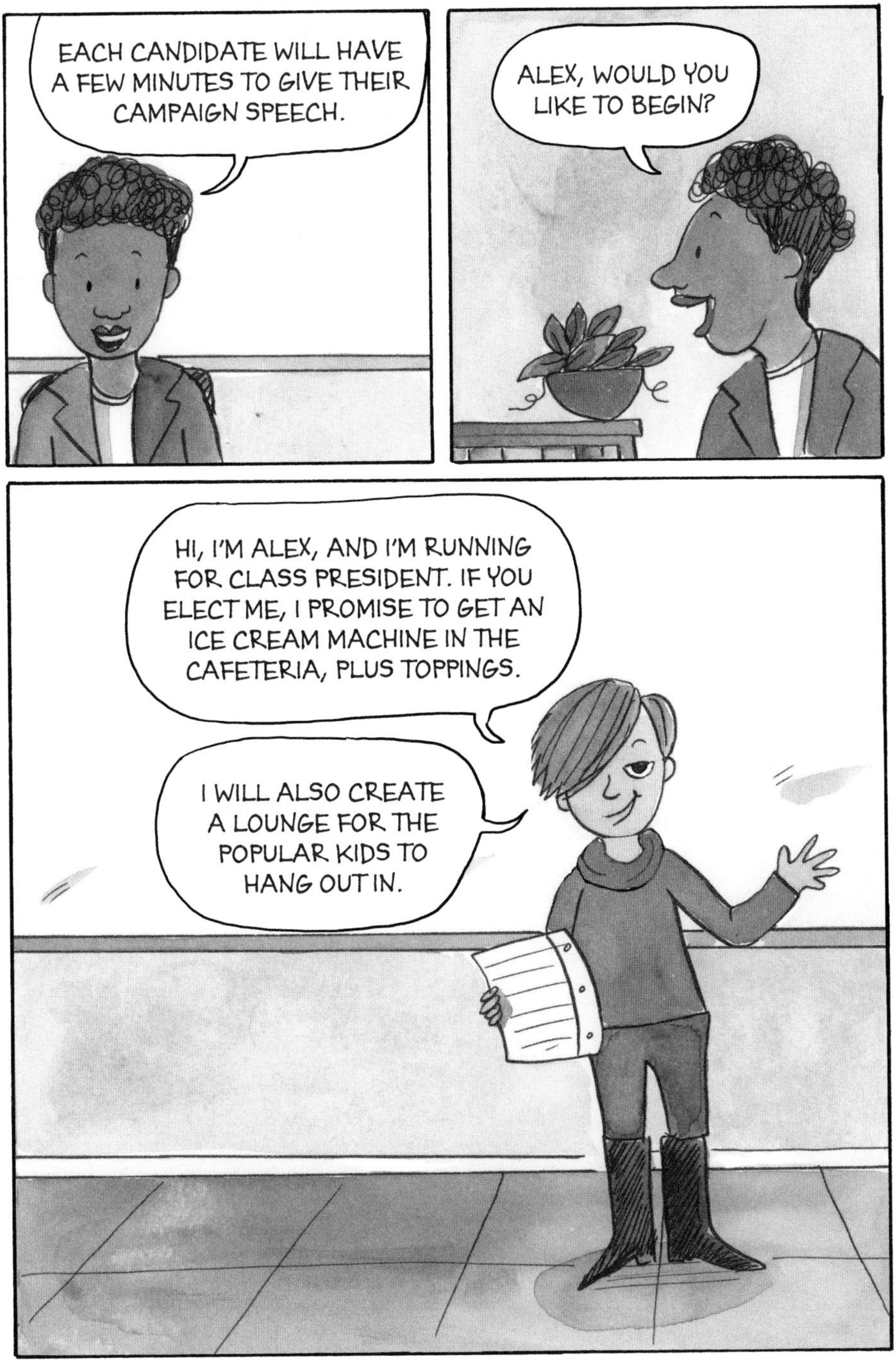
EACH CANDIDATE WILL HAVE A FEW MINUTES TO GIVE THEIR CAMPAIGN SPEECH.
ALEX, WOULD YOU LIKE TO BEGIN?
HI, I'M ALEX, AND I'M RUNNING FOR CLASS PRESIDENT. IF YOU ELECT ME, I PROMISE TO GET AN ICE CREAM MACHINE IN THE CAFETERIA, PLUS TOPPINGS.
I WILL ALSO CREATE A LOUNGE FOR THE POPULAR KIDS TO HANG OUT IN.

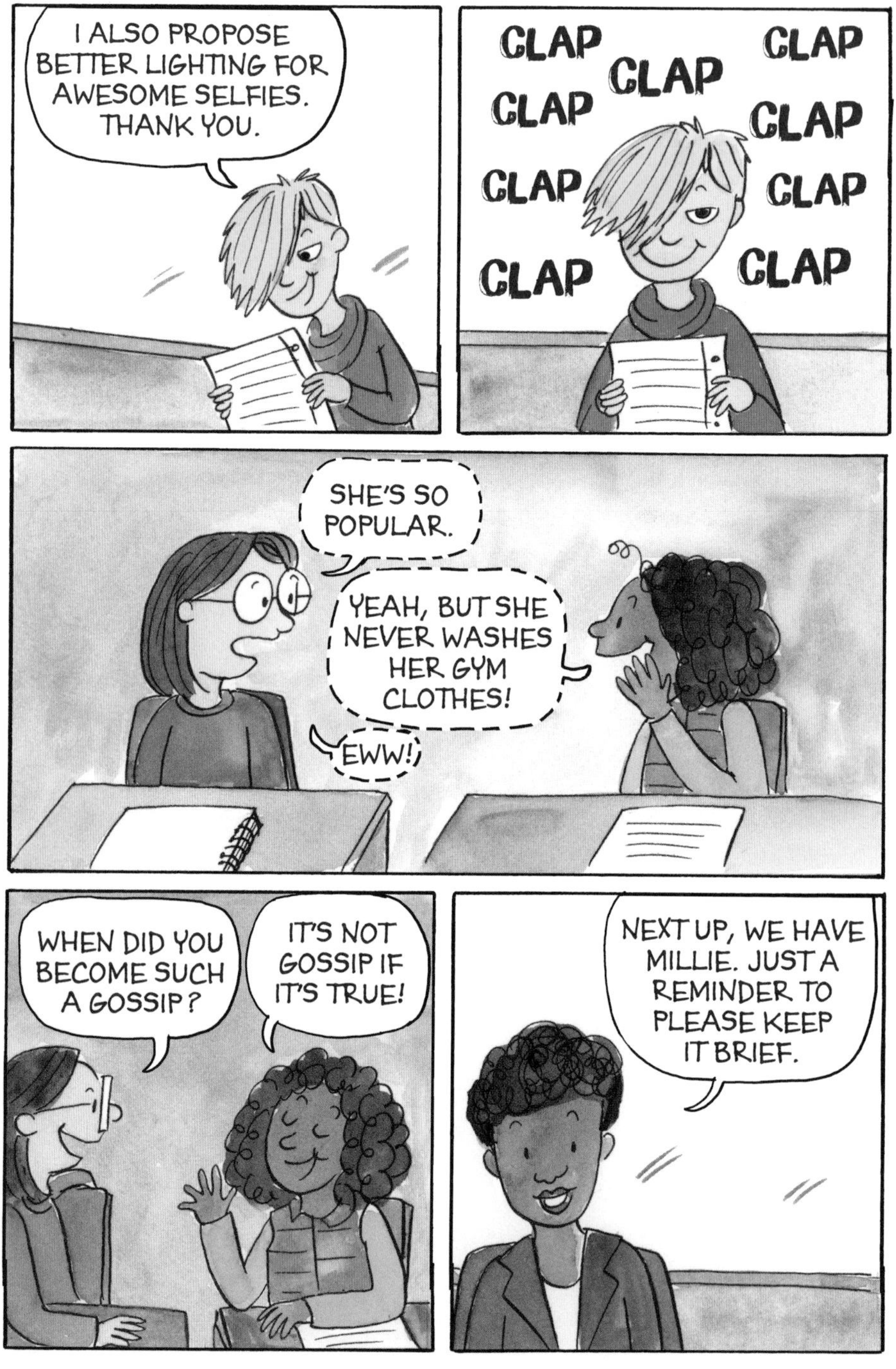
I ALSO PROPOSE BETTER LIGHTING FOR AWESOME SELFIES. THANK YOU.
CLAP CLAP CLAP CLAP CLAP CLAP CLAP CLAP CLAP
SHE'S SO POPULAR.
YEAH, BUT SHE NEVER WASHES HER GYM CLOTHES!
EWW!
WHEN DID YOU BECOME SUCH A GOSSIP?
IT'S NOT GOSSIP IF IT'S TRUE!
NEXT UP, WE HAVE MILLIE. JUST A REMINDER TO PLEASE KEEP IT BRIEF.

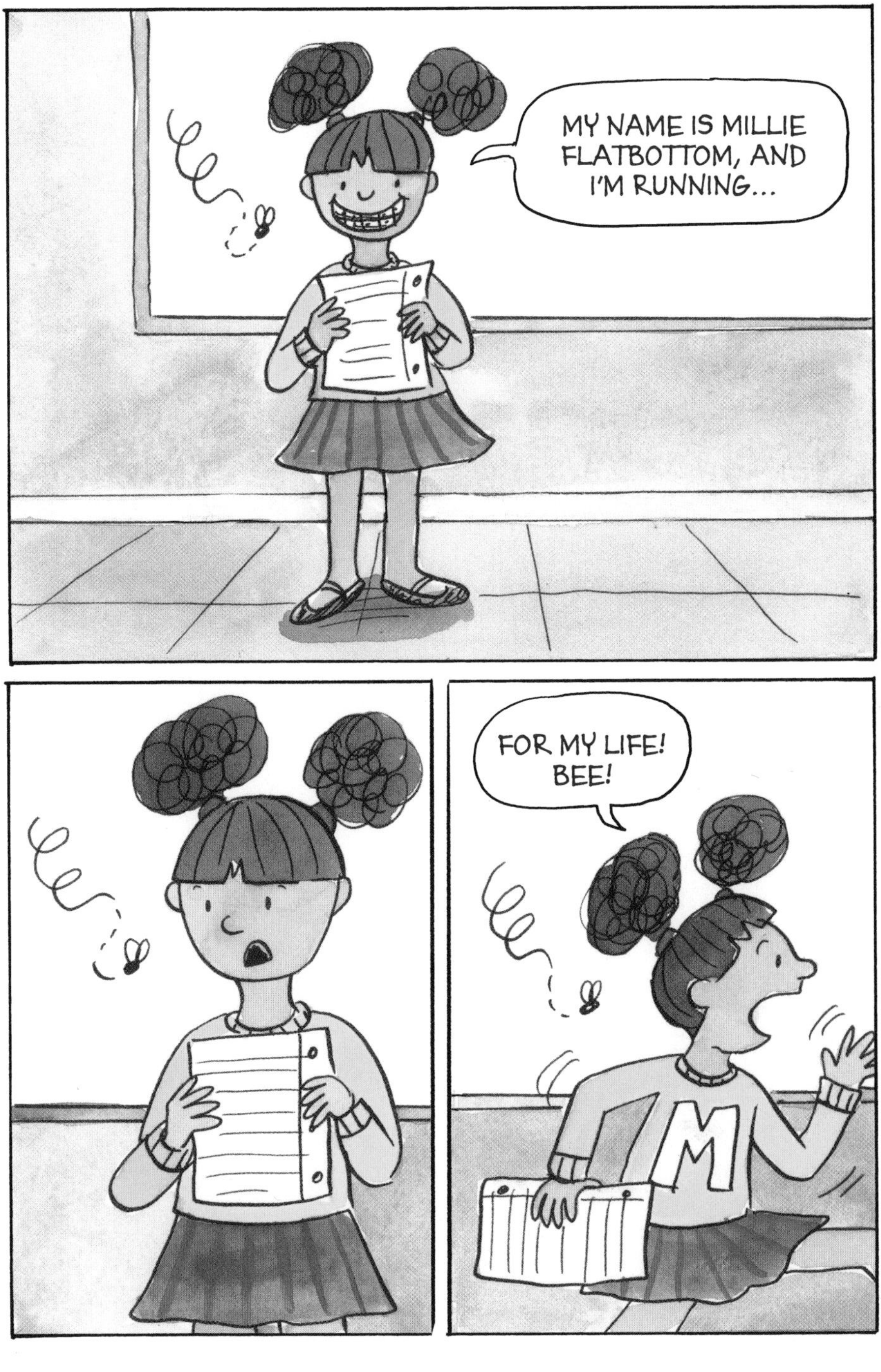
MY NAME IS MILLIE FLATBOTTOM, AND I'M RUNNING...
FOR MY LIFE! BEE!

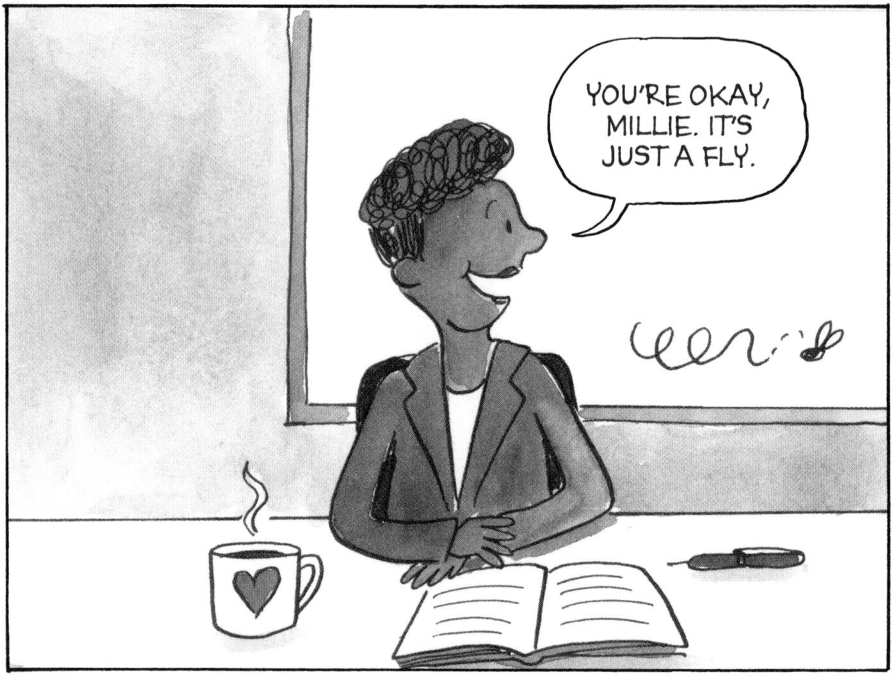
YOU'RE OKAY, MILLIE. IT'S JUST A FLY.

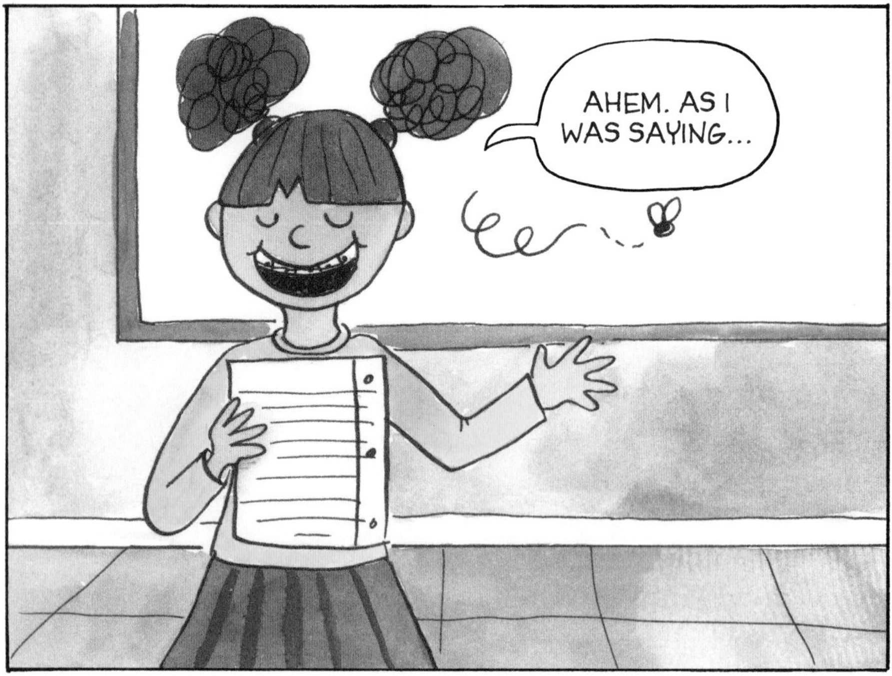
AHEM. AS I WAS SAYING...

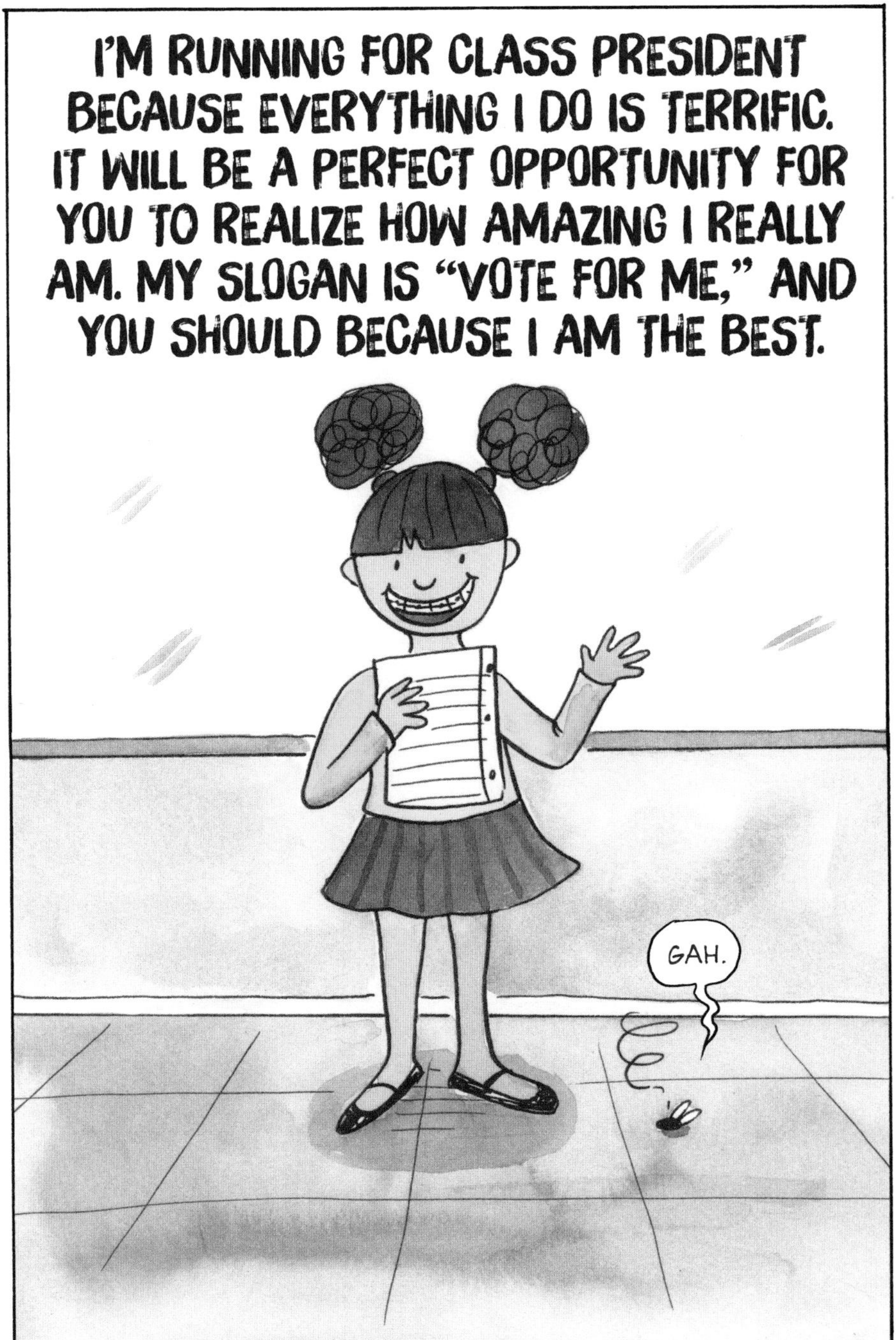
I'M RUNNING FOR CLASS PRESIDENT BECAUSE EVERYTHING I DO IS TERRIFIC. IT WILL BE A PERFECT OPPORTUNITY FOR YOU TO REALIZE HOW AMAZING I REALLY AM. MY SLOGAN IS "VOTE FOR ME," AND YOU SHOULD BECAUSE I AM THE BEST.
GAH.

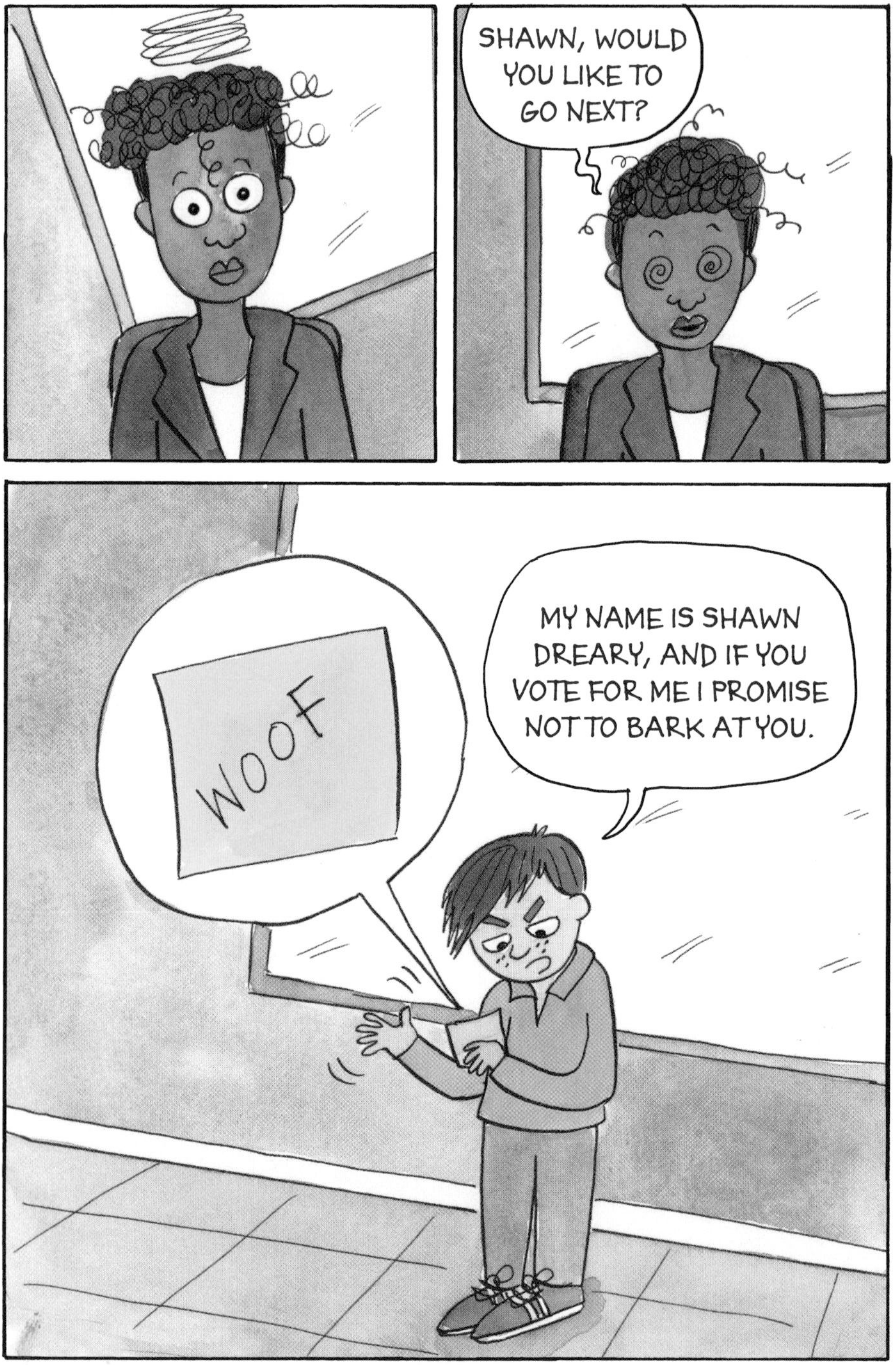

SHAWN, WOULD YOU LIKE TO GO NEXT?
WOOF
MY NAME IS SHAWN DREARY, AND IF YOU VOTE FOR ME I PROMISE NOT TO BARK AT YOU.

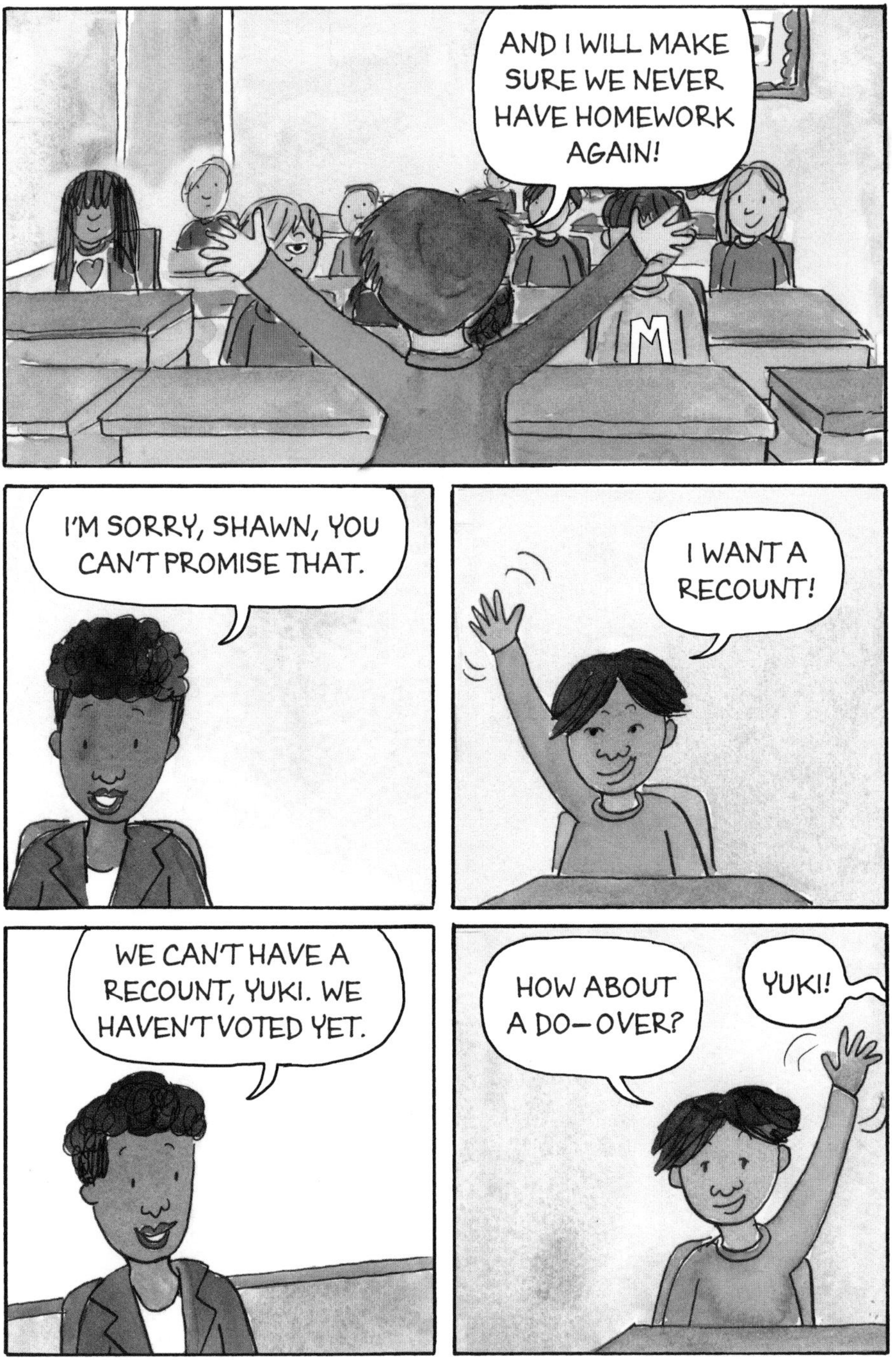
AND I WILL MAKE SURE WE NEVER HAVE HOMEWORK AGAIN!
M
I'M SORRY, SHAWN, YOU CAN'T PROMISE THAT.
I WANT A RECOUNT!
WE CAN'T HAVE A RECOUNT, YUKI. WE HAVEN'T VOTED YET.
HOW ABOUT A DO-OVER?
YUKI!

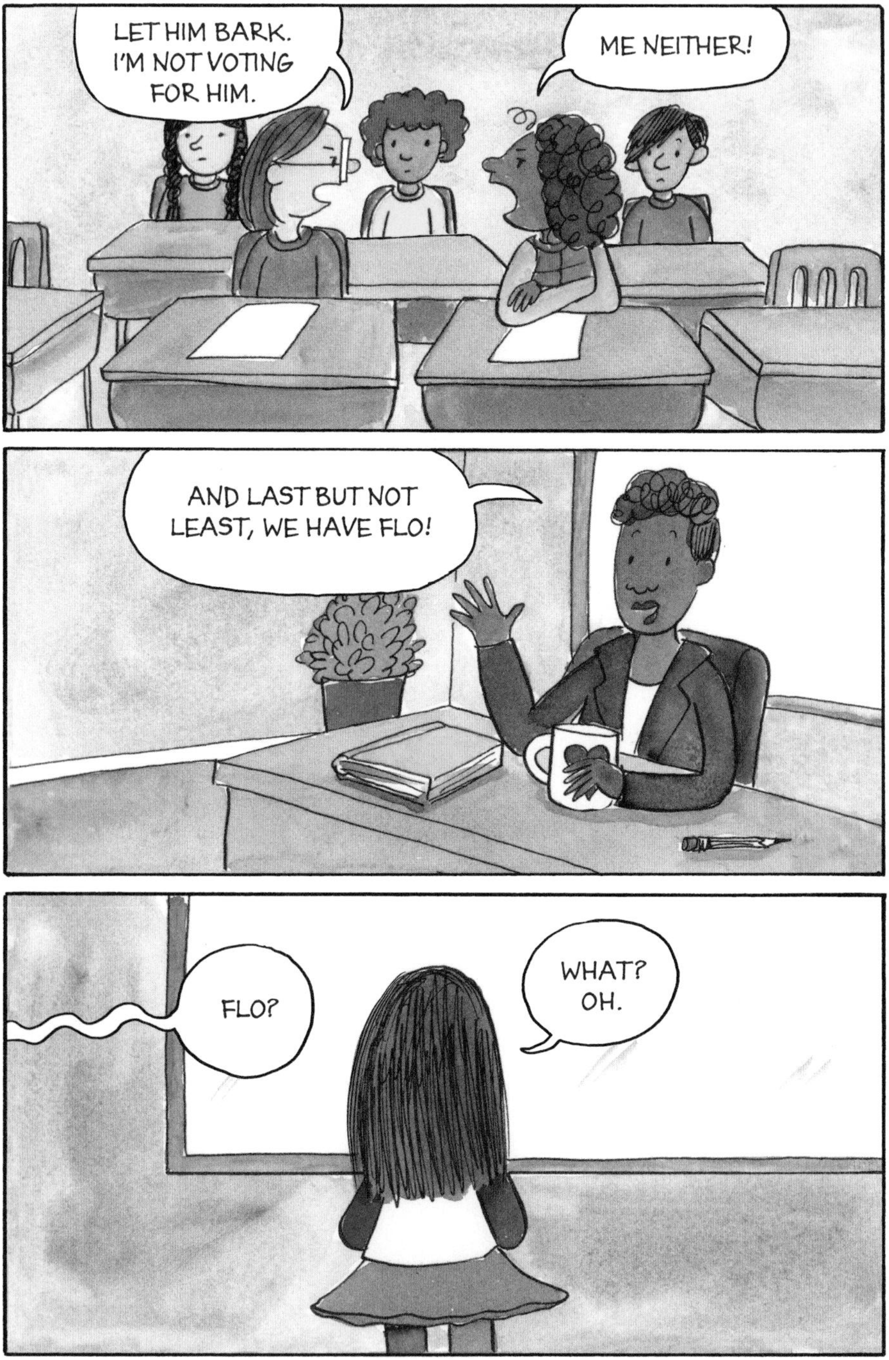
LET HIM BARK. I'M NOT VOTING FOR HIM.
ME NEITHER!
AND LAST BUT NOT LEAST, WE HAVE FLO!
FLO?
WHAT? OH.

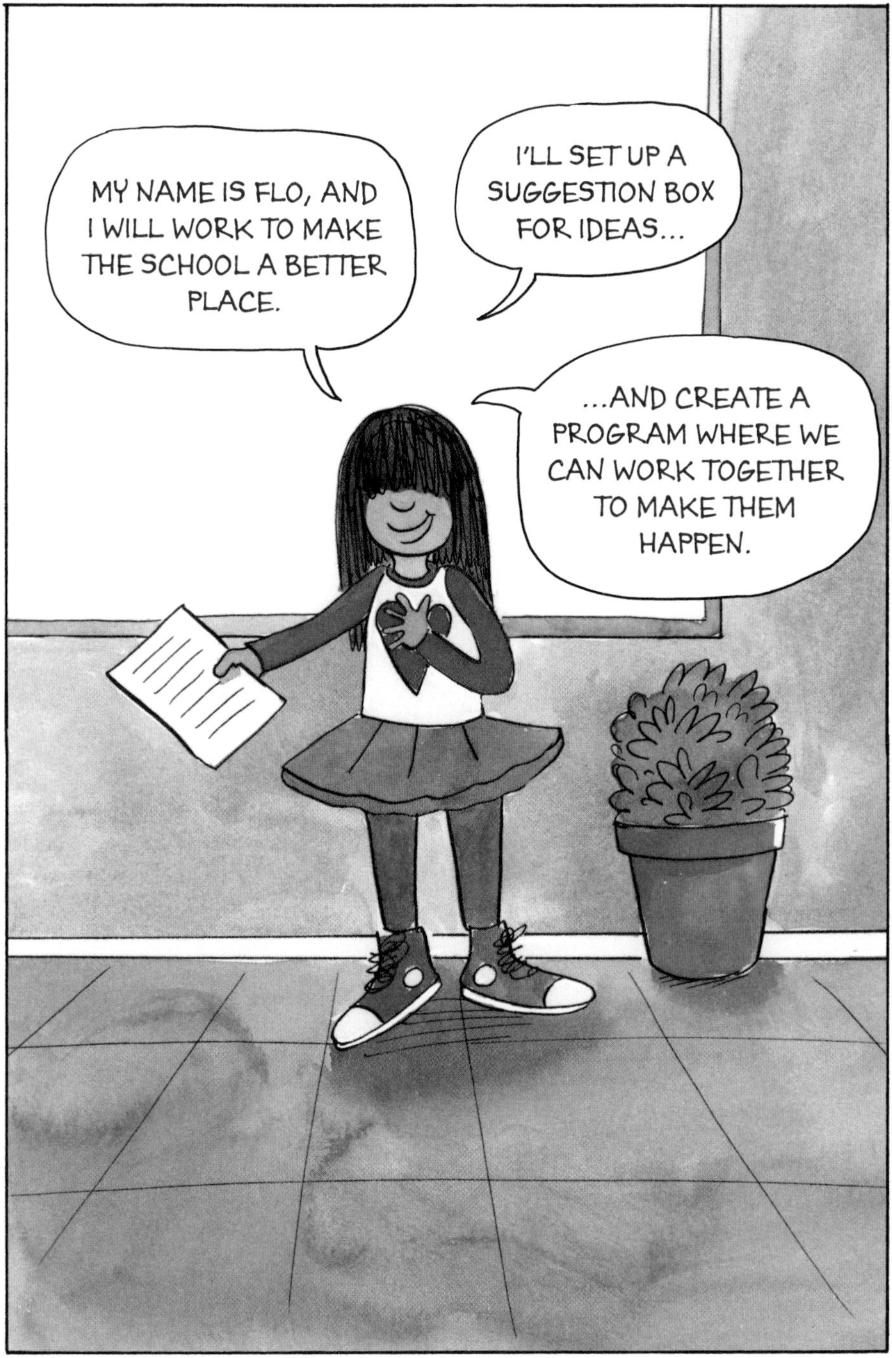
MY NAME IS FLO, AND I WILL WORK TO MAKE THE SCHOOL A BETTER PLACE.
I'LL SET UP A SUGGESTION BOX FOR IDEAS...
...AND CREATE A PROGRAM WHERE WE CAN WORK TOGETHER TO MAKE THEM HAPPEN.

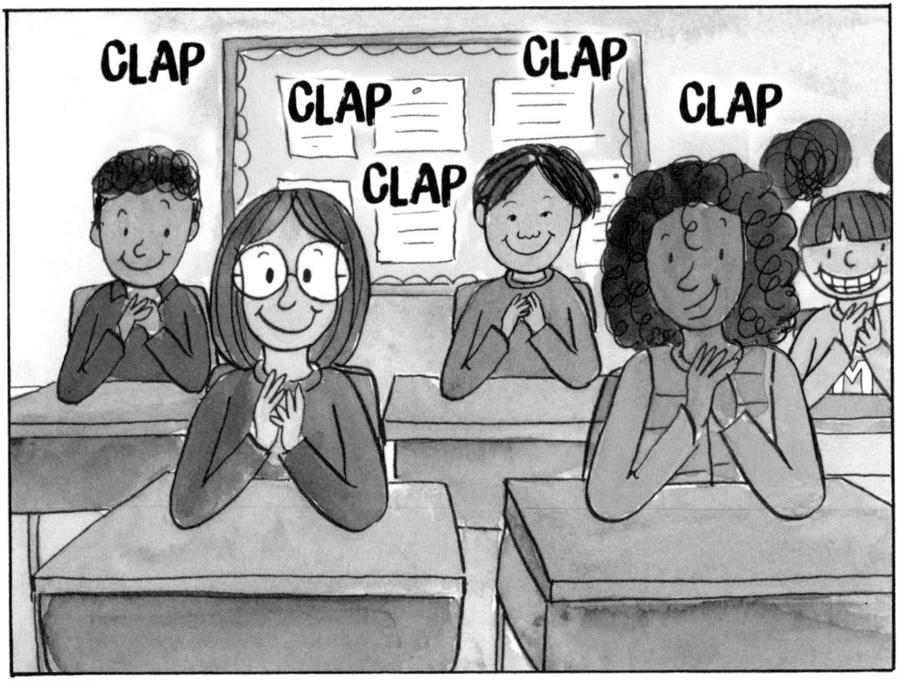
CLAP
CLAP
CLAP
CLAP
CLAP

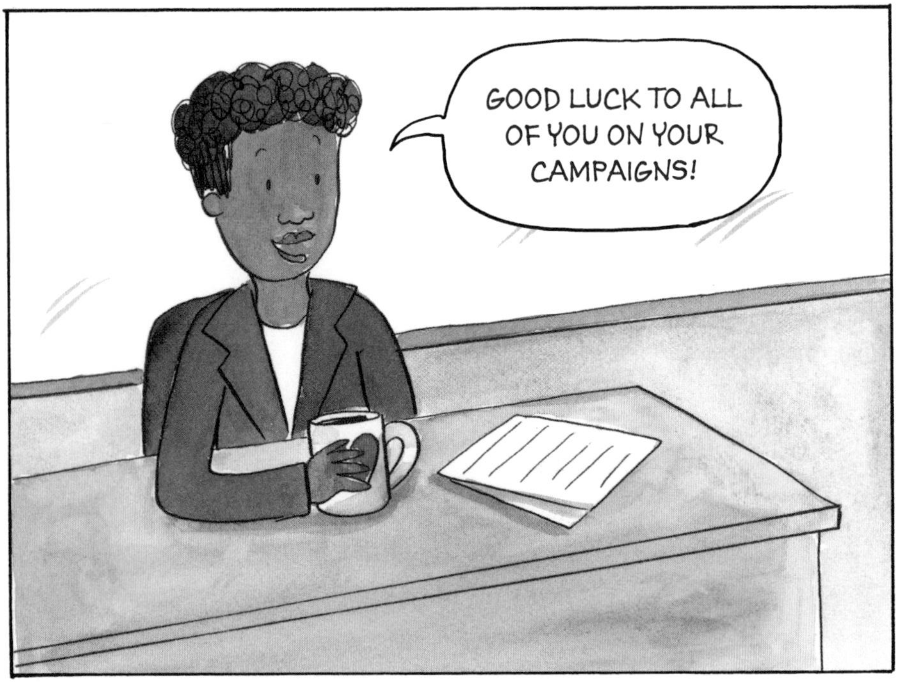
GOOD LUCK TO ALL OF YOU ON YOUR CAMPAIGNS!

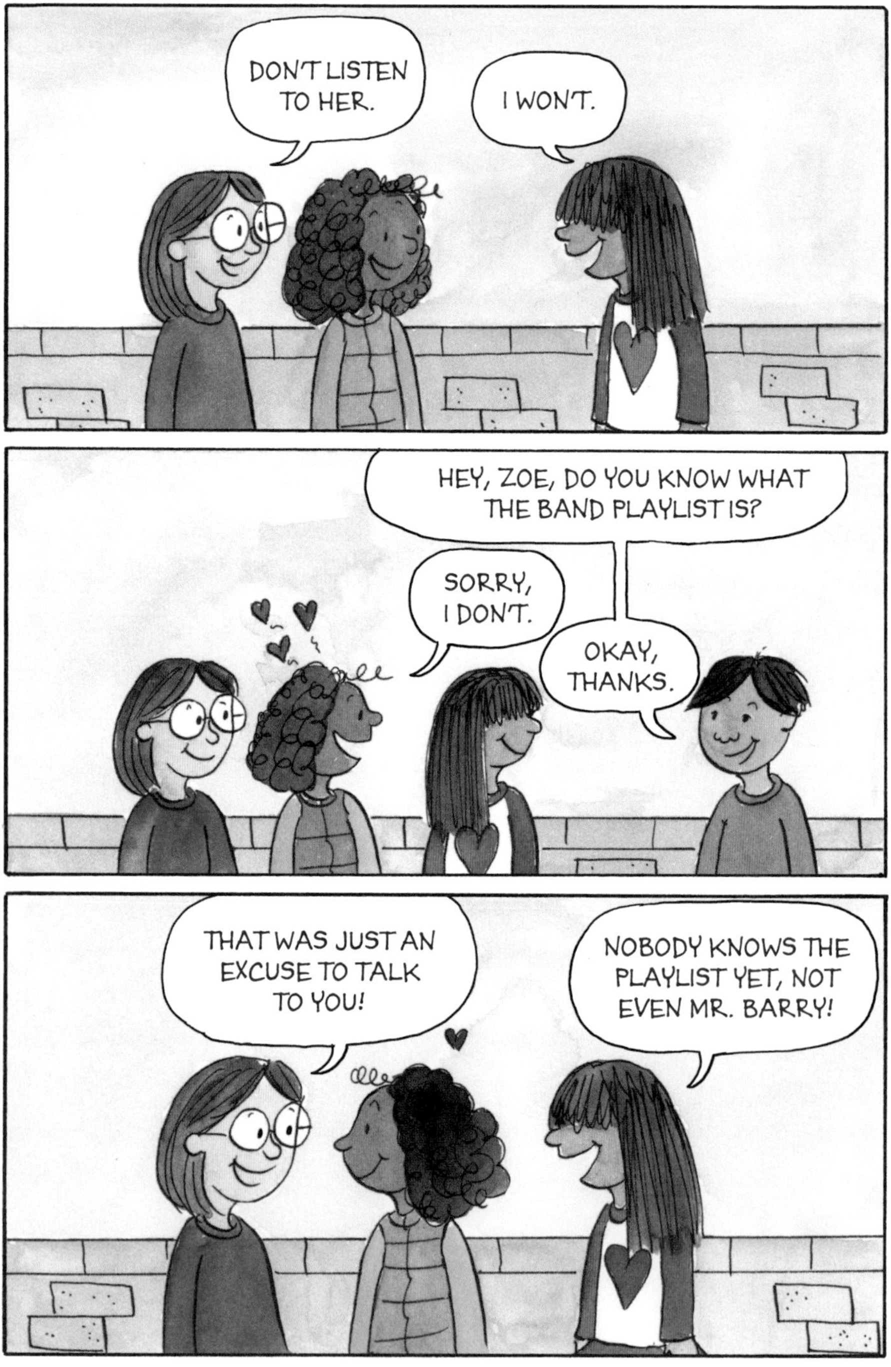
DON'T LISTEN TO HER.
I WON'T.
HEY, ZOE, DO YOU KNOW WHAT THE BAND PLAYLIST IS?
SORRY, I DON'T.
OKAY, THANKS.
THAT WAS JUST AN EXCUSE TO TALK TO YOU!
NOBODY KNOWS THE PLAYLIST YET, NOT EVEN MR. BARRY!

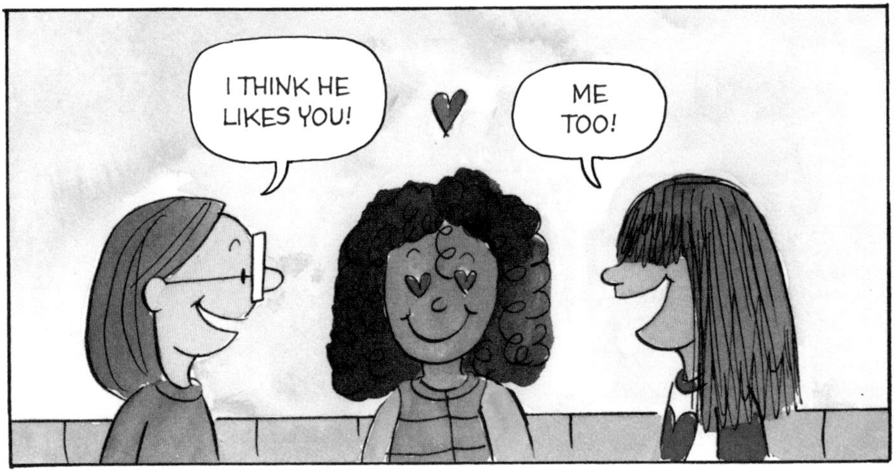
I THINK HE LIKES YOU!
ME TOO!

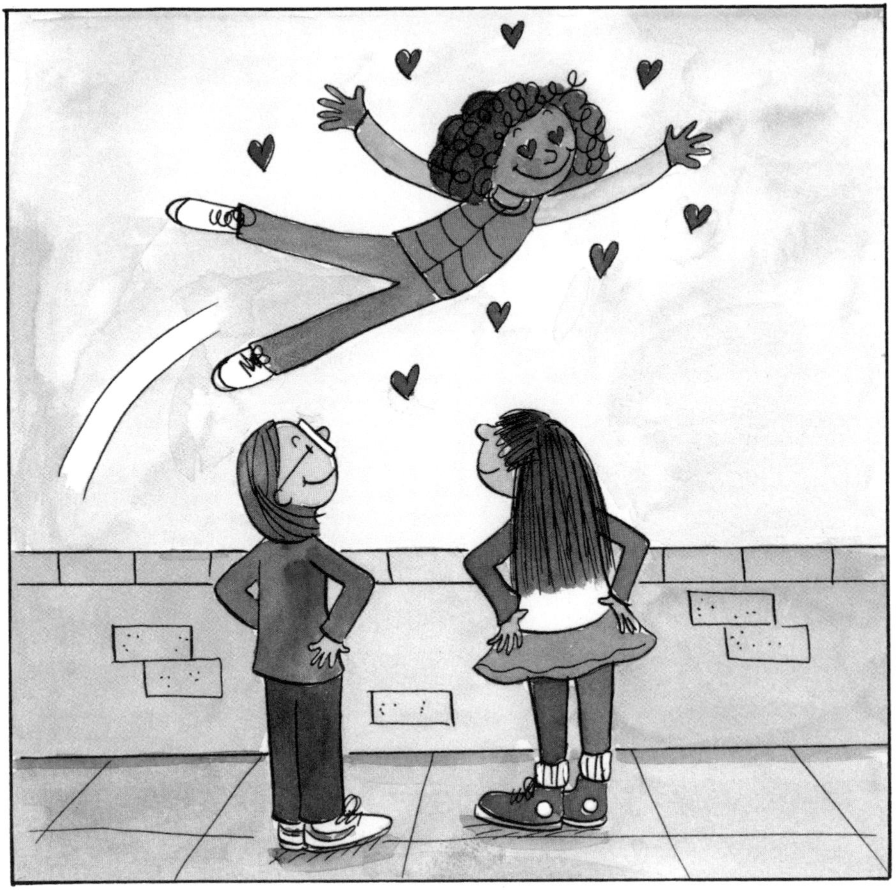

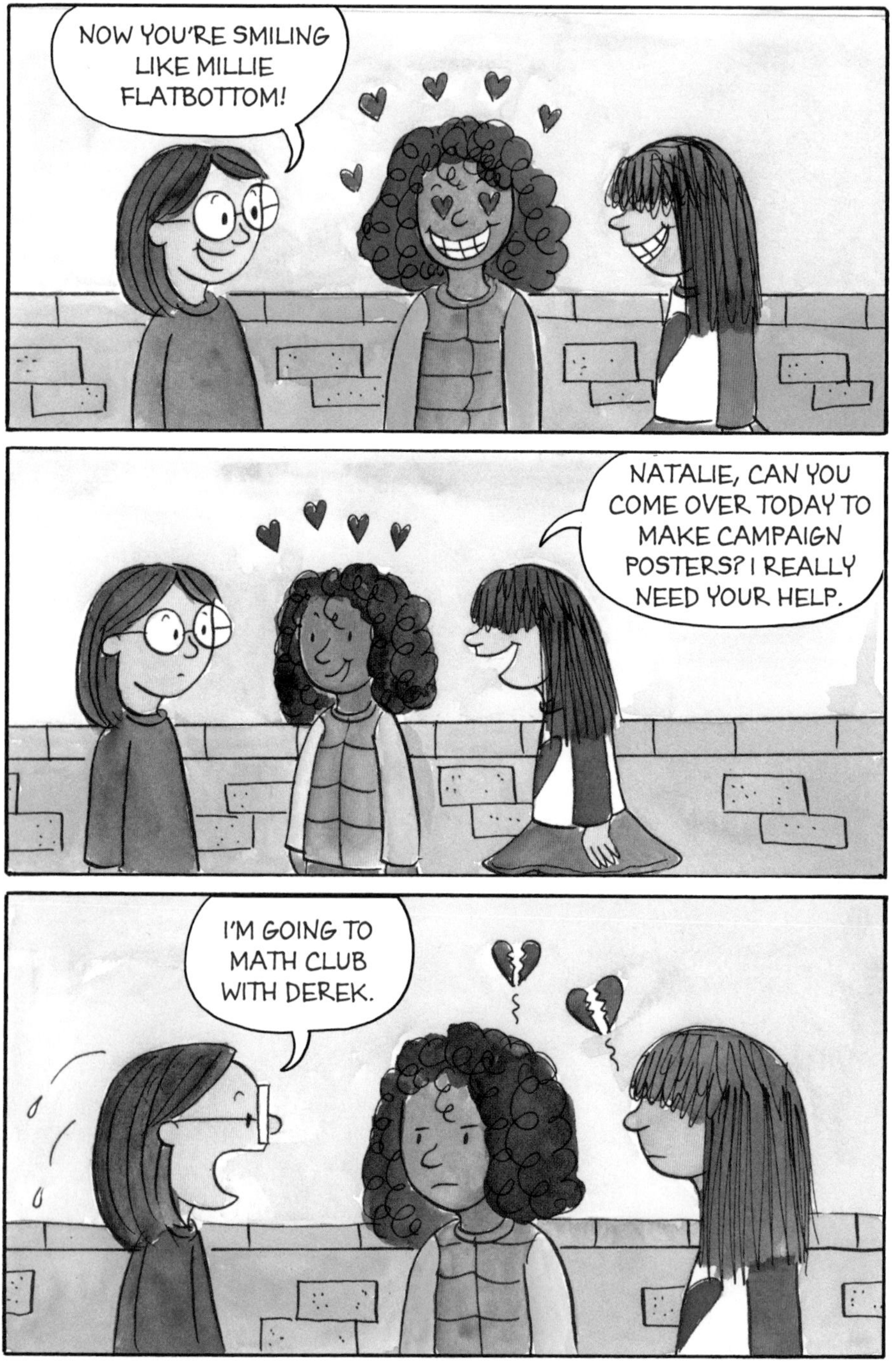
NOW YOU'RE SMILING LIKE MILLIE FLATBOTTOM!
NATALIE, CAN YOU COME OVER TODAY TO MAKE CAMPAIGN POSTERS? I REALLY NEED YOUR HELP.
I'M GOING TO MATH CLUB WITH DEREK.

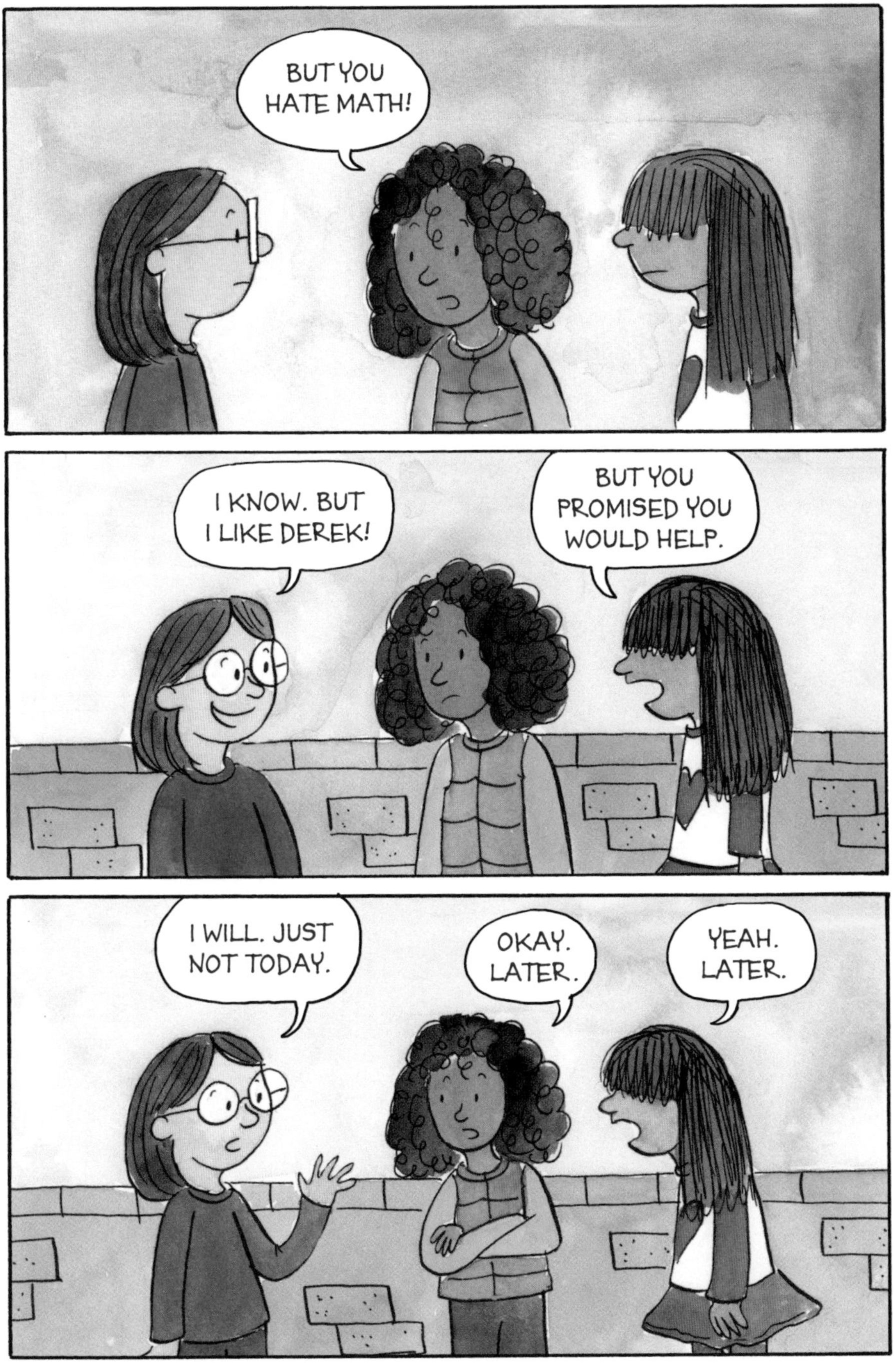
BUT YOU HATE MATH!
I KNOW. BUT I LIKE DEREK!
BUT YOU PROMISED YOU WOULD HELP.
I WILL. JUST NOT TODAY.
OKAY. LATER.
YEAH. LATER.

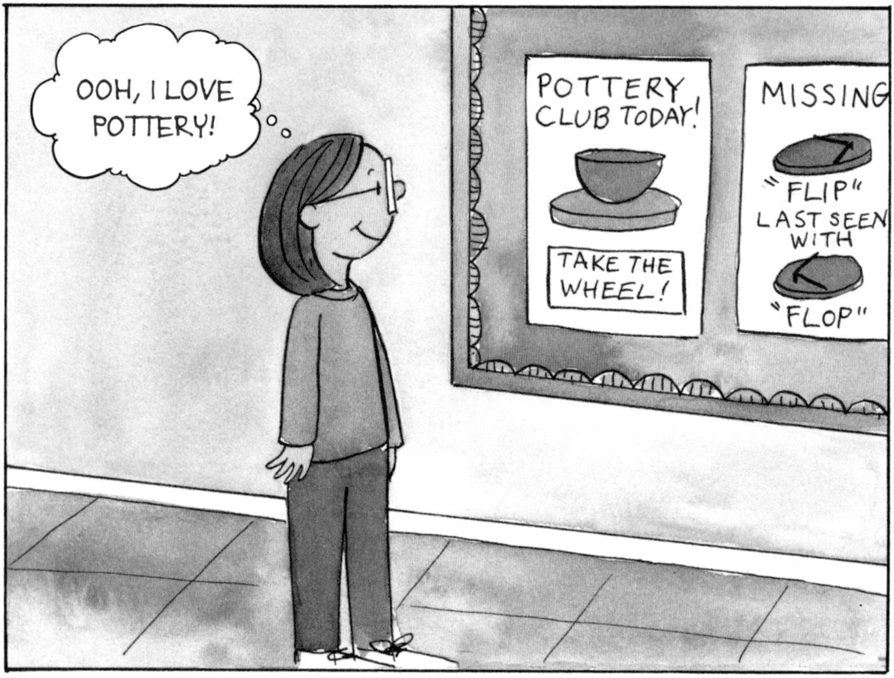
OOH, I LOVE POTTERY!
POTTERY CLUB TODAY!
TAKE THE WHEEL!
MISSING
"FLIP" LAST SEEN WITH
"FLOP"

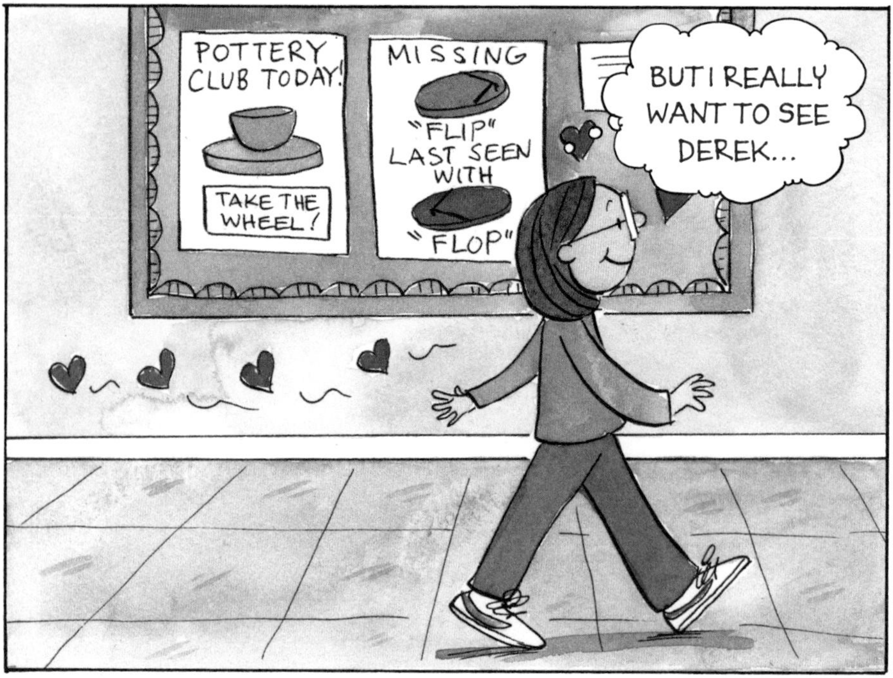
POTTERY CLUB TODAY!
TAKE THE WHEEL!
MISSING
"FLIP" LAST SEEN WITH
"FLOP"
BUT I REALLY WANT TO SEE DEREK...

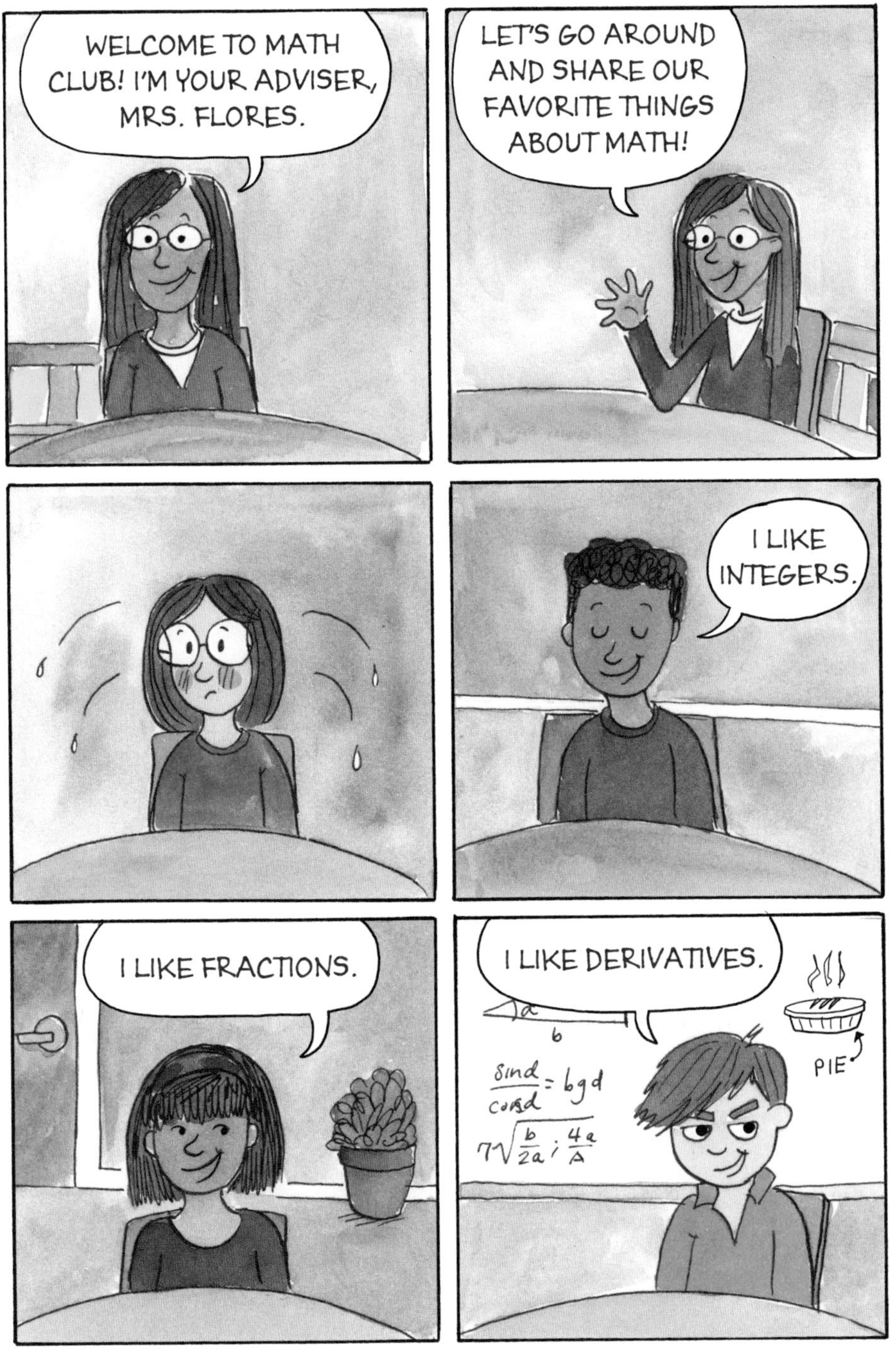
WELCOME TO MATH CLUB! I'M YOUR ADVISER, MRS. FLORES.
LET'S GO AROUND AND SHARE OUR FAVORITE THINGS ABOUT MATH!
I LIKE INTEGERS.
I LIKE FRACTIONS.
I LIKE DERIVATIVES.
PIE

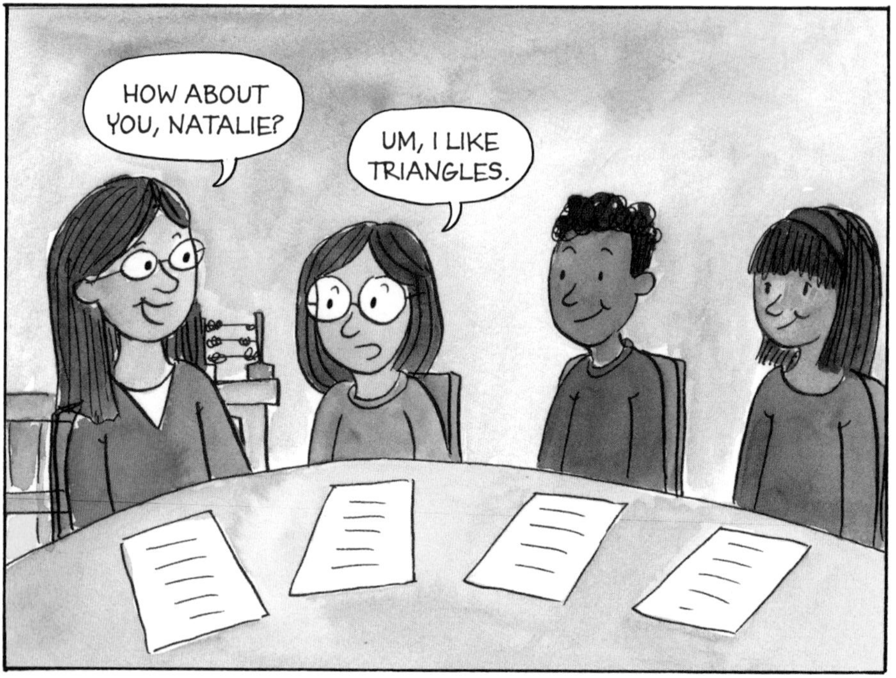
HOW ABOUT YOU, NATALIE?
UM, I LIKE TRIANGLES.

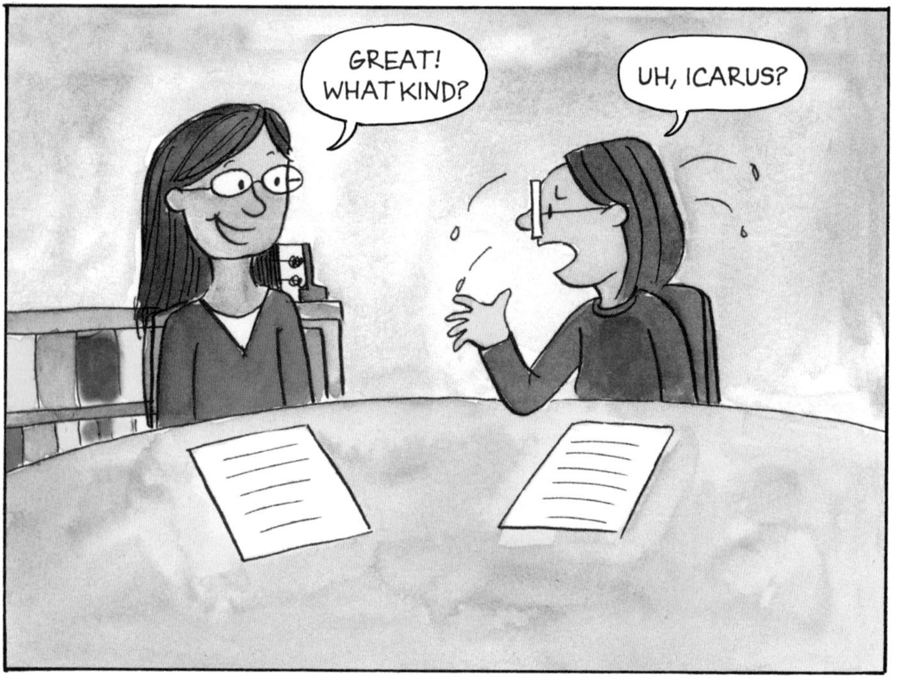
GREAT! WHAT KIND?
UH, ICARUS?

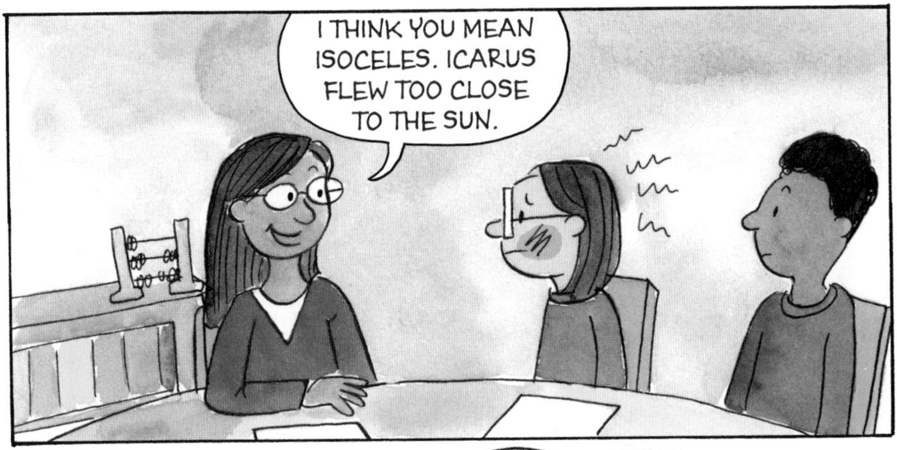
I THINK YOU MEAN ISOCELES. ICARUS FLEW TOO CLOSE TO THE SUN.

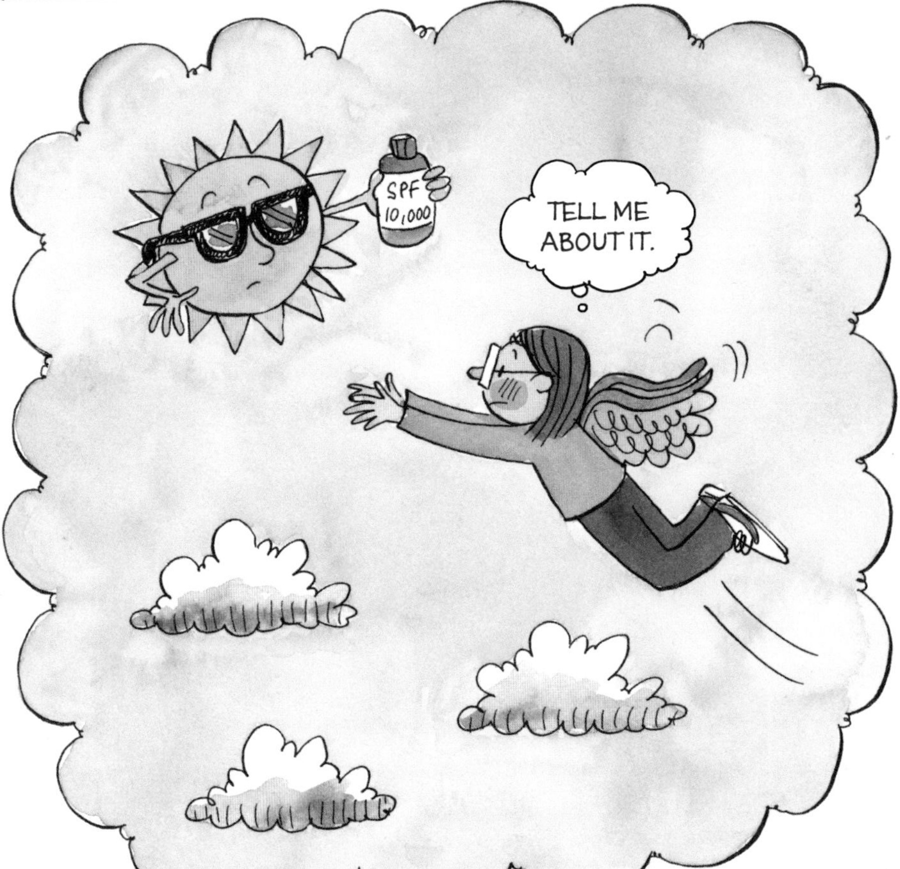
SPF 10,000
TELL ME ABOUT IT.

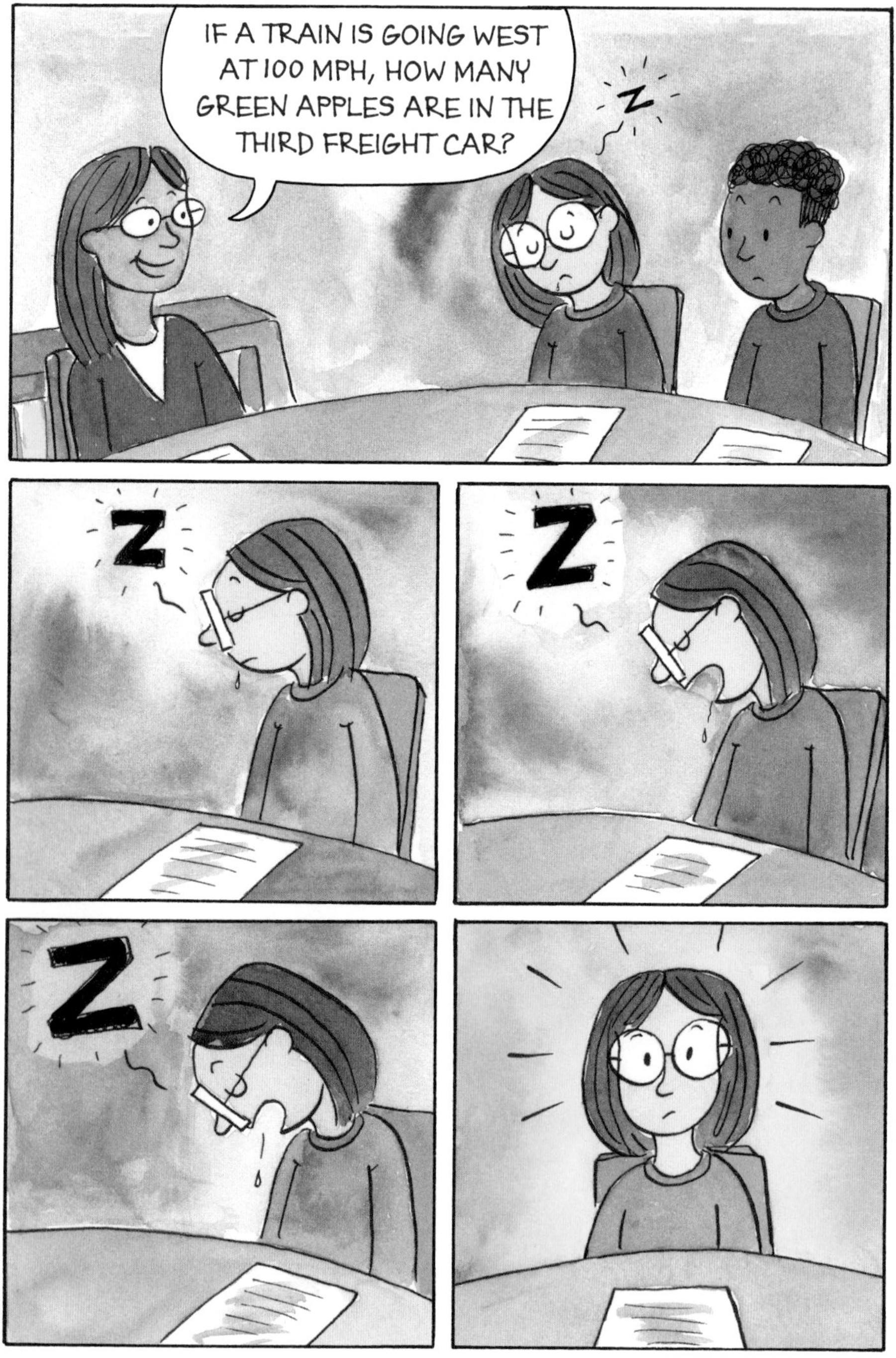
IF A TRAIN IS GOING WEST AT 100 MPH, HOW MANY GREEN APPLES ARE IN THE THIRD FREIGHT CAR?
Z
Z
Z
Z

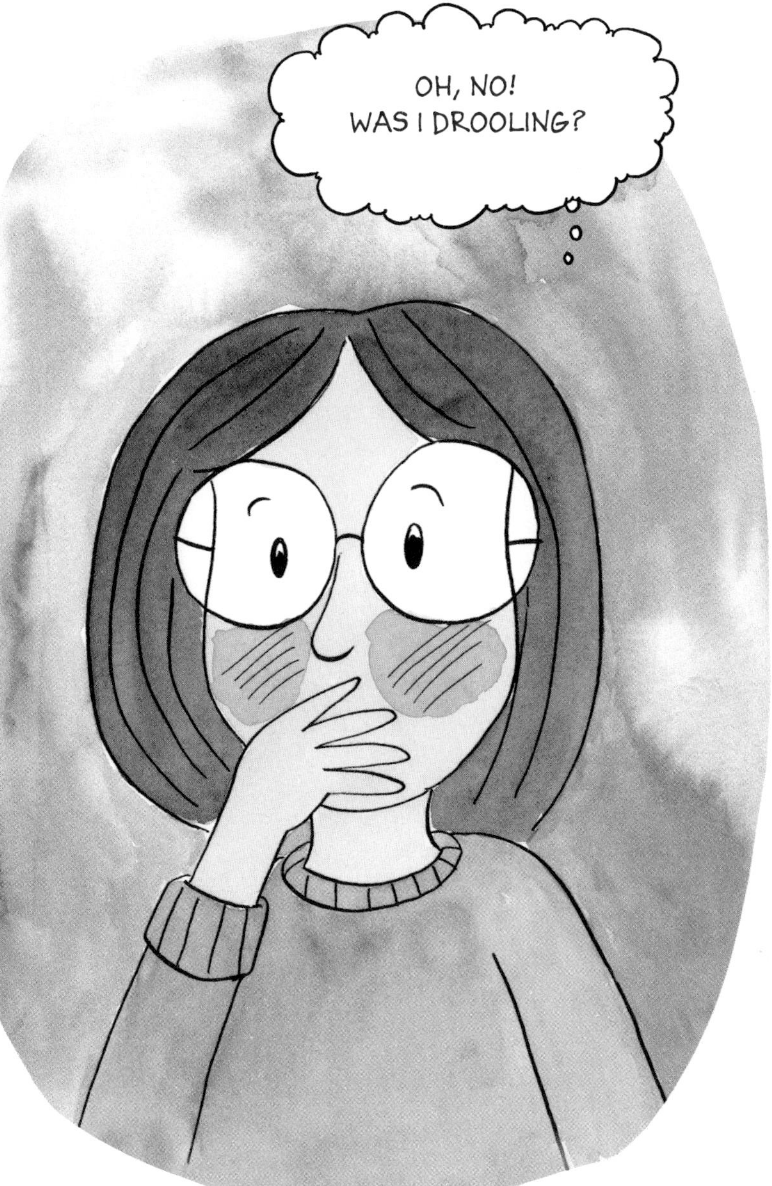
OH, NO!
WAS I DROOLING?

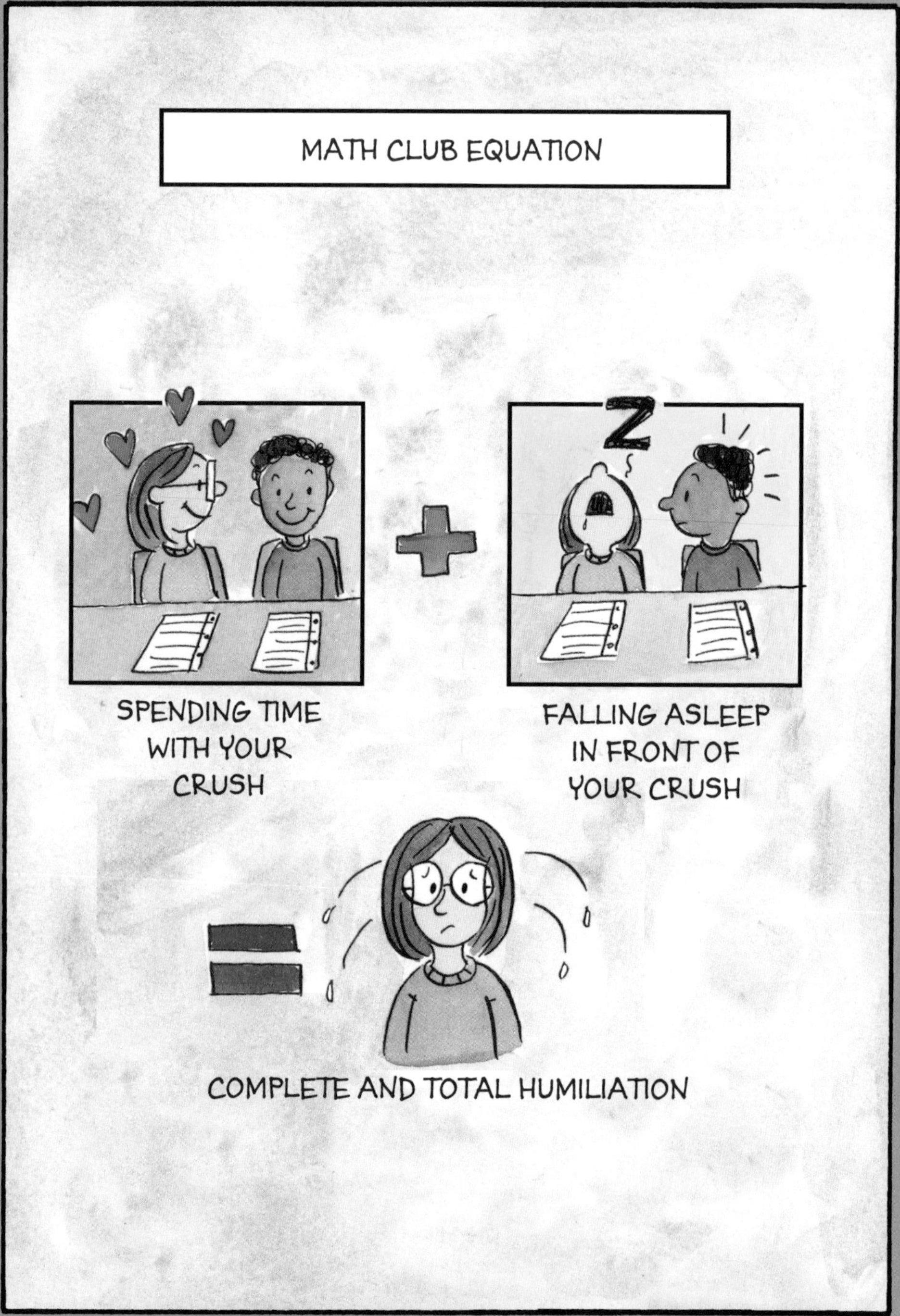
MATH CLUB EQUATION
SPENDING TIME WITH YOUR CRUSH
Z
FALLING ASLEEP IN FRONT OF YOUR CRUSH
COMPLETE AND TOTAL HUMILIATION

CHAPTER 5
BRACE YOURSELF

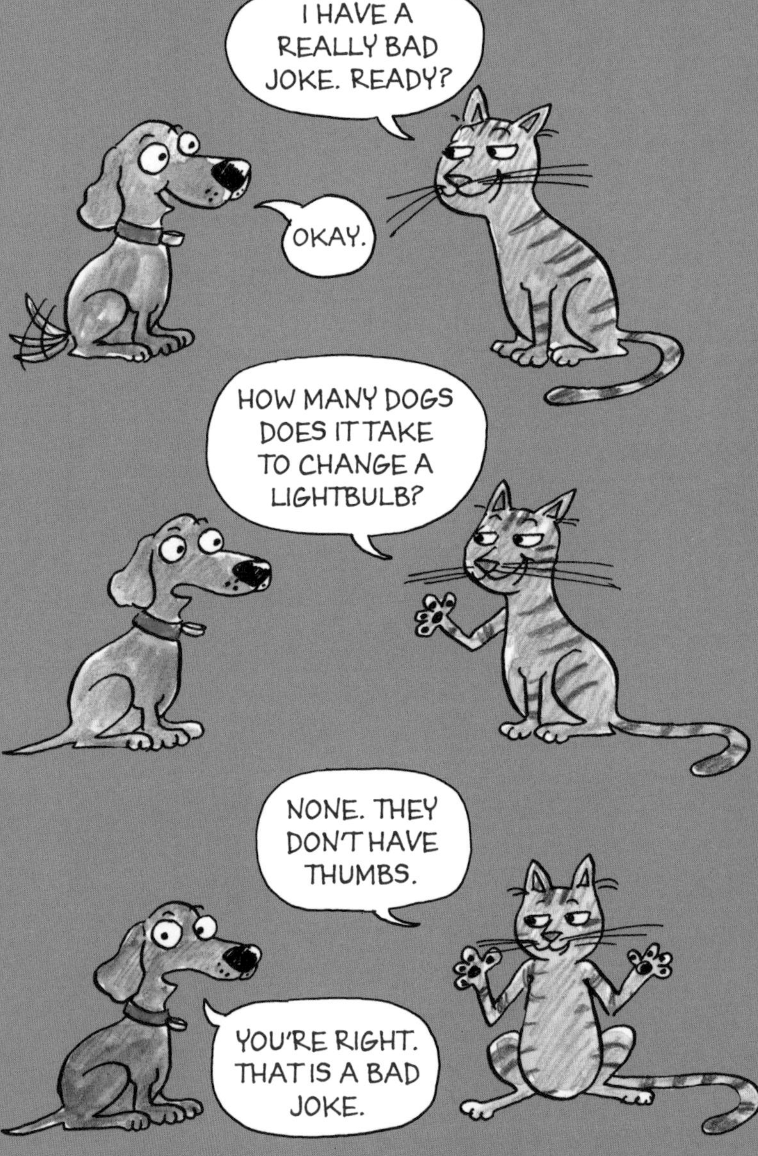
I HAVE A REALLY BAD JOKE. READY?
OKAY.
HOW MANY DOGS DOES IT TAKE TO CHANGE A LIGHTBULB?
NONE. THEY DON'T HAVE THUMBS.
YOU'RE RIGHT. THAT IS A BAD JOKE.

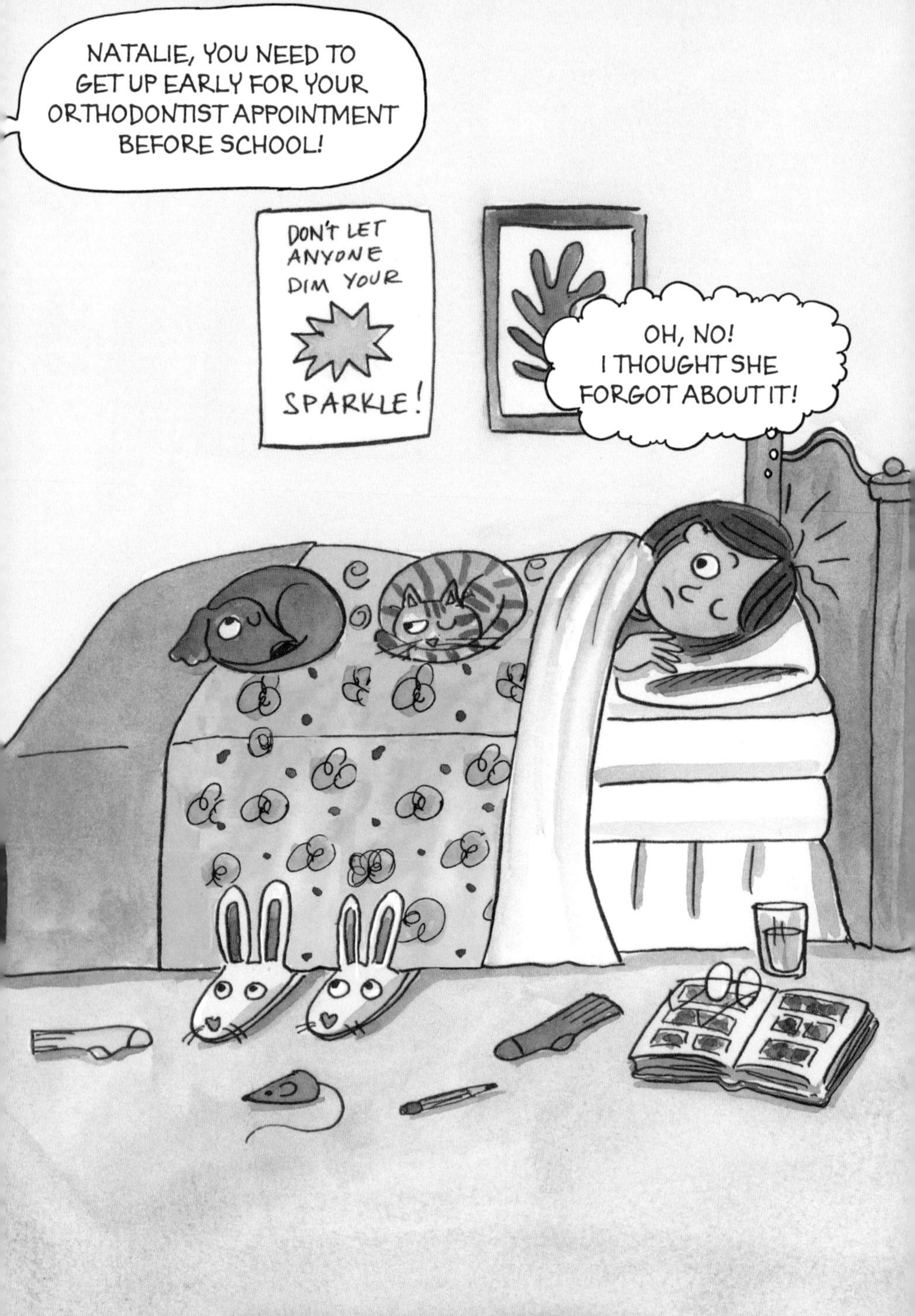
NATALIE, YOU NEED TO GET UP EARLY FOR YOUR ORTHODONTIST APPOINTMENT BEFORE SCHOOL!
DON'T LET ANYONE DIM YOUR SPARKLE!
OH, NO! I THOUGHT SHE FORGOT ABOUT IT!

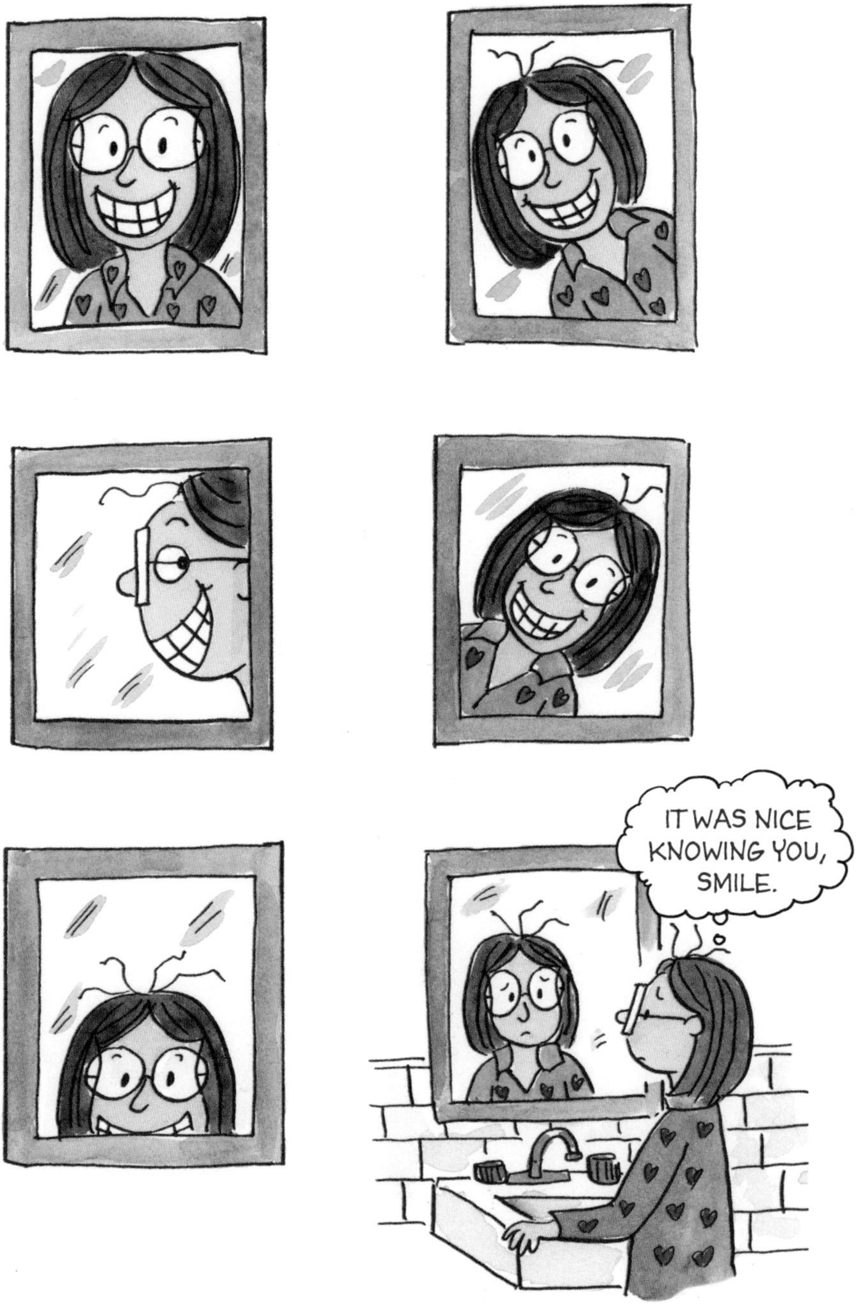
IT WAS NICE KNOWING YOU, SMILE.

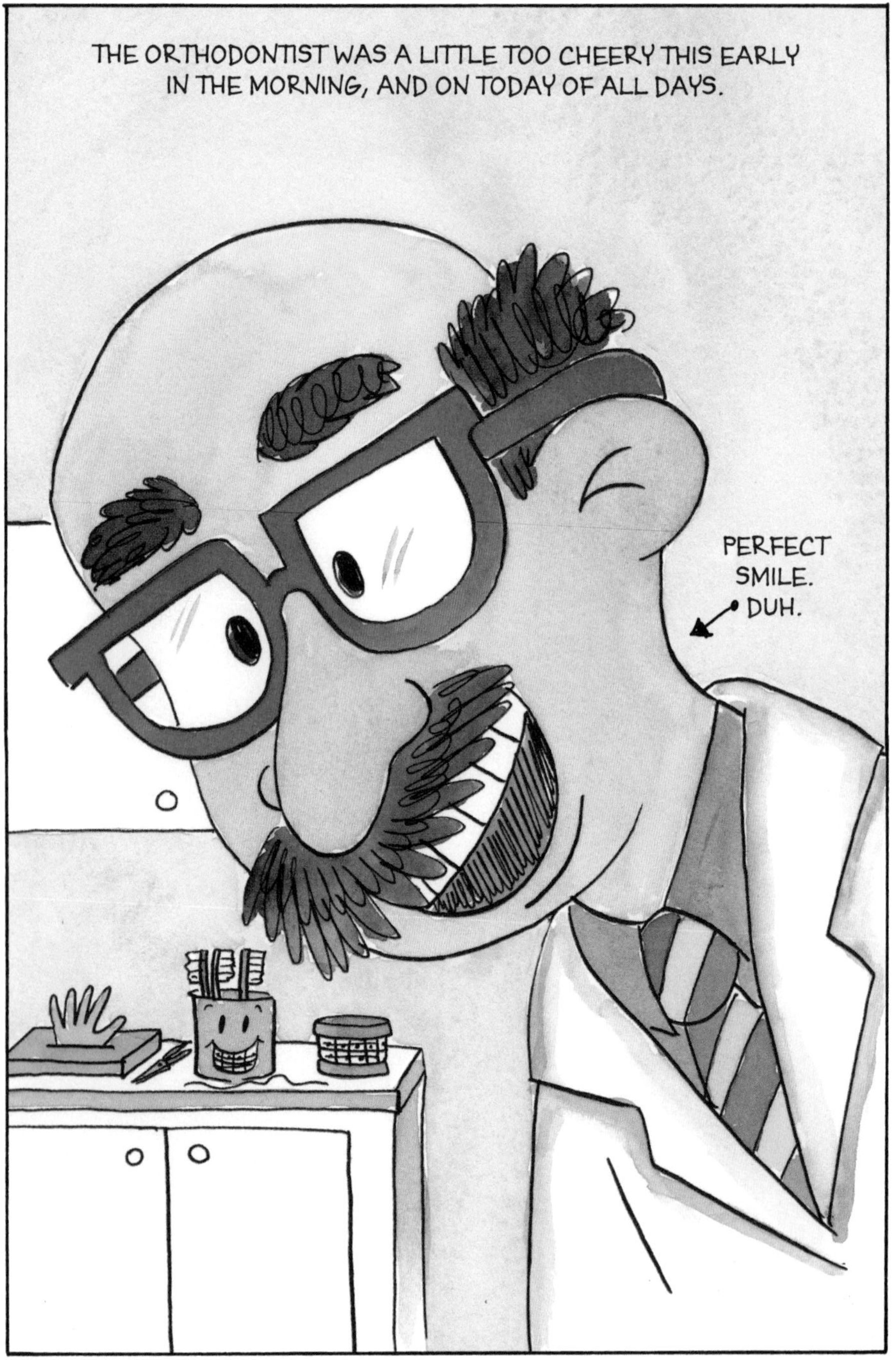
THE ORTHODONTIST WAS A LITTLE TOO CHEERY THIS EARLY IN THE MORNING, AND ON TODAY OF ALL DAYS.
PERFECT SMILE. DUH.

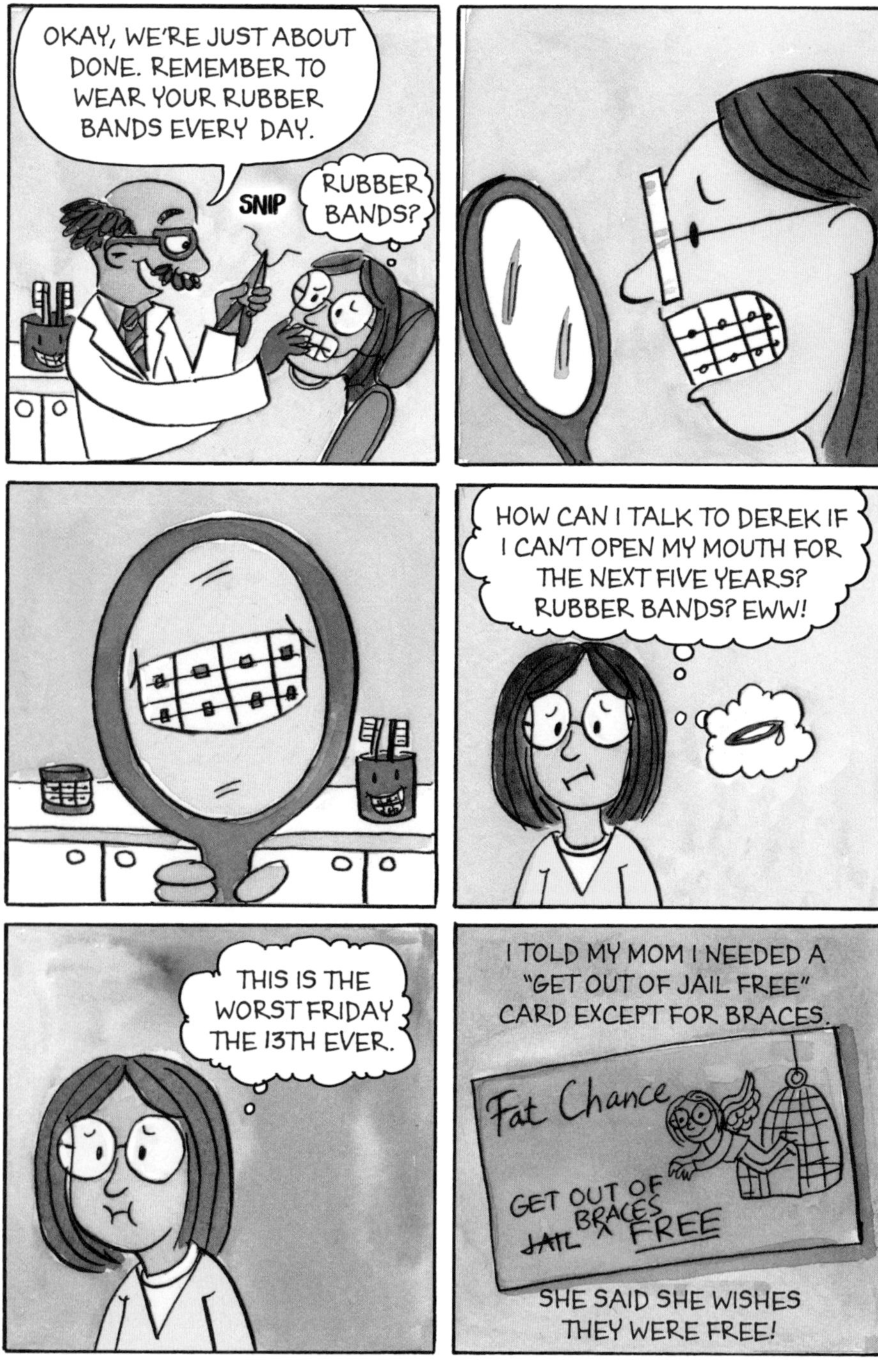
OKAY, WE'RE JUST ABOUT DONE. REMEMBER TO WEAR YOUR RUBBER BANDS EVERY DAY.
SNIP
RUBBER BANDS?
HOW CAN I TALK TO DEREK IF I CAN'T OPEN MY MOUTH FOR THE NEXT FIVE YEARS? RUBBER BANDS? EWW!
THIS IS THE WORST FRIDAY THE 13TH EVER.
I TOLD MY MOM I NEEDED A "GET OUT OF JAIL FREE" CARD EXCEPT FOR BRACES.
Fat Chance
GET OUT OF JAIL BRACES FREE
SHE SAID SHE WISHES THEY WERE FREE!

"BRACES" IS ONE OF THOSE WORDS THAT LOOKS EXACTLY LIKE IT SOUNDS, EXCEPT WHEN YOU'RE WEARING THEM. THEN IT'S MORE LIKE "BRATHES."

HERE ARE SOME OF THE THINGS I'M SUPPOSED TO AVOID WHILE WEARING BRACES:

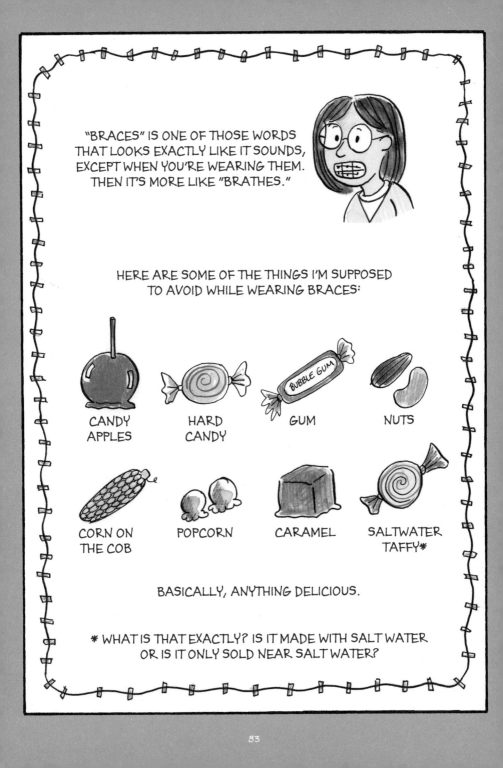

CANDY APPLES

HARD CANDY

GUM

NUTS

CORN ON THE COB

POPCORN

CARAMEL

SALTWATER TAFFY*

BASICALLY, ANYTHING DELICIOUS.

* WHAT IS THAT EXACTLY? IS IT MADE WITH SALT WATER OR IS IT ONLY SOLD NEAR SALT WATER?

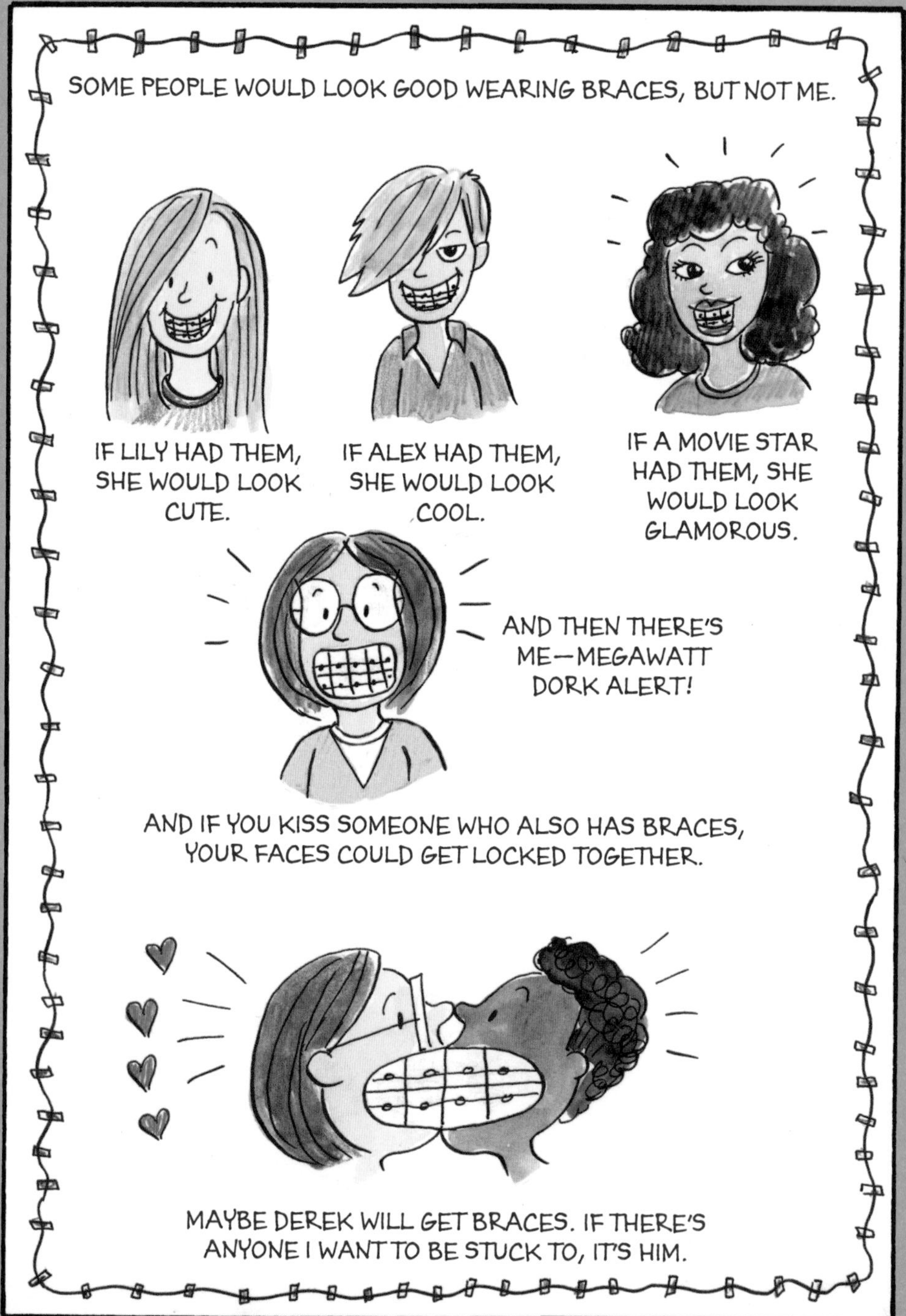
SOME PEOPLE WOULD LOOK GOOD WEARING BRACES, BUT NOT ME.
IF LILY HAD THEM, SHE WOULD LOOK CUTE.
IF ALEX HAD THEM, SHE WOULD LOOK COOL.
IF A MOVIE STAR HAD THEM, SHE WOULD LOOK GLAMOROUS.
AND THEN THERE'S ME—MEGAWATT DORK ALERT!
AND IF YOU KISS SOMEONE WHO ALSO HAS BRACES, YOUR FACES COULD GET LOCKED TOGETHER.
MAYBE DEREK WILL GET BRACES. IF THERE'S ANYONE I WANT TO BE STUCK TO, IT'S HIM.

I CAN'T BELIEVE I HAVE TO GO TO SCHOOL AFTER GETTING BRACES. I GUESS I CAN JUST TALK OUT OF THE SIDE OF MY MOUTH OR MAYBE THROUGH A VENTRILOQUIST PUPPET, BUT THAT MIGHT BE WEIRD.

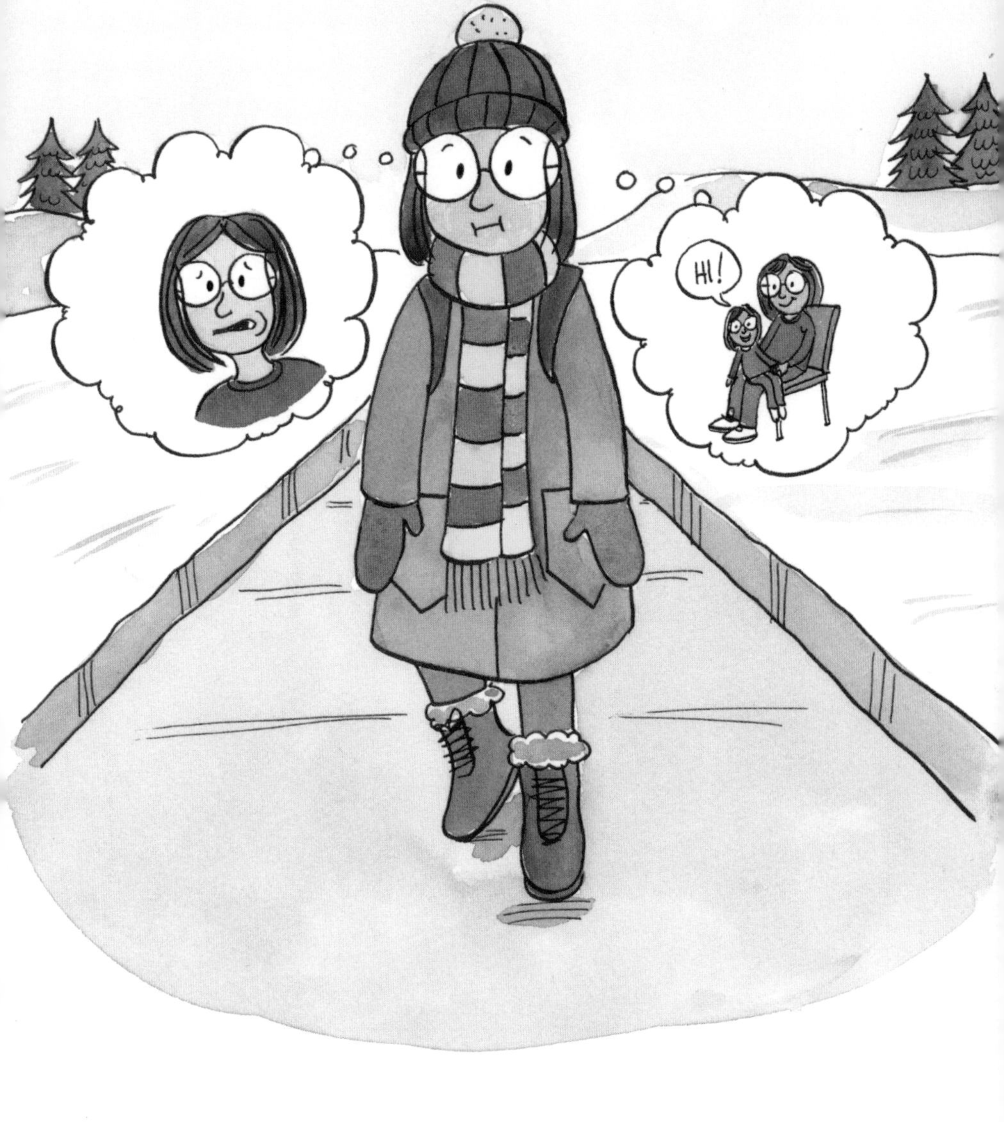
HI!

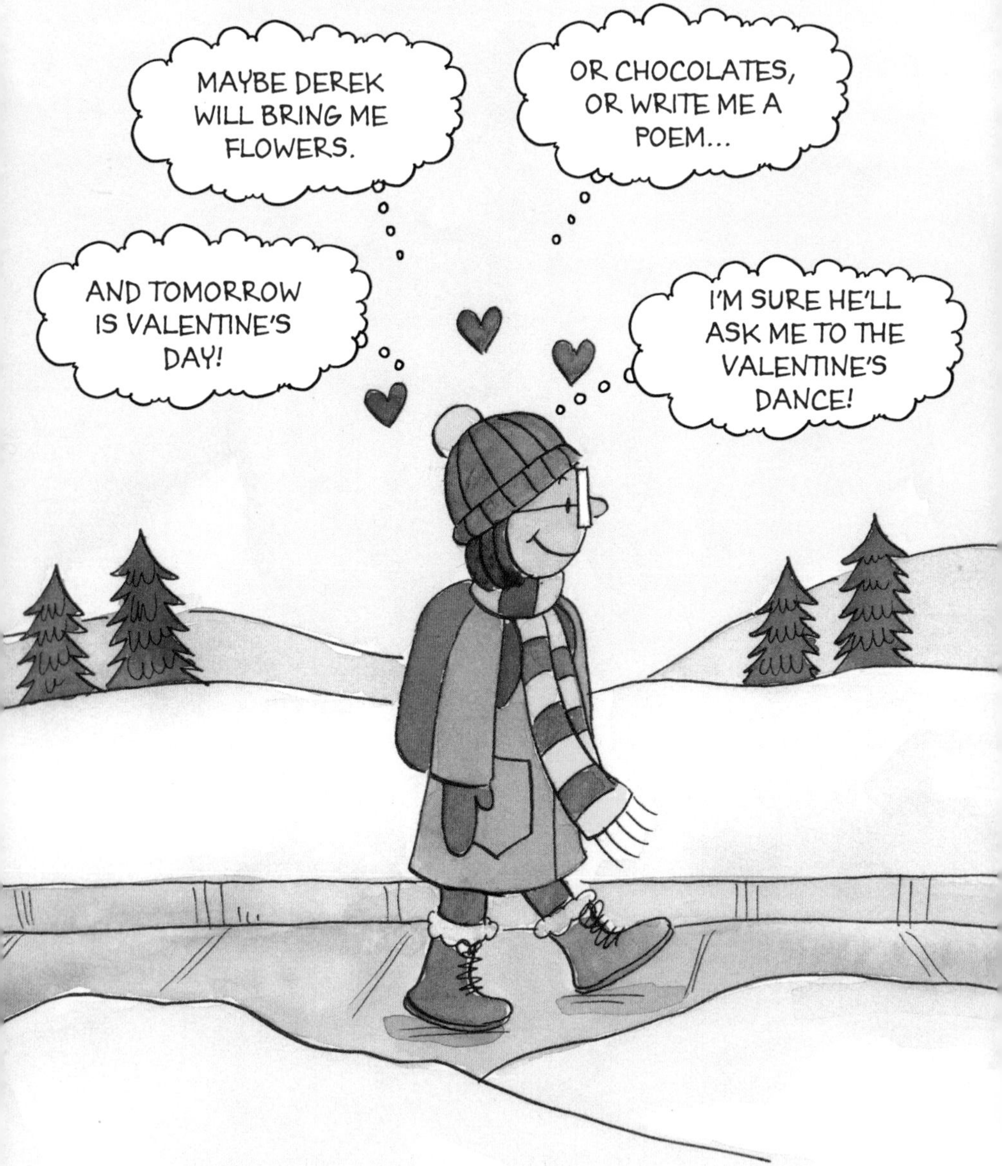
MAYBE DEREK WILL BRING ME FLOWERS.
OR CHOCOLATES, OR WRITE ME A POEM...
AND TOMORROW IS VALENTINE'S DAY!
I'M SURE HE'LL ASK ME TO THE VALENTINE'S DANCE!

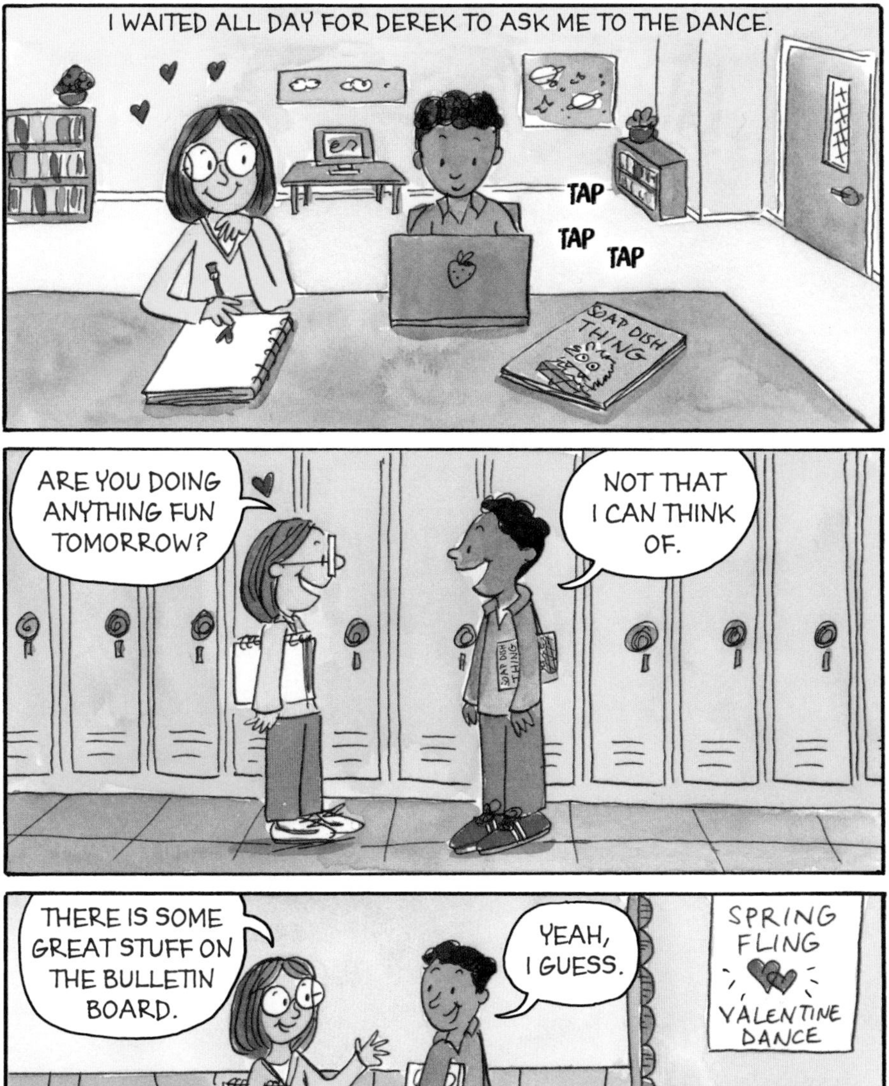
I WAITED ALL DAY FOR DEREK TO ASK ME TO THE DANCE.
TAP
TAP
TAP
SOAP DISH THING
ARE YOU DOING ANYTHING FUN TOMORROW?
NOT THAT I CAN THINK OF.
THERE IS SOME GREAT STUFF ON THE BULLETIN BOARD.
YEAH, I GUESS.
SPRING FLING
VALENTINE DANCE

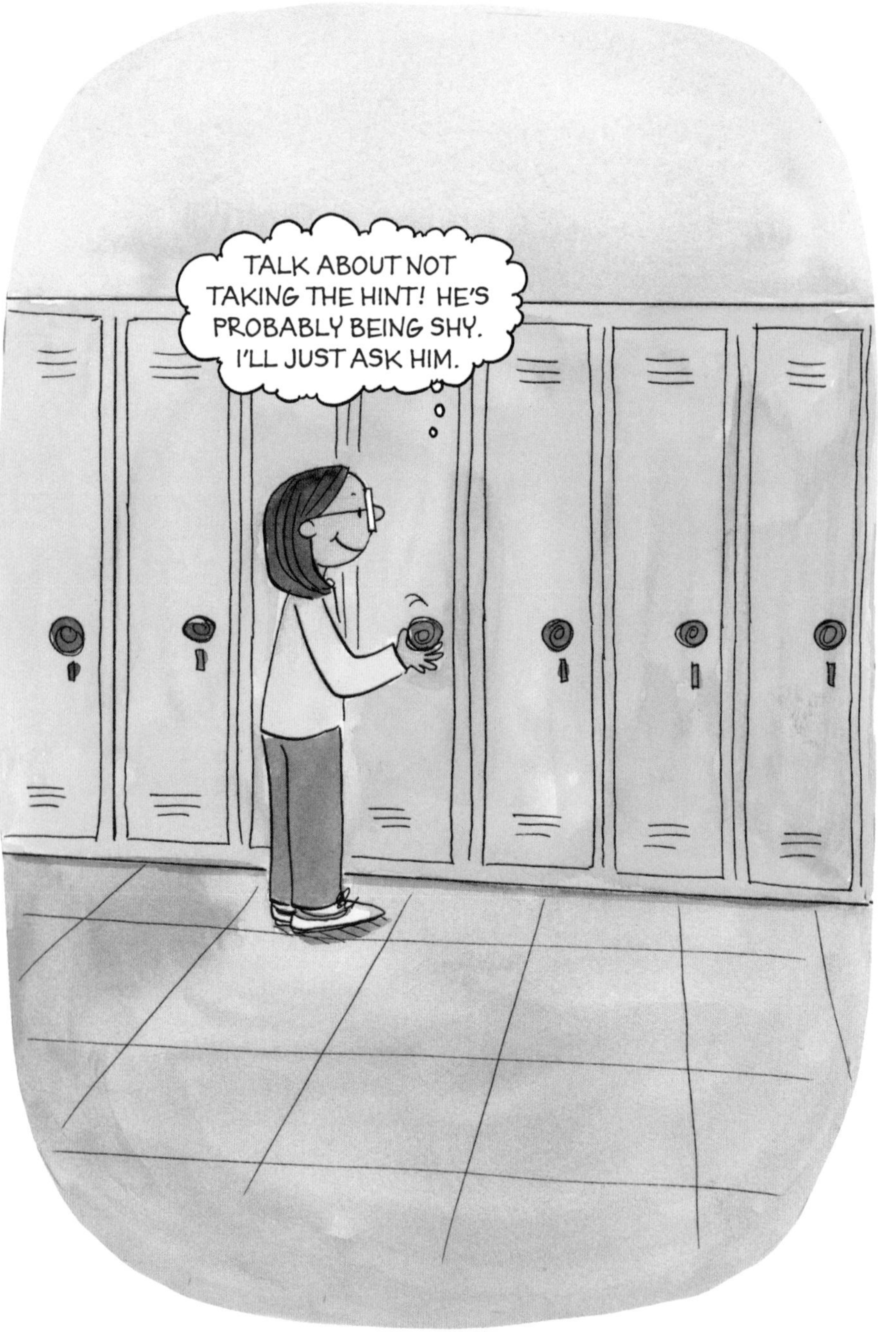
TALK ABOUT NOT TAKING THE HINT! HE'S PROBABLY BEING SHY. I'LL JUST ASK HIM.

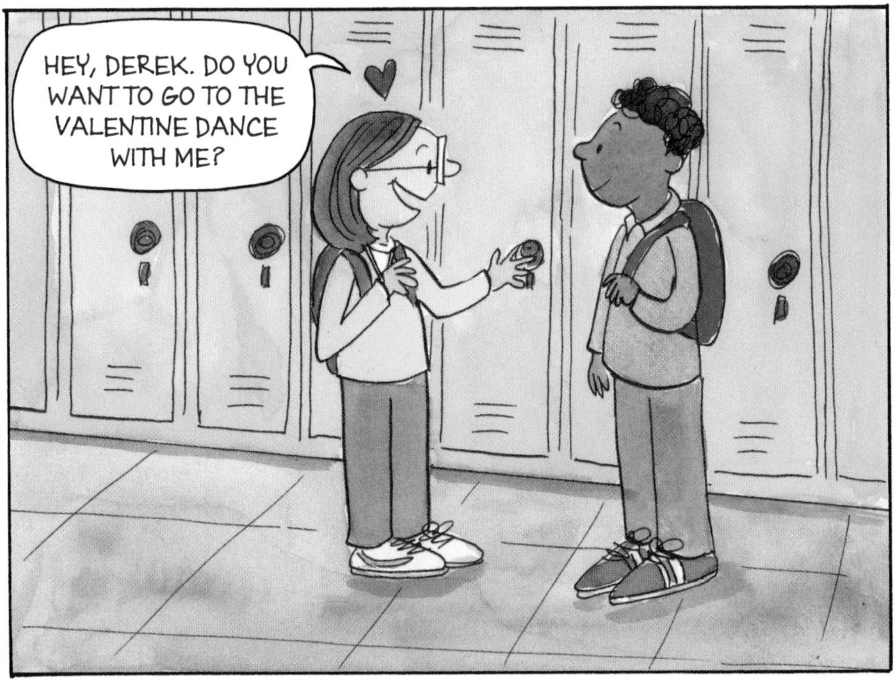
HEY, DEREK. DO YOU WANT TO GO TO THE VALENTINE DANCE WITH ME?

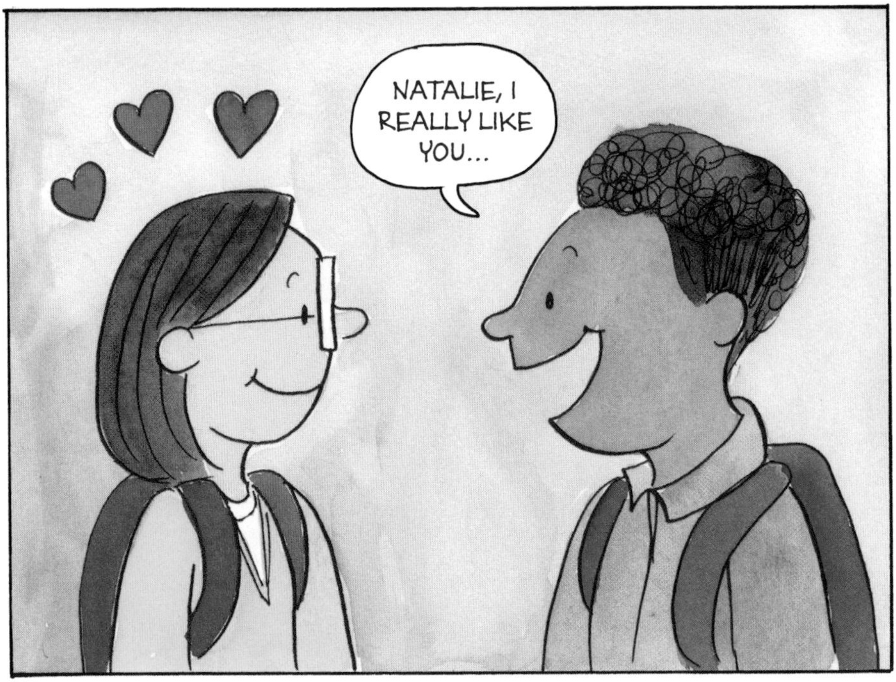
NATALIE, I REALLY LIKE YOU...

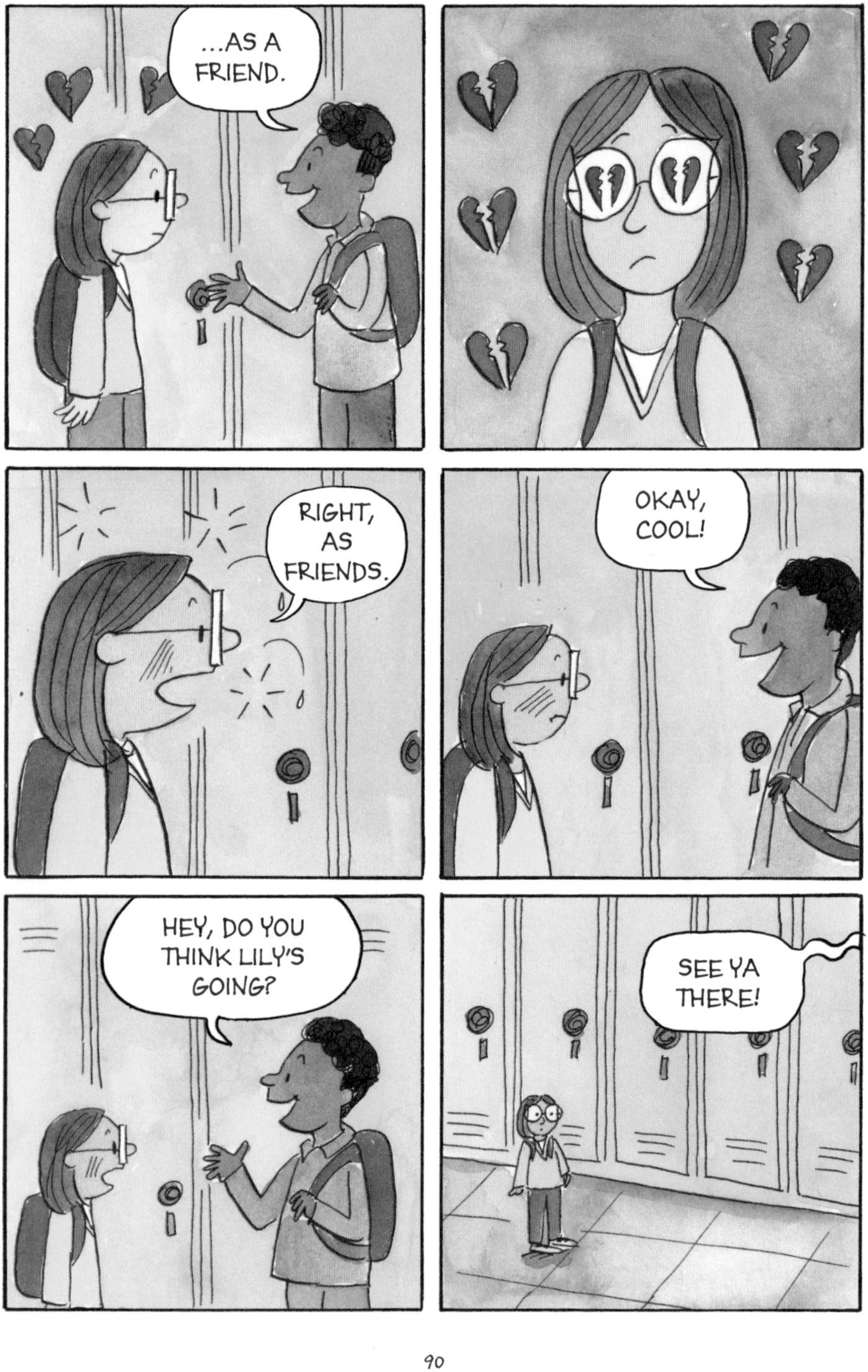
...AS A FRIEND.
RIGHT, AS FRIENDS.
OKAY, COOL!
HEY, DO YOU THINK LILY'S GOING?
SEE YA THERE!

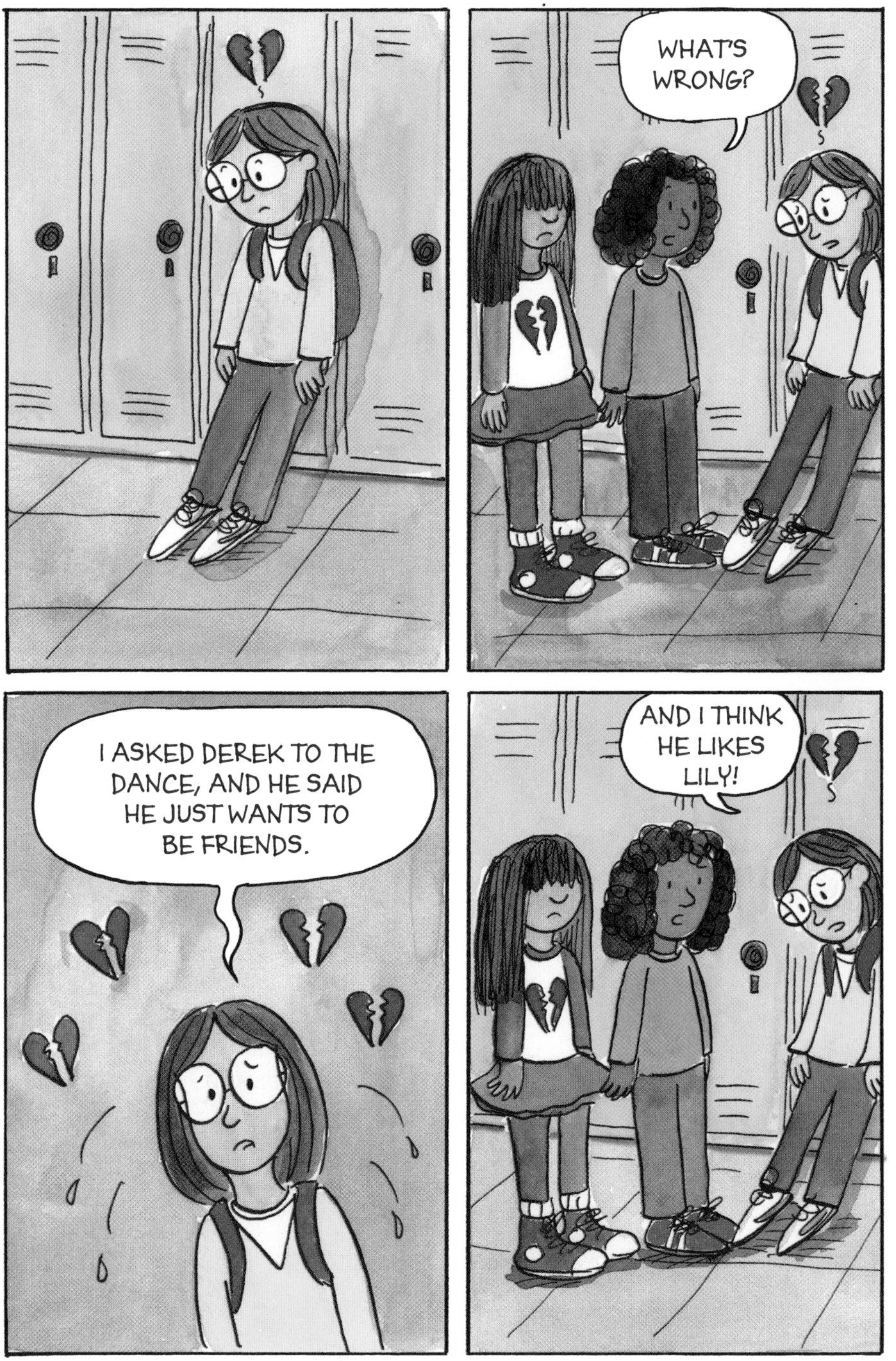
WHAT'S WRONG?
I ASKED DEREK TO THE DANCE, AND HE SAID HE JUST WANTS TO BE FRIENDS.
AND I THINK HE LIKES LILY!

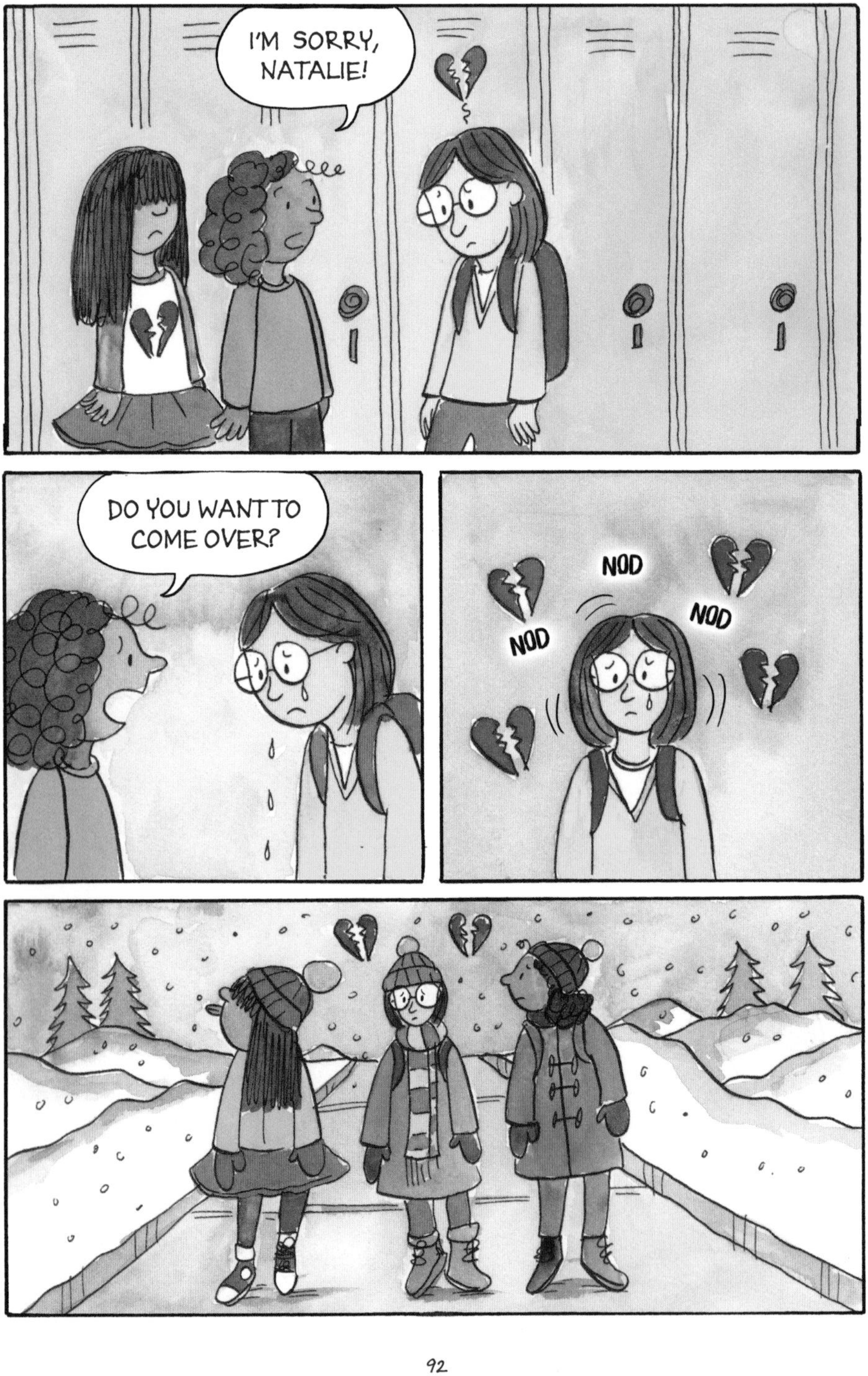
I'M SORRY, NATALIE!
DO YOU WANT TO COME OVER?
NOD
NOD
NOD

CHAPTER 6
THE DAY BEFORE VALENTINE'S DAY

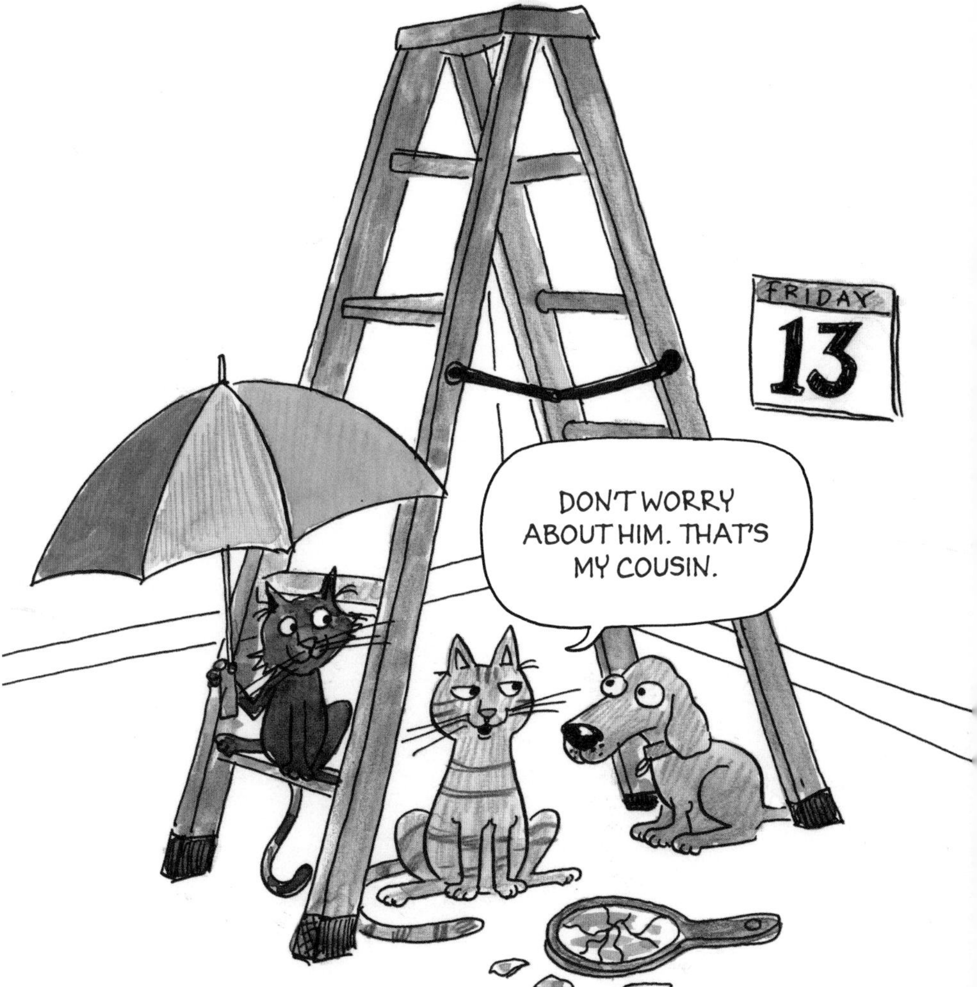
FRIDAY
13
DON'T WORRY ABOUT HIM. THAT'S MY COUSIN.

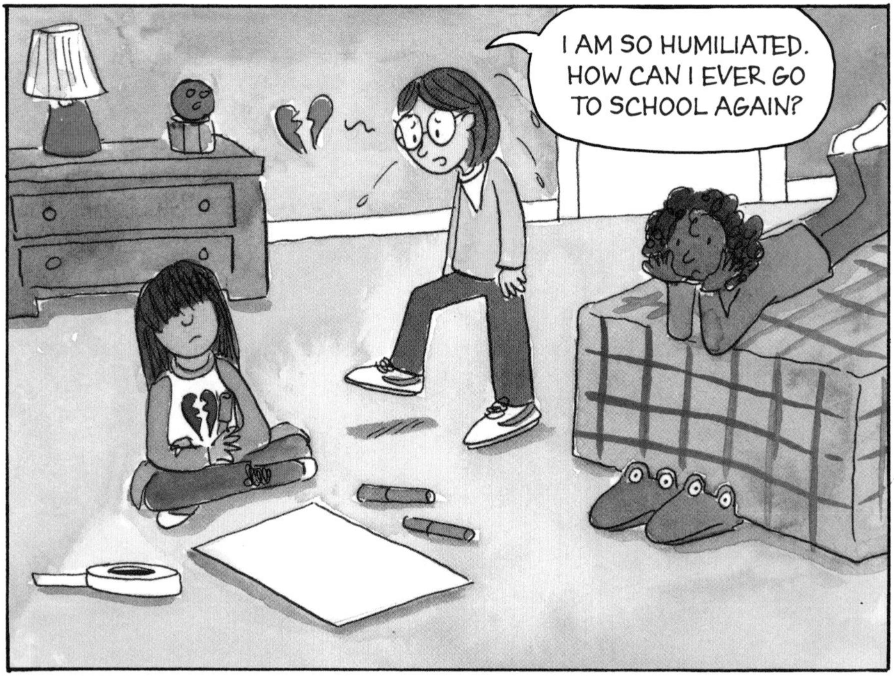
I AM SO HUMILIATED. HOW CAN I EVER GO TO SCHOOL AGAIN?

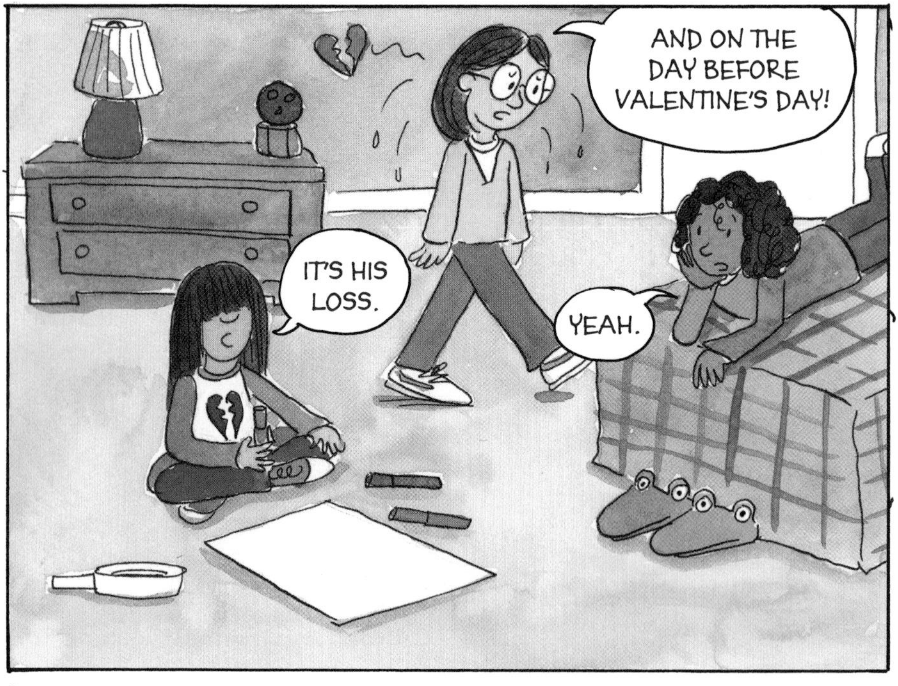
AND ON THE DAY BEFORE VALENTINE'S DAY!
IT'S HIS LOSS.
YEAH.

CHAPTER 7
STUCK ON YOU

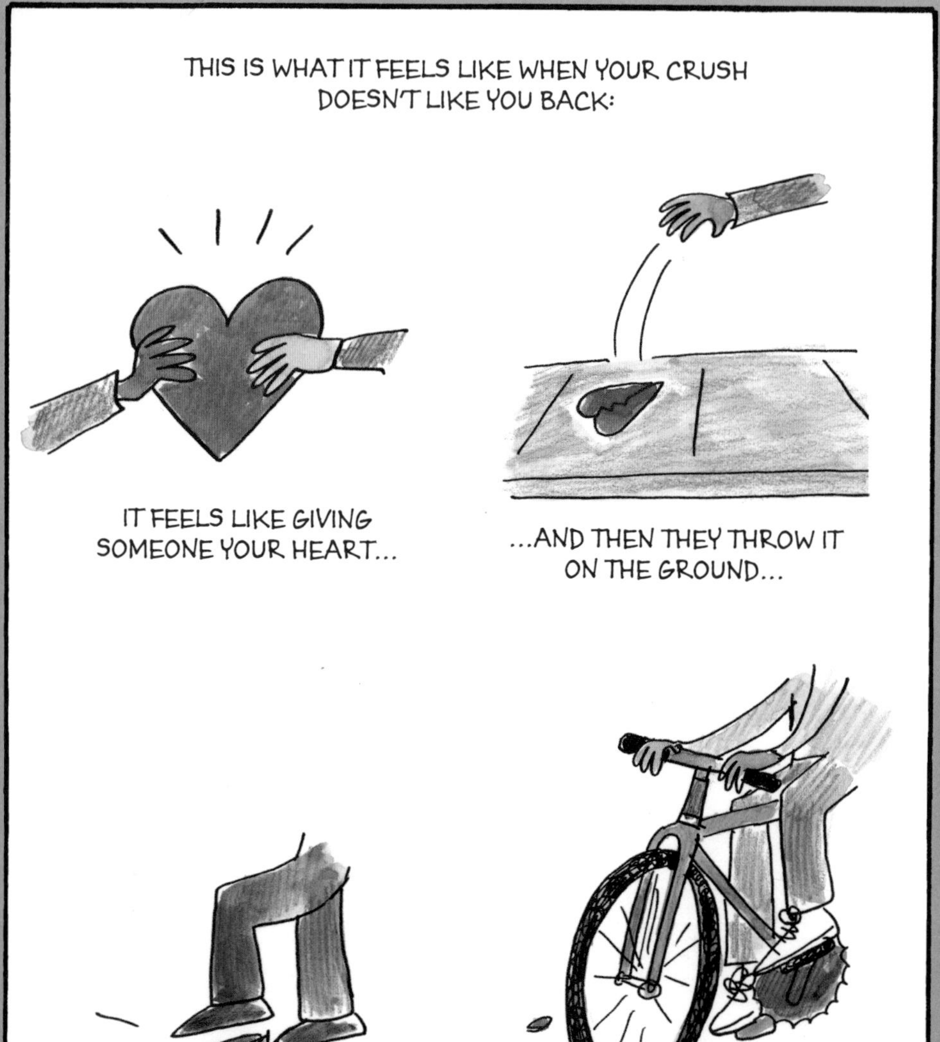
THIS IS WHAT IT FEELS LIKE WHEN YOUR CRUSH DOESN'T LIKE YOU BACK:
IT FEELS LIKE GIVING SOMEONE YOUR HEART...
...AND THEN THEY THROW IT ON THE GROUND...
...STOMP ON IT WITH THEIR FEET...
...RIDE OVER IT WITH THEIR BIKE...

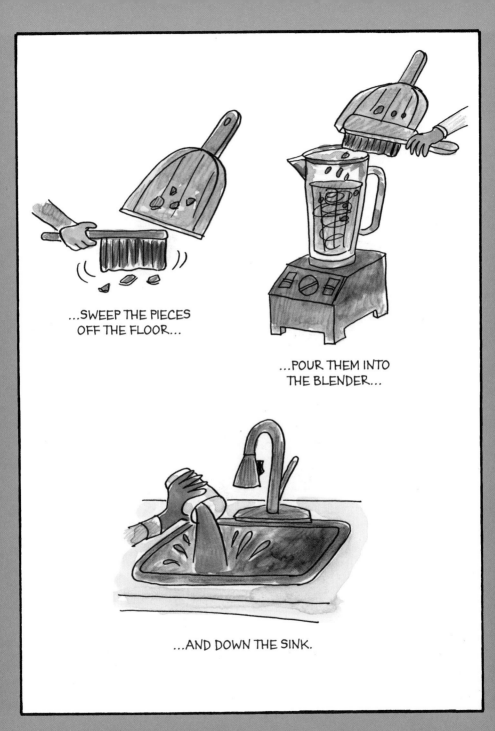

...SWEEP THE PIECES OFF THE FLOOR...

...POUR THEM INTO THE BLENDER...

...AND DOWN THE SINK.

CHAPTER 8
THE DANCE

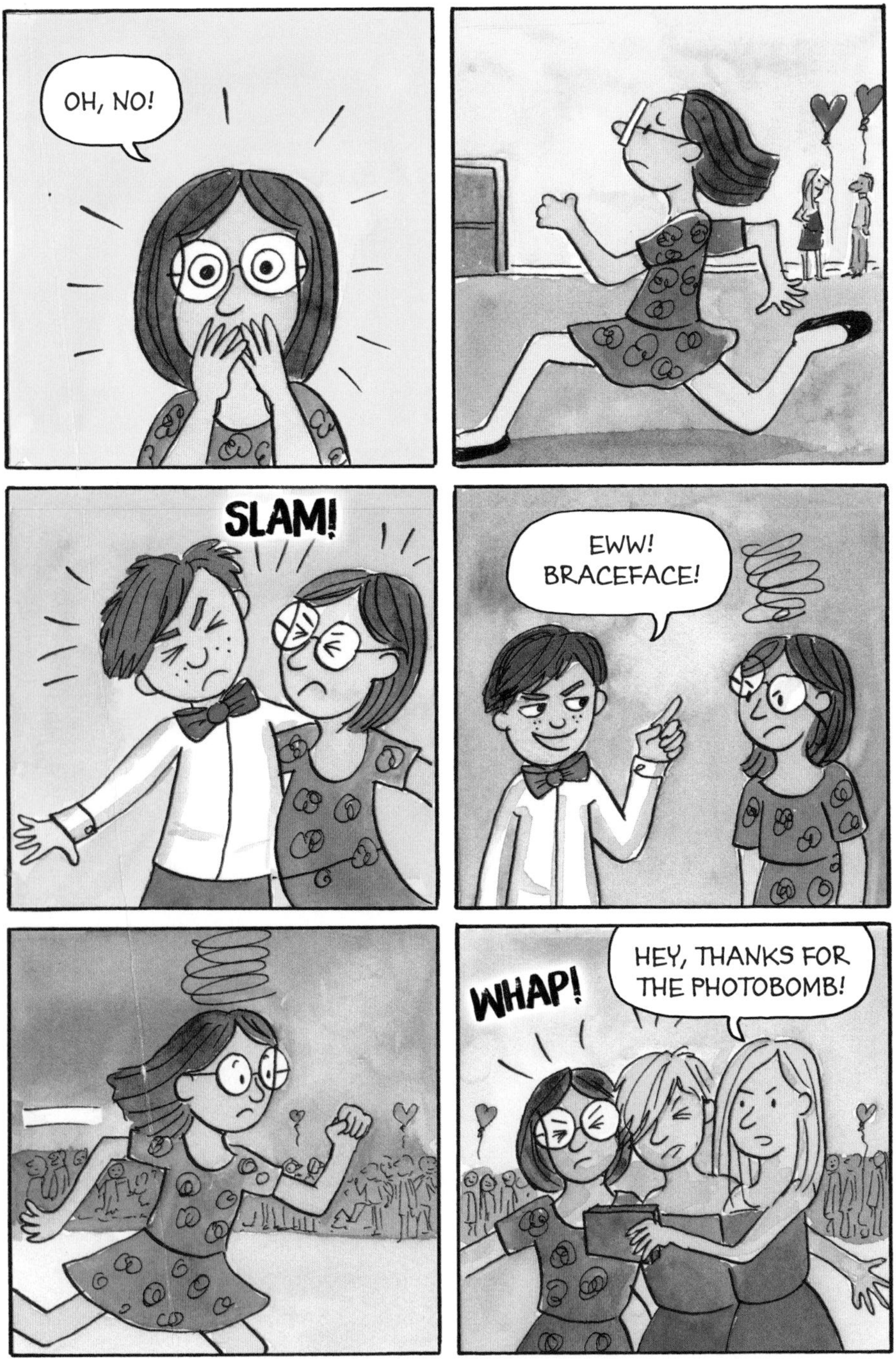
OH, NO!
SLAM!
EWW! BRACEFACE!
WHAP!
HEY, THANKS FOR THE PHOTOBOMB!

CHAPTER 9
SOUR GRAPES
(AND EVERYTHING ELSE)

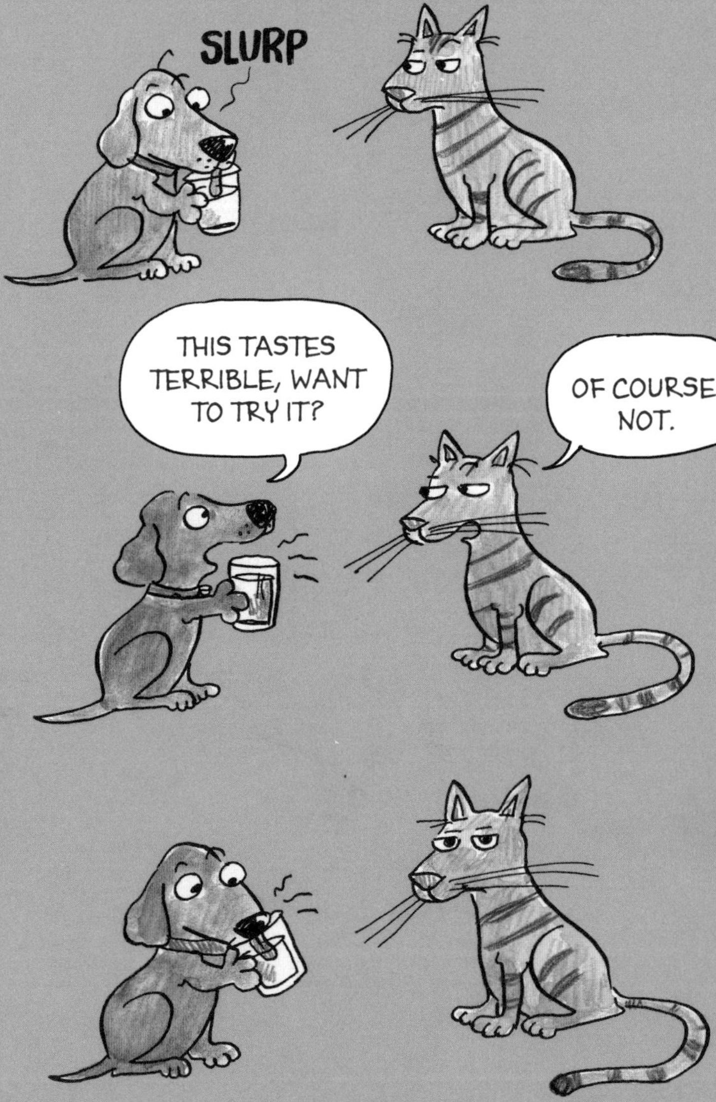
SLURP
THIS TASTES TERRIBLE, WANT TO TRY IT?
OF COURSE NOT.

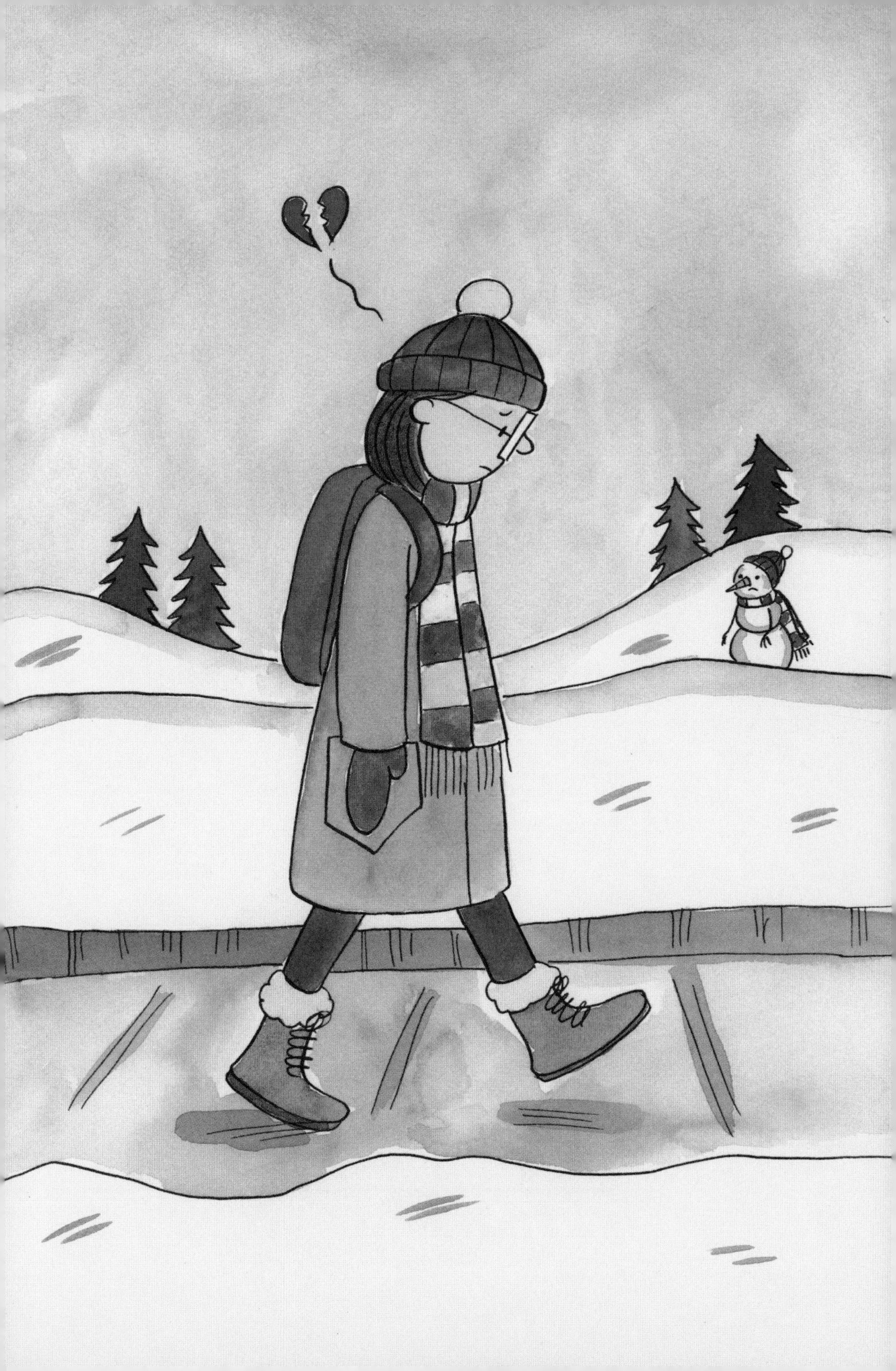

DEREK DIDN'T REALLY WANT TO TALK TO ME
AFTER THE SONG DEDICATION INCIDENT.

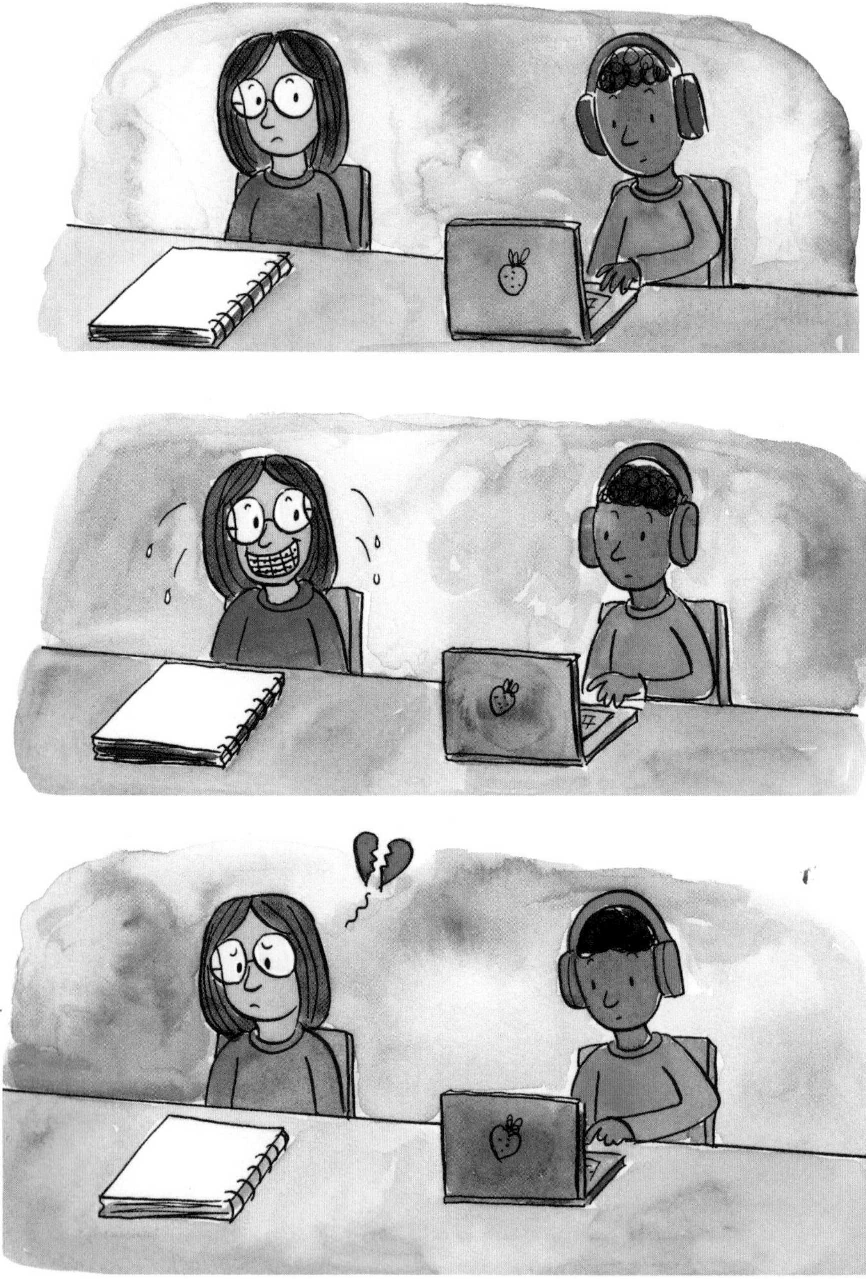

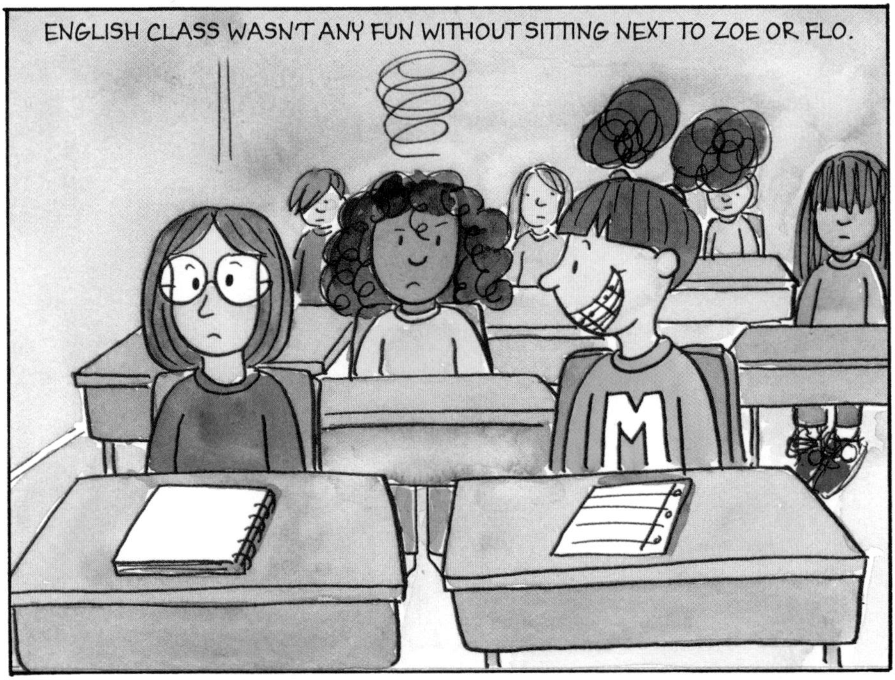
ENGLISH CLASS WASN'T ANY FUN WITHOUT SITTING NEXT TO ZOE OR FLO.

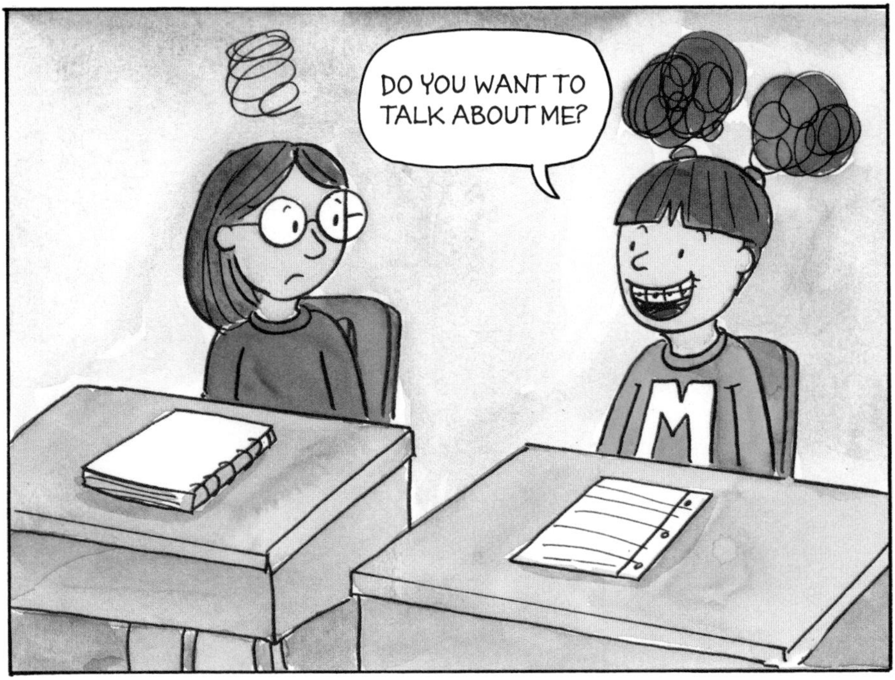
DO YOU WANT TO TALK ABOUT ME?

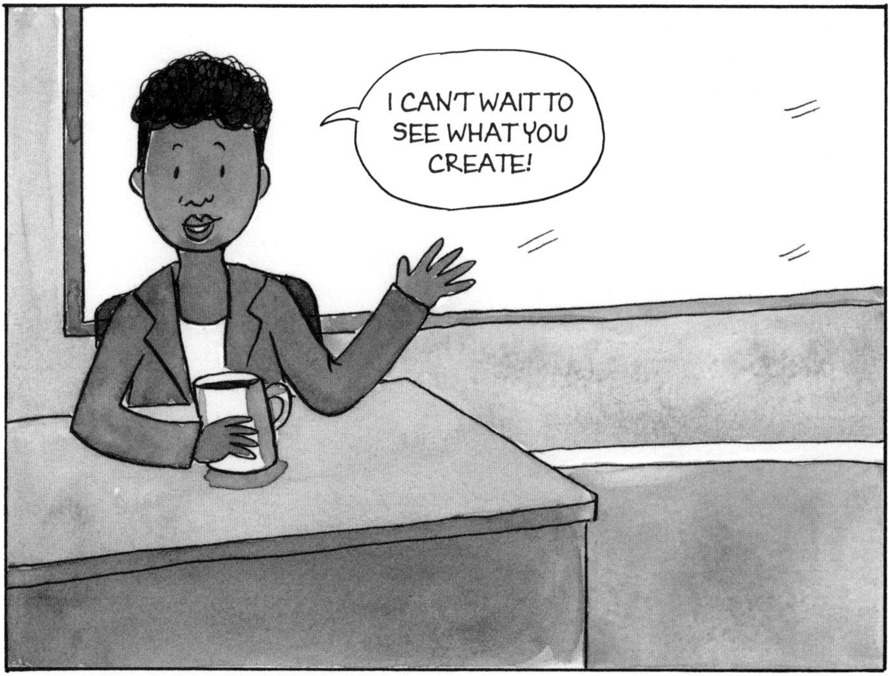
I CAN'T WAIT TO SEE WHAT YOU CREATE!

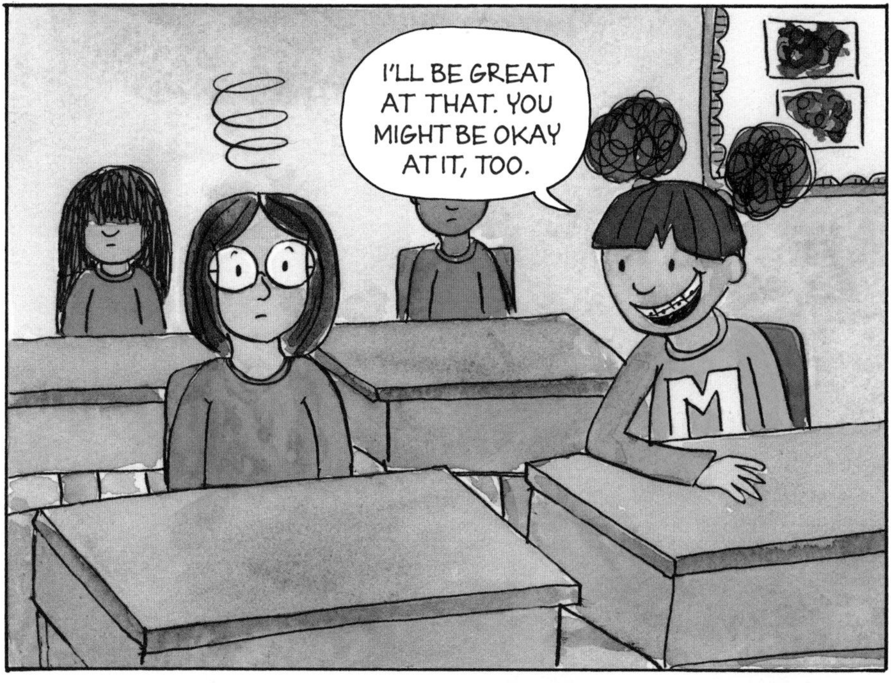
I'LL BE GREAT AT THAT. YOU MIGHT BE OKAY AT IT, TOO.

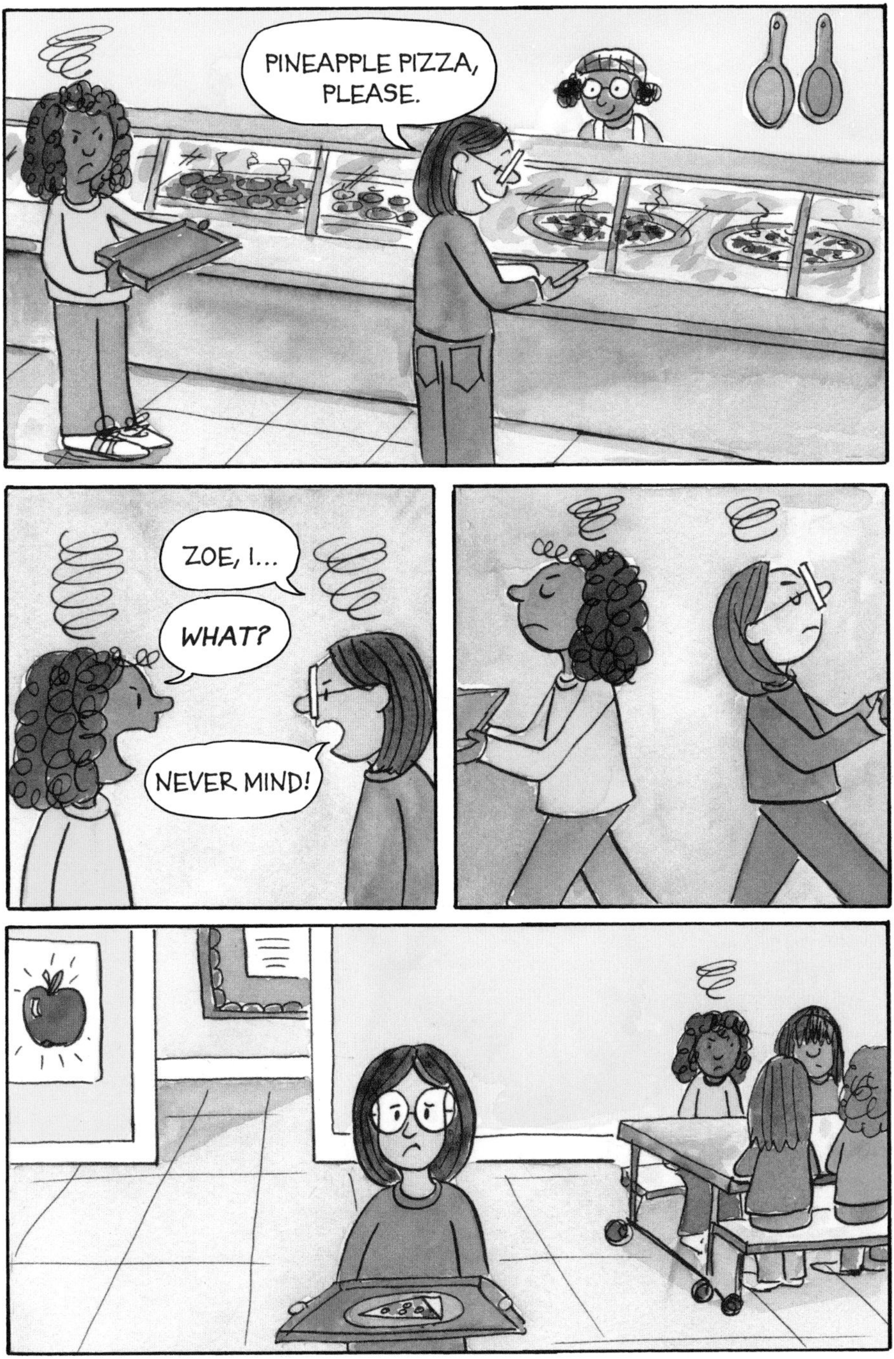
PINEAPPLE PIZZA, PLEASE.
ZOE, I...
WHAT?
NEVER MIND!

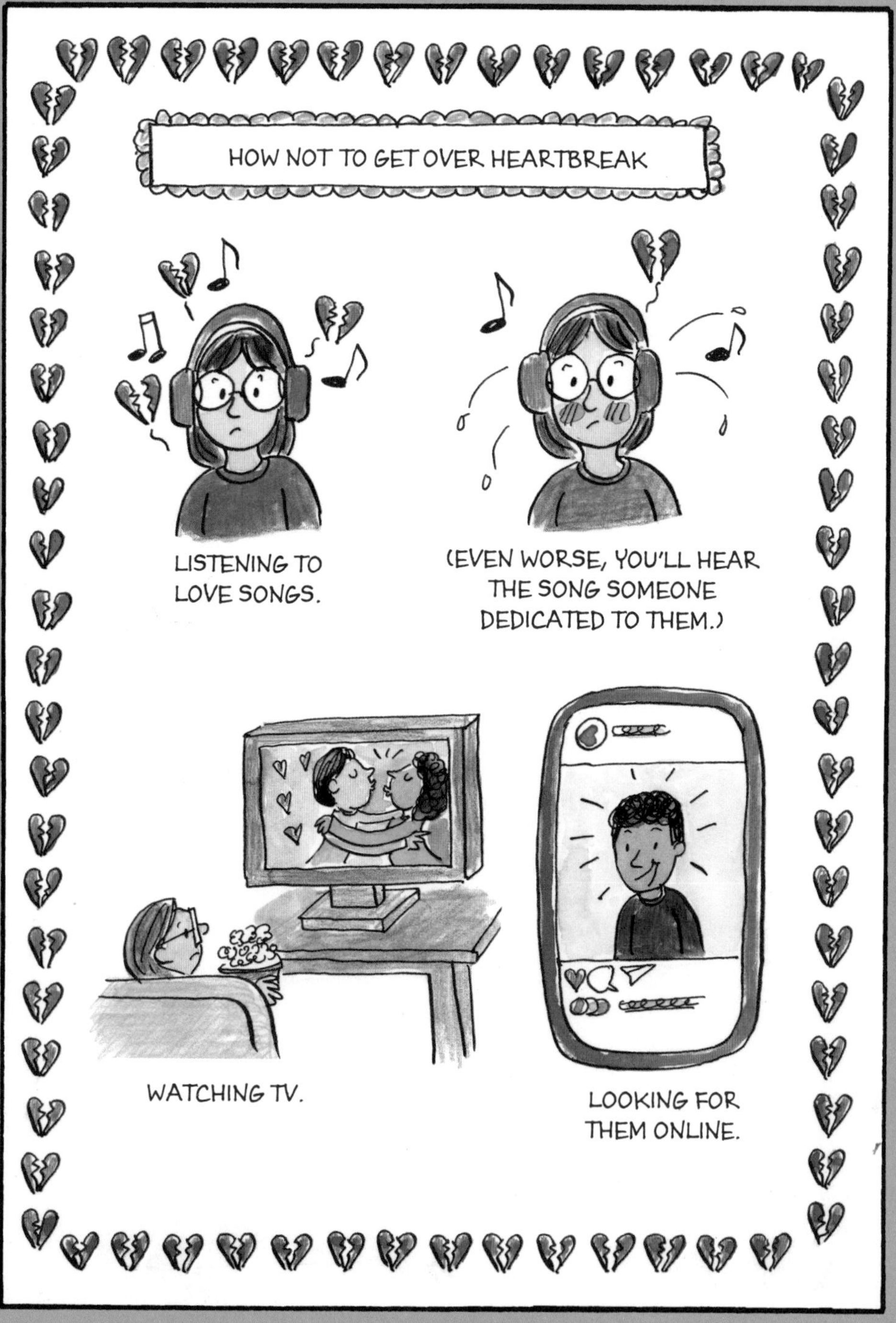
HOW NOT TO GET OVER HEARTBREAK
LISTENING TO LOVE SONGS.
(EVEN WORSE, YOU'LL HEAR THE SONG SOMEONE DEDICATED TO THEM.)
WATCHING TV.
LOOKING FOR THEM ONLINE.

CHAPTER 10
PRACTICE

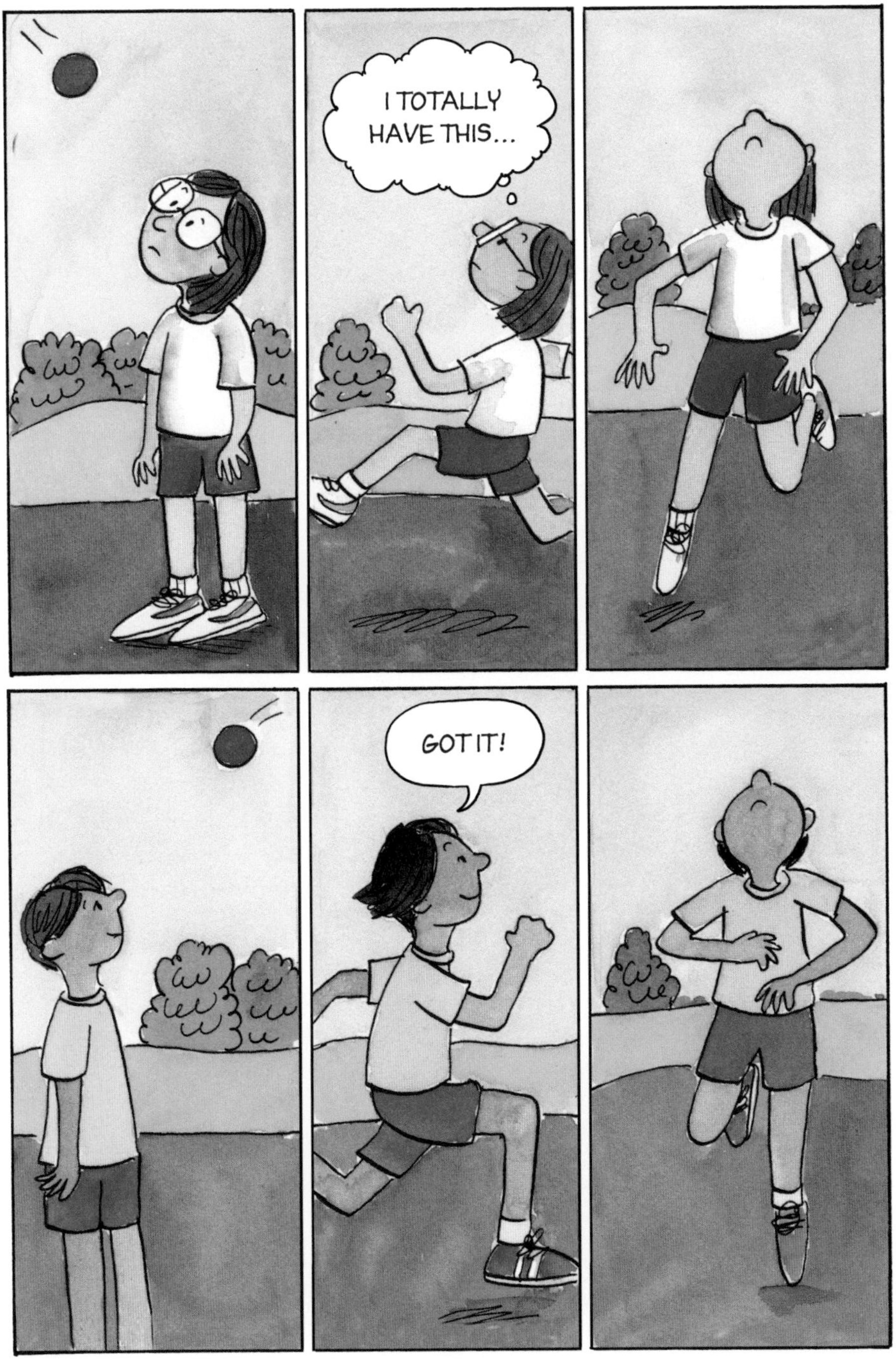
I TOTALLY HAVE THIS...
GOT IT!

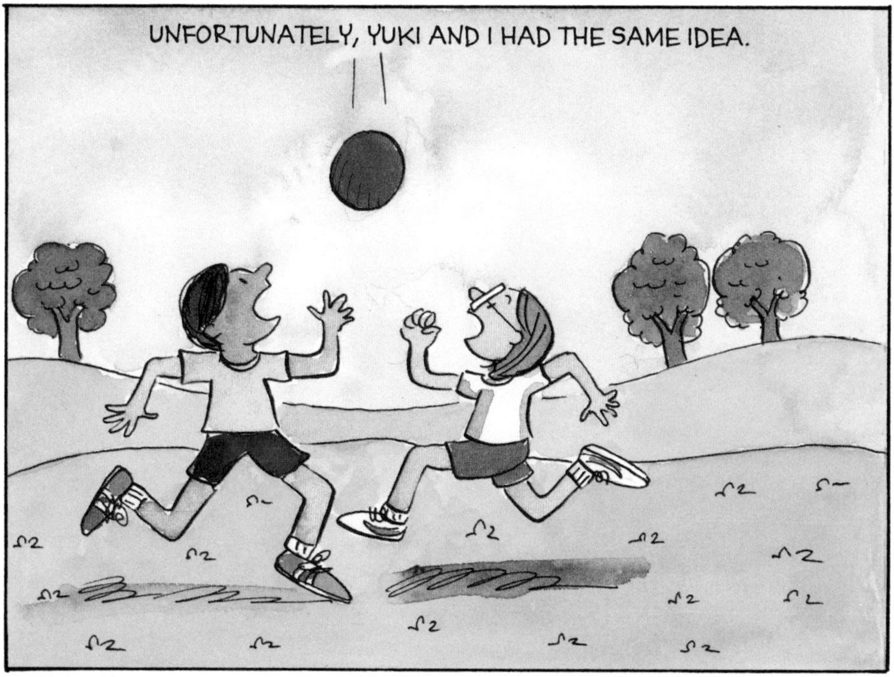
UNFORTUNATELY, YUKI AND I HAD THE SAME IDEA.

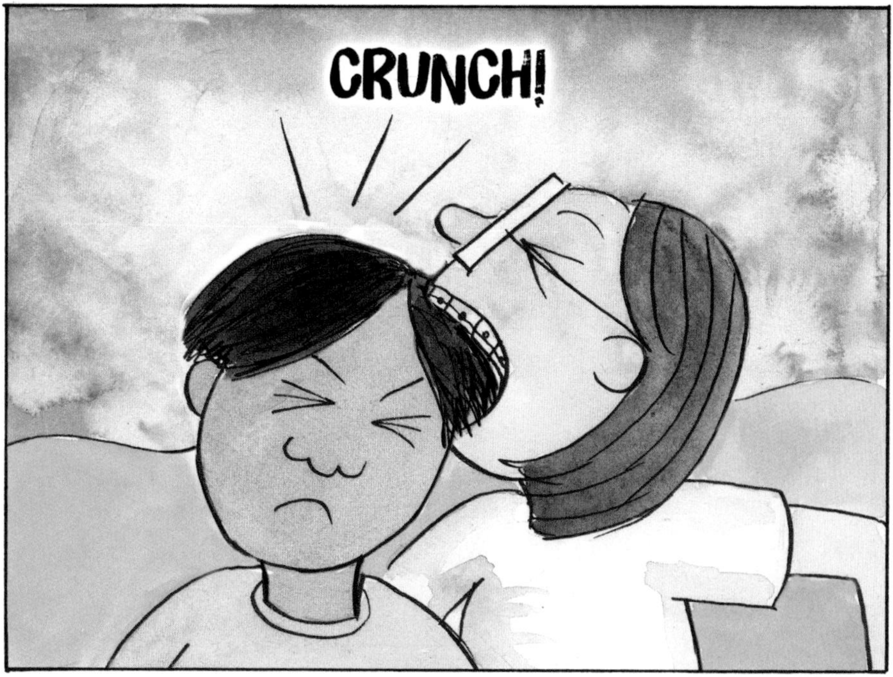
CRUNCH!

THERE AREN'T ENOUGH BANDAGES IN THE WORLD TO FIX MY BROKEN HEART.

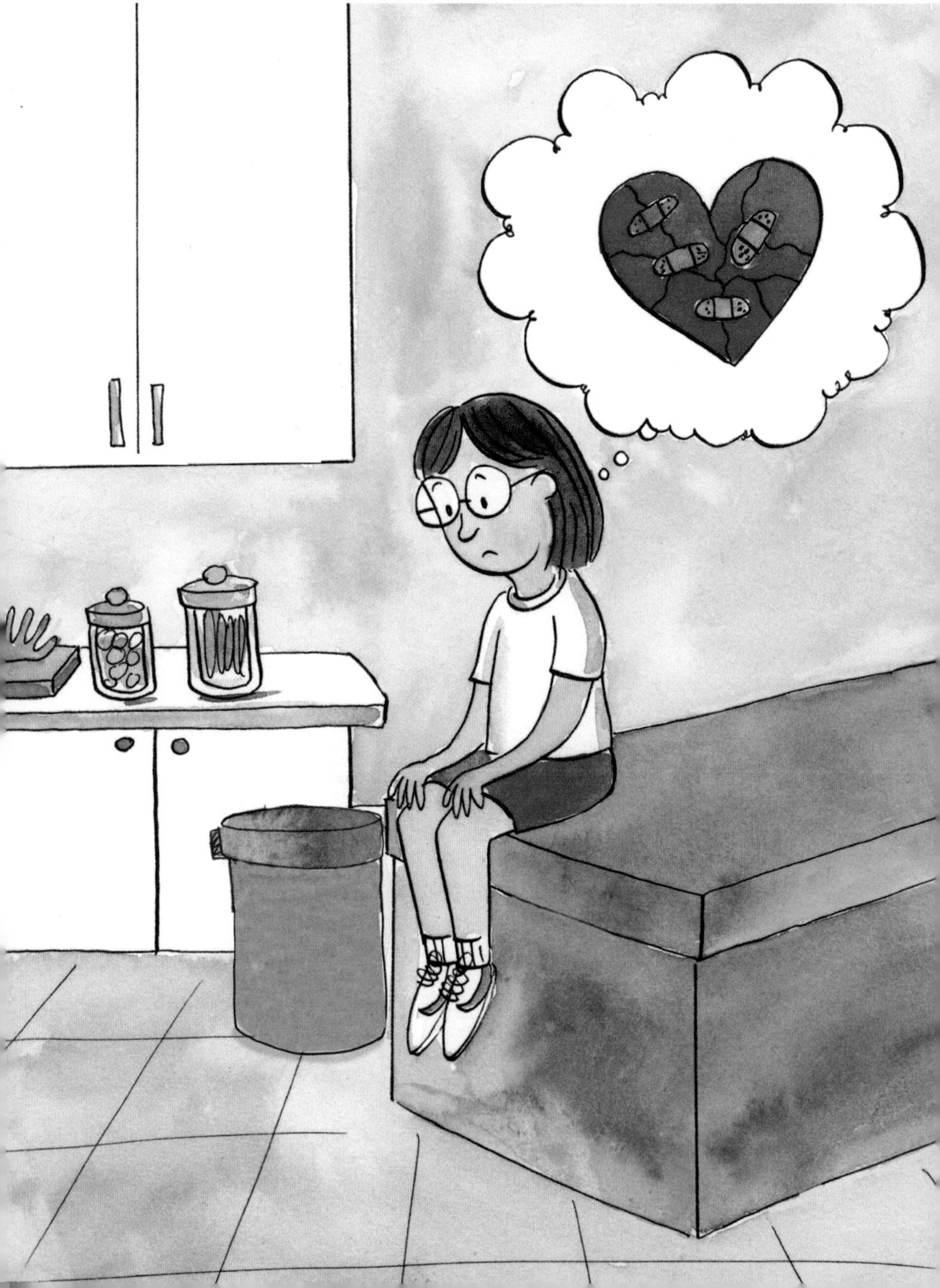

CHAPTER 11
PROMISES

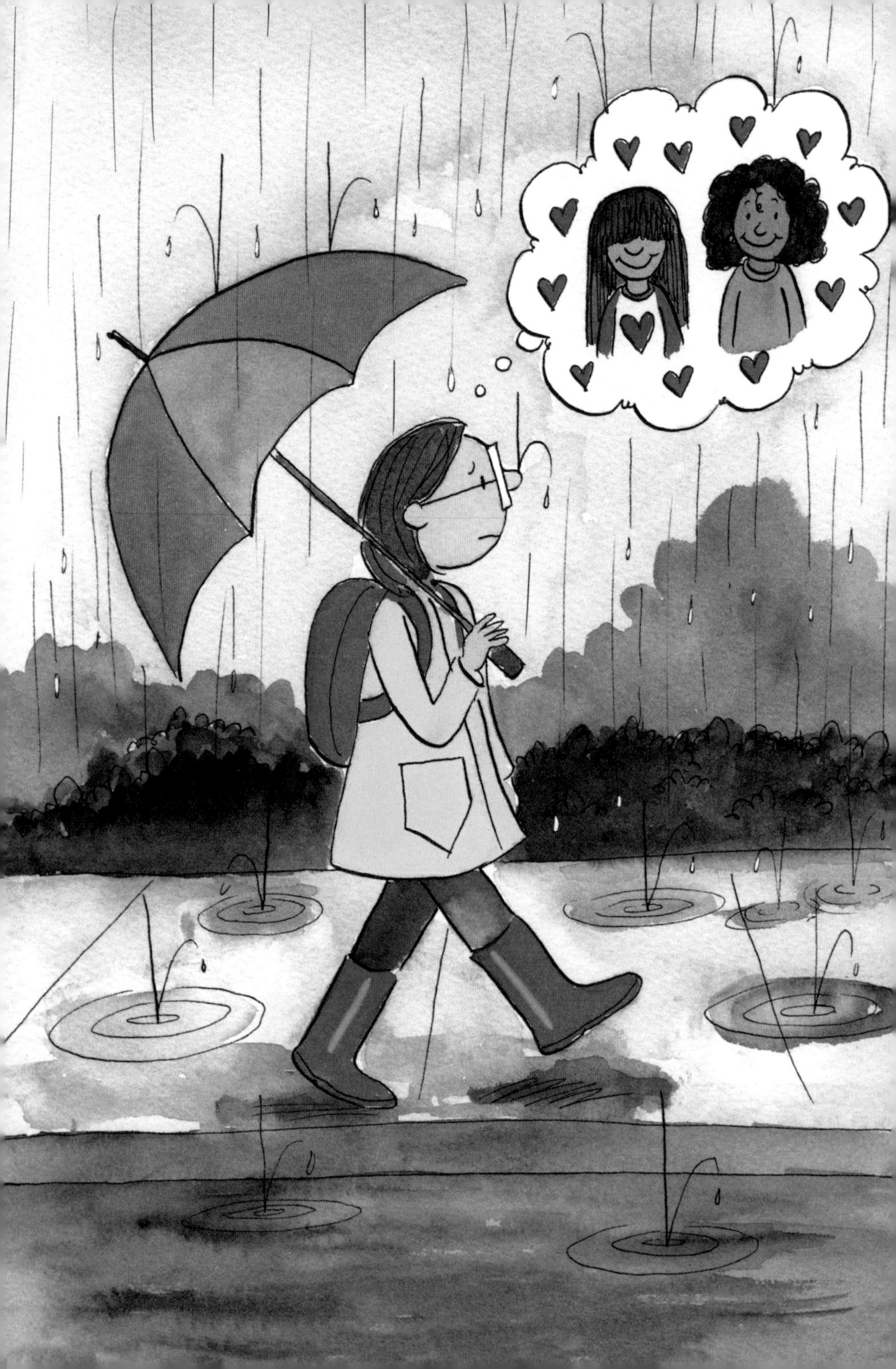

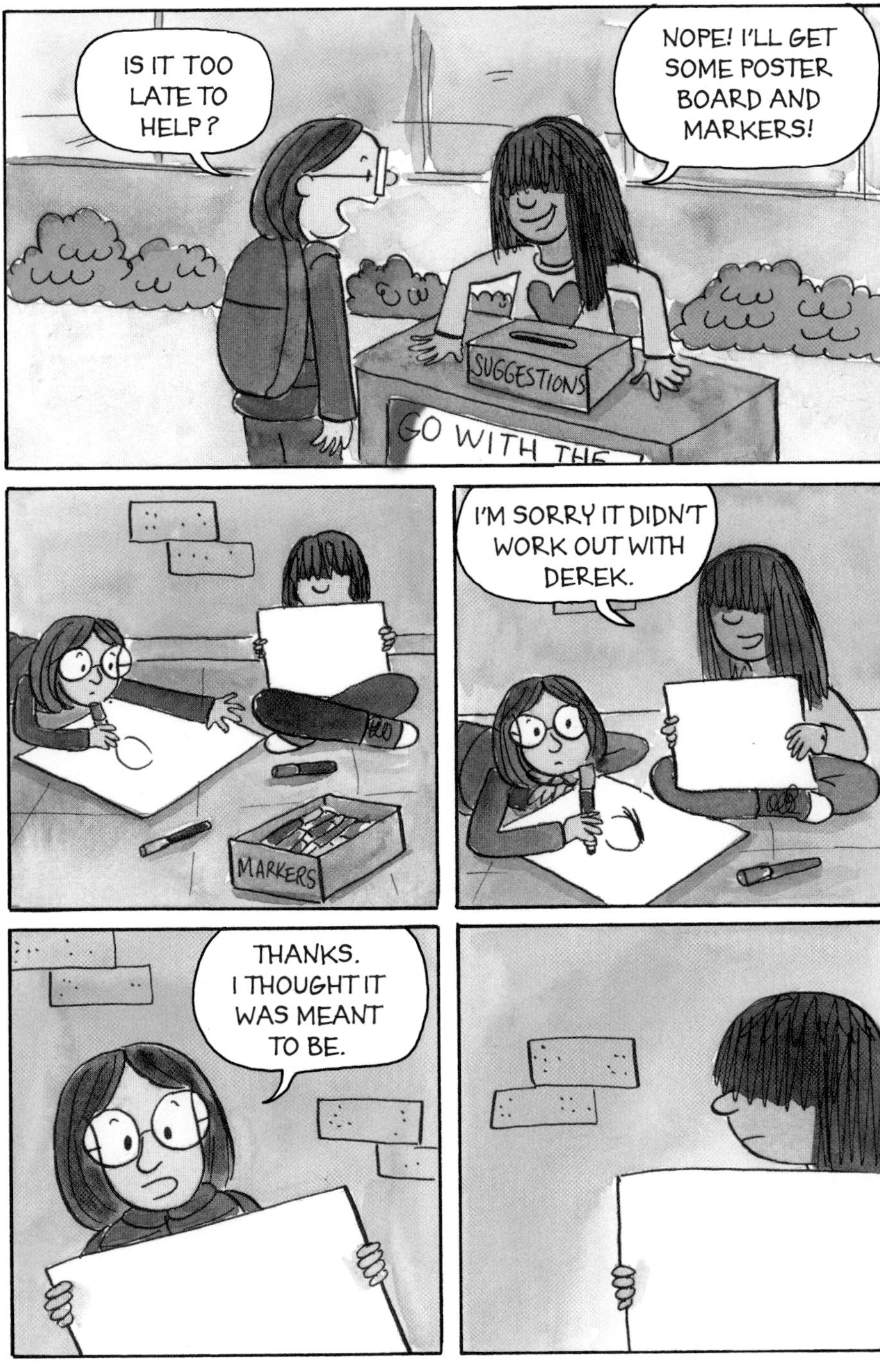
IS IT TOO LATE TO HELP?
NOPE! I'LL GET SOME POSTER BOARD AND MARKERS!
SUGGESTIONS
GO WITH THE
MARKERS
I'M SORRY IT DIDN'T WORK OUT WITH DEREK.
THANKS. I THOUGHT IT WAS MEANT TO BE.

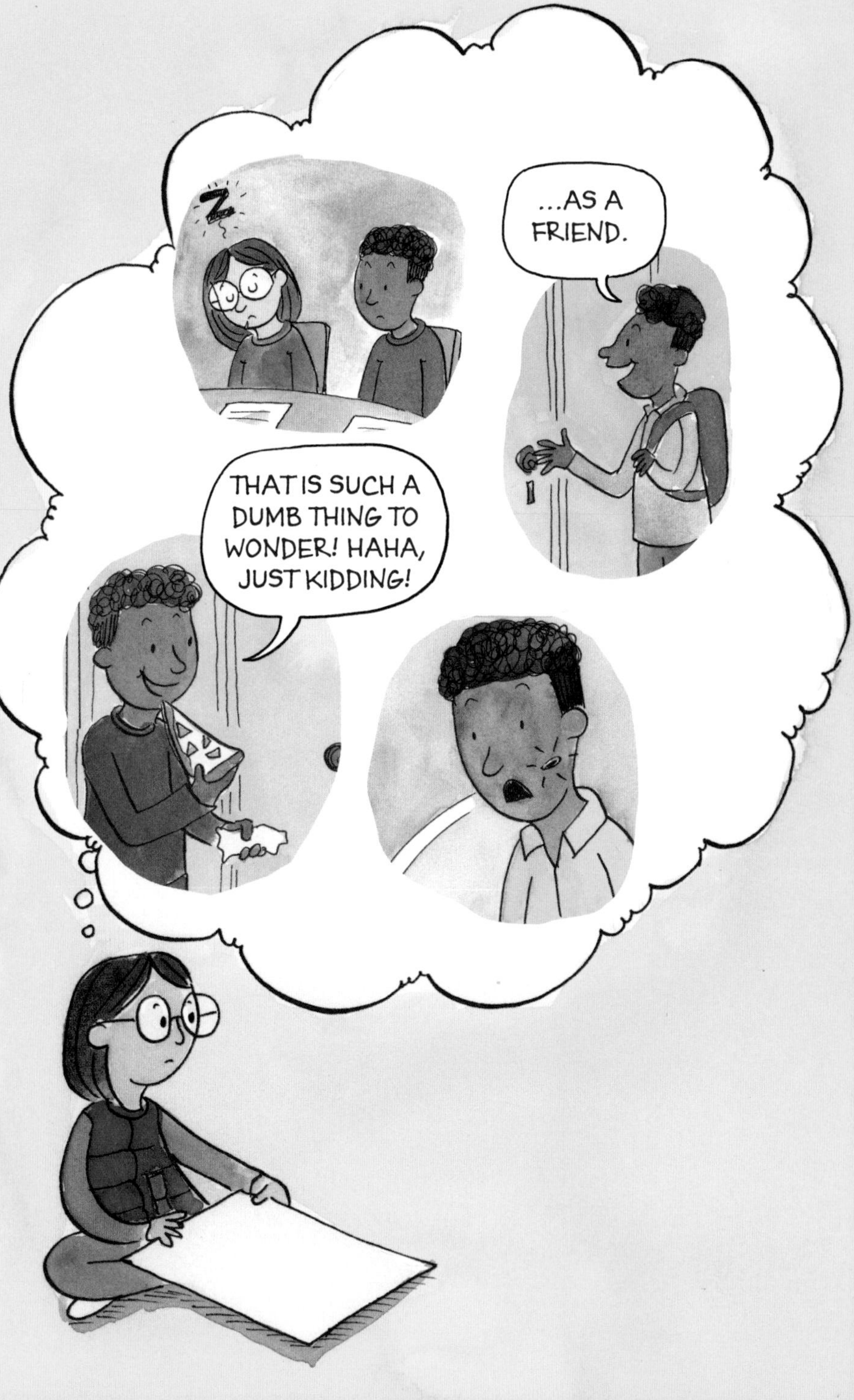
...AS A FRIEND.
THAT IS SUCH A DUMB THING TO WONDER! HAHA, JUST KIDDING!

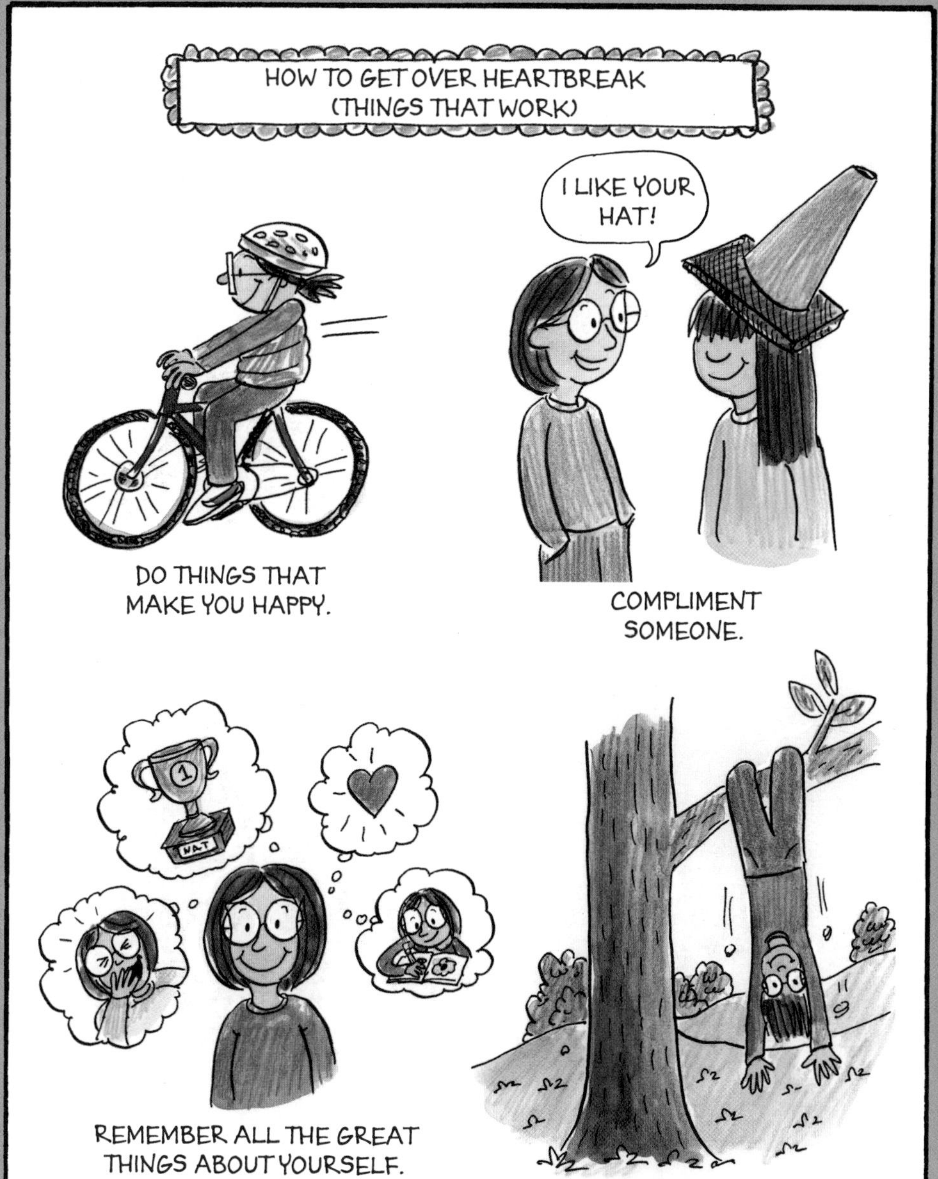
HOW TO GET OVER HEARTBREAK
(THINGS THAT WORK)
DO THINGS THAT MAKE YOU HAPPY.
I LIKE YOUR HAT!
COMPLIMENT SOMEONE.
1
HAT
REMEMBER ALL THE GREAT THINGS ABOUT YOURSELF.
DO SOMETHING FUN OUTSIDE.

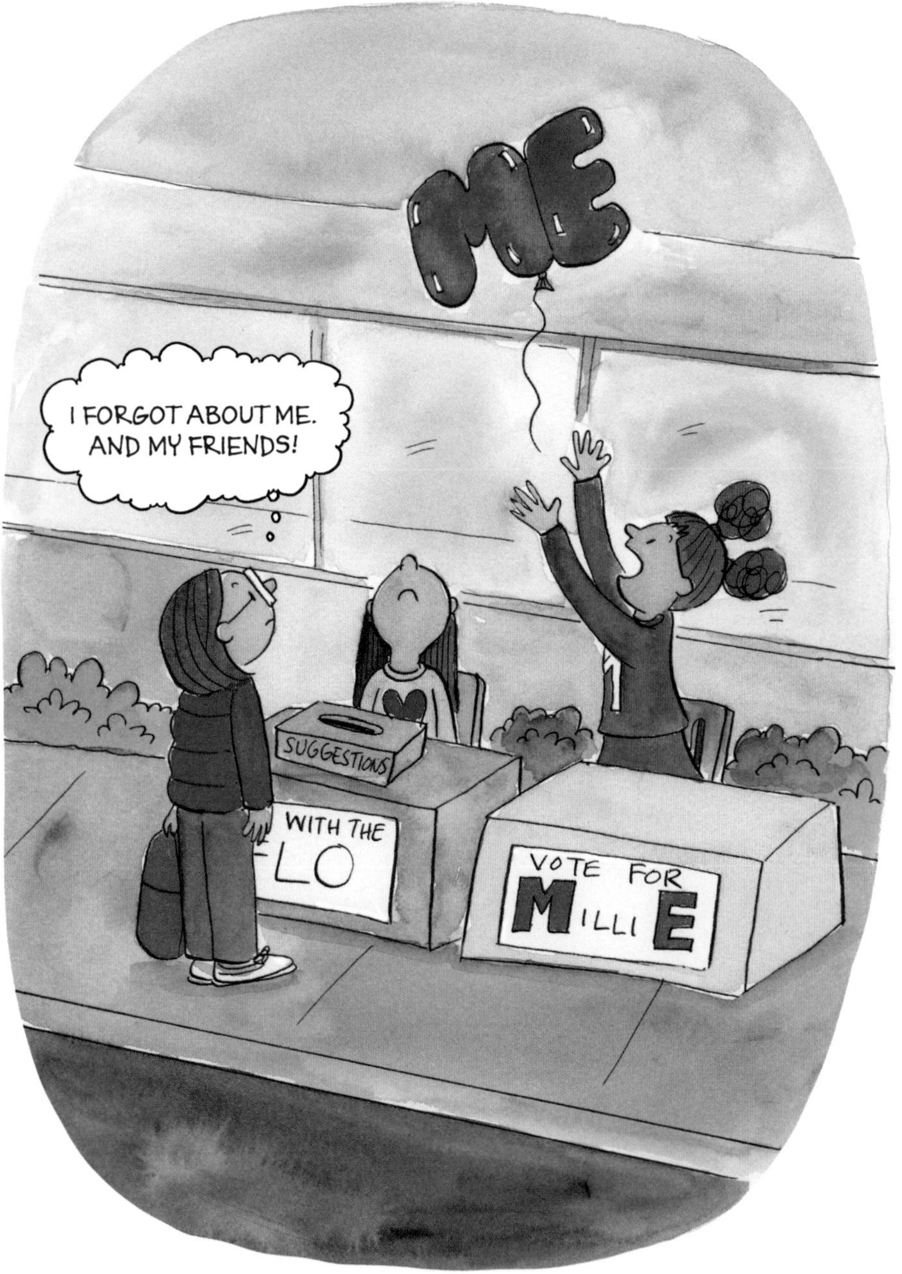
ME
I FORGOT ABOUT ME.
AND MY FRIENDS!
SUGGESTIONS
WITH THE
LO
VOTE FOR
MILLIE

CHAPTER 12
FRIENDS

CHAPTER 13
VOTE

* BARK LOUDLY AND CARRY A BIG STICK.

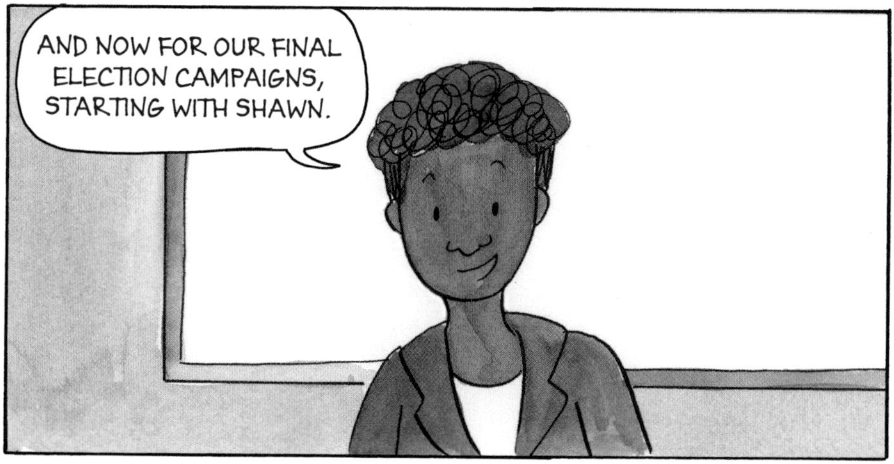
AND NOW FOR OUR FINAL ELECTION CAMPAIGNS, STARTING WITH SHAWN.

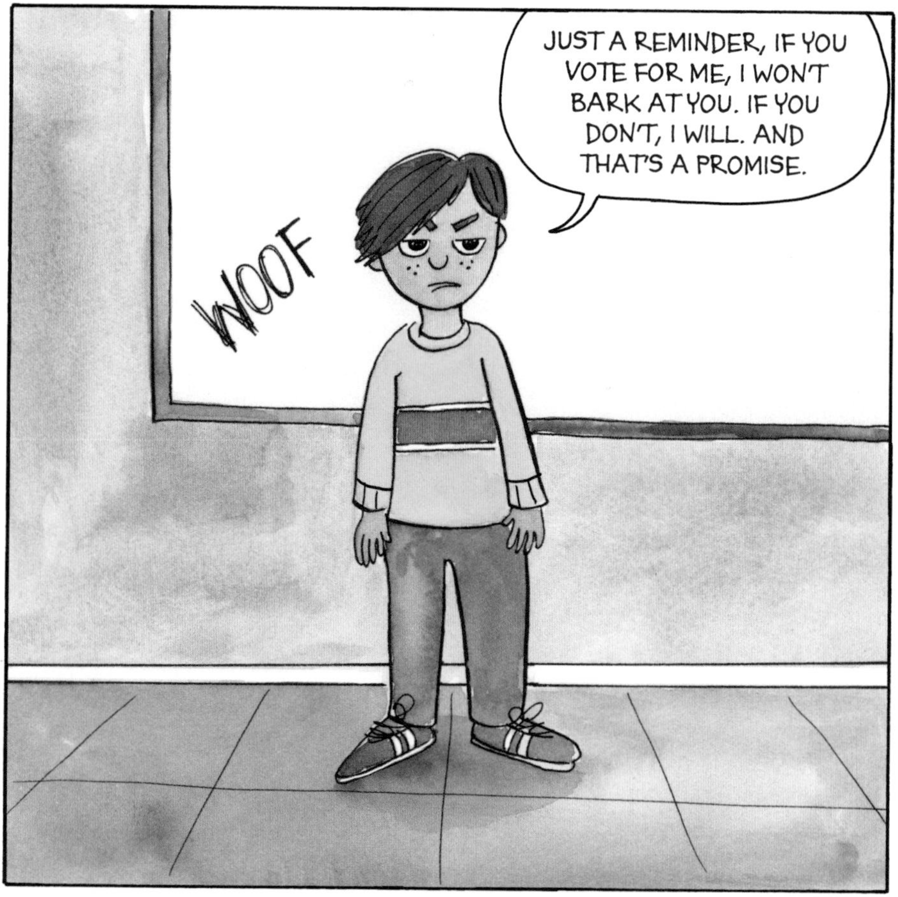
JUST A REMINDER, IF YOU VOTE FOR ME, I WON'T BARK AT YOU. IF YOU DON'T, I WILL. AND THAT'S A PROMISE.
WOOF

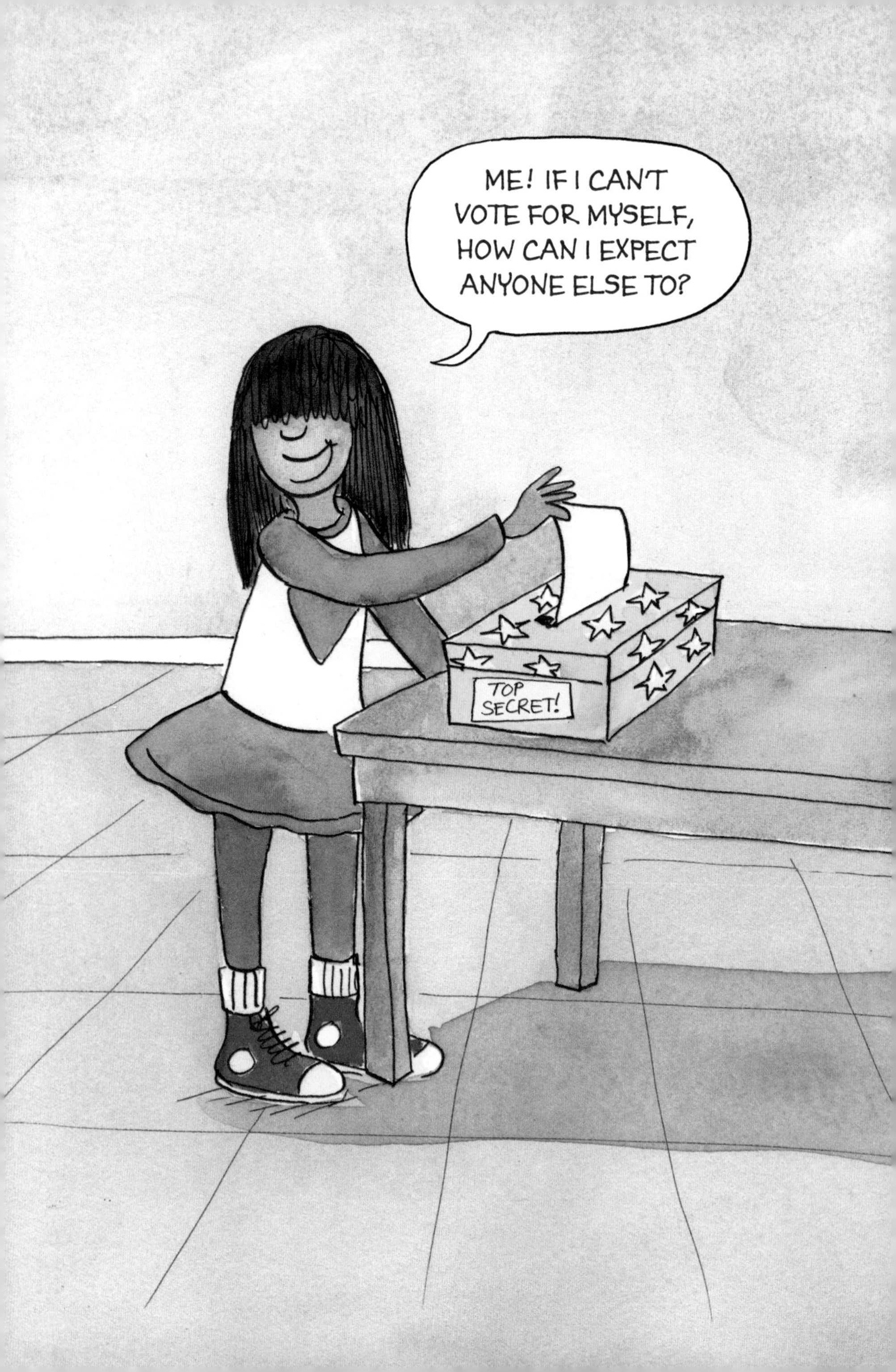
ME! IF I CAN'T VOTE FOR MYSELF, HOW CAN I EXPECT ANYONE ELSE TO?
TOP SECRET!

CHAPTER 14
RUBBER BAND

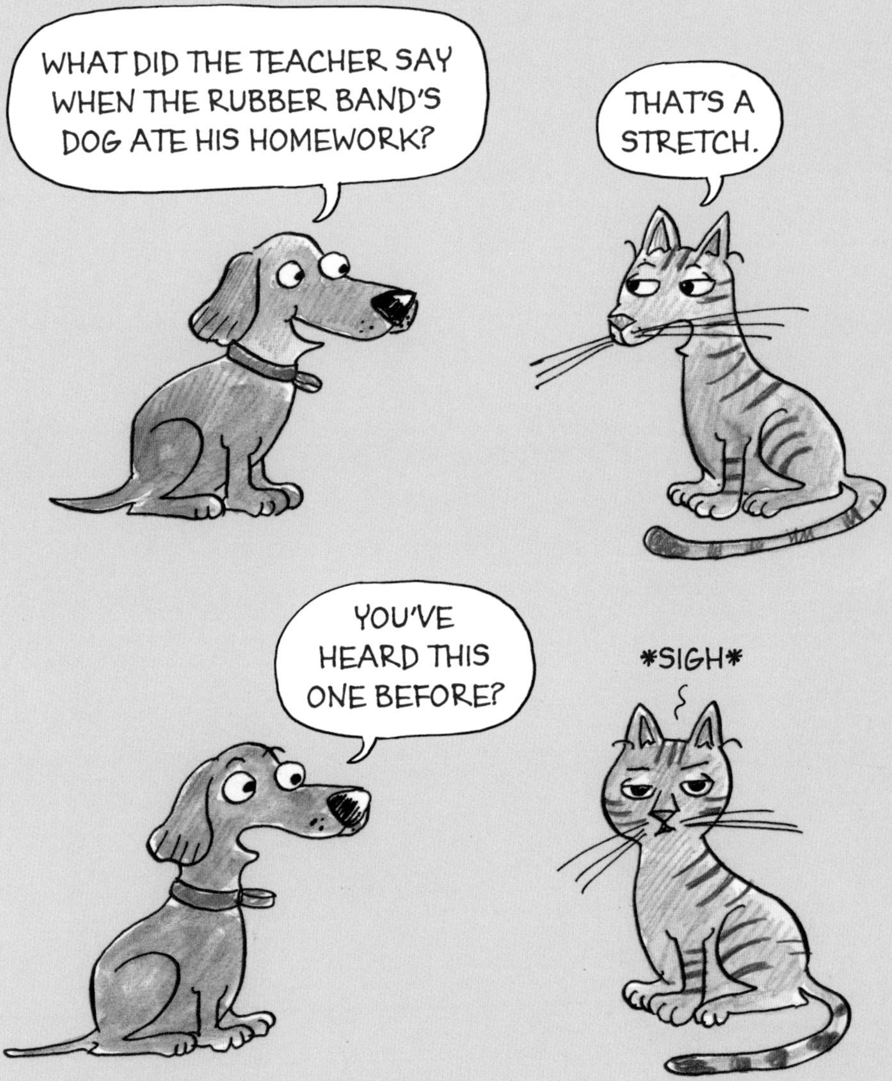
WHAT DID THE TEACHER SAY WHEN THE RUBBER BAND'S DOG ATE HIS HOMEWORK?
THAT'S A STRETCH.
YOU'VE HEARD THIS ONE BEFORE?
SIGH

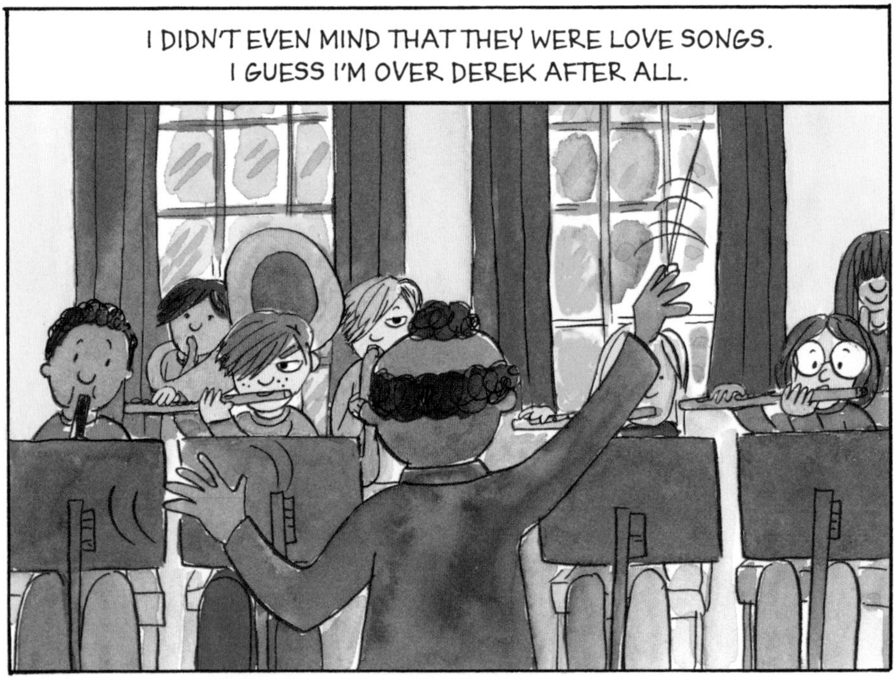
I DIDN'T EVEN MIND THAT THEY WERE LOVE SONGS.
I GUESS I'M OVER DEREK AFTER ALL.

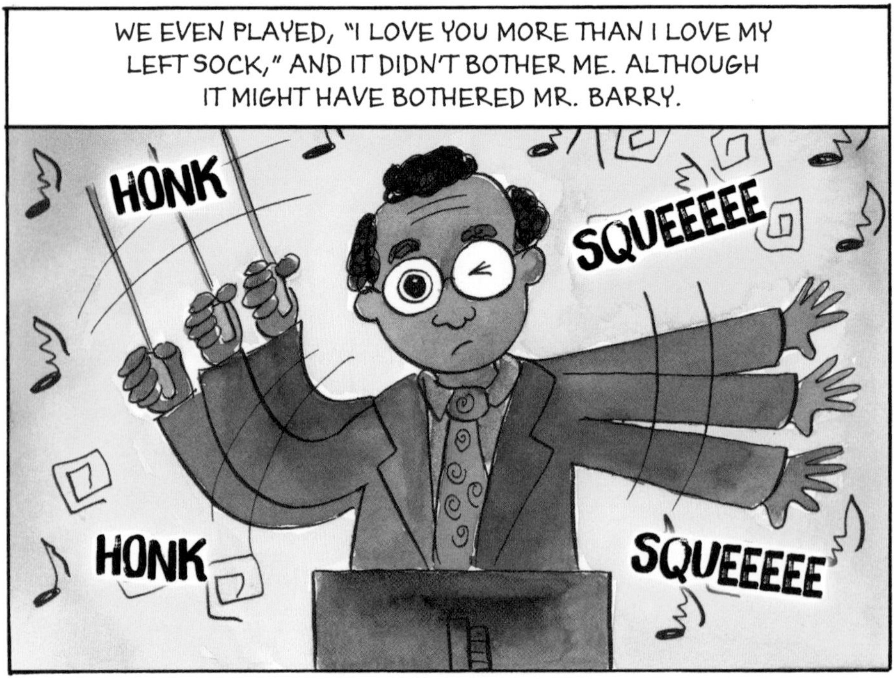
WE EVEN PLAYED, "I LOVE YOU MORE THAN I LOVE MY LEFT SOCK," AND IT DIDN'T BOTHER ME. ALTHOUGH IT MIGHT HAVE BOTHERED MR. BARRY.
HONK
SQUEEEEE
HONK
SQUEEEEE

MR. BARRY FIXED THE PROBLEM OF FLO MISSING HER CUE BY GIVING HER A SOLO.

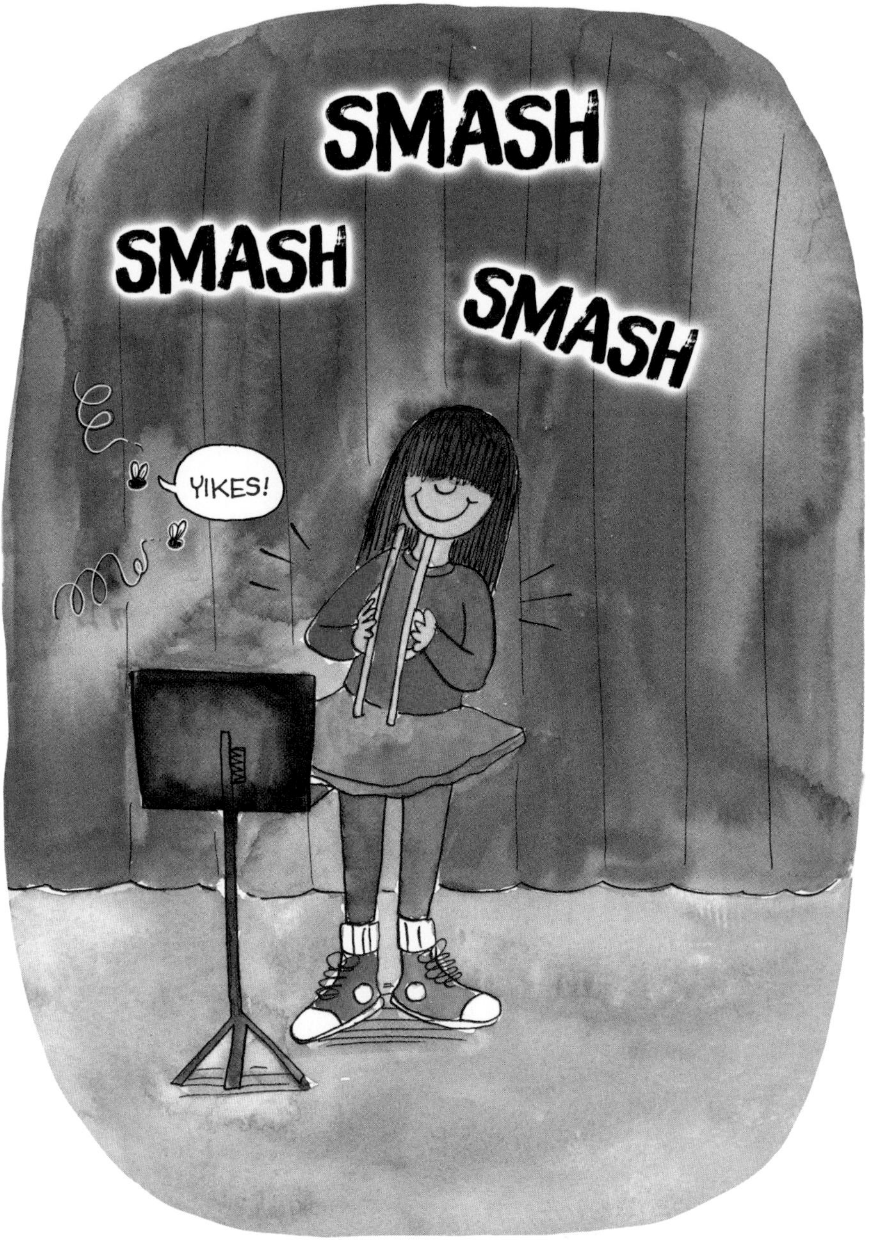
SMASH
SMASH
SMASH
YIKES!

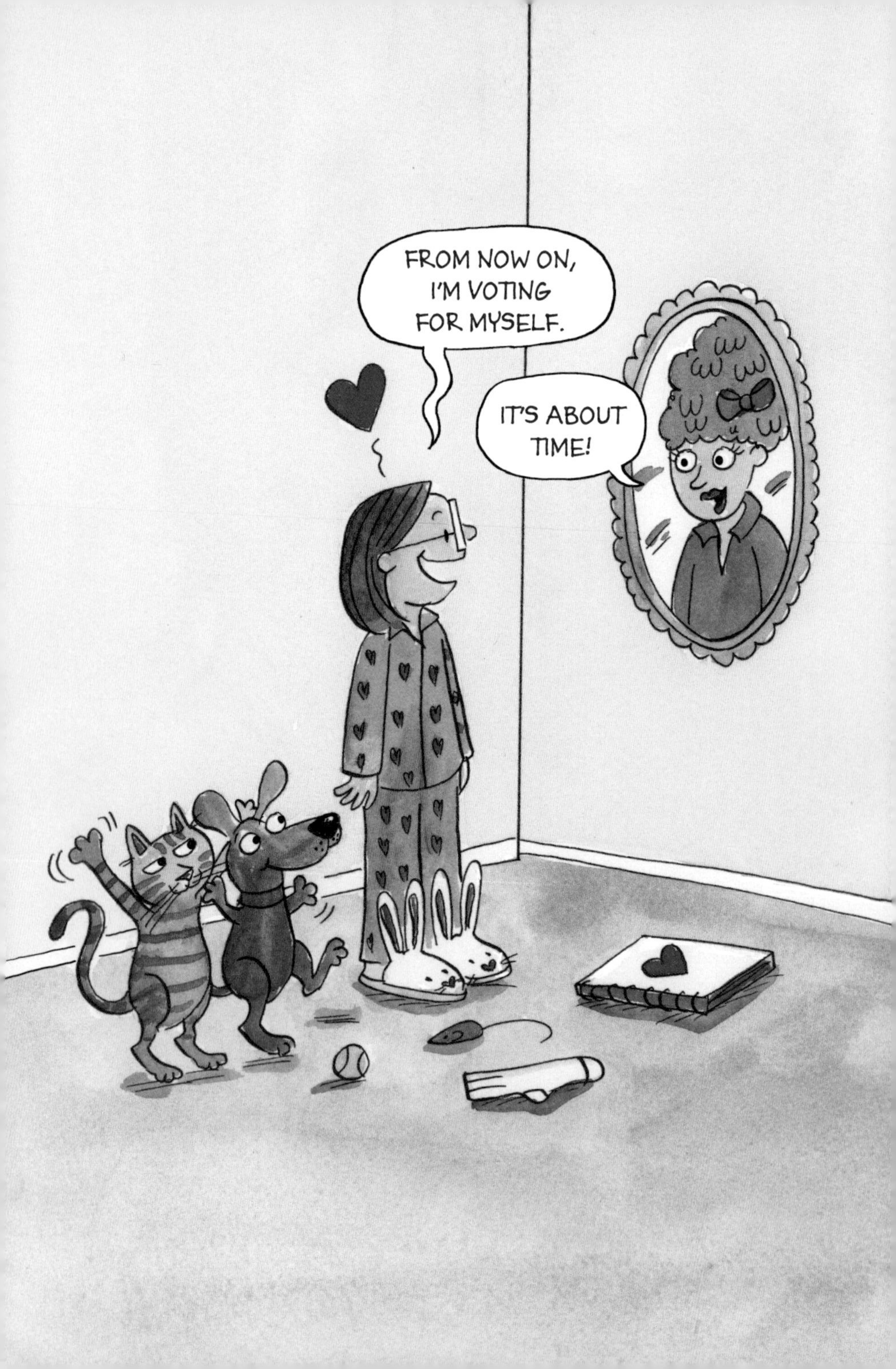
FROM NOW ON, I'M VOTING FOR MYSELF.
IT'S ABOUT TIME!

CHAPTER 15
ELECTION RESULTS

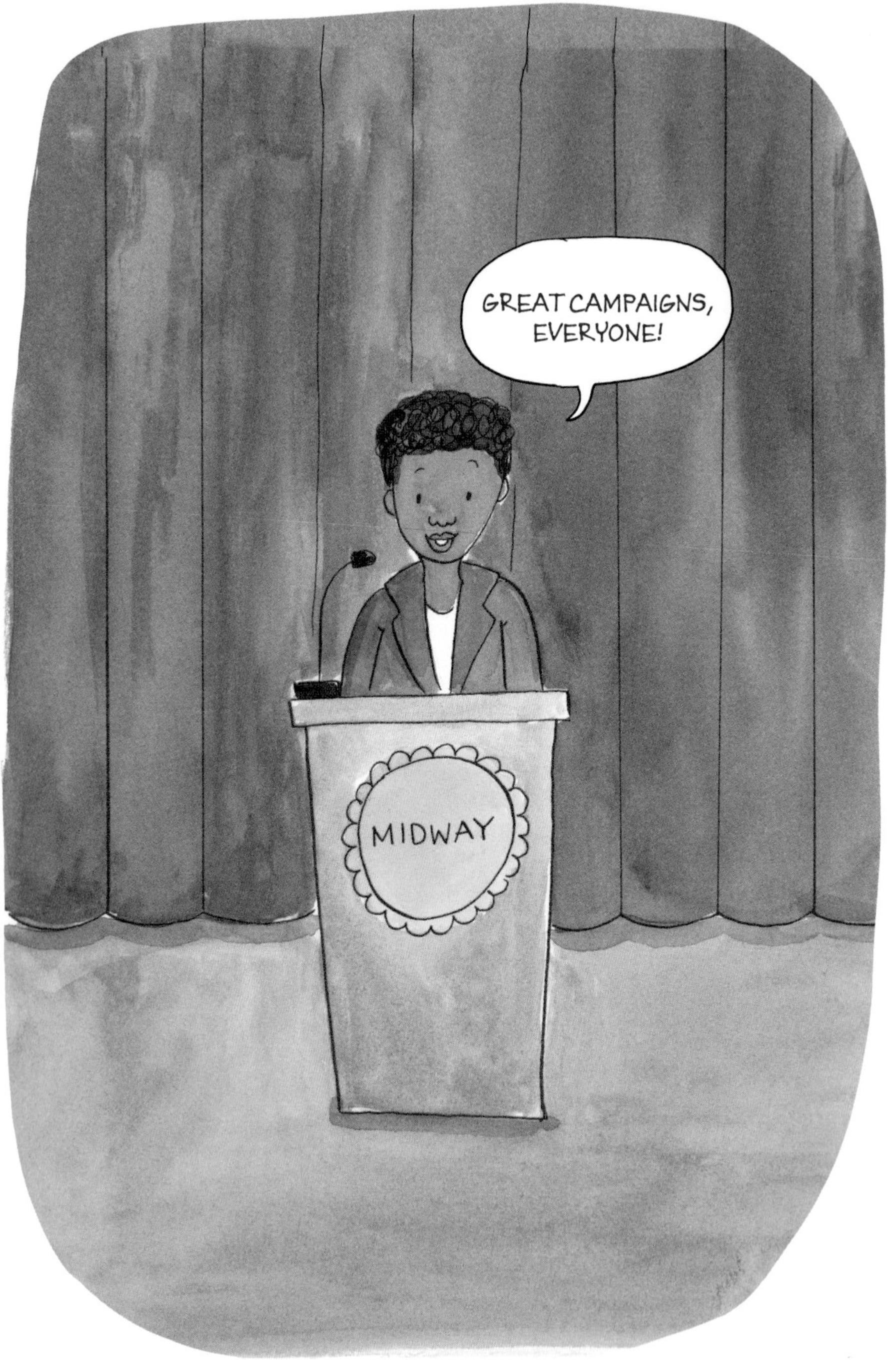
GREAT CAMPAIGNS, EVERYONE!
MIDWAY

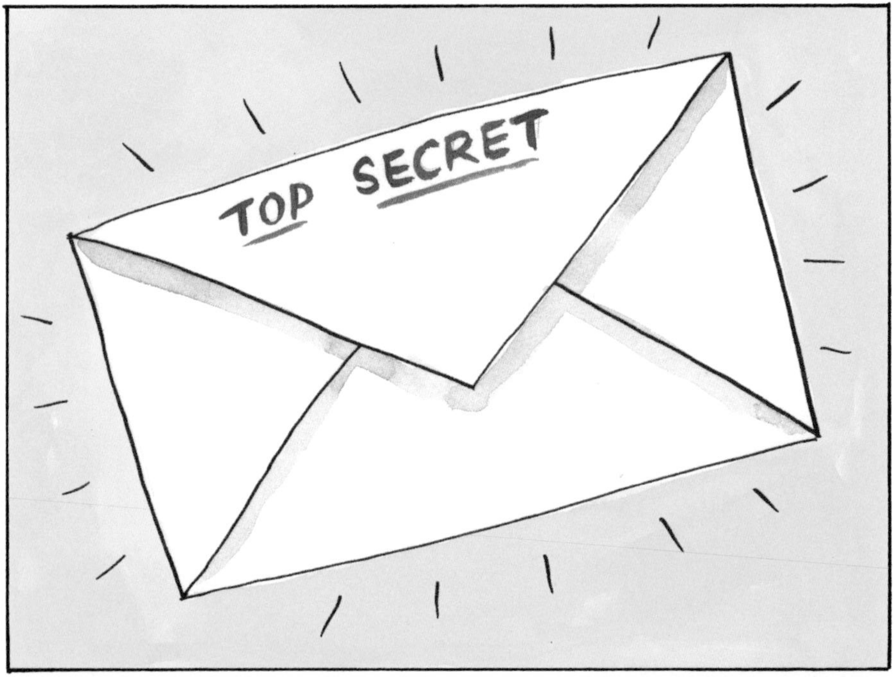
TOP SECRET

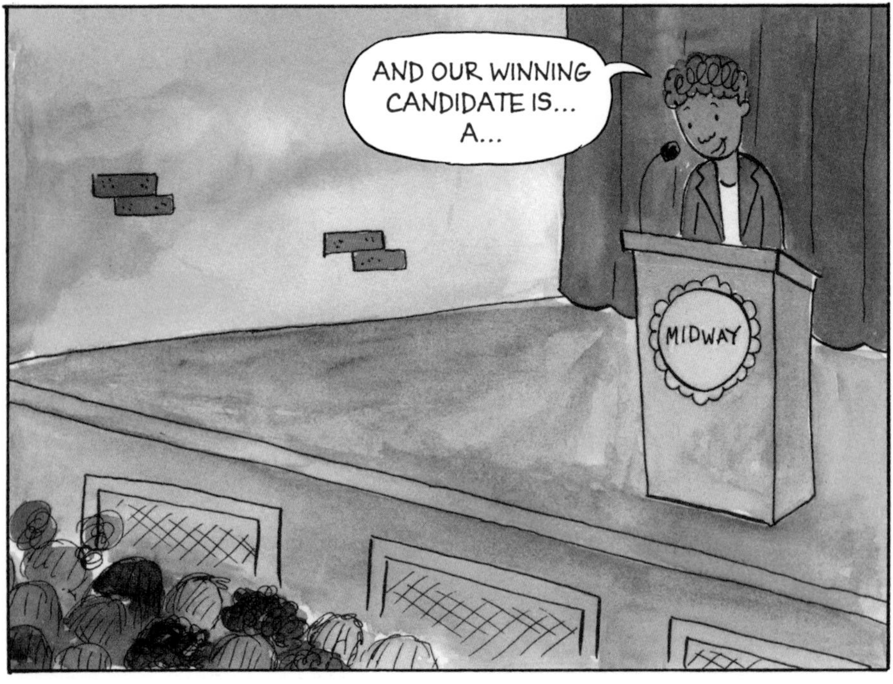
AND OUR WINNING CANDIDATE IS... A...
MIDWAY

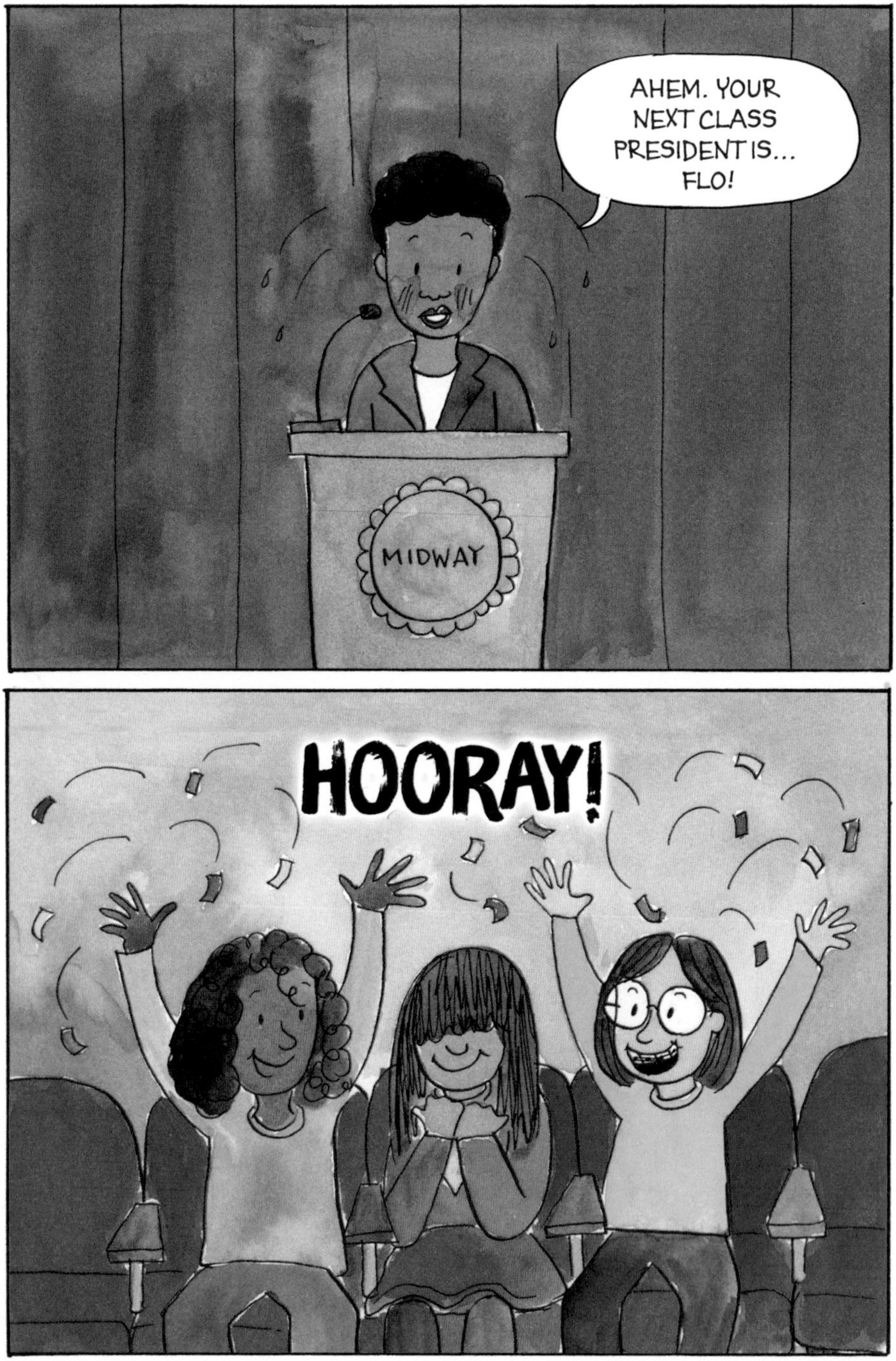
AHEM. YOUR NEXT CLASS PRESIDENT IS... FLO!
MIDWAY
HOORAY!

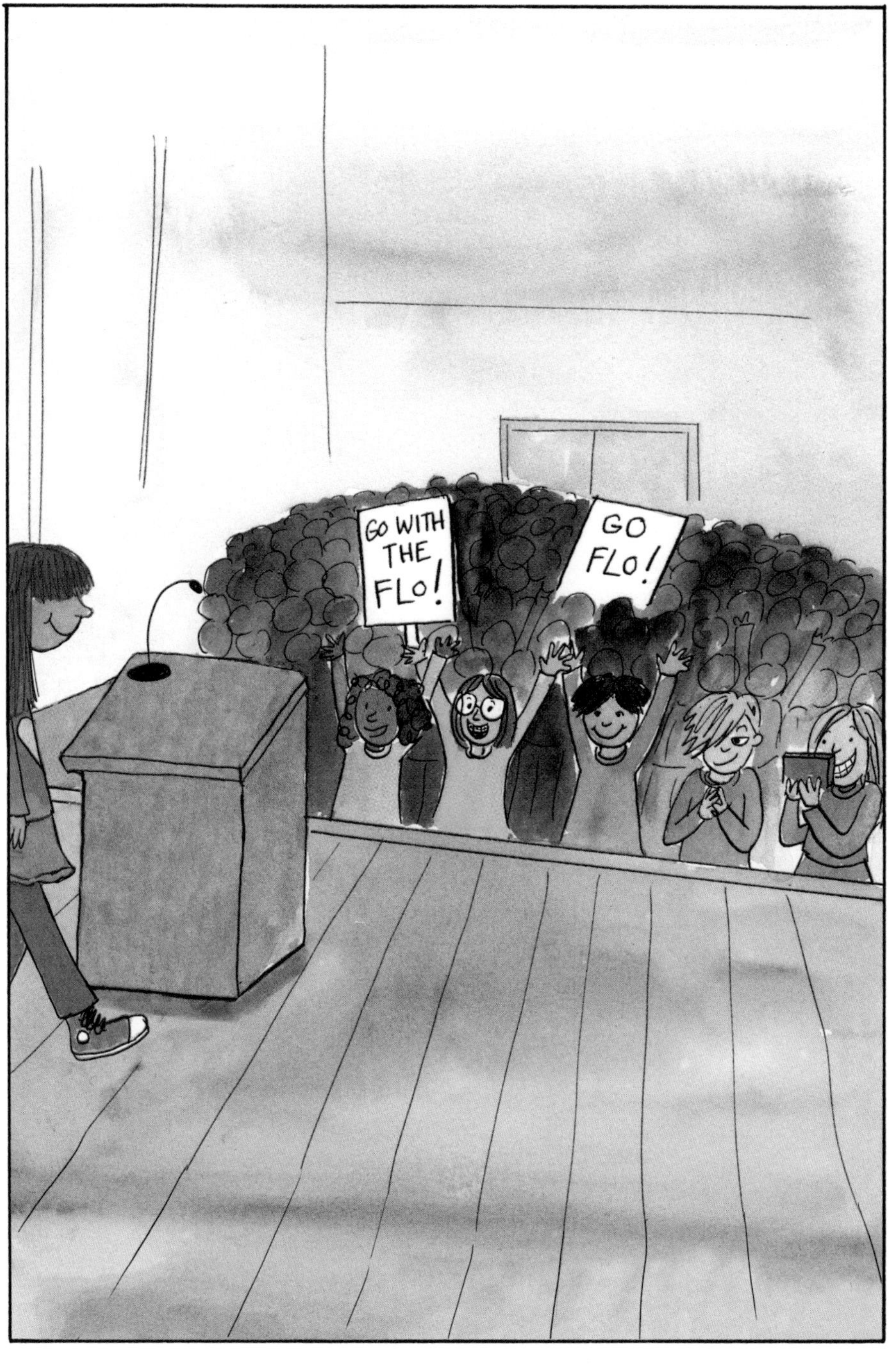
GO WITH THE FLO!
GO FLO!

CHAPTER 16
PROMISES TOO

HOW TO MAKE A PROMISE:
PINKY SWEAR

HOW TO BREAK A PROMISE:
CROSS YOUR FINGERS BEHIND YOUR BACK

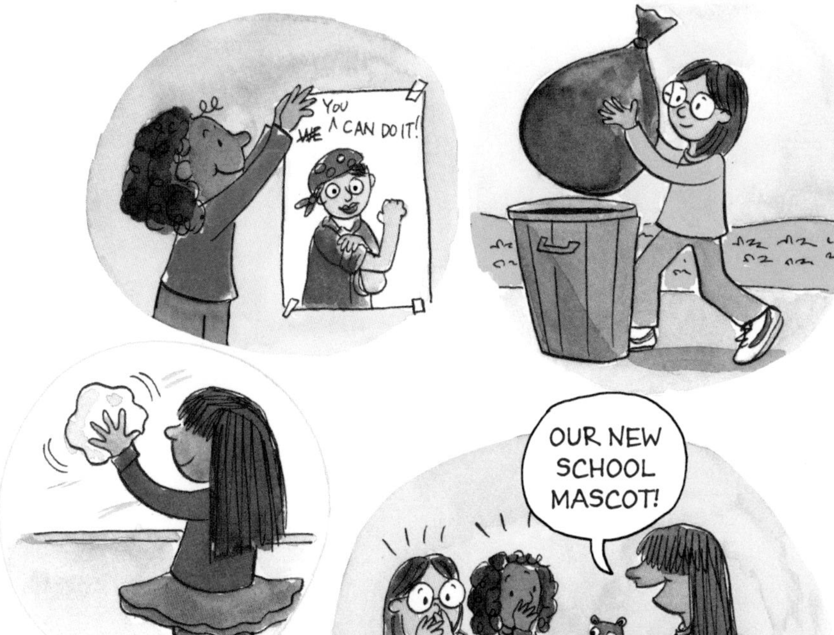
YOU
WE CAN DO IT!
OUR NEW SCHOOL MASCOT!
BOOK DONATION

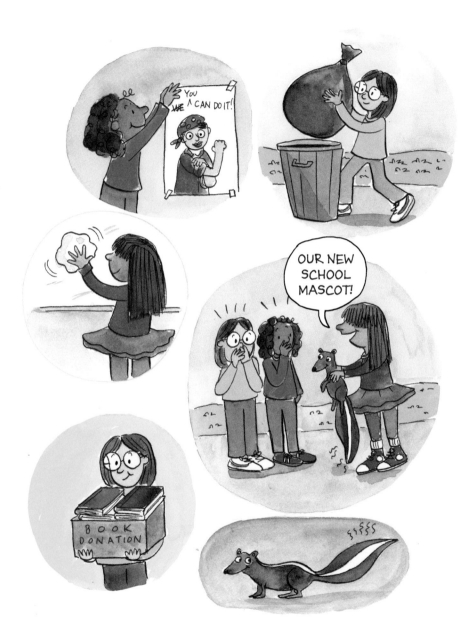

MY SKETCHBOOKS WERE FILLED WITH HEARTS
AND DEREK'S NAME ALL OVER THE PLACE.

AS I WAS WORKING ON MY ENGLISH ASSIGNMENT,
I THOUGHT ABOUT MY OUTTAKES WITH DEREK.

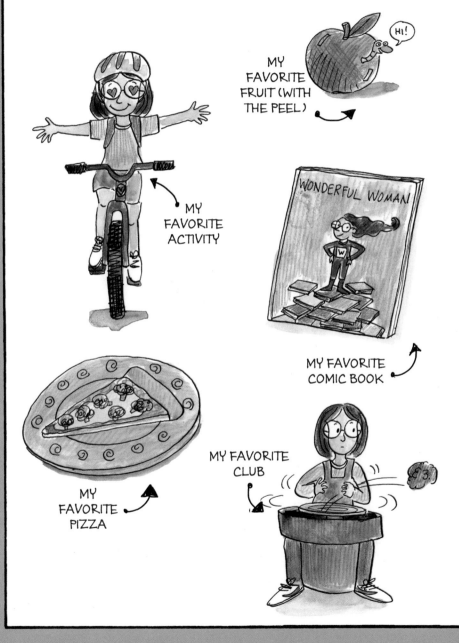

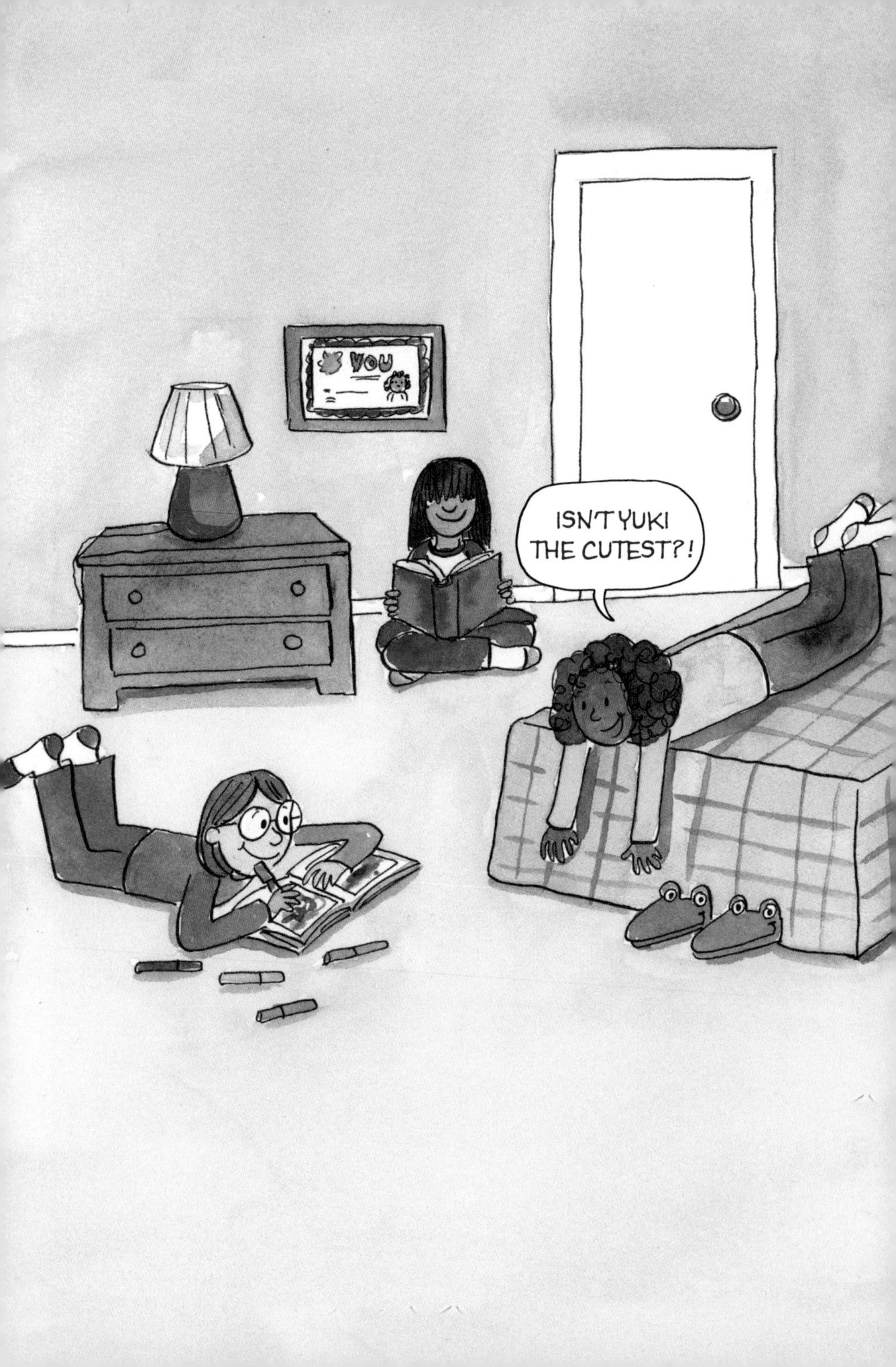
YOU
ISN'T YUKI THE CUTEST?!

CHAPTER 17
YEARBOOK

A FEW WEEKS LATER WE GOT OUR YEARBOOKS.

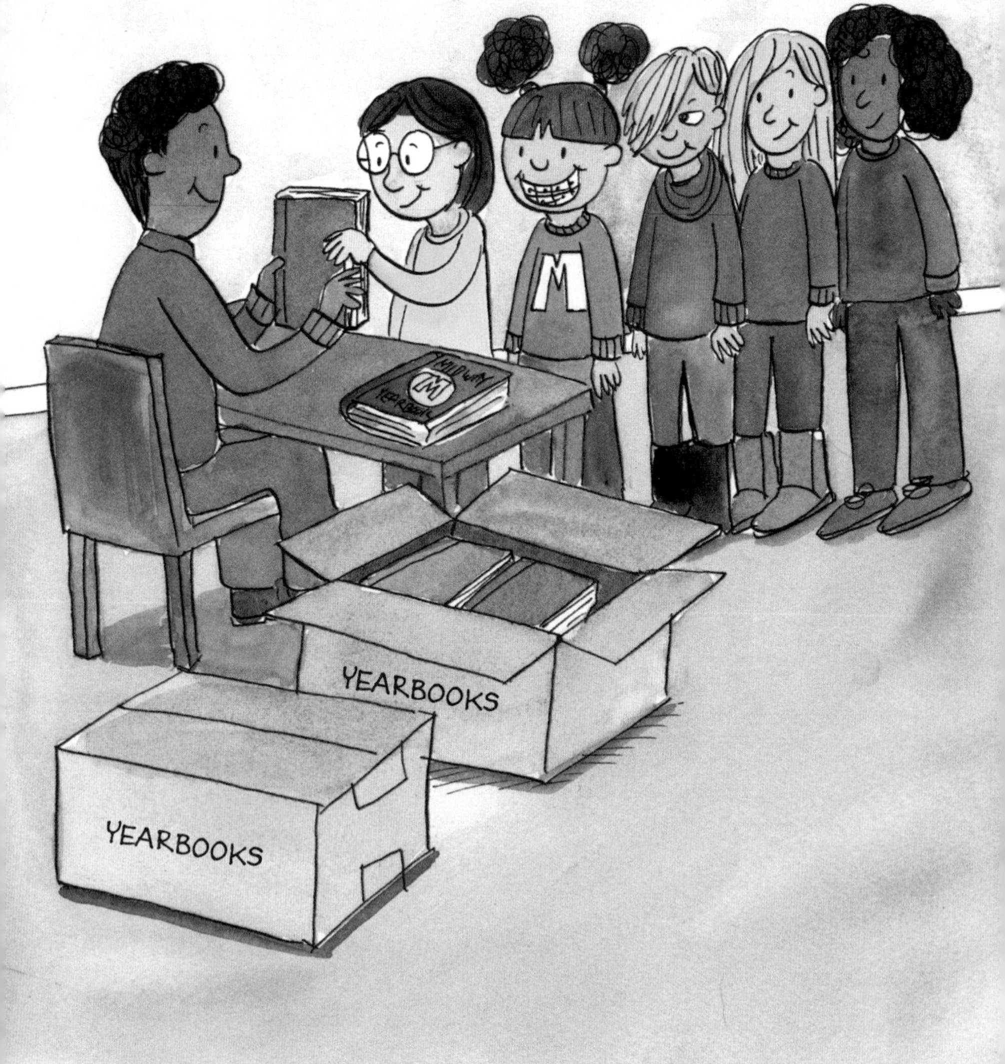
M
YEARBOOKS
YEARBOOKS

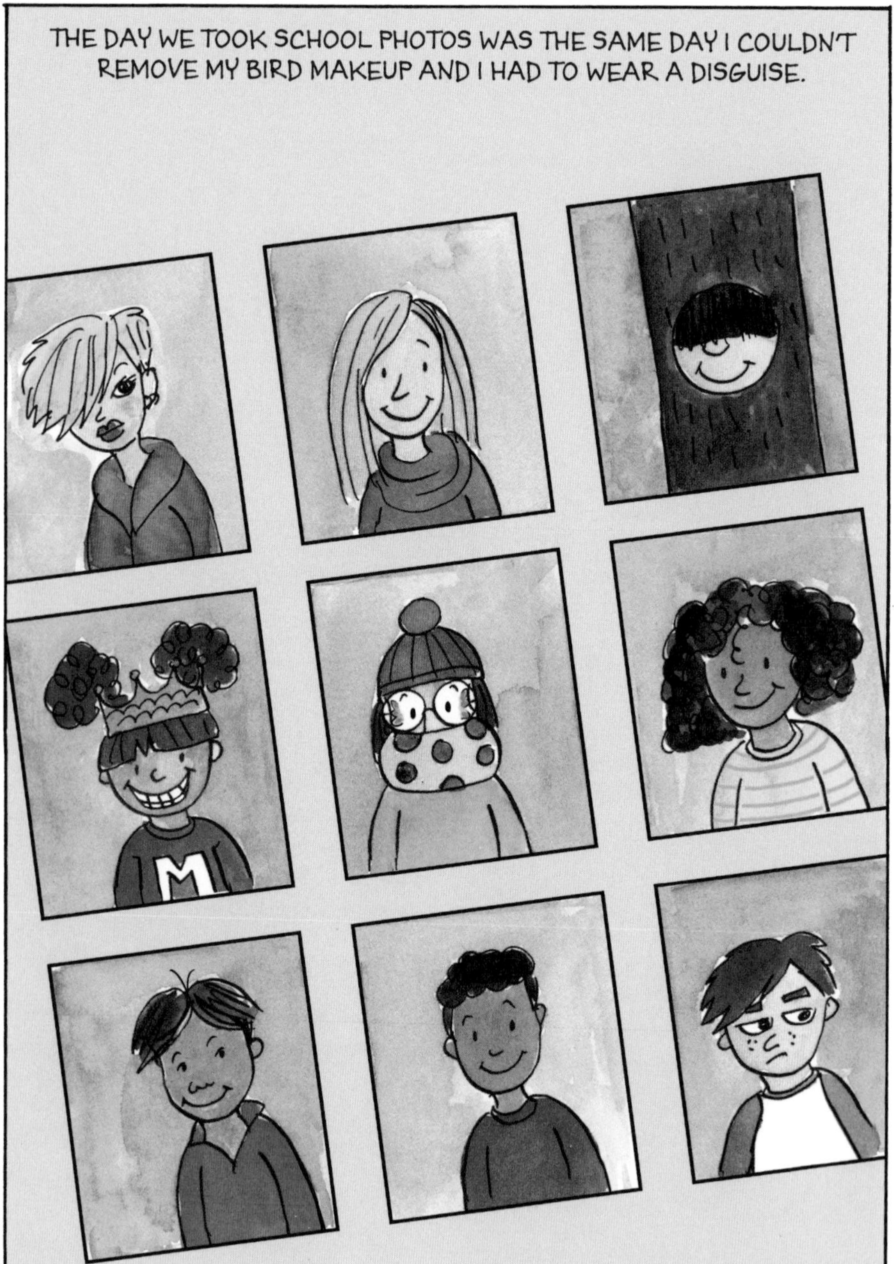
THE DAY WE TOOK SCHOOL PHOTOS WAS THE SAME DAY I COULDN'T REMOVE MY BIRD MAKEUP AND I HAD TO WEAR A DISGUISE.
M

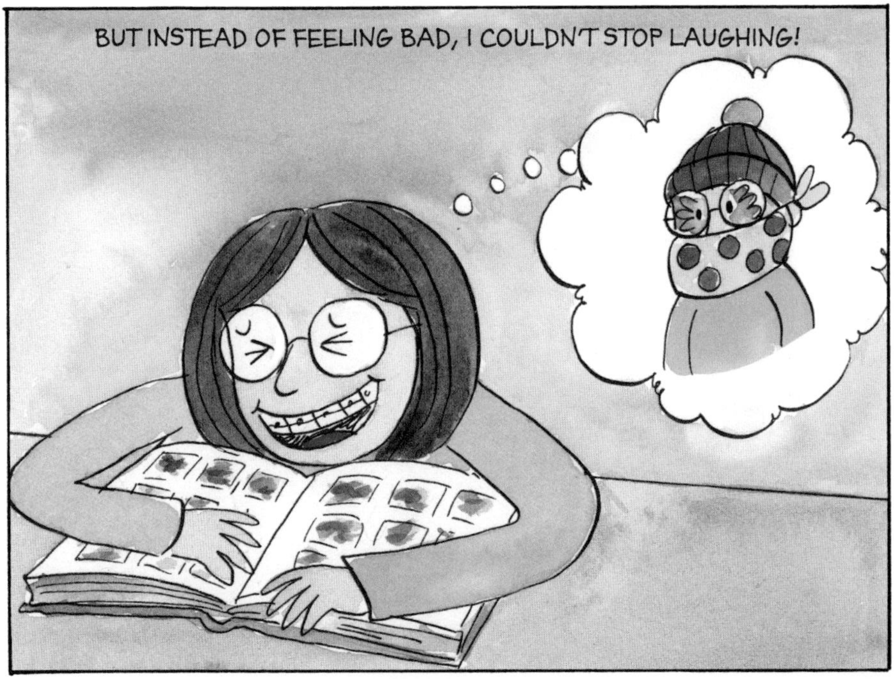
BUT INSTEAD OF FEELING BAD, I COULDN'T STOP LAUGHING!

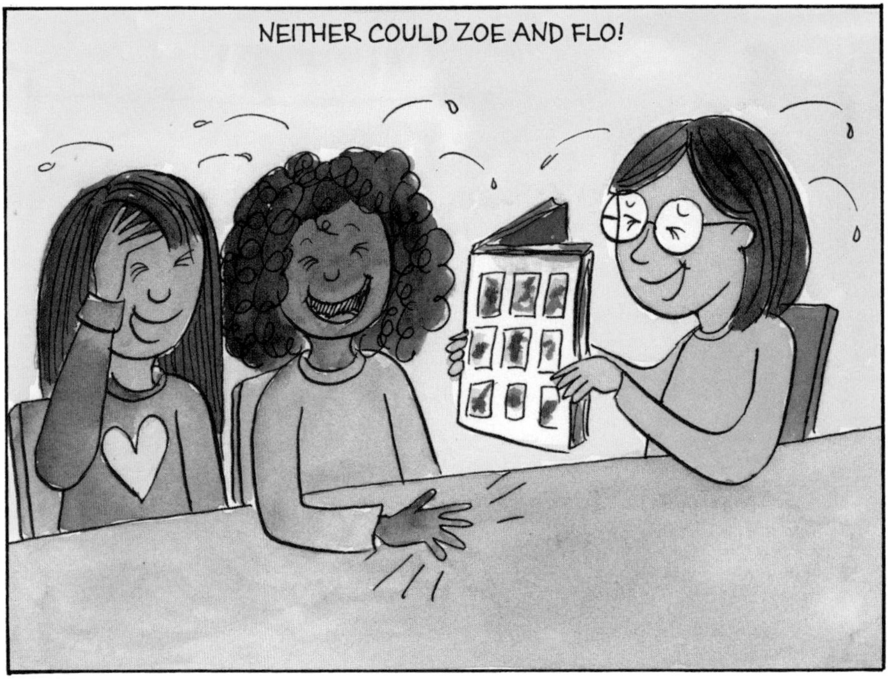
NEITHER COULD ZOE AND FLO!

I HAD SO MUCH FUN SIGNING EVERONE'S YEARBOOK AND MAKING BIRD JOKES.

AND IT WAS FUN TO READ WHAT EVERYONE WROTE TO ME.

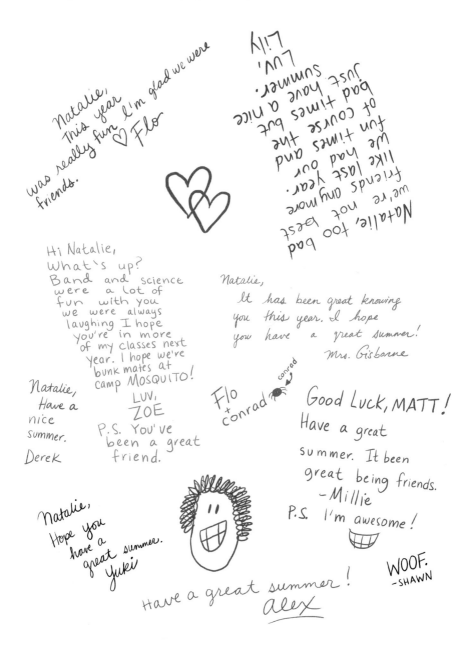

Natalie,
This year was really fun. I'm glad we were friends. ♡ Flo

Lily,
LUV,

Natalie, too bad we're not best friends anymore like last year. We had our fun times and of course the bad times but just have a nice summer.

Hi Natalie,
What's up?
Band and science were a lot of fun with you we were always laughing I hope you're in more of my classes next year. I hope we're bunk mates at camp MOSQUITO!
LUV,
ZOE
P.S. You've been a great friend.

Natalie,
Have a nice summer.
Derek

Natalie,
It has been great knowing you this year. I hope you have a great summer!
Mrs. Gisborne

conrad
Flo + conrad

Good Luck, MATT!
Have a great summer. It been great being friends.
-Millie
P.S. I'm awesome!

Natalie,
Hope you have a great summer.
Yuki

Have a great summer!
alex

WOOF.
-SHAWN

WHO'S WHO AT MIDWAY MIDDLE SCHOOL

LILY AND ALEX
MOST LIKELY TO
TAKE A SELFIE

YUKI
MOST LIKEY TO HAVE
A COMEDY SPECIAL

FLO
MOST LIKELY TO TALK
TO A HOUSEPLANT

DEREK
MOST LIKELY TO FIX
YOUR LAPTOP

WHO'S WHO AT MIDWAY MIDDLE SCHOOL

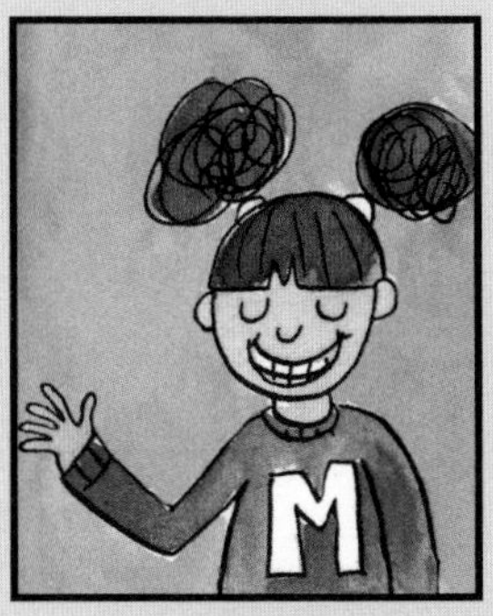

MILLIE
MOST LIKELY TO TALK
A LOT BUT SAY A LITTLE

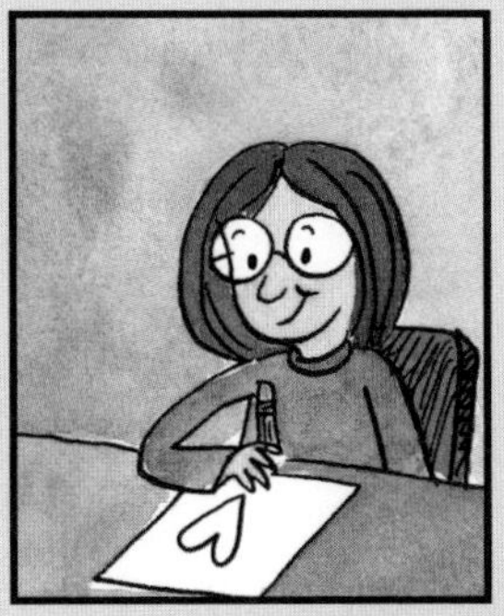

NATALIE
MOST LIKELY TO
DRAW HER WAY OUT
OF A CORNER

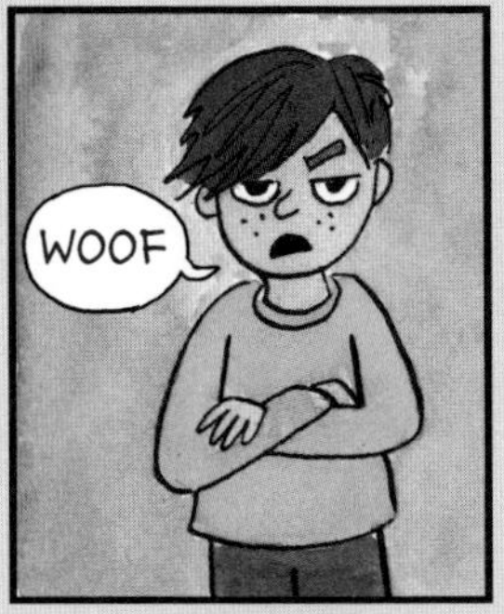
WOOF

SHAWN
MOST LIKELY
TO BARK

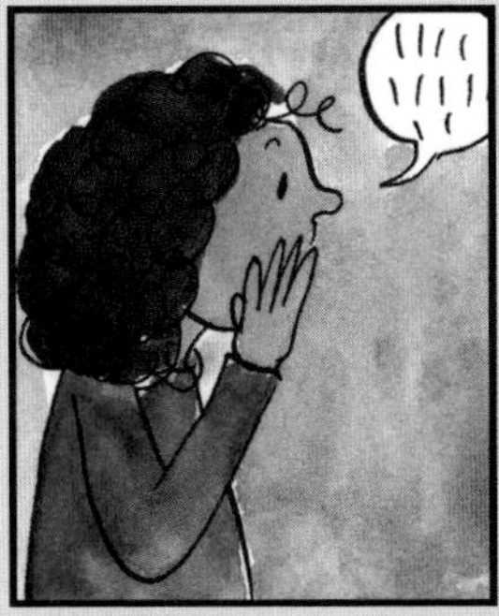

ZOE
MOST LIKELY TO
BE A REPORTER

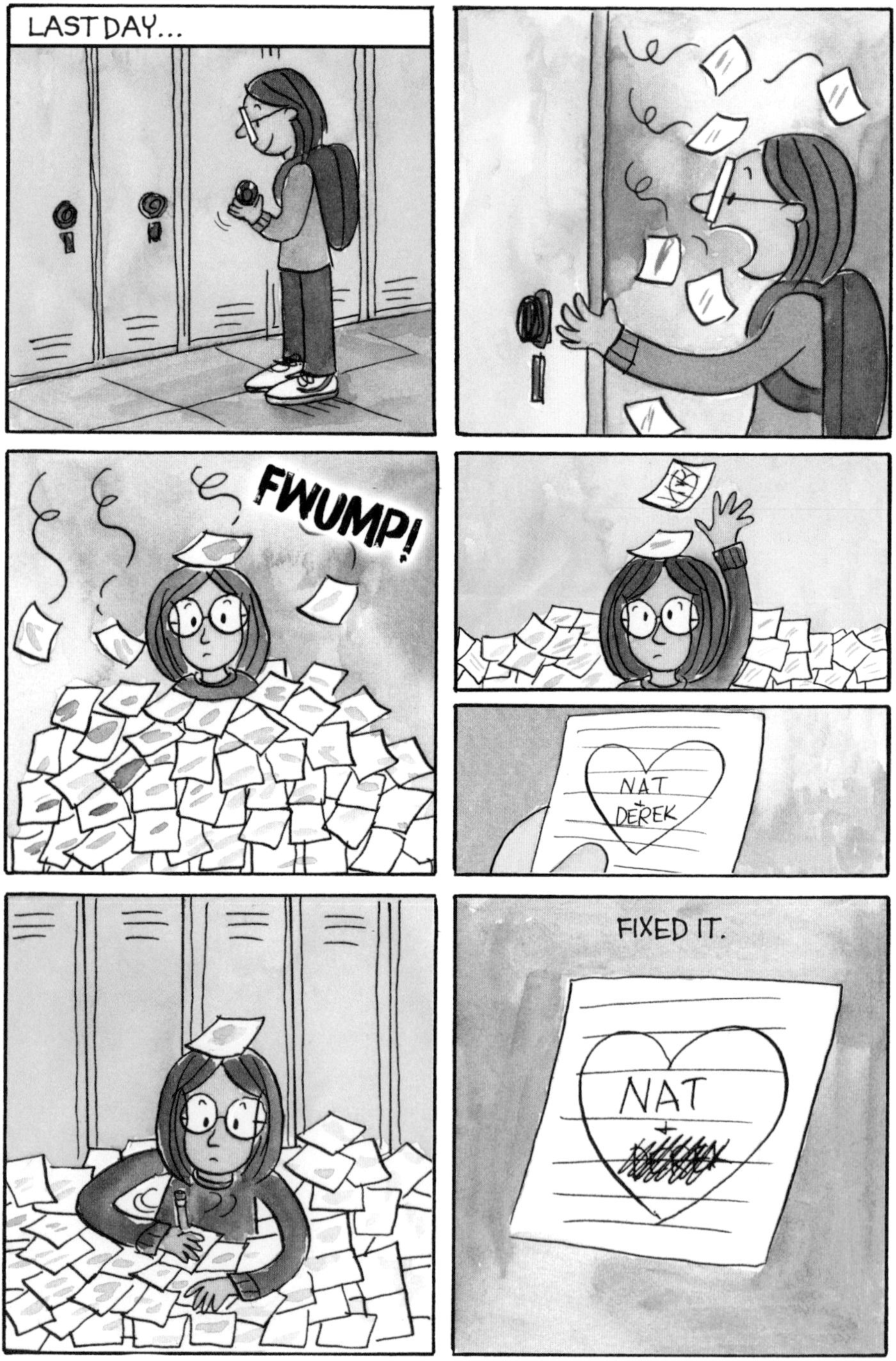
LAST DAY...
FWUMP!
NAT
+
DEREK
FIXED IT.
NAT
+

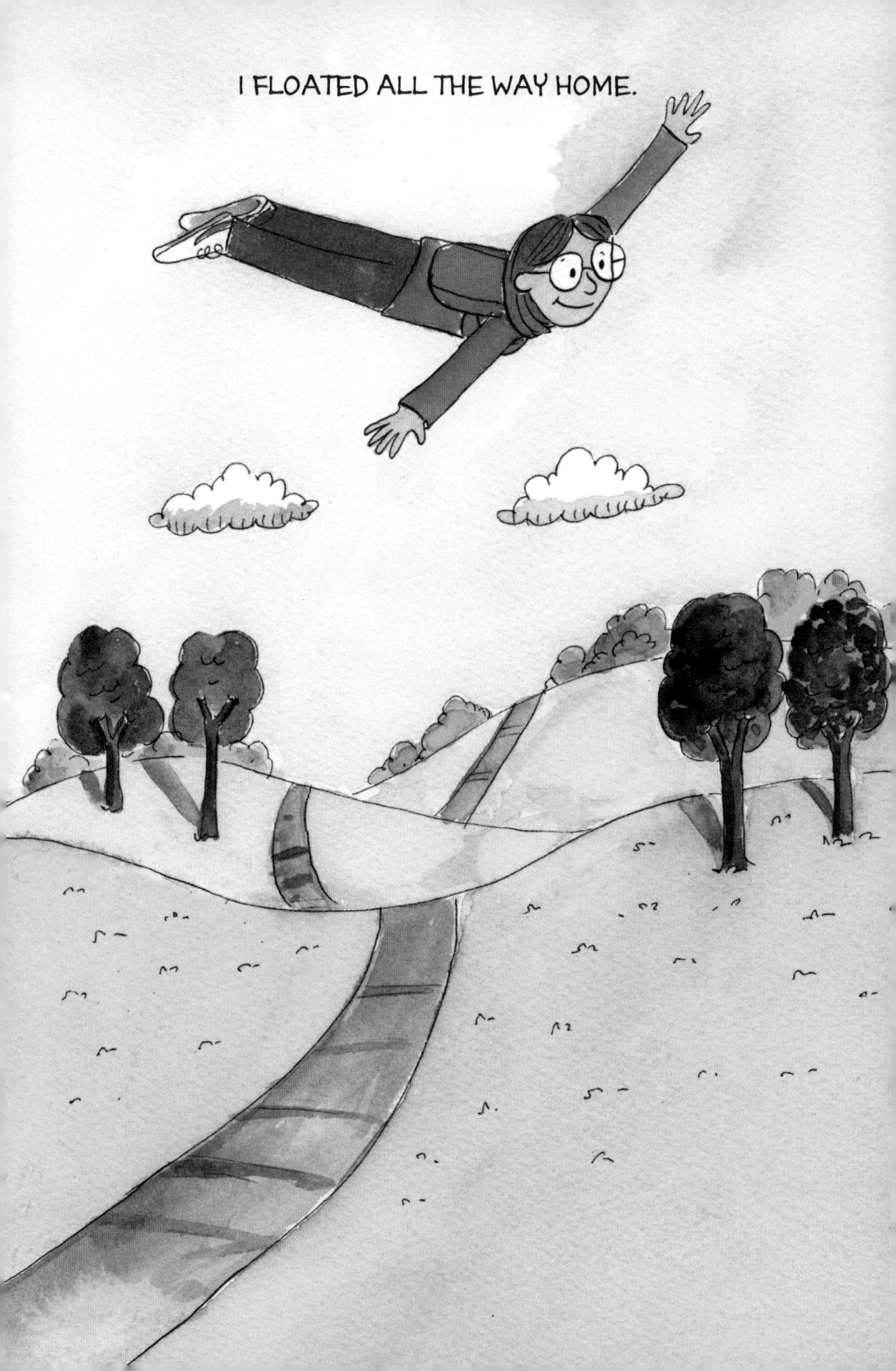
I FLOATED ALL THE WAY HOME.

THE OU TAKES

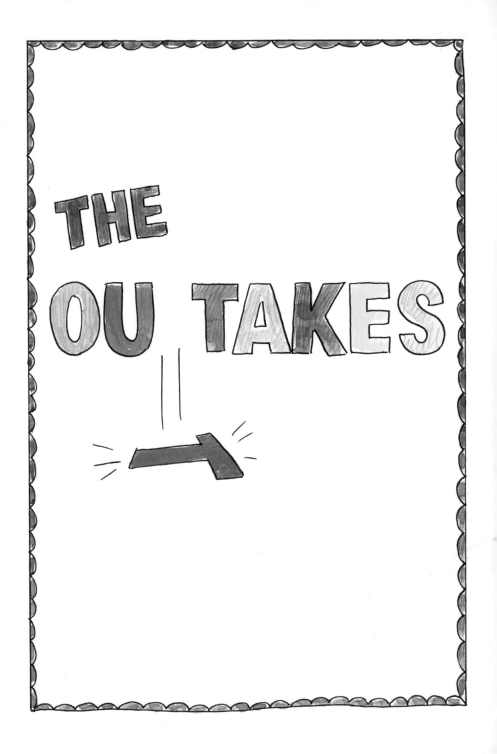

DEREK'S HOMERUN KICKBALL KICK

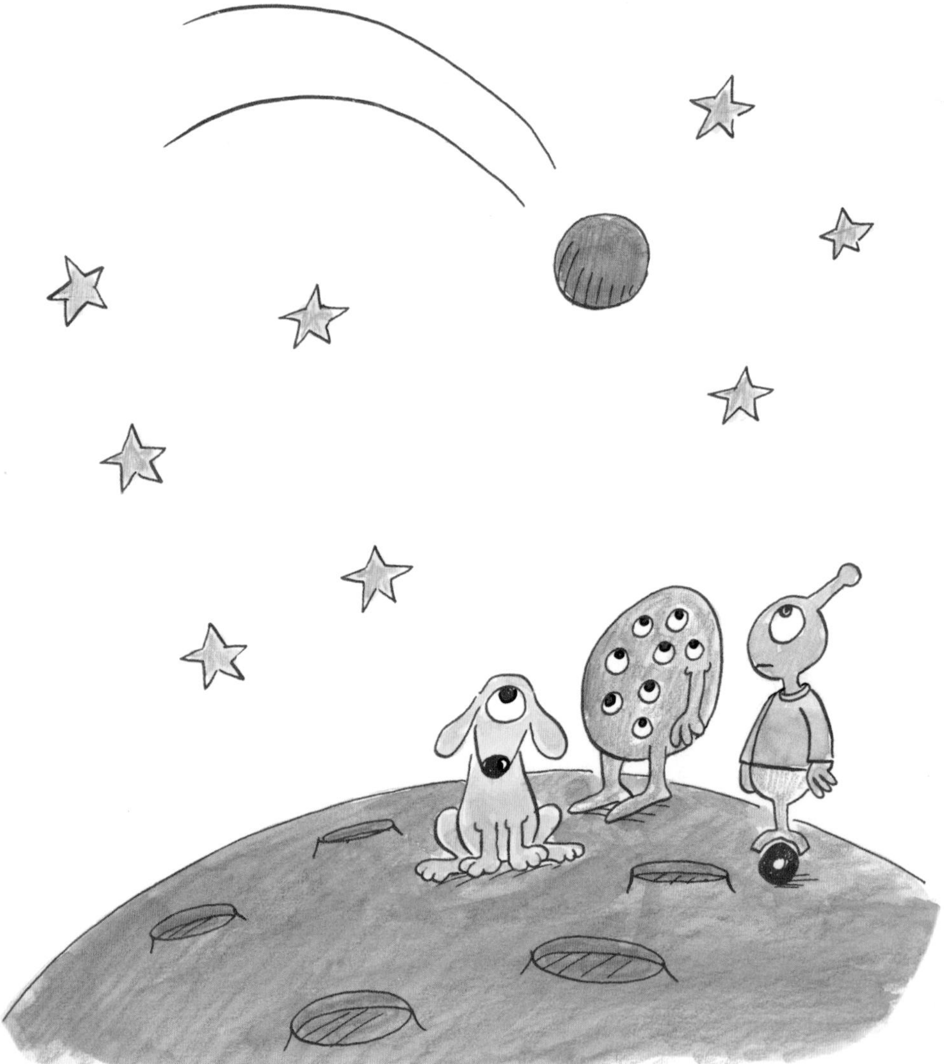

EVEN MORE LUNCHROOM UTENSILS

SPORK   FNIFE   STROON   FRAW

FLO'S SOLO

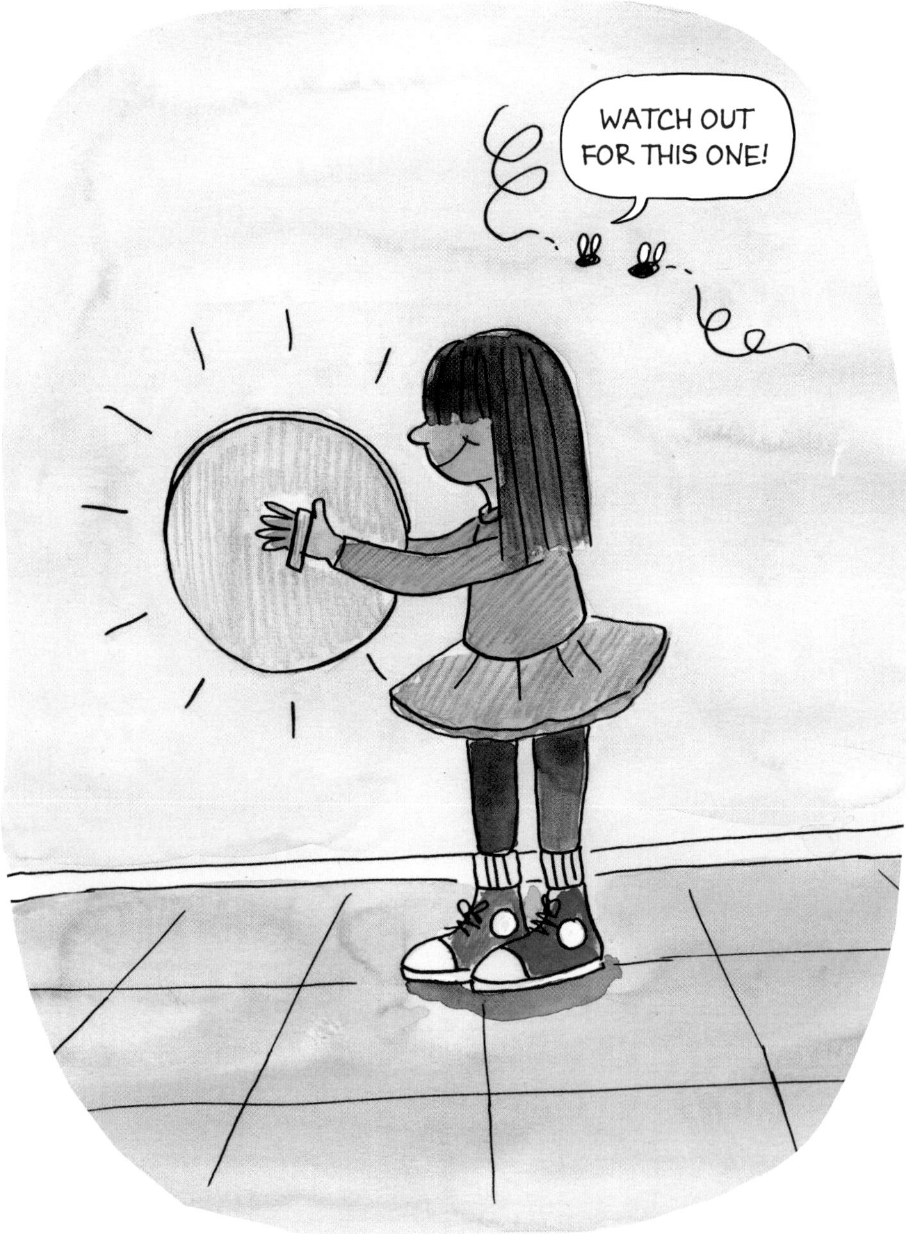
WATCH OUT FOR THIS ONE!

MR. BARRY'S CLOSET

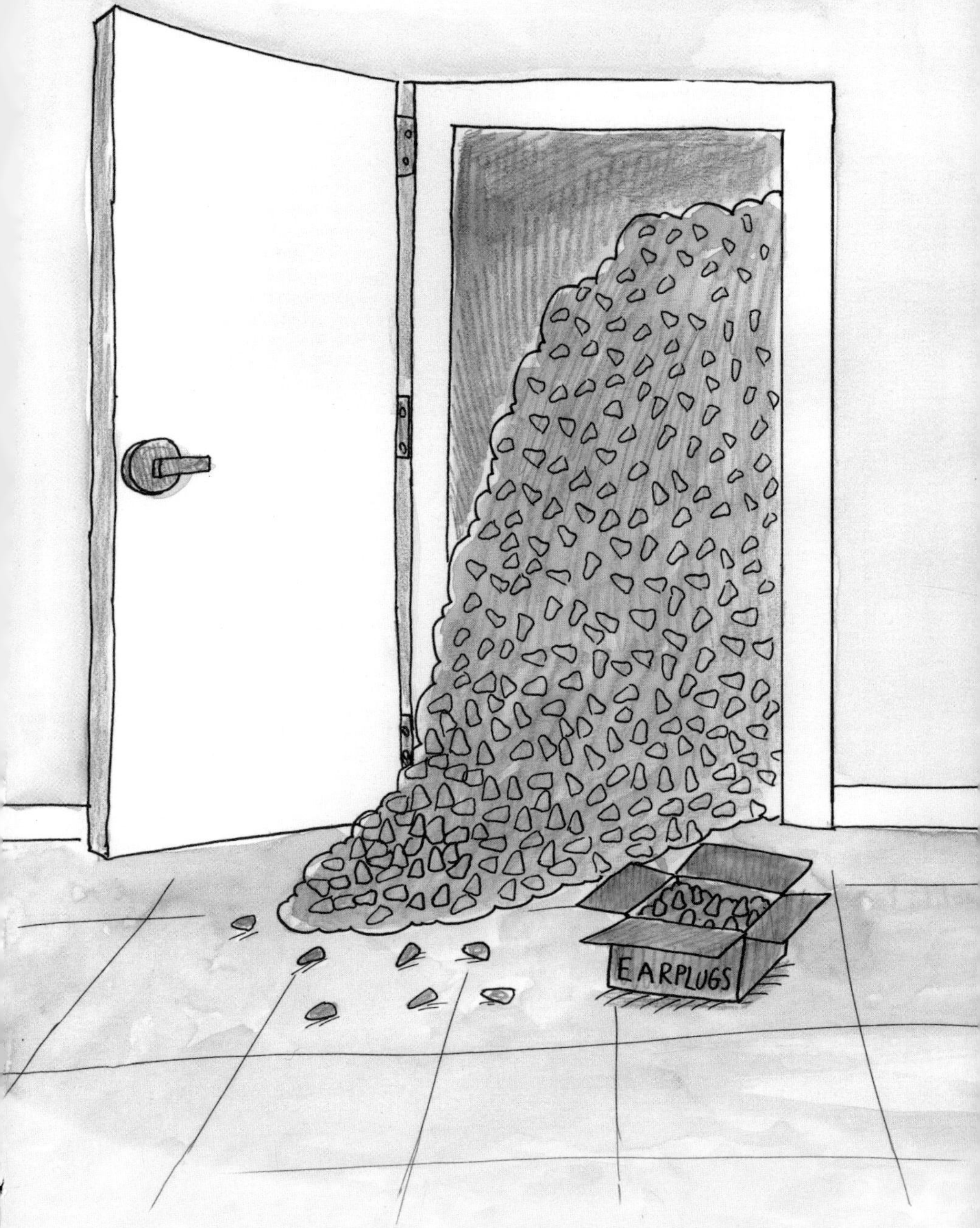
EARPLUGS

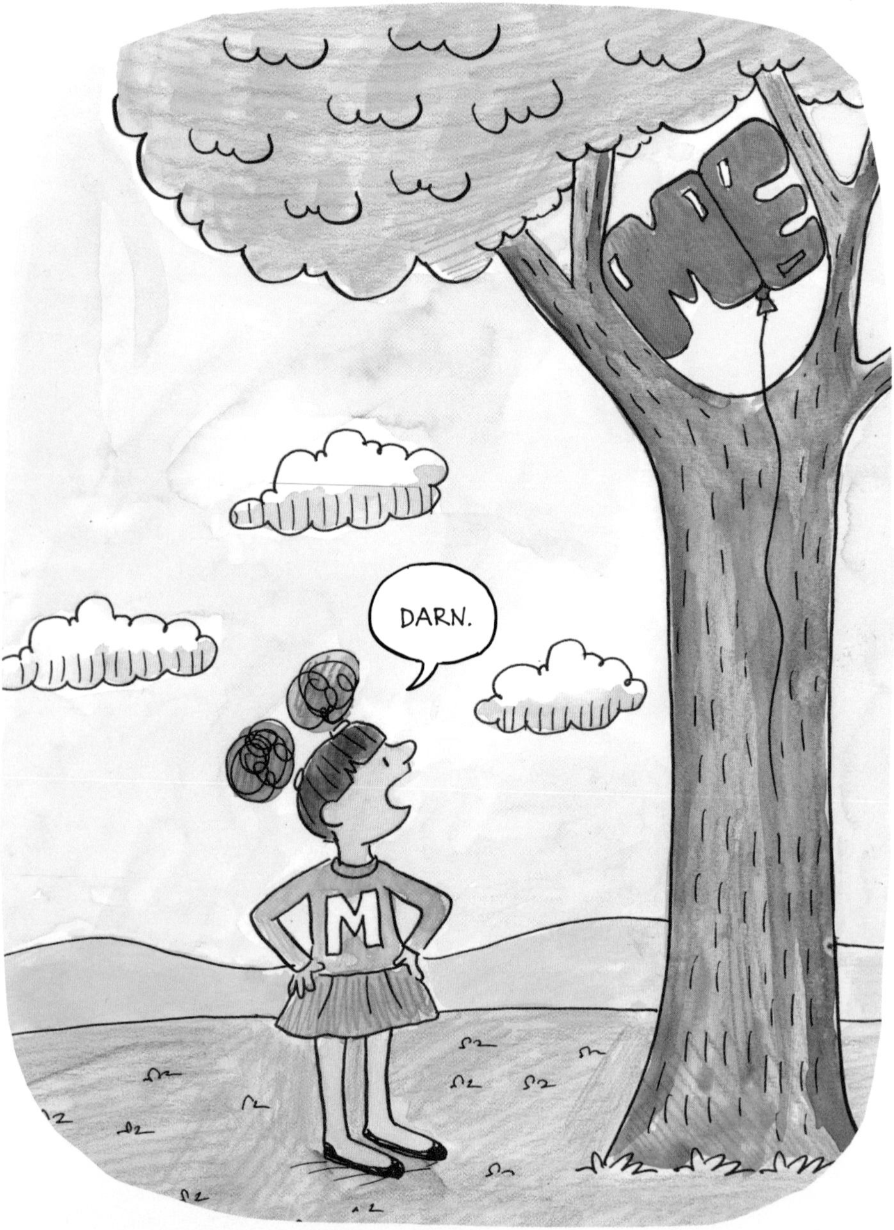

DARN.
M

MY UNSUCCESSFUL JUMPSHOT

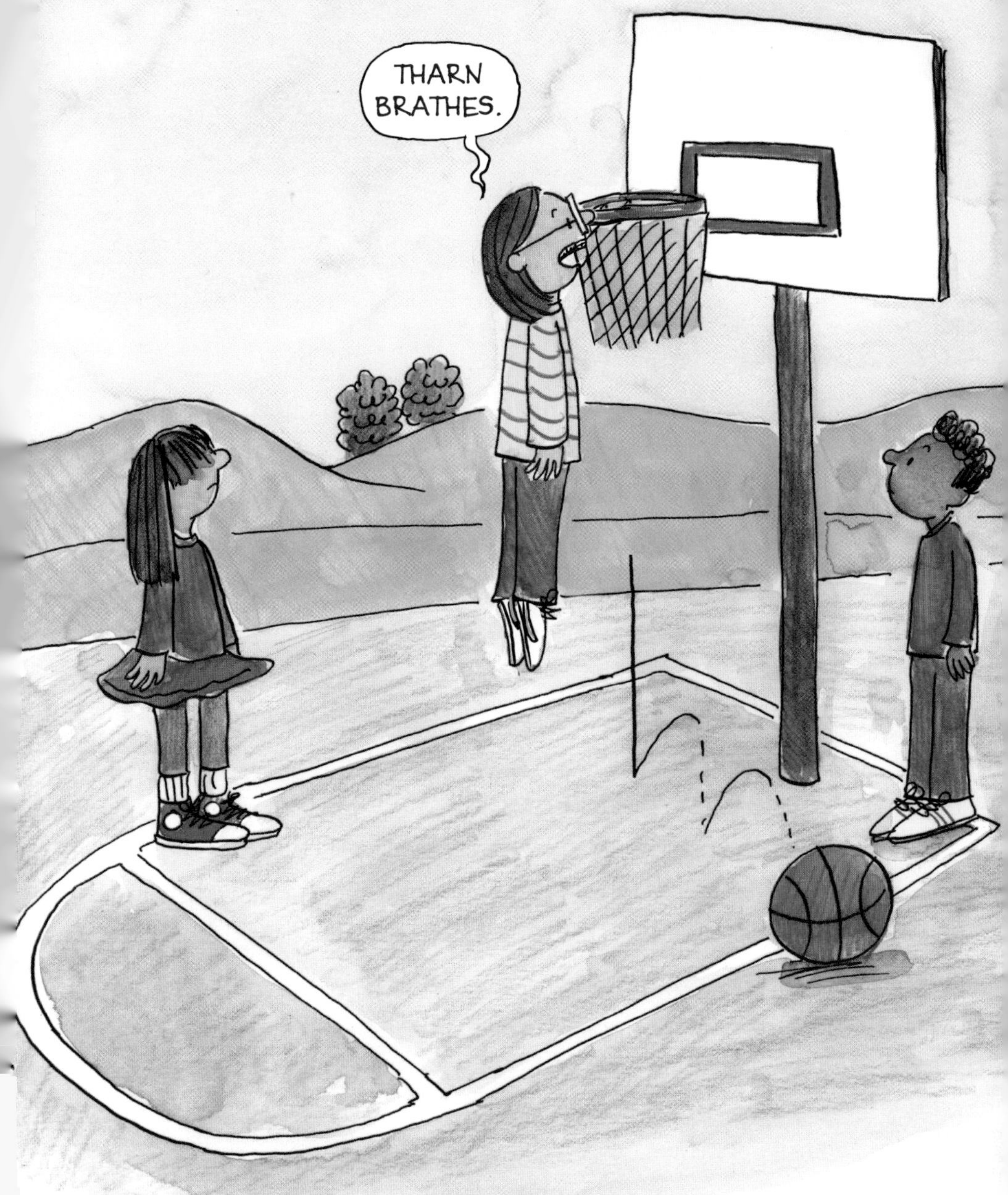
THARN BRATHES.

FLO'S SUGGESTION BOX

YUKI'S TUBA PRACTICE

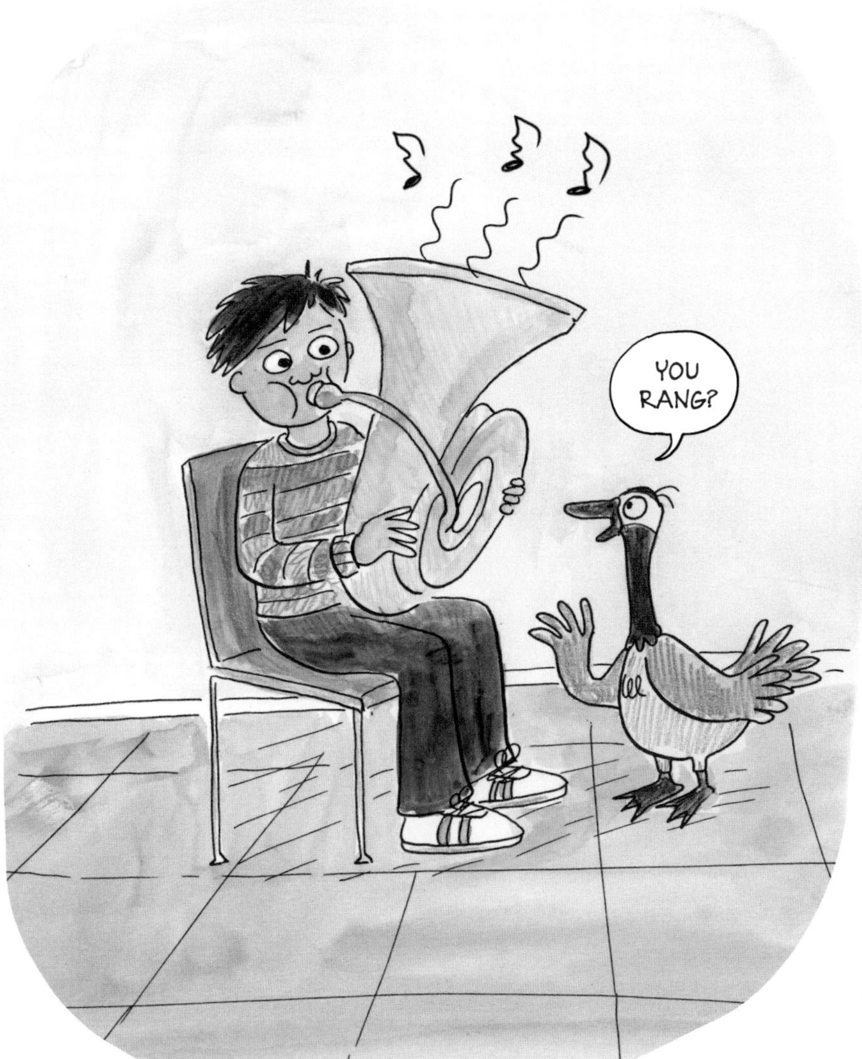
YOU RANG?

SHAWN BARKING

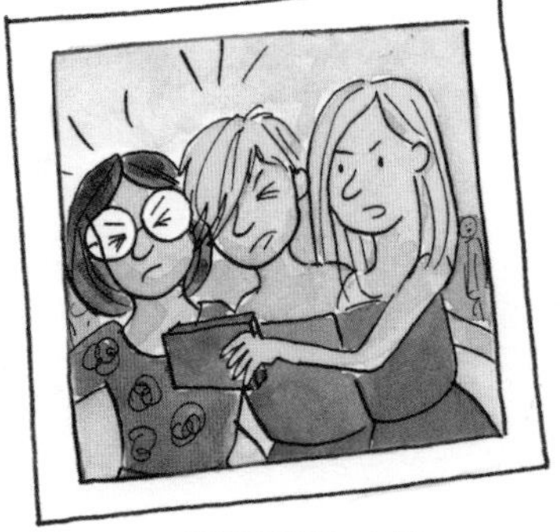

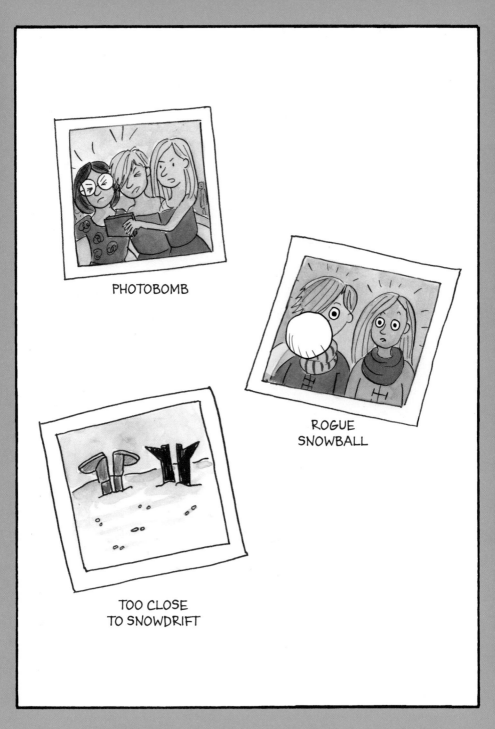

PHOTOBOMB

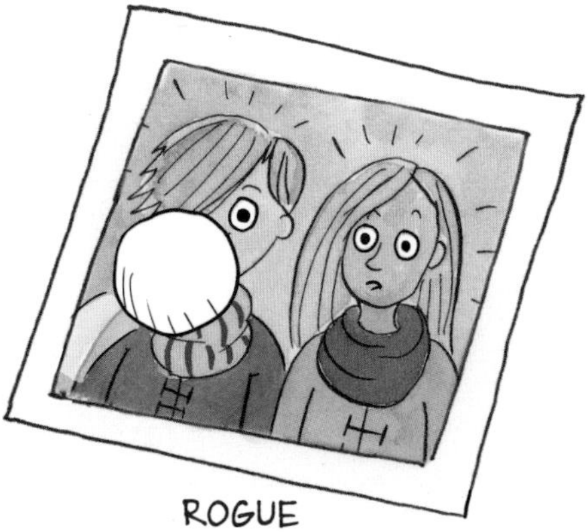

ROGUE
SNOWBALL

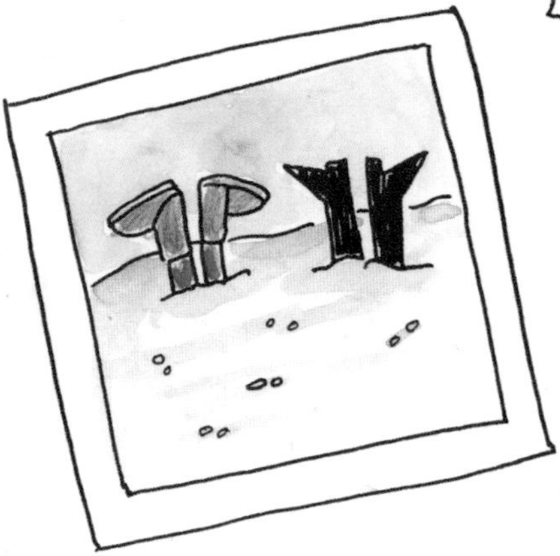

TOO CLOSE
TO SNOWDRIFT

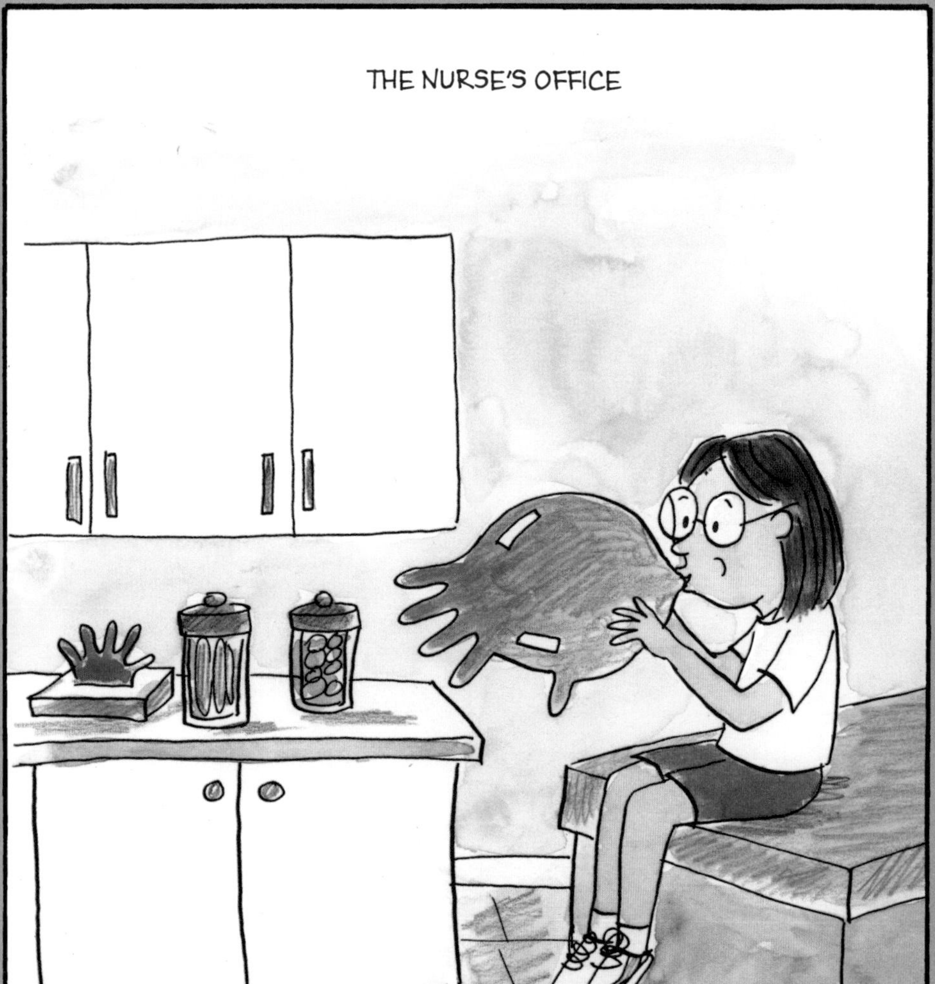
THE NURSE'S OFFICE

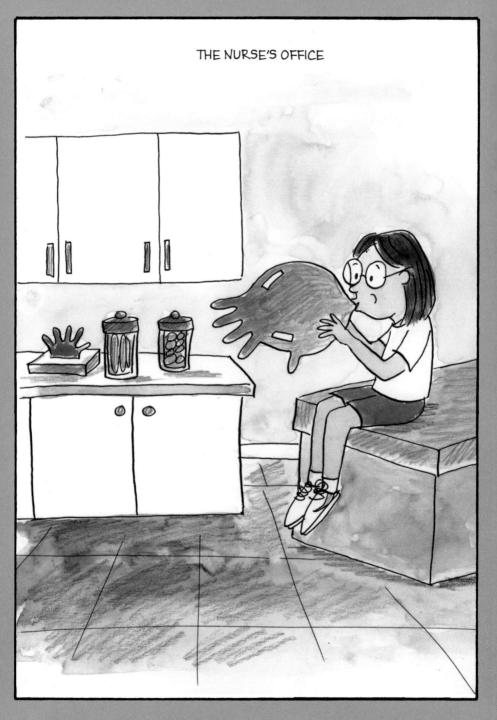

THE END

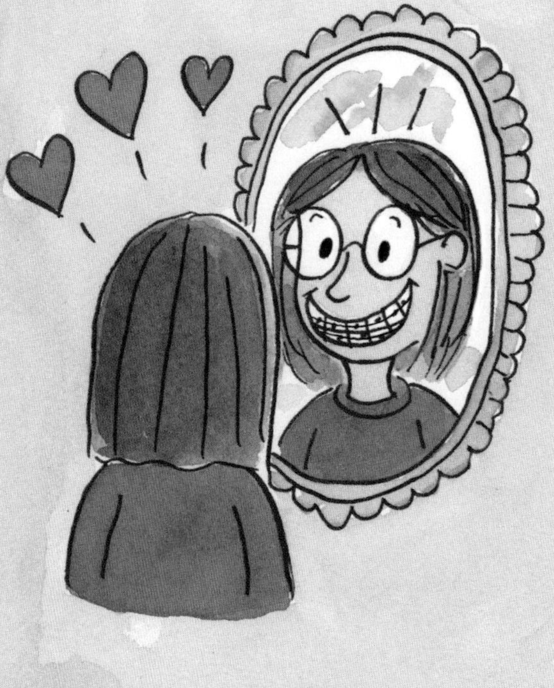

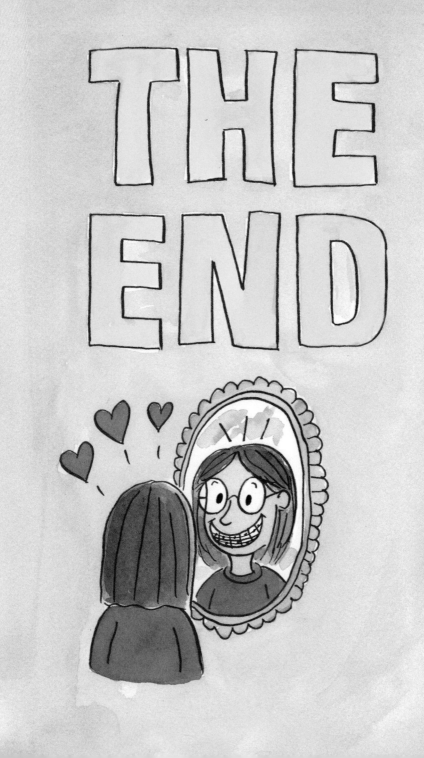

MARIA SCRIVAN is an award—winning cartoonist, illustrator, and author based in Stamford, Connecticut. Her debut graphic novel, *Nat Enough*, released to great acclaim, and her laugh—out—loud syndicated comic, *Half Full*, appears daily in newspapers nationwide and on gocomics.com. Maria licenses her work for greeting cards, and her cartoons have also appeared in *MAD Magazine*, *Parade*, and many other publications. Visit Maria online at mariascrivan.com.